Our Patriots
of the
American Revolution

Daughters of the American Revolution

*Stories of our Revolutionary Patriot Ancestors
Lake Minnetonka Chapter
National Society Daughters of the American Revolution*

Copyright © 2023
Lake Minnetonka Chapter
National Society Daughters of the American Revolution
All Rights Reserved

No part of this publication may be reproduced, distributed, or transmitted in any form without prior written permission of the publisher, except as permitted by U.S. copyright law. For permission requests contact: lakemtkadar@gmail.com.

ISBN 979-8-218-26856-5
Library of Congress Control Number: 2023917148

Published in the United States of America by
Lake Minnetonka Chapter
National Society Daughters of the American Revolution

Printed in the United States of America by
Smartpress in Chanhassen, Minnesota

Cover Photo:
Independence Hall as viewed through Congress Hall, Philadelphia, PA
Back Photo:
Mural in DAR Constitution Hall, Washington, D.C.

Revolutionary History Author
Linda LaBelle Kline

Patriot Story Authors
Members of the Lake Minnetonka Chapter DAR

Editors & Researchers in Chief
Georgetta Henrichsen Hickey
Linda LaBelle Kline

Editing & Research Assistants
Meghan Grace Flannery
Charlotte Clark Jenkins
Sarah Lynne Martin

Cover Design & Photography
Michelle Henderson White

Contents

Introduction: PATRIOTS   2

Chapter 1: RESOLVE   12

Chapter 2: DECLARATION   40

Chapter 3: HOPE   86

Chapter 4: PERSEVERANCE   118

Chapter 5: INDEPENDENCE   160

Chapter 6: VISION   208

Appendix   231

This book is dedicated to the Revolutionary War Patriots
who secured the American vision of liberty, equality, and justice
for their descendants, trusting us to continue their work and
make that vision a reality for all Americans.

DAR Memorial Continental Hall, Washington, D.C.
"Afternoon Light Shines on our House Beautiful"
Courtesy of Michelle Henderson White © 2022

Introduction:
PATRIOTS

America 250

The United States of America turns a glorious 250 years old on July 4, 2026. America is still a young nation by global standards, but this anniversary is a monumental achievement for a profoundly bold experiment in democratic government, nonetheless. Ancient Athens is widely credited with getting the democracy party started. The Greek words "demos," meaning common people, and "kratos," meaning power, were aptly combined to form the word "democracy" to describe the government of ancient Athens in which free male citizens had a voice. This model offered more than a little inspiration to America's founders. As did America's own imperial parent who first adopted a form of representative government with the Magna Carta in 1215. Iceland and the Isle of Man also both deserve hearty "huzzas" for their thousand-year-old representative parliaments.[1] And New Zealand is to be commended as the first modern nation to grant universal suffrage, having the good sense to do so in 1893.[2] America's 250 years as a continuous, independent democracy puts her in elite company.

Even more incredible than the longevity of America's democracy is the audacity of pursuing it in the first place. A disparate group of leaders from 13 unique entities with little history of cooperation dared to challenge the mightiest imperial and military power on earth for independence. Claiming that chartered colonists had the same constitutional rights as British citizens in England, they boldly criticized their monarch's heavy hand and insisted on reform. When that failed, they brazenly (however eloquently) declared their independence. All this was initiated without a standing army or even a unified vision of what a new independent government might look like. More astonishingly still, *ordinary American colonists risked their lives and livelihoods to join the cause.*

We are the proud descendants of these ordinary colonists. While the words and work of America's founding fathers have been carefully preserved, the efforts of common Patriots have largely been lost to history. The fragmented evidence of their service to the American Revolution lies in fading town records, obscure military rosters, and archaic pension applications. As a contribution to the America 250 celebrations, members of the Lake Minnetonka Chapter, National Society Daughters of the American Revolution have reconstructed our Patriot ancestors' historical roles in the American Revolution. The purpose of this book is to honor our Patriots by bringing the events and values of the Revolution to life through their experiences.

We hope these stories reveal the events of America's birth from a fresh perspective. In so doing, we trust they will renew pride in America, instill hope in the values on which it was founded, and inspire gratitude for those who earned her independence. Most importantly, we hope these stories of ordinary people make a compelling case that each of us can play an important role in advancing the work yet to be done to ensure that America's founding values of liberty, equality, and justice are realized for all Americans.

By understanding our nation's history – strengths and flaws alike – we can be encouraged to perpetuate America at its best and challenge it at its worst. That is our responsibility as contemporary American citizens. Our system of government was built by people who expected nothing less. As Patriot John Adams said to future Americans, "You will never know how much it cost the present generation to preserve your freedom! I hope you will make a good use of it."[3]

Daughters of the American Revolution

On a personal level, researching and writing the stories of our Patriot ancestors proved to be transformational. We learned that we inherit so much more than DNA from our ancestors. Their wisdom, values, and strengths are also passed on to us, having been shaped by the experiences of each subsequent generation. For example, my practical and resourceful grandmother, Eula Wilder Todleben, had the endearing gift of seeing potential. Nothing was too insignificant to save, including the turkey carcass she brought back home with her on the plane from Minnesota to Michigan one Thanksgiving. Where I saw bones, she saw soup. But I was never more grateful for her ability to see potential than when I inherited the fragments of genealogical information she had saved to piece together our family tree.

My grandmother's interest in genealogy was in finding long lost cousins; mine was in solving family mysteries. When I inherited her box of treasures, I set to work solving these mysteries. One mystery was a claim that we were related to President Calvin Coolidge. That turned out to be false. He was just a neighbor in Vermont. Another claim was our relationship to author, Laura Ingalls Wilder. That turned out to be true, by marriage at least. But the most intriguing mystery was a claim that read, "Hannah Warner, daughter of the younger Eleazer, grew up in Pittsford hearing stories of the Revolutionary War" where her father and grandfather "had served under the command of General George Washington." A few magnificent months of plundering census, birth, and marriage records across five states and two centuries revealed that I was descended from Revolutionary War Patriots. When I learned more about their stories, I was convinced that my grandmother's ability to see potential had been inherited from these courageous Massachusetts Minutemen who saw the potential of a new nation founded on liberty.

Having discovered my Patriot ancestors, I wanted to meet others who shared my interest in genealogy and American history, so I applied for membership in the Lake Minnetonka Chapter, National Society Daughters of the American Revolution (DAR). The DAR is a women's organization dedicated to community service whose members are descendants of Revolutionary War Patriots. This non-political organization proudly honors Patriots through historic preservation, promotes productive citizenship through education, and nurtures a love of country through patriotism. Our chapter is an enthusiastic, collaborative group of women of all ages who work to honor veterans, inspire students, and preserve our local history. We also enjoy gathering as friends for social events and excursions to historical sites around our beautiful state of Minnesota. Most of us would never have met if we hadn't discovered a Revolutionary Patriot in our family trees.

Our Patriots

A Patriot can be broadly defined as any person who supported the cause of independence during the American Revolution. A Loyalist, by contrast, is a person who remained loyal to the British crown.

The DAR recognizes Patriots who served during the Revolution in three different capacities. The first is patriotic service in government. When Great Britain dissolved the rebellious colonies' legislatures, colonists responded by setting up provisional representative governments of their own. The First Continental Congress recommended that each provisional government establish Committees of Correspondence, Safety, and Inspection. The purpose of these committees was to create efficient communication links to exchange news and ideas across the colonies, and to execute the Congress's resolves, such as boycotts of British goods. Service in the Continental Congress, a provisional colonial government, or on one of these committees demonstrated support for the cause of independence and establishes an ancestor as a Patriot. Some of the colonies urged citizens to sign documents such as Articles of Association declaring their allegiance. Such signers are also Patriots.

The second way the DAR recognizes Patriots is through military service. Military service in the Revolution began when local New England militias faced British regulars at the Battles of Lexington and Concord in 1775 and concluded in 1783 when the *Treaty of Paris* was signed, officially ending hostilities. Those who served in a local militia, a state line or navy, the Continental Army, or the Continental Navy are Patriots.

The third way the DAR recognizes Patriots is through civil service. In addition to dissolving colonial legislatures, Great Britain enacted laws restricting town gatherings that had been the heart of local government in many colonies. Those who served in a local governmental role in defiance of these laws are Patriots. Additionally, many colonists supported the cause of independence and became Patriots by paying supply taxes to fund the war or by providing food and supplies to the soldiers.

When we began our research, most of us knew very little about how our Patriot ancestors had served in the American Revolution. We undertook digital archaeological digs to sift through old colonial records looking for the pieces and parts that would comprise our Patriots' Revolutionary War stories. We searched through militia rolls, National Archive records, and soldier databases. We deciphered original, hand-written colonial town records where "s's" look like "f's", as well as family memoirs and letters.

Once we had determined the dates and places in which our Patriots served, we researched specific events to put their service into historical context. We read primary legal documents such as colonial charters and acts of the British Parliament, along with protest letters, pamphlets, newspaper articles, and eye-witness accounts of the historical events of the Revolution. The reconstruction of these fragments of information revealed fascinating pictures of our Patriots' personal lives and a clear sense of what they experienced living through America's Revolutionary times.

We knew that none of our Patriots was particularly famous, though we discovered that many crossed paths with well-known leaders like George Washington, the Marquis de Lafayette, John Adams, Benjamin Franklin, Patrick Henry, and even Benedict Arnold. None of their signatures appear on the Declaration of Independence, though many of them committed treason by signing oaths of allegiance long before the Declaration of Independence was written. Nor did they debate strategy in the Continental Congress, though many debated the events of the day while serving in leadership roles in their provincial and town governments. None of them wore the epaulets of military generals, though many fought courageously on the battlefield and suffered tremendous hardships such as hunger, imprisonment, and sickness far from home. Some sacrificed their lives for the cause of liberty.

Taken together, our Patriots represent a broad cross section of ordinary colonial life during an extraordinary chapter in American history. At the time of their service, their ages spanned a tender 13 years to a seasoned 85 years. While most were small farmers, their ranks also include blacksmiths, teachers, cobblers, tavern owners, laborers, weavers, merchants, and millers. They served their local communities as surveyors, jurors, sheriffs, selectmen, justices of the peace, and church deacons. Economically, they ranged from an indentured servant whose merchandising skills were put to excellent use during the war to wealthy plantation owners who contributed funds and supplies. Some descended from families who were among the colonies' earliest European settlers, including *Mayflower* passengers, while others were first generation immigrants. They lived in 12 of the 13 original colonies plus present-day Vermont. And we were deeply saddened to discover the heartbreaking truth that some of our Patriots enslaved other people.

Regretfully, few of our stories feature the contributions of female Patriots. Not surprisingly considering traditional gender roles of the times, Revolutionary era military, government, and town documents that recorded the service of women are scarce. However, women most definitely contributed to the Revolutionary War. Some women took on the arduous work of tending farms and raising children on their own so their husbands and older sons could join the military. Their efforts helped ensure supply taxes could be paid and goods could be provided to fuel the war. One story reveals the creative and resourceful ways in which a patriotic group of sisters contributed supplies to Washington's army. In other cases, women followed their soldier husbands to war and set up makeshift homes along the edges of the military encampments. Another story includes a woman who gave birth to twin boys in such a camp. Where possible, we included the names of our Patriots' spouses in our stories as a way to honor their valuable but unrecorded contributions to the Revolution.

The contributions of African American Patriots are similarly under-recorded. The words "we hold these truths to be self-evident that all men are created equal" written in the Declaration of Independence held a particularly profound meaning to those kept in bondage by slavery. Inspired by the hope and logic that a new nation seeking political freedom from a tyrannical king would decide to free its own people from slavery, African Americans enthusiastically volunteered for service in the Revolution. In addition to being present when the first shots were fired on Lexington Green to the final conflict at Yorktown, African Americans played critical intelligence gathering roles as spies as well as motivational roles as orators and writers. In honor of these contributions, the stories of ten African American Patriots are included in this book.

Revolutionary Values

As the details and chronology of our Patriots' service took shape to become stories, the values motivating their service became visible as well. Those who risked their lives to face the might of the British military surely demonstrated a blend of courage, resolve, and resilience that most of us will never be required to show. Those who served in provisional government roles in defiance of their imperial government demonstrated incredible ingenuity, resourcefulness, and a strong sense of justice. Those who funded the effort with the fruits of their labor on subsistence farms demonstrated selflessness and generosity.

Incredibly, most of our Patriots knew it was unlikely that they would personally benefit from their sacrifices. Perhaps they were inspired by Thomas Paine's widely read pamphlet, *The American Crisis,* that stated, "If there must be trouble, let it be in my day, that my child may have peace."[4] What they did, they did for their descendants. What they did, *they did for us*.

The values we discovered may be the most important part of our Patriot stories because they are as relevant to resolving the problems of today as they were to resolving those of 1776. Many Revolutionary War values are permanently written as a compelling vision in our founding documents. From America's imperfect start where more than one-fifth of her population was enslaved[5], where women had little voice in their government, and where indigenous First Nation people were oppressed, citizens have spent the last 250 years working toward the founding vision of liberty, equality, and justice for all. We are still an imperfect nation. And we live in difficult times. In the context of today's terrifying world events, America's divisive politics, prejudices, and inequalities can cause us to question our national character.

Statesman Daniel Webster anticipated difficult times like these. In a speech at the dedication of the Bunker Hill Memorial in 1843, he said,

> We wish that, in those days of disaster, which, as they come upon all nations, must be expected to come upon us also, desponding patriotism may turn its eyes hitherward, and be assured that the foundations of our national power are still strong.[6]

Not many Americans today find occasion to "turn their eyes hitherward." Such sentimentality can seem out of date. But maybe we should give it a try. Who knows? We might see some ideas that could help solve the problems of our day. At the very least, we may discover a Patriot whose story in this book assures us that the foundations of America are still strong.

Paul Revere's Engraving of the Boston Massacre[1]
Source: Library of Congress

Chapter 1:
RESOLVE

To say the English colonists in North America had an independent streak would be an understatement. Self-determination was their way of life from the start. The colonies were founded by people who cherished their constitutional rights as free English citizens and had risked their lives traveling a continent away for the right to work, worship, and live independently. Their societies were developed through generations of representative governments designed to preserve those rights. And they were ruled for decades by distant monarchs who were perfectly content with this arrangement – as long as it was profitable.

Massive debt from an expensive war upset this status quo. When a series of laws initially meant to restore the British treasury escalated from "concerning" to "intolerable," the colonists resolved to defend what they believed were their natural and constitutional rights.

Foundations of Liberty

As an emerging naval superpower at the close of the 16th century, England was quick to see the potential economic opportunities in North America. King James I began granting charters to private investors to set up colonies and unlock resources that could create wealth back in England. In 1606 he granted a joint-stock charter for the southern part of the Atlantic coast to the Virginia Company of London. This company sold shares to investors whose capital would fund the colonies' development. The Virginia Company set up the first permanent colonial settlement in Jamestown in 1607.

The constitutional rights and liberties of Jamestown's settlers as English citizens were embedded in this first charter. The charter stated that the colony's inhabitants and their children "shall have and enjoy all liberties, franchises and immunities as if they had been abiding and borne [sic] within this our realme [sic] of England."² Many of these liberties dated back to the 1215 Magna Carta, including the right to due process under the law as guaranteed in the famous clause, "To no one will we sell, to no one deny or delay right or justice," as well as the right to a trial by a jury of one's peers.³ The charter also granted the colony the right to create its own currency to facilitate trade.

A decade later, the Jamestown settlers took an important step toward another cherished principle found in the Magna Carta: establishing a freely elected representative government. To improve living conditions in Jamestown, the Virginia Company Board voted to replace martial law with what would be the first representative legislative assembly in the English colonies.⁴ Inspired by the House of Commons in Parliament, the board decided "two Burgesses from each plantation freely to be elected by the inhabitants" of the colony would "enact, constitute, and frame such just and equal laws."⁵ The original assembly met for the first time on July 3, 1619, and was comprised of 22 burgesses, the governor, and four council members.⁶

This foundation of liberty and representative government continued as new English colonial settlements were established. In 1620 a group of religious separatists wanting to break from the Church of England set sail for the Virginia Colony aboard the *Mayflower*. They missed Virginia and landed in present-day Massachusetts where they planted the Plymouth settlement. Since the Virginia Charter did not apply to this territory, these settlers drafted a document called the "Mayflower Compact" in which they agreed to join "together into a civil body politick [sic], for our better ordering and preservation" and "by virtue hereof do enact, constitute, and frame such just and equal Laws."⁷ On this precedent, King Charles I granted a charter to the Massachusetts Bay Company in 1629 to establish a colony. Like the Virginia charter, this charter guaranteed that the colonists and their children "shall have and enjoy all liberties and immunities of free and naturall [sic] subjects … borne [sic] within the Realme [sic] of England."⁸

By 1663 charters had been granted for the creation of 12 English colonies in North America. While the colonies' government structures varied according to their charters and would continue to evolve, they each had a governor to execute the law, a council that served as a supreme court, and an elected representative legislature. At this point, Virginia, New Hampshire, New York, New Jersey, North Carolina, and South Carolina all had royal charters in which the governor was appointed by the King.[9] Pennsylvania, Delaware, and Maryland had proprietary charters in which a person with a relationship to the King served as governor.[10] Massachusetts (which would later be given a royal charter), Rhode Island, and Connecticut had joint-stock charters granted to a group of investors in which the colonists elected their governor.[11] The New England colonies also held town meetings which gave free male colonists the opportunity to participate in their local governments.

More than 3,000 miles away across the Atlantic Ocean, the English government was undergoing a democratic transformation that would powerfully influence and embolden the American Revolution. In 1687 King James II had dissolved the elected Parliament and attempted to replace it with a Parliament willing to grant him unconditional support.[12] In a movement dubbed the "Glorious Revolution," King James was removed from power and in 1689 the British Bill of Rights was created. This document's stated purpose was to ensure that English citizens' "religion, laws and liberties might not again be in danger of being subverted" by a monarch.[13] English citizens were guaranteed the right to freely elect "persons to represent them as were of right to be sent to Parliament," and the government was forbidden from "keeping a standing army within the kingdom in time of peace" without the consent of Parliament.[14] English subjects were also guaranteed freedom from taxation not approved by Parliament and the right to keep arms for their self-defense. Although application to the colonies was not expressly written, the colonists reasonably assumed this Bill of Rights extended to them as English citizens.

During this time, England relaxed its authority and ruled the American colonies with an unofficial policy that Member of Parliament, Edmund Burke, later termed "wise and salutary neglect."[15] England maintained the right to regulate colonial trade in order to maximize wealth for the benefit of the entire British Empire. However, trade laws such as the Navigation Act and the Molasses Act that were designed to discourage trade with foreign nations were not enforced under the policy of salutary neglect. The colonies were effectively left to independently manage their own trade and internal taxation. This arrangement bolstered economies on both sides of the Atlantic. The colonies exported much needed raw materials to the rapidly industrializing England and, in turn, increasingly consumed finished goods imported from England. As such, neither the colonists nor their imperial government pressed for representation of the colonies in Parliament in the manner described in England's new Bill of Rights.

The colonies' autonomy from England was matched by their autonomy from one another. The colonies, now 13 strong with the addition of Georgia in 1732, had developed unique economies and social structures based on their geographical resources and opportunities.[16] They had little need or desire for interaction. The inquisitive Pennsylvania writer and scientist, Benjamin Franklin, had studied the centuries-old Six Nations Confederacy comprised of the Seneca, Cayuga, Onondaga, Oneida, Mohawk, and Tuscarora nations who so effectively collaborated to manage political and resource issues that jointly impacted them.[17] He proposed a similar alliance between the 13 colonies to manage issues of common interest such as trade, taxation, and defense.[18] Delegates from seven colonies met at the Albany Congress in 1754 to discuss a plan for potential union. Fearing encroachment on their individual self-interests, colonial assemblies rejected the plan. The benefit of cooperation was not worth trading the autonomy they enjoyed. It was not yet time to "join or die."

The French and Indian War

The English were not the only Europeans to have colonized North America. Eager to accumulate gold, Spanish conquistadors established the settlement of St. Augustine in present-day Florida in 1565 and claimed the territory west to present-day California.[19] The French established their first settlement in Quebec in 1608, claiming present-day Canada and the Great Lakes region as French territory, and setting up trading posts with indigenous First Nation leaders to supply Europe with furs.[20] Borders between the territorial claims of

England (called Great Britain starting in 1707), France, and Spain were not always clear.[21] Tensions developed between these three imperial nations and their settlers.

The British had promised First Nation leaders that their colonists would not settle west of the Allegheny River and Blue Ridge Mountains.[22] However, eager British settlers pushed westward and eventually clashed with French merchants expanding southward. A dispute over land in present-day Pennsylvania erupted in 1754, igniting the French and Indian War.[23] In 1756 Great Britain declared war on France, escalating the conflict into the global Seven Years War across five continents. In the French and Indian War in North America, the French, with their First Nation and Spanish allies, engaged the British Army reinforced by colonial militia and Iroquois League nations for control of the continent. Among the colonial militia leaders was a young, ambitious Virginian named George Washington who would gain invaluable experience from this conflict.

Hostilities finally ended in a British victory with the *First Treaty of Paris* in 1763. Under this treaty, France ceded Canada and its territory east of the Mississippi River to Great Britain. The Spanish ceded Florida to Great Britain in a trade to recover lost territory in Cuba and the Philippines. With this huge territorial gain, Great Britain became the dominant European power in North America as well as an undisputed world power. "Rule Britannia!" was sung by proud British citizens across the American colonies.[24]

But the war to secure North American dominance had been costly, nearly doubling Great Britain's national debt and severely stressing its treasury.[25] An expensive force of 10,000 British regulars remained in North America to protect territorial borders along the frontier.[26] Tax increases in Great Britain proved insufficient. Radically new revenue raising schemes would be required.

At the same time, the American colonies had fallen into an economic depression after the French and Indian War. War-related business had evaporated. British merchants eager to recoup losses during the war further exacerbated the problem by tightening credit to colonial businesses. As a result of this capital restriction, unfortunate merchants across Massachusetts, New York, and Pennsylvania fell into bankruptcy.[27]

Provocation

King George III and Parliament reasoned that some of the needed revenue should be raised in the North American colonies as compensation for their protection during French and Indian War. Conversely, the economically beleaguered colonists felt they had already contributed sacrificially by fighting alongside British regulars during the war. In the absence of mutual empathy and understanding, the political era of salutary neglect was abruptly replaced with an era of authoritarian provocations.

The first of these provocations was designed to prevent another costly war with First Nation tribes. After the *First Treaty of Paris*, colonists continued moving west to settle Great Britain's newly claimed territory. This expansion was met with opposition from a First Nation coalition led by Ottawa Chief Pontiac. To put a stop to the resulting conflicts, Parliament imposed the Proclamation Line of 1763 which forbade British colonists from settling land west of the Appalachian Mountains. This frustrated the ambitions of colonists planning to expand their fortunes by settling this territory, some of whom had been awarded land there for service in the French and Indian War. Among those frustrated colonists was Virginia House of Burgess member and former colonial militia officer, George Washington, who petitioned both the Virginia Assembly and British King George III to move the line further west.[28]

The next provocation came in the form of the Sugar Act of 1764. This act imposed duties on foreign imports of sugar, indigo, coffee, herbs, textiles, and non-French wine to the American colonies. The act also reduced the duty on foreign molasses from the unenforced Molasses Act of 1633. The language of the act made its purpose clear: "it is just and necessary that a revenue be raised, in your Majesty's said dominions in America, for defraying the expenses of defending, protecting, and securing the same" with the intent of "raising the said revenue in America."[29] While previous acts had been passed for the innocuous purpose of regulating and encouraging trade within the British empire, the Sugar Act was the first law ever imposed on the American colonies with the express purpose of raising revenue.[30] And these duties were being imposed by a British Parliament in which the American colonies were not represented.

Unlike previous acts impacting trade, the Sugar Act outlined strict enforcement provisions that appeared to further encroach on colonial liberties. An increased naval presence and higher-level customs agents were put in place to monitor trade and collect Sugar Act duties. Consistent with the rights guaranteed in the Magna Carta and the British Bill of Rights, American colonists had been accustomed to jury trials. However, alleged violators of the Sugar Act would instead be tried in a Vice-Admiralty Court without a jury of their peers.[31]

Concerns were published in local newspapers and Sugar Act protests sprang up spontaneously across the colonial governments. Five colonies sent formal petitions to Parliament and four others sent grievances.[32] The Massachusetts Bay Colony legislature's written appeal to the House of Commons protested not only the economic hardship of the Sugar Act, but also stressed its enforcement "deprived the colonies of one of the most valuable of English liberties, trials by juries."[33] Other leaders published critiques in pamphlets. Rhode Island Governor Stephen Hopkins contended in his essay, *The Rights of Colonies Examined*, "British subjects are to be governed only agreeable to laws to which they themselves have in some way consented."[34] Massachusetts General Assembly representative, James Otis, agreed in his essay *The Rights of the British Colonies Asserted and Proven* in which he argued, "Taxes are not to be laid on the people, but by their consent in person, or by deputation."[35]

Parliament further exacerbated the colonies' economic concerns two weeks later by passing the Currency Act of 1764. Denying a right dating back to the original Virginia charter, this act forbade the colonies from printing their own paper currency, instead requiring them to pay for imported goods, as well as Sugar Act duties, in gold or silver.[36] Since the colonies' imports exceeded their exports, access to this required gold and silver became increasingly difficult.[37]

Parliament was not persuaded by the colonies' petitions. Arguing that the House of Commons represented all British subjects regardless of geography, Parliament went on to pass an even more controversial law: the Stamp Act of 1765. This act required colonists to pay taxes through the purchase of stamps to be affixed to written material on "every skin or piece of vellum or parchment, or sheet or piece of paper" used to conduct business, legal, and church matters.[38] While the Sugar Act was an *external* tax paid in the form of duties on foreign imports, the Stamp Act was the first *internal* tax paid on goods traded *within* the colonies. Under the policy of salutary neglect, such internal taxes had been the exclusive domain of the representative colonial legislatures for more than a century. As with the Sugar Act, alleged violators of the Stamp Act would be tried in an admiralty court without a jury of their peers.

News of this act sparked widespread opposition in colonial assemblies. Patrick Henry led the passage of a bold resolution in the Virginia House of Burgesses stating, "the habitants of this colony are not bound to yield obedience to any law or ordinance designed to impose any taxation whatsoever other than the laws of their own general assembly."[39] In Massachusetts, John Adams wrote a resolution adopted by 40 Massachusetts town assemblies[40] asserting, "We have always understood it to be a grand and fundamental principle of the English Constitution that no free man should be subject to any tax to which he has not given his own consent."[41] He declared it unconstitutional that "we should be Subjected to any Tax imposed by the British Parliament because we are not Represented in that assembly in any sense."[42] Assemblies in seven other colonies passed resolutions in opposition to the Stamp Act.[43]

While law makers protested with words, merchants and laborers protested with actions. American businesses organized non-importation agreements to disrupt trade with British merchants.[44] Merchants and tradesmen in Massachusetts organized a group called the Sons of Liberty whose members intended to resist collection of the Stamp Act tax.[45] Angry mobs rioted across the colonies and attacked stamp masters appointed by Parliament to administer the tax.

By fall of 1765 the colonies finally concluded that a unified response to Parliament may be more powerful than individual petitions. Delegates from nine colonies met to discuss their concerns in what became known as the Stamp Act Congress.[46] They issued a *Declaration of Rights and Grievances* affirming their allegiance to the King and his government. However, echoing previous individual petitions, the declaration firmly stated, "subjects in these colonies are entitled to all the inherent rights and privileges of his natural born subjects within the kingdom of Great Britain" and therefore "[i]t is inseparably essential to the freedom of a people, and the undoubted right of Englishmen, that no taxes be imposed on them, but with their own consent, given personally, or by their representatives."[47]

That same year, Parliament passed the Quartering Act, requiring the colonies to provide supplies and barracks to house British troops. The colonists protested that this act violated the British Bill of Rights which forbade maintaining a standing army in times of peace.[48] When 1,500 soldiers were sent to New York in 1766, the New York Provincial Assembly flatly refused to house and supply them.[49] In a response that was more punitive than practical, Parliament suspended the New York Assembly until it agreed to comply.

To quell colonial disorder and to appease angry London merchants whose trade had been disrupted, Parliament reluctantly repealed the Stamp Act in March 1766. However conciliatory this may have appeared, Parliament simultaneously passed an ominous new law affirming its authority to tax the colonies. The Declaratory Act unequivocally stated that Parliament held "full power and authority to make laws and statutes of sufficient force and validity to bind the colonies and people of America, subjects of the crown of Great Britain, in all cases whatsoever."[50]

Escalation

Putting this "full power and authority" into action, Parliament passed the controversial Townshend Revenue Act in 1767. As with the Stamp

Act, the stated purpose of this law was to raise revenue in the American colonies. This act imposed a duty on glass, china, paper, lead, paint, and tea imported to the American colonies from Great Britain. In a horrifying measure to enforce this law, the act authorized customs officials armed with writs of assistance to "go into any house, shop, cellar, warehouse, or room or other place, and, in case of resistance, to break open doors, chests, trunks … to seize … any kinds of goods or merchandize [sic] whatsoever prohibited."[51]

This escalation in Parliament's authority was met with an escalation in colonial opposition. Two widely distributed writings protested the Townshend Revenue Act and encouraged colonists to join together to boycott British imports.[52] The first was a series of letters written by Philadelphia attorney, John Dickinson, and printed in newspapers across the colonies.[53] While acknowledging Parliament's authority to regulate colonial trade, Dickinson denied its authority to regulate internal matters, which included raising revenue. Invoking the long-standing policy of salutary neglect, he rejected the Townshend duties as an unreasonable expansion of Parliament's power, rhetorically asking,

> What but the indisputable, the acknowledged exclusive right of the colonies to tax themselves, could be the reason, that in this long period of more than one hundred and fifty years, no statute was ever passed for the sole purpose of raising a revenue on the colonies?[54]

The second influential writing was a letter authored by Samuel Adams and James Otis representing the Massachusetts legislative assembly and calling for a unified colonial response to the Townshend Revenue Act. They declared the Townshend duties were "infringements of their natural and constitutional rights; because, as they are not represented in the British Parliament, his Majesty's commons in Britain, by those Acts, grant their property without their consent."[55] "As it is a subject in which every colony is deeply interested," they wrote, "it seems to be necessary that all possible care should be taken that the representatives of the several assemblies, upon so delicate a point, should harmonize with each other."[56]

The Virginia House of Burgesses sent separate petitions of protest to King George III and Parliament. The respectful petition sent to the King underscored their loyalty, even pledging "at all times to exert their best Endeavours [sic], even at the expense of their Lives and Fortunes, to promote the Glory of your Majesty's Reign," while requesting that he intervene to repeal the Townshend Revenue Act.[57] The more blunt petition sent to the House of Commons condemned the Townshend duties as a violation of their constitutional right to be taxed only with the consent of their elected representatives.[58] Though stating they were not interested in independence from Great Britain, the Burgesses claimed to be the sole representatives of Virginia colonists and added that Parliamentary representation was impractical given the distance between Virginia and London.[59]

Arguments like those made by Dickinson, Adams, and Otis began to motivate a coordinated response among ordinary colonists. Merchants in 24 towns across Massachusetts, Rhode Island, and Connecticut agreed to boycott the importation of British goods for one year.[60] This strategy proved to be a brilliant mechanism for including and encouraging women to participate in protests. Although they did not have a voice in town meetings, women could express their political opinions by participating in boycotts as consumers. By refusing to purchase and consume British-made goods, they loudly expressed their opposition to the Townshend Revenue Act and the unconstitutional overreach of power it represented.[61]

In addition to the boycotts, violent street demonstrations continued. Angry protesters vandalized stores carrying British goods.[62] Customs officials were harassed and attacked as they attempted to collect Townshend duties. Exasperated with colonial insubordination, the King sent 2,000 British troops to Boston to suppress such protests.[63] In a town of only 16,000 people, this military presence was visible and threatening.[64] On March 5, 1770, a skirmish erupted between protesters and soldiers guarding the Boston Customs House. Five colonists were killed in the incident that would be characterized in newspapers as "the Boston Massacre."

Following this highly publicized tragedy, British troops were withdrawn from Boston and the Townshend duties were repealed in 1770. However, the duty on tea was intentionally kept in place to assert Parliament's power to tax the colonies. This would prove to be a costly assertion.

Committees of Correspondence

In the wake of this alarming chain of provocations, ordinary colonists began taking a greater interest in learning about the political events shaping their lives. Newspapers had been instrumental in publishing the acts of Parliament and reporting the discussions in colonial assemblies that followed. Vocal leaders across the colonies continued to print pamphlets that articulated the rights of the colonies and their grievances against Parliament, widely distributing them for discussion at local meetings.[65]

To facilitate even faster and more efficient communication of Parliament's decisions and potential colonial responses, these leaders formed organizations called Committees of Correspondence. Early committees had been set up temporarily to organize protests against Parliament's tax laws. The first longstanding Committee of Correspondence was formed in Massachusetts in 1772 to protest a British proposal that would shift payment of colonial governors' and judges' salaries from the colonies to the crown with the intent of securing their loyalty.[66] By March 1773, the Colony of Virginia had formed its own Committee of Correspondence and called for the other colonies to do the same.[67] Within two years, 12 colonies had formed such committees.[68] The information flow created by these committees transformed local meetings. Now instead of discussing only local affairs, people attending these meetings were equipped to debate matters that impacted the colonies as a whole.

Unified by this free exchange of ideas on issues of joint concern, the colonies began to shape and share an identity that was becoming uniquely American.[69] The dubious motives behind Parliament's decisions toward the American colonies raised questions about whether those in the social aristocracy an ocean away were really best suited to govern them.[70]

Rebellion

Over time, commitment to boycotts began to weaken and Parliament took the opportunity to reassert its authority to tax the colonies by enacting the Tea Act in 1773. This act granted a tea monopoly in the American colonies to the East India Company and eliminated the duty paid by the company when the tea was transported through Great Britain.[71] The duty would instead be paid on receipt of the tea in the American colonies. Consignee merchants were appointed in the colonies to accept shipment of the East India Tea and pay the duty upon its arrival.

On the surface, the law was designed to rescue the failing East India Tea Company whose profits had suffered under the sizable duty it paid before its tea was exported abroad. Parliament hoped the now-cheaper tea would be welcomed by the American colonists. However, many colonists believed the act was deviously designed to force them to accept Parliament's right to tax them.[72]

Patriots across the colonies organized ways to avoid paying the duty as ships carrying the East India Tea began arriving at their ports. In New York and Philadelphia, Patriots convinced the appointed consignees to resign and sent the ships back to England.[73] In Charleston the tea was unloaded but stored untouched in a warehouse controlled by Patriots without paying the duty.[74]

The situation was more complicated when the *Beaver*, the *Dartmouth*, and the *Eleanor* sailed into Boston Harbor carrying 92,000 pounds of East India Tea.[75] The Sons of Liberty organized a town meeting in Boston on November 29, 1773, that was attended by thousands of people from Boston and nearby towns.[76] Samuel Adams proposed a resolution "that the tea shall not only be sent back but that no duty shall be paid thereof" that was affirmed with cheers and nods of support from the assembled crowd.[77] Nevertheless, Massachusetts Lieutenant Governor Thomas Hutchinson and the ships' owners refused to send the tea back to Great Britain.

On December 16, the eve of the tea duty deadline, over a thousand colonists from across Massachusetts again gathered in Boston.[78] When the governor continued to refuse to return the ships to Great Britain, Samuel Adams uttered the coded words, "This meeting can do nothing more to save the country."[79] This phrase was the signal to proceed with a secret plan to destroy the tea rather than allow it to be unloaded and incur the duty. Accompanied by a crowd of cheering supporters, approximately 200 Sons of Liberty boarded the three ships and flung the 340 chests of tea they were carrying into Boston Harbor.[80] They were careful not to damage any other property on the ship, even sweeping the decks when they were finished and replacing a padlock they had broken.[81]

Response to Boston's defiance was a mixture of condemnation and praise. Unsurprisingly, Lieutenant Governor Hutchinson declared it an act of high treason.[82] George Washington condemned the destruction of property.[83] Benjamin Franklin agreed and favored compensation to the East India Company, believing "a speedy Reparation will immediately set us right in the Opinion of all Europe."[84] Boston businessman, John Hancock, foresaw the "Tea Party's" potential to galvanize broad colonial support, writing a week later, "No one circumstance could possibly have taken place more effectively to unite the colonies than this maneuver of the tea."[85] Massachusetts lawyer and politician, John Adams, jubilantly recorded in his diary that the destruction of the tea was "the most magnificent movement of all," believing it "was absolutely and indispensably" appropriate because the governor and customs officials could have saved the tea by sending it back to London but refused.[86] However, Adams also understood that the tea's destruction would undoubtedly heighten tensions with King George III and Parliament. He privately wondered in his diary,

> What Measures will the Ministry take, in Consequence of this? Will they resent it? Will they dare to resent it? Will they punish Us? How? By quartering Troops upon Us? By annulling our Charter? By laying on more duties? By restraining our Trade? By Sacrifice of Individuals, or how?[87]

Royal Fury

Adams would not wait long for answers. News of the destruction of the tea in Boston Harbor arrived in London in January. After dismissing the idea of charging individuals with treason, King George III and Parliament swiftly formulated a harsh plan that would punish the entire Massachusetts Bay Colony and send a strong message to deter other colonies from such insubordination.

This punitive response came in a series of four oppressive laws that Parliament collectively called the "Coercive Acts" and colonists characterized as the "Intolerable Acts." The first was the Boston Port Act passed in March 1774, designed to paralyze the Massachusetts Bay Colony's economy by closing Boston Harbor until the people of Boston paid restitution for the destroyed tea. The act forbade exports by discontinuing "the landing and discharging, lading or shipping, of goods, wares, and merchandise, at the town, and within the harbour [sic], of Boston, in the province of Massachusets [sic] Bay, in North America."[88] The only imports allowed were supplies for the British military and essentials such as wheat and fuel.

The second act stripped Massachusetts Bay colonists of their elected representative government. The Massachusetts Government Act passed in May 1774 revoked the colony's charter and dissolved its elected representative government. The act ordered the elected Massachusetts Assembly to be replaced with crown-appointed members and authorized the governor to appoint judges, justices of the peace, and sheriffs. Town meetings throughout the colony were restricted to once a year because Parliament claimed that "a great abuse has been made of the power of calling such meetings" resulting in the passage of "dangerous and unwarrantable resolves."[89] The third was the Act for the Impartial Administration of Justice passed in May 1774, threatening the colonists' right to a trial by jury by granting the governor of Massachusetts the power to move trials to another colony at his discretion.[90]

None other than the mighty British military was installed to administer these punitive acts. British General Thomas Gage arrived in Boston in

May to replace Thomas Hutchinson as governor of Massachusetts. Eleven regiments of British regulars were garrisoned there to enforce the Government and Administration Acts, while the Royal Navy was dispatched to enforce the Boston Port Act.[91]

A fourth ominous act was passed in June 1774 and applied to all the colonies. Replacing the previously expired quartering law, the new Quartering Act authorized military leaders to demand better and more convenient accommodations for British troops, including uninhabited houses and barns.[92] To colonial leaders monitoring events in Massachusetts, the intent behind this veiled threat was unmistakable.

Colonial Outrage

The text of the Intolerable Acts was published in newspapers across the colonies, eliciting shock and outrage throughout the summer of 1774. In June, newspapers began printing the reactions of several legislative assemblies. The House of Representatives in Connecticut denounced the acts as "justly alarming to every British colony in America" and a threat to "their lives, liberties, and properties."[93] The legislative assembly of New Jersey declared the Coercive Acts "depriv[ed] his Majesties [sic] American subjects of their undoubted and constitutional rights and privileges."[94] When legislative assemblies in the Colony of New Hampshire, the Province of Maryland, and the Colony of Virginia similarly opposed the Coercive Acts, their royal governors dissolved the assemblies.[95] The members of these dissolved assemblies simply formed their own independent provincial assemblies to continue their deliberations. In a letter to a friend, an incensed George Washington declared, "the cause of Boston [against] the despotick [sic] Measures . . . now is and ever will be consider[e]d as the cause of America."[96]

Ordinary colonists agreed. As Boston's trade evaporated under the Royal Navy's enforcement of the Port Act, supplies and aid poured in from colonies sympathetic to the city's painful crisis.[97] Town assemblies passed supportive resolutions and called for days of fasting and prayer in support of Boston.[98]

Bolstered by this outpouring of colonial support, Patriots in Massachusetts were determined to defy every aspect of the Coercive Acts. Some merchants and political moderates still called for restitution for the destroyed tea.[99] But when the Massachusetts Government Act went into effect on August 1, large crowds across the colony prevented county courts, with their new crown-appointed judges, from operating.[100] Similarly, all 36 men appointed to Governor Gage's Council were harassed by angry groups who forced them to resign.[101]

In open defiance of the new law forbidding their meetings, town residents gathered as usual to elect delegates to the Massachusetts Bay Colony's legislative assembly.[102] When Governor Gage refused to meet with this assembly as scheduled in October, the defiant delegates met anyway and resolved to create a new representative governing body called the Massachusetts Provincial Congress.[103] In a foreboding anticipation of future conflict, this illegal body recommended that each town recruit, organize, and elect officers for militia who would "hold themselves in Readiness to march at the shortest Notice."[104] Towns all over Massachusetts complied and began to equip and train their units of "Minutemen."[105]

Our Patriots

Many of our Patriots were proud descendants of the settlers who had established the 13 American colonies and built the foundation of self-governance. Some had fought alongside British regulars during the French and Indian War. They undoubtedly read the newspaper coverage of each new revenue-raising act from Parliament with increasing concern. As town selectmen and representatives in colonial assemblies, many openly discussed these concerns and debated ideas for response. Some became influential members of Committees of Correspondence. Many compassionately participated in the call to support the people of Boston with supplies.

As alarming as previous provocations had been, the Intolerable Acts were the most contemptable to the colonists. The acts went beyond *challenging* the colonists' constitutional rights as British citizens to *denying* them outright. And if these rights could be stripped from the Massachusetts Bay Colony, the other 12 reasoned, they could surely be stripped from any of them. Individual colonial petitions to London had proven ineffective. The time for a united response to defend their rights and liberties had come.

Weller Tavern in Manchester, Vermont
Courtesy of Manchester Historical Society

Eliakim Weller A214108
(ante 1748 - circa 1780)
Kathleen Barrett Huston

Eliakim Weller was born in New Milford, Connecticut, and migrated to Dutchess County, New York. A proprietor in the New Hampshire Grants, Eliakim was a long-time selectman of Manchester, Vermont, and immersed in conflicts between New York and Vermont landowners whose rights the Green Mountain Boys fiercely defended.

Eliakim owned Weller Tavern which served as an important meeting place at the outset of the American Revolution. The tavern is on the National Register of Historic Places and a plaque above its fireplace reads:

"On March 1, 1774, the seeds of American Independence were sown at a special meeting held here in Eliakim and Anna Weller's Tavern. On that day, the Freemen of Manchester and the Committees of Safety from surrounding townships openly challenged the political authority of the British Governor of New York ... The following year, Allen's militia captured Fort Ticonderoga in a surprise attack that marked the first offensive actions in American's War for Independence."

In 1776 Eliakim served on the Committee of Correspondence for Manchester. Meetings continued to be held in Weller Tavern throughout the Revolution. Eliakim's children intermarried with Green Mountain Boys and, interestingly, Tories. His daughter, Catharine, first married John Vail, son of Green Mountain Boys Captain Micah Vail, and second, Alexander Barrett, son of Bartholomew Barrett (A208181), a Revolutionary soldier for New York.

Captain Edward Converse A025168
(baptized 1720 - 1800)
Nina Bentley

Edward Converse was born in Killingly, Connecticut, in 1720. He married Mary Davis and the couple settled on a farm along the French River on land from the estate of Mary's father and where Edward was named Captain of the 7th Company, 15th Regiment militia.

The couple relocated to the newly incorporated town of Gageborough in the northwest corner of Massachusetts. The town was named in honor of General Thomas Gage who had served as the Commander in Chief of British Armed Forces in North America after the French and Indian War. Edward became a prominent leader in his new community and was voted selectman for nine consecutive years beginning in 1771.

In 1774 Parliament passed the Coercive Acts to punish Massachusetts for the destruction of East India Company tea. The Coercive Acts dissolved the colony's representative government and severely restricted town meetings. General Thomas Gage was appointed governor of Massachusetts to enforce these unjust acts. Outraged at their namesake's oppressive leadership, the inhabitants of Gageborough voted to rename the town "Windsor" four years later. As town selectman, Edward would have led this patriotic and rebellious gesture.

Edward and Mary remained in Windsor after the Revolution. Edward died there in 1800.

Richard Langhorn (Clarke) Clark A134150
(1753 - 1814)
Charlotte Clark Jenkins

Richard Langhorn Clark was a fourth-generation colonist of The Province of Maryland. Maryland was chosen by his family for the religious freedom the province offered to Catholics. In 1774 Richard became a member of the St. Mary's County Committee of Correspondence.

Committees of Correspondence had operated for years prior to the American Revolution as a way for the colonists to communicate with the British Parliament. By the 1770s, opposition to British imperial policies drove the committees to develop a more well-organized and deliberate mission: resistance. The local committees, besides participating in the communication system between colonies, selected delegates to the First Continental Congress, acted as local enforcers of the Continental Association decisions, such as nonimportation and nonexportation agreements, and worked with Committees of Safety to secure militias. Records show Clark acted as a collector, gathering and dispersing funds and supplies as needed. Once "the shot heard 'round the world" was fired at Lexington and Concord, the Committees of Correspondence acted as defacto governments before provincial assemblies were established.

In 1778 Clark signed the Oath of Fidelity, renouncing the King of England and pledging allegiance to the revolutionary government of Maryland. By signing this oath and serving on the Committee of Correspondence, Clark had committed two acts of treason by the age of 25!

Major Hezekiah Smith A105490
(1726 - 1800)
Michelle Henderson White

Major Hezekiah Smith was born in 1726 in Woodstock, Connecticut, and died in Colrain, Massachusetts, on August 19, 1800, at age 74. He married Eunice Morris on December 19, 1747. Hezekiah and Eunice moved to the beautiful valley of Colrain around 1764, settling on the "Wells lot" on the west side of the scenic North River.

Hezekiah was a prominent Massachusetts statesman during the American Revolution. He was a member of the Committee of Correspondence in 1773, a delegate to the Massachusetts Provincial Congress in 1775, and a member of the convention that developed the constitution of Massachusetts in 1780 written by John Adams. Chosen as a moderator for Colrain, he was tasked with reading the constitution drafts aloud and recommending amendments to residents.

Hezekiah also served in the military throughout the war. He enlisted in 1775, immediately following the Lexington Alarm. By April 1777, he was a major in the regiment of his neighbor, Colonel David Wells, serving in the Commissary Department at Fort Ticonderoga. In July he experienced General Burgoyne's Siege of Fort Ticonderoga and the American evacuation to Saratoga where he witnessed Burgoyne's surrender in October 1777. Five of Hezekiah's sons also served in the Revolutionary War, including my ancestor, David (A213166), who served alongside his father at Saratoga.

Thomas Johnson A063768
(1735 - 1803)
Michelle Henderson White

Thomas Johnson was a prominent leader in the colony of Virginia. He descended from early settlers of Virginia and resided at Roundabout Castle on family property received as a land grant from the King. Thomas served in the Virginia House of Burgesses and as Sheriff in Louisa County. He was also a justice of the peace, becoming chief justice and vestryman by 1787. During the American Revolution, he was named to serve on Louisa County's Committee of Safety in 1775.

In 1762 Sheriff Johnson was sued for failing to enforce a clergy compensation law. He hired a young lawyer named Patrick Henry to defend him. Henry's passionate arguments against the tyranny of King George unfortunately resulted in a loss for Johnson, but the plaintiff clergyman was awarded only one penny in compensation. Johnson and Henry became friends and then neighbors at Roundabout.

As a result of Johnson's faithful mentorship, Henry assumed Johnson's seat in the House of Burgesses upon Johnson's retirement in 1765. Henry used this position to introduce the Stamp Act Resolves to protest British Parliament's taxation of the colonies. Henry's powerful "Give me liberty or give me death!" speech made during the Second Virginia Convention on March 20, 1775, would inspire people across the colonies to join the cause of independence.

Captain John Fox A215188
(circa 1740 - 1803)
Michelle Henderson White

John Fox was born in Hanover, Virginia, to Joseph and Susanna Smith Fox. John married Grace Young in 1764. They made their home in Louisa County, Virginia.

Louisa County was home to people of strong convictions about the rights and liberties of colonists. Virginians met in Richmond, Virginia, for eight days beginning March 20, 1775, to discuss the many injustices levied upon them by the English Crown. In anticipation of this convention, a group of concerned citizens including John Fox and the man who would become his son Meredith's father-in-law, John Ragland (A132445), wrote a letter dated March 17, 1775, to delegates admonishing them not to allow small-sum gambling in the colony. The letter stated such a thing would surely "open the Door to all that Excess, injustice, idleness, fraud, deception, and Idleness" that they perceived would be the ruin of society. Theirs was not the only well-written outrage presented at the Virginia Convention. Fellow Louisa resident, Patrick Henry, delivered his famous "Give Me Liberty or Give Me Death!" speech at this gathering.

When the Revolution began, John was a captain in the Louisa County militia. He additionally provided patriotic service by paying for supplies for himself and his officers. Captain Fox died in 1803 at age 63 at his Louisa County home named Mount Harmony.

John Ragland A132445
(circa 1721 - circa 1785)
Michelle Henderson White

John Ragland was born in 1721 in Hanover, Virginia. He married Anne Beverly Dudley in 1758 and they had 11 children. They lived in Louisa County, Virginia, during the American Revolution.

John provided patriotic service by supplying beef to the Continental Army. In 1775, the Continental Congress approved a Ration of Provisions that would be provided to each enlisted soldier. The first items listed were "One pound of fresh beef, or ¾ of a pound of Pork, or one pound of Salt Fish, pr diem." Meeting this daily provision was a difficult task. Patriots like John Ragland provided the beef the army needed to keep the soldiers fed and able to fight for the cause of liberty.

When Virginia delegates met in Richmond in March 1775 to discuss British oppression of the American colonies, John joined his daughter's future father-in-law, Captain John Fox (A215188), to express their deeply held convictions. The two presented a letter to the delegates articulating the threats to society posed by small-sum gambling.

John remained in his beloved Virginia his entire life. He died in Louisa County in 1785, just one year after the *Treaty of Paris* ending hostilities with Great Britain was ratified by Congress.

*Thomas Jefferson's Original Draft
of the Declaration of Independence*[1]
Source: Library of Congress

Chapter 2: DECLARATION

---   ★   ---

The Coercive Acts punishing the Massachusetts Bay Colony for the destruction of British East India Company tea ignited the chain of events that would finally galvanize Patriots across the colonies to unite. They issued a unified response to King George III and Parliament asserting their rights while at the same time seeking reconciliation. When martial law replaced representative government in Massachusetts Bay, the first armed conflict erupted between colonial militia and British regulars. Astonishing Patriot military victories in Boston emboldened the Revolution, but enraged King George III.

At the very moment the largest military force ever assembled by Great Britain arrived in New York City to subdue the rebellion, people across the colonies directed their Continental Congress delegates to break from Great Britain. These delegates drafted and ultimately signed their Declaration of Independence. Under the direction of the people themselves, this document transformed 13 separate colonies into the United States of America. However, humbling defeats in New York sent a painful message that true independence would cost a great deal more than a treasonous declaration.

A Grand Continental Congress

The ruthlessness of the Coercive Acts, coupled with the subsequent dissolution of several colonial assemblies by royal governors, struck the spark that ignited colonial unity. Determined leaders across the colonies agreed to meet to discuss the potential for a joint response to these developments. At the invitation of the Virginia Committee of Correspondence, delegates from 12 colonies met in secret on September 5, 1774, in Philadelphia's Carpenters' Hall for a "Grand Continental Congress."

The delegates unanimously agreed that the Coercive Acts were an unconstitutional violation of their liberties as British citizens. They drafted a *Declaration and Resolves* to express their grievances to King George III and Parliament. This document unequivocally stated that the Coercive Acts were "impolitic, unjust, and cruel, as well as unconstitutional, and most dangerous and destructive of American rights."[2] The document resolved that the colonists had the constitutional rights to "life, liberty and property," to participate in their own government, to peaceably assemble, to be tried by a jury of their peers, and to be subject to taxation only with their consent or representation.[3] The delegates also boldly asserted that any government officials appointed by the crown could not be objective and were therefore "unconstitutional, dangerous and destructive to the freedom of American legislation."[4]

Despite widespread agreement on the importance of these grievances, there was less alignment among the delegates on how best to address them. Massachusetts delegate, John Adams, and Virginia delegate, Patrick Henry, advocated for independence from Great Britain and proposed the colonies prepare for conflict by building a strong military.[5] This proposal was dismissed as an act of war. Others argued reconciliation with Great Britain was still possible. Pennsylvania delegate, Joseph Galloway, presented a narrowly defeated proposal for the creation of a Colonial Parliament that would collaborate with the British Parliament.[6] Citing the previous success of boycotts in forcing the repeal of the Stamp and Townshend Acts, other delegates proposed imposing economic measures to encourage Parliament to similarly repeal the Coercive Acts.[7]

Finally agreeing that economic restrictions would be the wisest course, the delegates drafted the *Continental Association* in which the colonies jointly agreed to ban the importation and consumption of British goods, including the importation of enslaved people.[8] The articles instructed each town to elect local Committees of Observation and Inspection responsible for enforcing this embargo and openly exposing the "enemies of American Liberty" who refused to comply.[9]

If the Coercive Acts were not repealed within one year, the colonies further agreed to ban all exports to Great Britain.

In his diary, John Adams captured the sense of unity that emerged during the First Continental Congress. He recorded the words of Patrick Henry, who declared, "The distinctions between Virginians, Pennsylvanians, New Yorkers, [a]nd New Englanders, are no more. I am not a Virginian, but an American."[10]

Bloody Conflict Begins

As illegal political gatherings escalated from town and province levels to a continental level, British General Thomas Gage faced increasing pressure from London to take military action to bring the American colonies under control. Alarmed by colonial militias observed drilling in towns across Massachusetts, Gage decided on a plan to seize their military supplies. British regulars successfully seized colonial arms in Cambridge, but angry colonists had defended their supplies in Salem without firing any shots.[11] Gage devised a secret plan to confiscate a large store of weapons and ammunition in Concord, Massachusetts.

Patriot spies learned of the plan and on the evening of April 18, 1775, dispatched a network of riders, including Paul Revere and William Dawes, to warn Massachusetts towns between Boston and Concord to anticipate the arrival of British regulars.

At 5:00 a.m. on April 19, a company of 77 militiamen led by Captain John Parker stood ready in Lexington to intercept 700 British regulars led by Lieutenant Colonel Francis Smith.[12] As the militiamen began to disperse, one shot from an unknown source was fired. The British regulars then opened fire, leaving eight militiamen dead.[13]

Within hours of the conflict, Joseph Palmer of the Watertown, Massachusetts Committee of Safety learned of the attack, along with the news that the unnerved Colonel Francis had called for reinforcements from Boston. Palmer wrote a pivotal letter addressed "To all friends of American liberty" informing them that eyewitnesses had reported a brigade of British regulars had met a company of colonial militia at Lexington "upon whom they fired without any provocation."[14] This letter, now known as the Lexington Alarm, was immediately dispatched by riders through Massachusetts and Connecticut who copied the letter at each stop and sped the message along via fresh riders.[15]

From Lexington the British regulars advanced toward their destination in Concord. After setting the courthouse on fire and securing the town's North Bridge, the regulars found themselves facing a force of 400 well-organized Patriot militiamen who had arrived from surrounding towns.[16] The British regulars first fired warning shots, but then fired directly into the gathered militia. In what would be the Revolution's first direct order to fire on British troops, colonial leader, Major John Buttrick, shouted, "Fire, for God's sake, fellow soldiers, fire!"[17] Throughout the afternoon, thousands of Minutemen arrived in response to the Lexington Alarm to fight the retreating British column from behind stone fences and woods along the entire road back to Boston. By the end of the day, 3,800 colonial militiamen had engaged with 1,500 British regulars in twenty hours of continuous fighting.[18]

Committees of Correspondence rapidly spread the news of the conflicts at Lexington and Concord throughout the colonies. Though colonial newspapers typically did not use headlines, the *New Hampshire Gazette* in Portsmouth headlined the front page with "Bloody News" in its April 21, 1775 edition.[19] The article cited a letter received by the chairman of the Portsmouth Committee of Correspondence blaming the conflict on British troops who "marched out of Boston to make some attack on the country."[20] Within two weeks, 20,000 colonial militiamen from across New England responded to this news and surrounded the British Army in Boston in a siege of the city.[21]

Other colonial leaders eager to harass the British launched plans of their own. Frontier leader, Ethan Allen, along with the Green Mountain Boys of Vermont, set out to attack British-held Fort Ticonderoga in New York.[22] He was joined enroute by Connecticut merchant and militiaman, Benedict Arnold, who held orders to capture the fort from the Massachusetts Provincial Congress. The two leaders reluctantly agreed to share command of the operation and easily captured the fort in a surprise attack on May 10, 1775.

The stunned General Gage declared martial law in the besieged city of Boston and made plans to occupy the city's high grounds on Bunker Hill and Dorchester Heights. Learning of this plan, colonial Colonel William Prescott led 1,200 Massachusetts and Connecticut militiamen to build a fortification on Bunker Hill before dawn on June 19, 1775.[23] The British launched an immediate attack. While warships bombarded the Patriot fortification with cannon fire, British Major General William Howe led a ground assault. The determined militia successfully repelled three waves of British attacks before they ran out of ammunition and were forced to retreat.

Despite being a military defeat, the Battle of Bunker Hill was celebrated as a victory by American Patriots. Nearly half of Howe's 2,200 troops had been killed or wounded by a significantly smaller Patriot force.[24] The spirited Massachusetts soldier, Peter Brown, described the fierce fighting in a letter to his mother, recounting how British regulars "advanc[e]d towards us in order to swallow us up, but they found a Choaky mouthful of us."[25] The elated Patriot went on to write,

> God in Mercy to us fought our battle, and tho[ugh] we were but few in number, and suffer[e]d to be defeated by our enemy, yet we were preserv[ed] in a most wonderful manner, far beyond our expectation.[26]

The defiant rebellion against Parliament to protest oppressive laws had now become a violent conflict against the powerful British military to preserve colonial liberties. With convincing shows of resistance at Concord, Boston, and Fort Ticonderoga, the colonists began to believe it was a conflict they could win.

The Second Continental Congress

In the midst of these armed clashes in the spring of 1775, the Second Continental Congress met in Philadelphia to determine a new course of action. With Georgia's three delegates, all 13 colonies were now represented. Convinced by eye-witness accounts that escalation in Boston was inevitable, the delegates decided to create a Continental Army. They resolved to arm and supply the militia already gathered in Boston, raise additional troops, and appoint French and Indian War veteran, George Washington, as Commander in Chief of the new army.[27] Each colony was directed to provide regiments and military supplies according to their populations.[28] At full strength, each company in the Continental Army was intended to be comprised of a captain, two lieutenants, one ensign, four sergeants, four corporals, two drummers, two fifers, and seventy-six privates.[29]

Within months, the Continental Congress also resolved to create a navy. The delegates knew they could not create a navy capable of competing with Great Britain's, but they could use a nimble fleet to harass British commercial ships. Without time to build ships, Congress resolved to equip privateers with letters of marque authorizing them to attack and seize British ships and their cargo as prizes.[30] Over the course of the war, almost 800 ships would be commissioned as privateers that would capture or destroy nearly 600 British ships.[31]

Though united on the need for defense, the Second Continental Congress remained divided on the question of independence. Several provincial assemblies had specifically instructed their delegates to vote against independence, hoping reconciliation with Great Britain may still be possible. Consequently, at the same time the delegates resolved to create a military force in preparation for war, they also prepared an offer of peace. The resulting *Olive Branch Petition* reaffirmed the colonies' loyalty to the King and expressed gratitude for the historic "union between our Mother country and these colonies" that had "produced benefits so remarkably important, and afforded such an assurance of their permanency and increase, that the wonder and envy of other Nations were excited."[32] However, the petition criticized Parliament for disrupting this union by "proceeding to open hostilities" to enforce its unjust laws that now "have compelled us to arm in our own defence [sic]."[33] The petition closed with an appeal to the King to intervene and restore the relationship between Great Britain and the American colonies. Congress dispatched former Pennsylvania Governor, Richard Penn, to London to hand-deliver the petition to the King.

Open and Avowed Rebellion

If the thousands of colonial militiamen still surrounding the British army in a siege of Boston wondered about the consequences of their actions, a royal proclamation answered the question. King George III rejected the *Olive Branch Petition* and on August 23, 1775, issued a royal proclamation declaring the colonies to be in a state of "open and avowed rebellion."[34] The proclamation required all British civil servants, and indeed all British subjects in the colonies, "to suppress such Rebellion, and to bring the Traitors to Justice."[35] The proclamation broadened its condemnation beyond those carrying arms, unequivocally stating "all Persons who shall be found carrying on Correspondence with, or in any Manner or Degree aiding or abetting the Persons now in open Arms and Rebellion against Our Government within any of Our Colonies" will be punished.[36]

On the heels of the King's proclamation, Parliament passed another act designed to cripple the colonial economy. The American Prohibitory Act made all American trade with foreign nations illegal. The act removed British protection from colonial ships, declared them to be enemies, and permitted the cargo from their capture by the Royal Navy to be prizes of war.[37]

Under the weight of this news, General George Washington worked to organize, train, and supply the disorderly, disjointed collection of militia companies he had discovered in Boston upon his arrival in July 1775. As winter set in, the Siege of Boston remained in a stalemate. The Continental Army outnumbered the British regulars but could not blockade the port without a navy and could not attack without artillery.[38] The British were too weak to attack, but too strong to overtake.[39]

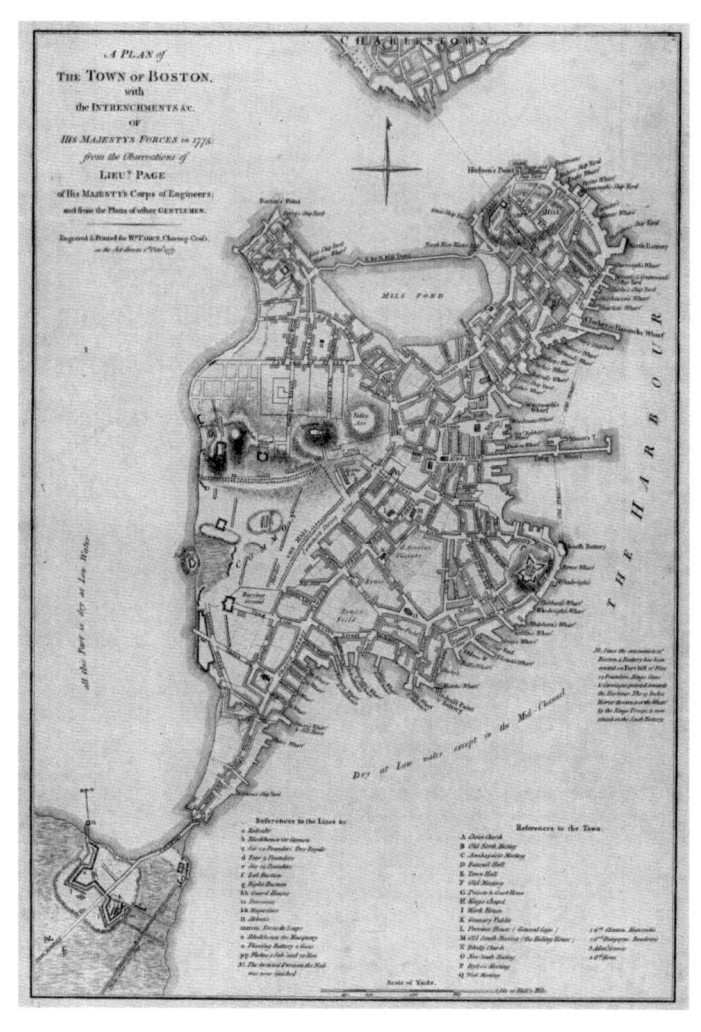

Map of Boston with British Military Positions
Siege of Boston, 1775[40]
Source: Library of Congress

Canadian Campaign

Hoping to generate a victory on another front while the stalemate in Boston wore on, General Washington ordered an invasion of Canada. The first stage of the campaign began in August 1775 when American General Richard Montgomery with troops from Fort Ticonderoga successfully captured British Fort St. John and the city of Montreal. Washington then sent Colonel Benedict Arnold with 1,100 Continental troops to capture Quebec City in collaboration with Montgomery.[41] However, General Montgomery was killed in the first attack of the conflict. Colonel Arnold was shot in the leg and forced to retreat. Further obstructed by blizzard conditions and hindered by severe hunger and unrelenting sickness among the troops, the Quebec mission ended in failure on New Year's Eve 1775. After a series of skirmishes in the Battle of the Cedars outside of Montreal, American troops were forced to retreat back to New York in the spring.

Common Sense

A fresh vision of hope lifted Patriot spirits when a little-known writer and English immigrant named Thomas Paine published his 48-page pamphlet entitled *Common Sense* in January 1776. One hundred thousand copies were sold and excerpts were reprinted in newspapers throughout the colonies.[42] Written in language ordinary colonists could understand, the pamphlet laid out sound and convincing arguments for independence from Great Britain. Appealing to the colonists' values of equality and justice, Paine first criticized the British form of government. He argued a monarch was "not to be trusted" because the "thirst for absolute power is the natural disease of monarchy" and "the state of monarchy shuts him from the world, yet the business of a king requires him to know it thoroughly." [43] "Of more worth" he bluntly stated, "is one honest man to society, and in the sight of God, than all the crowned ruffians that ever lived."[44] Equally absurd, Paine continued, is government by a hereditary aristocracy such as the House of Lords because "all men being originally equals, no one by birth could have the right to set up his own family in perpetual preference to all others forever."[45]

Paine then appealed to the colonists' proud ancestral roots, reminding them "the same tyranny that drove the first emigrants from [England], pursues their descendants still."[46] He also appealed to their economic ambitions, arguing an independent America would be wealthier with unrestricted global trade and safer if free from Britain's powerful French and Spanish enemies.[47] He painted a compelling vision of a more just form of government that could correct the inherent flaws of a monarchy. Paine believed the people themselves had a historic opportunity to create an entirely new form of central government with its own "Continental Charter" of individual rights where "the law is king."[48] Failure to do so now, he warned, would be "using posterity with the utmost cruelty."[49]

Delighted to see *Common Sense* generate so much enthusiasm for independence but concerned that Paine's central government ideas were too radical and vague, John Adams offered an alternative in *Thoughts on Government* published in April 1776. Adams believed "that the form of government, which communicates ease, comfort, security, or in one word happiness to the greatest number of persons, and in the greatest degree, is the best."[50] To that end, Adams advocated for separate executive, legislative, and judicial branches of a government equipped with checks on each other's powers set out in a written constitution.[51] He proposed two legislative bodies. The first body would be an elected, representative assembly who would choose the second body as a council to provide a counterbalance to the first.[52] These assemblies would then choose an executive governor who would command the military and appoint the judiciary.[53] All officials, Adams firmly believed, should be elected annually as, "[t]his will teach them the great political virtues of humility, patience, and moderation, without which every man in power becomes a ravenous beast of prey."[54]

In Adams's mind, the question of whether the colonies should assume governments separately or together should be their decision.[55] If a continental government should be formed, it should consist of "a fair and adequate Representation of the Colonies" and confine itself to governing issues of war, trade, disputes between colonies, and the post office.[56]

Knowing her husband was imagining such future government structures, Abigail Adams urged him to expand his vision and create a more inclusive government. In a letter written in March 1776, she implored him to "remember the ladies" and "not put such unlimited power into the hands of the Husbands."[57] If not, she warned, "we are determined to foment a Rebelion [sic], and will not hold ourselves bound by any Laws in which we have no voice."[58]

As colonists studied and debated these pamphlets, the arguments for independence from Great Britain in *Common Sense* and the clear vision of a representative government worth fighting for in *Thoughts on Government* combined to rally support for the Revolution to new heights.

Victory in Boston

Aware that the British Army would undoubtedly be reinforced in spring, General Washington decided to launch an offensive operation to break the siege in Boston. The decision was made clear when Boston bookseller and self-taught artillery expert, Henry Knox, successfully hauled the cannons from Fort Ticonderoga on sleds pulled by 80 yoke of oxen across New England to Boston.[59] On March 5, 1776, while part of the Continental Army created a distraction of bombardments from their siege positions, another group stealthily positioned the Fort Ticonderoga cannons on the high ground at Dorchester Heights overnight. Shocked by the realization that the Continental Army was now positioned to fire on the British warships and army positions below the Heights, British General William Howe abandoned plans for an assault and evacuated Boston without a single casualty on either side.[60]

With the evacuation of Boston, General Washington feared that the important port of New York would be the next British military target. The Continental Congress passed an ominous resolution to warn the city. On May 18, 1776, the *Pennsylvania Gazette* printed the resolution, "That it be recommended for the present to the inhabitants of New-York, that if troops which are expected should arrive, the said colony act on the defensive" and repel hostilities "force by force."[61] In June Washington mobilized the Continental Army to march to defend New York City.

Declaration of Independence

With revolutionary fervor at its height and in the face of an impending British attack in New York, the colonists decided it was finally time to "join or die." On May 4, 1776, Rhode Island became the first colony to declare its independence from Great Britain. Throughout the spring, more than 90 local declarations poured into other provincial assemblies in support of independence.[62] By the middle of May, eight colonies were ready to instruct their Continental Congress delegates to support a call for independence.[63] With this groundswell of popular support, the Continental Congress recommended that each colony form a new government and constitution of its own.[64]

Virginia planter, merchant, and politician, Richard Henry Lee, was authorized by members of the Virginia Conference to submit a unified, colony-wide proposal for independence from Great Britain to the Continental Congress. On June 7, Lee introduced the proposal "that these united colonies are and of right ought to be free and independent states."[65] A geographically diverse committee made up of John Adams from Massachusetts, Roger Sherman from Connecticut, Benjamin Franklin from Pennsylvania, Robert Livingston from New York, and Thomas Jefferson from Virginia was appointed to write the formal Declaration of Independence. After debating its provisions and consulting with their provincial assemblies, delegates from 12 of the 13 colonies approved the document on July 2.[66] New York's delegates abstained.

The Declaration of Independence painted a broad vision of ideals as the cornerstone for the new nation. Its most famous line states, "We hold these truths to be self-evident, that all men are created equal, that they are endowed by their Creator with certain unalienable Rights, that among these are Life, Liberty and the pursuit of Happiness."[67] "To secure these rights," the authors asserted, "[g]overnments are instituted among Men, deriving their just powers from the consent of the governed."[68] The authors reasoned therefore, "[t]hat whenever any Form of Government becomes destructive of these ends, it is the Right of the People to alter or to abolish it, and to institute new Government."[69] After listing the King's history of destructive abuses, the authors boldly declared "[t]hat these United Colonies are, and of Right ought to be Free and Independent States; that they are Absolved from all Allegiance to the British Crown."[70] The delegates agreed "for the support of this Declaration, with a firm reliance on the protection of divine Providence, we mutually pledge to each other our Lives, our Fortunes and our sacred Honor."[71]

The Continental Congress met in the Pennsylvania State House on July 4, 1776, and approved the final text of the Declaration of Independence. A copy was delivered to a local printer so that the first broadsides could be published the following day. On July 8, citizens of Philadelphia were called to the State House, later renamed Independence Hall, by the ringing of celebratory bells to hear the words of the Declaration read publicly for the first time.[72] Abigail Adams wrote to inform her husband that the Declaration had been read from the balcony of the State House. "As soon as [the reader] ended," she wrote, "the cry from the Belcona [balcony], was God Save our American States and then 3 cheers which rended the air, the Bells rang, the privateers fired, the forts and Batteries, the cannon were discharged."[73]

On August 2, 1776, members of the Continental Congress began signing the Declaration of Independence. The document was eventually signed by 57 people. Fifty-six of the signers were the men who represented their colonies as delegates in the Continental Congress when the document was written and approved. However, the document also contains the signature of a woman. The fifty-seventh signature is that of Baltimore Postmaster, Mary Katharine Goddard, who was hired by the Continental Congress to produce a second printing of the document that included the original signers' names.[74] In January 1777, she signed, "Baltimore, in Maryland: Printed by Mary Katharine Goddard."[75]

While Lee's proposal for independence had referred to the colonies' union as the "United *Colonies*," the Declaration of Independence had thrown off that submissive term and elevated the union to the "United *States* of America." On September 9, 1776, the Continental Congress formally resolved that the new independent nation would indeed be called the United States of America.[76] Under this new name, Congress dispatched a delegation including Benjamin Franklin; Connecticut politician, Silas Deane; and Virginia physician, Arthur Lee, to negotiate trade treaties and loan agreements with potential European allies.[77]

Disaster in New York

Congress had also dispatched a copy of the Declaration of Independence to General Washington in New York where the Continental Army was positioned to defend the city. On Washington's orders, the troops marched to the parade grounds in Lower Manhattan at 6:00 in the evening on July 9 to hear the public reading of the Declaration of Independence.[78] Just one week earlier, these inexperienced soldiers had observed with awe the largest military ever assembled by Great Britain sail into New York Harbor. By the end of July, 32,000 British and Hessian troops with a fleet of 400 ships assembled under the command of British brothers, General William Howe and Admiral Richard Howe.[79]

The Howe brothers had initially arrived in North America intent on negotiating peace. To minimize bloodshed, they had agreed to lead the British military only if they were appointed to be peace commissioners as well.[80] On August 22, the British began to transport 20,000 troops to Long Island in a show of force they hoped would intimidate the Americans.[81] Within the week, the superbly trained British military launched an attack against a divided Continental Army in the Battle of Long Island. British regulars attacked the American line under General Israel Putnam at Brooklyn Heights while Hessian mercenaries attacked those led by General John Sullivan on the Heights of Guam. After a fierce day of fighting, the Americans were overpowered and nearly surrounded on Brooklyn Heights. Rather than surrender, Washington evacuated the 9,000 trapped

Continental soldiers in rowboats from Long Island to Manhattan throughout the night under the cover of a miraculous fog.[82] However, the American defense of New York City had failed.

After such a resounding defeat, the British hoped to negotiate a peace agreement. The Continental Congress appointed Benjamin Franklin, John Adams, and South Carolinian, Edward Rutledge, to meet with Admiral Howe on Staten Island on September 11, 1776.[83] Howe proposed they negotiate solutions to the issues the colonies raised in their petition to the King, on the condition that they withdraw their Declaration of Independence. The American delegates flatly refused this condition and the meeting ended without a negotiated peace.

Throughout the remainder of the fall, the exhausted Continental Army experienced additional defeats in New York at Kips Bay, Harlem Heights, and White Plains. After the capitulation of American-held Forts Washington and Lee within days of each other in November, the British were firmly in control of New York City and the important lower Hudson River territory. The victorious General Howe issued a proclamation offering pardons to the people of New York who had been "forced into Rebellion."[84] In his position as peace commissioner, Howe promised in the proclamation that they would be "received as faithful Subjects" with "full protection for their Persons and Property" if they turned themselves in at British headquarters.[85]

The Continental Army, rapidly reduced to a few thousand soldiers as enlistments expired, retreated across New Jersey into Pennsylvania. The British Army chased the Continental Army along their retreat, placing groups of Hessian forces at key towns along the Delaware River. As the British Army neared Philadelphia, the Continental Congress fled in fear to Baltimore.[86] The enthusiasm generated by the victories in Boston and the Declaration of Independence began to evaporate.

Victories at Trenton and Princeton

In desperate need of a victory to boost morale among his troops, Patriot citizens, and Continental Congress alike, General Washington decided to cross back over the freezing Delaware River in December

1776 to launch a surprise attack on the Hessian garrison at Trenton, New Jersey. To inspire his troops before the conflict, he distributed copies of Thomas Paine's new pamphlet, *The American Crisis*. The soldiers, many of whom were barefoot and without winter clothing, were motivated to fight after reading Paine's captivating words. "These are the times that try men's souls: The summer soldier and the sunshine patriot will, in this crisis, shrink from the service of their country," Paine wrote, "but he that stands it now, deserves the love and thanks of man and woman."[87] "Tyranny, like hell, is not easily conquered," Paine argued, "yet we have this consolation with us, that the harder the conflict, the more glorious the triumph."[88] After a ten-mile march in blizzard conditions on Christmas Day, the Continental soldiers defeated the unprepared Hessians in a surprise attack at Trenton in one hour on December 26.[89]

When General Washington's report of the Battle of Trenton to the Continental Congress was reprinted in newspapers, American Patriots read with satisfaction, "Finding from our disposition, that they were surrounded, and they must inevitably be cut to pieces, if they made any further resistance, [the Hessians] agreed to put down their arms."[90] Ten days later, the Continental Army crossed the Delaware again and defeated British regulars at Princeton, New Jersey.

The weary but triumphant Continental Army established its winter quarters in Morristown, New Jersey, where General Washington answered General Howe's New York proclamation with a proclamation of his own. Washington's proclamation instructed anyone who signed an oath of fidelity to Great Britain to "retake the oath of allegiance to the United States of America" or retreat behind British lines.[91] Anyone who did not do so within 30 days, Washington wrote, "will be deemed adherents to the King of Great-Britain [sic], and treated as common enemies of the American States."[92]

Our Patriots

In the early days of the Revolution, our Massachusetts Patriots experienced firsthand both the economic hardships and political suppression of liberties brought on by the Coercive Acts in 1774. They were no doubt grateful when Patriots from their sister colonies sent supplies and joined in the days of fasting and prayer to show their support. Our Patriots across the colonies participated in the non-consumption agreements of the Continental Association and served on Committees of Inspection to enforce those agreements.

Our New England Patriots were among the first to join the military fight for independence in 1775. Several belonged to their local militias and responded to Joseph Palmer's Lexington Alarm. Many of these soldiers gathered at Boston to participate in the siege and went on to fight in the Battle of Bunker Hill and the victory at Dorchester Heights. Others served in the grueling Canadian Campaign. Still others joined the new Continental Army and fought in the tragic defeats in New York in 1776.

Whether or not they supported the *Olive Branch Petition*, our Patriots and their families would have read the King's proclamation of rebellion with horror. But when the Declaration of Independence of the United States of America was published in July 1776, they each made the courageous decision to support the cause of liberty.

*Gravestone of Abraham Winsor
Foster, Rhode Island
Courtesy of Nate Bramlett*

Captain Abraham Winsor A128863
(1740 - 1813)
Kathleen Winsor Petit

My fourth great-grandfather, Abraham Winsor, was born in 1740 in Glocester, Rhode Island. The people of Glocester vehemently protested the unfair taxation imposed by the British in the 1773 Tea Act. After a day of fasting and prayer on January 19, 1774, the town formally resolved "that there can be no property in which another can of right take from the owner without his consent." The following spring, an "army of observation" was created to defend Rhode Island.

Abraham Winsor enlisted and served as captain of the 3rd Company Glocester militia. In April 1775, they marched to Massachusetts when the Lexington Alarm was raised in response to the first conflict of the American Revolution. Abraham continued to serve as captain until 1780. For his loyal service, he was awarded land in what is present-day Ohio on which one of his sons eventually settled.

Abraham's gravestone in Foster, Rhode Island, became illegible over time. I am forever grateful to the Nathanael Greene Chapter DAR for marking Abraham's grave with a monument in 1981. I have since had the original stone repaired. The original inscription tells the story of his tragic death: "His end was sudden occasioned by the running of a horse with a wagon."

Private Burkhardt Musser A083545
(1736 - 1807)
Lois Abromitis Mackin

Burkhardt Musser was born in 1736 in Philadelphia County, Pennsylvania. He was the fifth child of Johann Martin Moser and Margaretha Kunkel, who arrived in 1728 and settled at New Goshenhoppen, near the present-day border of Montgomery, Berks, and Lehigh Counties. Burkhardt was confirmed in 1750 at Falkner Swamp Church, New Hanover Township, Philadelphia County. Within ten years he and brothers moved to Lynn Township, Northampton (now Lehigh) County. About 1760 Burkhardt married Maria Agatha Lichtenwalner, a widow with two children. Together Burkhardt and Maria Agatha had six more children.

Burkhardt's community was deeply divided during the American Revolution. Burkhardt chose the side of the Patriots and was appointed to the Northampton County Committee of Observation and Inspection in 1775. In 1776 Burkhardt attended a meeting at his brother Philip's house held by Tory sympathizer, William Thomas. The next day a document protesting the turning in of firearms was signed at Burkhardt's house. Burkhardt and Philip were jailed, required to pay security, and released. Philip testified that the purpose of their protest was to defend themselves against the depredations of lawless militiamen and Connecticut settlers from the Wyoming Valley. Burkhardt later served in Captain Adam Stahler's Company of Northampton County militia in 1782.

Burkhardt died in 1807 in Lynn Township, Northampton County.

Private David Haskell A052362
(circa 1755 - 1828)
Michelle Henderson White

David Haskell was baptized on October 12, 1755, the son of John Haskell and Eunice Low in Thompson Par, Windham County, Connecticut. He served four enlistments across three states during the American Revolution. He first enlisted on April 23, 1775, in Roxbury, Massachusetts, under Captain Healey and Colonel Learned, who had just arrived in Boston after responding to the Lexington Alarm. He then served in Muddy Brook, Connecticut, in 1776 under Captain Lyon and Colonel Chester in the Connecticut Line. Next, he served in Dudley, Massachusetts, in 1777 under Captain Carter and Colonel Whitney in the Massachusetts Line.

After his Massachusetts service, David moved to Cornish, New Hampshire, where he married Elizabeth Putnam in 1779. Elizabeth was the daughter of Patriot Daniel Putnam (A092404), the half-great nephew of General Israel Putnam of Bunker Hill fame.

Finally, David enlisted in Cornish, New Hampshire, in 1781 under Captain Moody Dustin and Captain Dearborn in the New Hampshire Line and served until the end of the war in 1783. His final discharge was signed by General Henry Knox at West Point, New York.

After the Revolution, David and Elizabeth moved to Madrid, New York, and purchased "ninety-two acres of wild and uninhabited land" for $483. His family is buried in the Haskell Family Cemetery in Madrid.

Corporal Jacob Barber A005849
(1738 - 1817)
Michelle Henderson White

Jacob Barber was born in Simsbury, Connecticut, in 1738 to Thomas Barber and Elizabeth Adams. He was part of the Barber family who settled throughout colonial Connecticut. Jacob began his military service in 1761 during the French and Indian War. At the time of his service, he was 37 years old, married to Patience Lawrence, and had 11 children.

In April 1775 escalations by the British resulted in the march of British regulars toward Concord, Massachusetts, to seize munitions. When bloody skirmishes followed in Lexington and Concord, an alarm was raised among New England militias to march to Boston where the British had retreated. Along with 60 other men from Simsbury, Jacob answered that call and served in Captain Amos Wilcox's company.

Jacob continued to serve in the military during the Revolutionary War. He joined the 18th Regiment of Connecticut militia and served under Captain John Brown. Brown's Company marched to New York, arriving on August 19, 1776, and participated in the devastating American loss in the Battle of Long Island. General Washington evacuated the Continental Army to Manhattan and the British went on to occupy New York City. Jacob served until he was discharged from service on September 1, 1776.

Captain Eleazer Warner, Sr. A121074
(1729 - 1810)
Linda LaBelle Kline

One hundred years before Eleazer Warner, Sr. was born in Hadley, Massachusetts, his ancestors migrated from England to the Massachusetts Bay Colony. Given his family's deep roots in the colonies, Eleazer served in the French and Indian War. He returned to become a leader in Granby, Massachusetts, serving as a surveyor, assessor, and selectman.

Eleazer was a Massachusetts Minuteman during the American Revolution. As tensions escalated in 1775, he first served on his town's Committee of Inspection. When the Lexington Alarm was raised on April 19, he marched to Boston the following day to help trap the British in a siege. Then on June 17, he raced under cannon fire with Colonel Ruggles Woodbridge's Regiment to fight in the Battle of Bunker Hill. Though a British victory, the battle was an unmistakable statement of American resolve.

As town selectman, Eleazer likely participated in his town's historic vote for independence. On June 20, 1776, the people "Voted that we of this town will support the Independence of the American Colonies with our lives and our fortunes provided the American Congress shall declare these Colonies Independent."

Eleazer went on to fight in the American victories at Bennington, Vermont and Saratoga, New York. After the war, he and his wife, Mary Chapin, remained in their beloved town of Granby.

Private David Glazier A045383
(1741 - 1824)
Kathleen Barrett Huston

David Glazier and his wife, Sarah Pratt, were born in Hardwick, Massachusetts, and married there in 1766. His father, Isaiah Glazier, fought in the French and Indian War as did Sarah's father, Ezekiel Pratt. On August 21, 1761, David was granted land in Rupert, Vermont.

David contributed both patriotic and military service during the American Revolution. He signed an association test in Westmoreland, New Hampshire, in support for American independence. He served in the military as a private in Captain Jacob Hind's 8th Company, Colonel James Reed's Regiment. This regiment fought at the Battle of Bunker Hill on June 17, 1775. David also served in General John Stark's Brigade from New Hampshire and fought in Captain Kimball Carleton's Company, Colonel Moses Nichols' Regiment at the Battle of Bennington on August 16, 1777.

Sarah's family also had strong ties to the American Revolution. Her father was the nephew of Captain Stephen Fay of the Green Mountain Boys who captured Fort Ticonderoga on May 10, 1775. Captain Fay operated the Catamount Tavern in Bennington, Vermont, which served as the headquarters for the Green Mountain Boys.

David and Sarah moved to Manchester, Vermont, after 1783. They died in Manchester and are buried at Factory Point Cemetery.

Private Ard Godfrey A045896
(ante 1758 - 1795)
Barbara Peterson Burwell

Ard Godfrey was born in Taunton, Bristol County, Massachusetts, to Richard and Theodora Godfrey. Richard Godfrey (A045946) served as a member of the Taunton Committee of Inspection and Correspondence in 1775, a step toward self-governance on the eve of the Revolutionary War.

As a very young man, Ard Godfrey enlisted in Captain Oliver Soper's Company to join the Siege of Boston during the summer and fall of 1775. Upon returning to Taunton, he married Tamerson Austin and their son Ard Godfrey, Jr. was born in 1777/78.

Private Ard Godfrey, Sr. marched from Bristol County to Rhode Island with Captain Ichabod Leonard's Company in July 1778 and likely fought in the Battle of Rhode Island. His pension application states he also served on an armed vessel of war. He was captured by the British and carried to England where he remained a prisoner until the end of the war.

Ard Godfrey, Sr. later married Abigail Cooper in Taunton. He died there in 1795. Ard C. Godfrey (1813-1891) – the grandson of Patriot Ard Godfrey, Sr. and the son of Ard Godfrey, Jr. – moved to Minnesota in 1847 to construct a sawmill at St. Anthony Falls. He became a prominent figure in early Minnesota history.

Portrait of Thomas Truxtun
Source: Library of Congress

Commodore Thomas Truxtun A116510
(1755 - 1822)
Virginia "Ginny" Morrison and Adrienne "Adie" Bendickson

Thomas Truxtun, a first-generation colonist of a British-born father, began his sea career at the age of 12. On March 23, 1776, the Continental Congress passed an act to permit private citizens to fit their ships with arms to pursue enemy vessels. Truxtun became the first privateer to be fitted out to serve in this capacity. Throughout the Revolution, this privateering strategy severely disrupted the British economy, prices of imported goods, and maritime insurance rates.

Through his command of four ships, *Mars, Congress, Independence,* and *St. James*, Truxtun saw action in the English Channel, the Caribbean, and the Azores. Never suffering defeat, Truxtun carried gunpowder and military supplies back to America and successfully delivered the United States Consul-General Thomas Barclay and his family to France. George Washington toasted Truxtun's ability to capture enemy ships, calling Truxtun's services equal to those of a regiment. In 1785 then Captain Truxtun transported an ailing, eighty-year-old Benjamin Franklin back from France to his beloved America aboard the *London Packet*.

"…the Navy—a member of which I became, not from any pecuniary consideration, but from motives of Patriotism, and a pure love of Country and the Service." - Thomas Truxtun

Private Jonathan Hall A049847
(1756 - 1827)
Shirleen Hoffman and Vicki Hoffman Musech

Jonathan Hall was among the earliest Patriots to join the American Revolution. In 1775 he enlisted at the age of 19 in the Massachusetts Line in Captain Isaac Wood's Company, Colonel Cotton's Regiment, where he served for eight months.

Jonathan's pension application describes his subsequent four re-enlistments and protracted military service. During the year 1776 he served in the Massachusetts Line, under the command of Colonel Shepherd. For nine months in 1777, Jonathan served under Colonel Putnam, after which he was employed for one year as a driver of a "field piece," such as a cannon placed on a cart and pulled by horses or oxen. Jonathan then served three years in Colonel Crane's artillery regiment. According to military experts at American Revolution.org, "artillerymen were considered elite troops. In an age of widespread illiteracy, soldiers who could do the geometric calculations necessary to place a cannonball on target must have seemed almost as wizards."

In 1785 Jonathan married Abigail Bisbee. Abigail herself was of Patriot stock, the daughter of Hopestill Bisbee (A010409) and granddaughter of Nathaniel Churchill, Sr. (A021950). Jonathan died in Oswego County, New York, in 1827. The Fulton Chapter DAR dedicated a bronze plaque at his grave in the Caughdenoy cemetery in New York on Memorial Day, 1941.

Private Charles Hilton A056408
(1754 - 1812)
Deborah Wood Blum

Born in New Hampshire, 21-year-old Charles Hilton served with Continental Army troops led by Colonel Benedict Arnold on the 1775 expedition through the wilderness from Cambridge, Massachusetts, to Quebec City, Canada. The purpose of the expedition and invasion was to encourage French-Canadian support for the American Revolution.

The soldiers on this treacherous mission found no game and were in a state of continual hunger. After exhausting their provisions, the men were reported to have eaten two dogs that accompanied the expedition, as well as to have boiled and eaten leather straps and moccasins. More than one-third of the soldiers turned back. Hilton did not.

When they finally arrived in Quebec, Arnold's troops found the city to be well-fortified. Freezing temperatures prevented digging protective trenches for their attempted siege. In addition to a smallpox outbreak and starvation, blizzard conditions and insufficient ammunition ultimately resulted in a resounding American defeat in the Battle of Quebec on New Year's Eve. The American side suffered 515 casualties while the British suffered only 19. Hilton was taken prisoner during this battle. Released seven months later, he tenaciously returned to join the New Hampshire Regiment, serving under Colonel Nicholas Gilman.

After the war, Hilton married Mary Wadleigh and became a prominent citizen of Andover, New Hampshire.

Private Daniel Putnam A092404
(1739 - 1809)
Michelle Henderson White

Daniel Putnam was born in Sutton, Worcester, Massachusetts. He married Anne Chase and the couple was among the first inhabitants of Cornish, New Hampshire, settling land purchased by Anne's father, Judge Samuel Chase, Sr. (A021210). In 1767 the town elected Daniel to be town clerk. His half-great uncle was Major General Israel Putnam of Bunker Hill fame.

The 1st New Hampshire Regiment was formed following the Lexington Alarm in 1775. In January 1776 Daniel enlisted with this regiment and marched under Colonel Timothy Bedel to Quebec, Canada, where he became ill and was abandoned by his regiment. After the war he petitioned the New Hampshire government for reimbursement of 14 pounds for the lost clothing and 16 pounds for doctor's service for this ordeal.

His experience in Quebec did not deter him from serving in the Revolution. He recovered and joined Captain Jason Wait's Company. Then in 1777 he joined Captain House's Company, Colonel Joseph Cilley's Regiment where he was stationed in Albany "on Command of ye Armory." Here he was described as age 35, six feet tall, with black hair, a dark complexion, and dark eyes. He continued to serve throughout the Revolution. In 1781 he joined Captain Moody Dustin's Regiment and served until the end of the war in 1783.

Private Nathaniel Webster A121332
(1753 - 1836)
Julie Anson Schaefer

Nathaniel Webster was raised in a frontier family that supported American independence. His father, Abel Sr. (A121122), served their town of Plymouth in four New Hampshire Provincial Congresses and on the town's Committee of Safety during the American Revolution.

In 1776 Nathaniel served in Captain Edward Everitt's Company, Colonel Timothy Bedel's New Hampshire Regiment as a private during the Canadian Campaign led by Colonel Benedict Arnold. He was first garrisoned at Montreal, then Isle aux Noix following the regiment's surrender at the Battle of the Cedars west of Montreal.

After his first enlistment, Nathaniel returned home and married Mehitable Smith in 1777. He served a final year with his previous regiment in Captain William Tarlton's Company starting April 1, 1778, first on the frontier and then in a detachment at Albany, New York.

Nathaniel's younger brother, Abel, Jr., enlisted in a militia regiment raised to reinforce General George Washington. He fought in the Battle of White Plains, New York, on October 28, 1776, where the Americans were forced to retreat. Abel, Jr. then enlisted with the Continental Army where he rendezvoused at Fort Ticonderoga, fought in the Battle of Saratoga, and endured the hardships of Valley Forge. He died in service on July 4, 1778, after fighting in the Battle of Monmouth, New Jersey.

Gravestone of Real Daughter Mary Lyman Alexander
Sakatah Cemetery, Waterville, Minnesota
Courtesy of Mary Helen Ellison Peterson

Captain Thomas Alexander A001253
(1727 - 1801)
Mary Helen Ellison Peterson "Mary Ellis"

Captain Thomas Alexander was born May 30, 1727, in Northfield, Massachusetts, the son of Ebenezer "The Fighting Deacon" Alexander and Mehitable Buck. Thomas's great-grandfather, George Alexander, and his great-great grandfather, John Alexander, had immigrated from Scotland to Massachusetts in 1643 with his father, John Alexander. On December 11, 1754, Thomas married Azubah Wright. The couple had at least 13 children.

Captain Alexander served in both military and political roles during the American Revolution. He marched to Quebec in March 1776 with a company in Colonel Porter's Regiment. After enduring what he described as "unparalleled scenes of danger, hardships, and distress," his company retreated through Fort Ticonderoga and Albany to join General Washington's army in New Jersey in December 1776. On his walk home in 1777, Thomas fell on the ice near Peekskill and dislocated his hip and broke his thigh, resulting in his permanent disability. In 1779 he served as the Northfield representative to the Massachusetts General Court and as a member of a Committee of Correspondence.

Thomas died March 23, 1801, in Northfield, Massachusetts. His son, George, married Mary Lyman, the daughter of Revolutionary War Sergeant Seth Lyman (A072622). Mary's grave was marked as a Real Daughter by Anoka and Josiah Edson Chapters DAR in 2000 at Sakatah Cemetery, Waterville, Minnesota.

Private Hugh (Osborne) Osborn A084449
(1763 - 1847)
Martha Mason

Descended from three *Mayflower* passengers, the Osborne family has unique links to the birth of our nation. George Osborne (A084440) and his sons served during the Revolutionary War. George was a Minuteman who enlisted on April 21, 1775, in response to the Lexington Alarm.

George's son, Hugh, was born in 1763 in Bridgewater, Massachusetts. In 1776 he enlisted at age 13 to serve with his father in Captain Joseph Stetson's Company at Dorchester Heights, Massachusetts. Defensive fortifications at Dorchester Heights allowed Washington's Continental Army to achieve one of its first victories. Hugh then served in Rhode Island in Captain Hatch's Company in 1776 and in Colonel Titcomb's Regiment in 1777. Between 1778 and 1779 he served in Pennsylvania, New York, and New Jersey in Colonel Bailey's Regiment.

Hugh and some of his brothers served in 1781 and 1782 as marines on the Continental frigates *Deane* under Captain Nicholson and *Alliance* under Captains Park and Berry. The *Alliance* was the fastest ship in the Continental Navy and never experienced a defeat. Hugh served when the *Alliance* transported the Marquis de Lafayette back to France and returned to America carrying diplomatic messages from Benjamin Franklin in Paris.

After the war Hugh married his cousin, Azuba Wade, who had also descended from *Mayflower* passengers. They raised their family in Kennebec County, Maine.

Captain John Willoughby A127077
(1735 -1834)
Ann Inez Knickrehm Winegar, Katherine Ann Winegar Tunheim, and Kristi Jane Winegar Wieser

Captain John Willoughby, Jr., my fifth great-grandfather, was born in 1735 in Billerica, Massachusetts. In 1758 he married Azubah Wheeler. John joined the party that explored Plymouth, New Hampshire, in 1762 and as one of the original grantees, was among the first to settle in the new town in 1764. He faithfully served Plymouth for many years as a selectman and church deacon. Prior to the American Revolution, he served in the French and Indian War.

John, Jr. served in patriotic, military, and civil roles during the Revolutionary War. He served in Captain Eames's Company on the northern frontiers in 1776 and led his own company into service twice in 1777 as a captain in Colonel Hobart's regiment. He was a member of Plymouth's Committee of Safety in 1777 and 1778. Finally, he served as a selectman in 1779.

Two of John, Jr.'s sons, John III and Josiah, also fought in the Revolution. Josiah enlisted on March 12, 1777, at the age of 15 and tragically died in October 1777.

Captain Willoughby died at the age of 98 in his beloved Plymouth. According to Stearns's *History of Plymouth*, he was remembered as "a useful citizen [...] His good service as a soldier was consistent with his excellent record in the conscientious discharge of every duty."

*Gravestone of Zebulon Sutton's wife, Sarah
Martinsburg Presbyterian Cemetery, Ohio
Courtesy of Terry Anderson*

Private Zebulon Sutton A111425
(1752 - 1840)
Terry Anderson

Zebulon Sutton was born in Somerset County, New Jersey, in 1752. Zebulon was a deeply committed Patriot throughout the American Revolution, enlisting in the New Jersey militia on June 1, 1776. According to his pension application, he experienced numerous battles as part of General George Washington's New York Campaign.

The newly enlisted Zebulon's initial engagement was the devastating Battle of Long Island under the command of Colonel Joseph Phillips where the defeated Americans retreated under cover of an opportune fog. Zebulon then marched to White Plains where he likely dug trenches for the defense of the city. After another American loss at the Battle of White Plains on October 28, 1776, Zebulon's unit retreated to Fort Washington. Colonel Phillips wrote a letter to General Washington recommending and receiving permission for his unit to "finish the Battery on the Rocks near the River side" of the fort that "will annoy the Enemies Shipping abundantly." However, the Battle of Fort Washington that followed on November 16, 1776, resulted in yet another American retreat.

The demoralizing losses of the New York Campaign would lead many Patriots to abandon hope and return home. Zebulon steadfastly persevered and continued serving until he was mustered out in 1780. He later married Pennsylvania-born Sarah Hull.

Private Levi Hayden A052558
(1747 - 1821)
Leilani Peck and Marjorie Brinkley

Levi Hayden was born May 28, 1747, and died August 24, 1821, living his entire life in Connecticut in an area of Windsor known as Hayden Station or Haydens. He was the fourth generation born in America after the arrival of his English great-great-grandfather William Hayden in 1630. Levi's life was largely spent farming, but he also held civil offices and represented the town of Windsor in the Connecticut General Assembly in 1814.

Three patriotic Hayden brothers served during the American Revolution. Levi was drafted twice for short terms during the Revolutionary War and served in the cavalry under Captain Skinner and Colonel Sheldon. Levi's brothers, Nathaniel and Hezekiah, fought with General George Washington in the Battle of Long Island during the summer of 1776. Nathaniel held a captain's commission in the first train-band (militia) in Windsor, Connecticut. After heavy fighting, he was safely evacuated as the outnumbered Continental Army retreated at night under the cover of fog. Hezekiah was not so fortunate. He served in Captain Ebenezer F. Bissell's Company, Colonel Huntington's Regiment. Hezekiah's company was cut off during the retreat and was captured by the British. He, along with all the men in his company except the captain, tragically starved to death while imprisoned.

Private Jabez Tuttle A131803
(1753 - 1799)
Pamela Wilbur Greinke

Jabez Tuttle was born in Wallingford, New Haven, Connecticut, on July 30, 1753. During the American Revolution, he served in the Tenth Regiment of militia, under Lieutenant Benham and Colonel Baldwin. He would bravely serve with this regiment in one of the most fearsome and precarious moments of the war.

After the British evacuated Boston in the winter of 1776, they chose New York as their next target. In July, 400 British warships carrying 32,000 soldiers arrived in New York Harbor. Jabez's regiment marched to New York City on August 9, 1776. The Battle of Long Island ensued on August 27 and the badly outnumbered Americans were overwhelmed. The next day, British General Howe ordered his troops to begin digging trenches to surround the American positions. Rather than surrender, 9,000 American soldiers successfully retreated to Manhattan under cover of a miraculous fog.

After the war, Jabez and his wife, Mary Todd, settled in Herkimer County, New York, where Jabez helped run a sawmill. They had 12 children, six of whom died before the age of ten. The Tuttle family were generous community members. According to family lore, they once donated more than 600 board feet of lumber to help raise a barn for one of their neighbors.

Corporal Elisha Clark A022276
(1755 - 1840)
Jacqueline Purcell Anderson

Elisha Clark was born in Milford, Connecticut, and served during one of the most difficult periods of the American Revolution. He first enlisted as a privately paid substitute soldier in a company formed by Captain Smith in Darby, Connecticut, in 1776. Clark's company responded to General George Washington's call for reinforcements to the Continental Army positioned to defend New York City. Clark marched to New York and fought on the Brooklyn front during the Battle of Long Island on August 27, 1776.

Following the American loss at Long Island, Clark returned to Milford and was promoted to corporal in Captain Samuel Peck's Company. He marched back to New York City and was stationed at Harlem. When the British finally forced the Continental Army to abandon New York City, Clark marched on to White Plains, New York. On October 28, he participated in the American loss in the Battle of White Plains.

Clark enlisted for a final time during the fall of 1777 and served in Captain Jehiel Bryan's Company, Colonel Joseph Thompson's Regiment. His company was employed to stop the progress of British General Burgoyne's march down the Hudson River. Clark served until Burgoyne's surrender at Saratoga, New York. At age 77, he received a military pension for his service.

Private Michael Zirkle A131099
(1735 - 1811)
Sarah Lynne Martin

Michael Zirkle was born in 1735 in Pennsylvania, the fourth of ten children of Johann Ludwig Zirkle and Maria Eva X. About 1765 Michael and his wife Catherine settled near Holman's Creek, in the Shenandoah Valley, Virginia. The couple had 14 children, all of whom were baptized at St. Mary's Lutheran Church in New Market, Virginia.

Michael was aged 41 at the start of the Revolutionary War. He served as a private in Captain Jacob Holeman's Dunmore County militia. The muster roll contains the names of Michael and his younger brothers, Andrew (A131097) and Peter (A131100). Michael also contributed 420 pounds of beef to the war effort on August 29, 1782.

The patriotic Zirkle and Roush families intermarried. Patriot George Roush (A098975) married Michael's eldest daughter, Catherine, in 1781. Michael's siblings, Lewis and Mary Jane, married George's siblings, Mary Magdalene Roush and Lewis Roush, respectively.

After the war, Michael was an elder in the Old Pine Lutheran Church, Mill Creek, Virginia. He died in fall 1811, near Forestville in the Shenandoah Valley and is buried in the Zirkle-Nehs Cemetery with his wife, who outlived him by nearly 20 years. The epitaph on his headstone is written in German. Many of their children moved west and were among the early settlers of Ohio.

*Sarah Pearson and Cecil Martin at Gravestone of Hendrick Cortelyou
Ten Mile Run Cemetery, New Jersey
Courtesy of Lindal Martin*

Hendrick Cortelyou A026240
(1736 - 1800)
Sarah Martin Pearson and Cheryl Lynn Stanga Despathy

Hendrick Cortelyou lived his entire life in Somerset County, New Jersey. Hendrick and his wife, Johanna Stoothoff, married in 1759 and had 11 children between 1761 and 1780.

The Cortelyou farm at Ten Mile Run was not far from a strategic intersection of colonial-era roads to Princeton and New Brunswick, New Jersey, and consequently saw extensive military action during the Revolutionary War. A DAR marker placed at Millstone Courthouse near Ten Mile Run states, "By this Route, WASHINGTON with his army Retired after his Victory at Princeton, January 1777."

Late in 1776, just prior to Washington's victory at Princeton, British and Hessian troops plundered the properties of New Jersey residents who refused to take an oath of allegiance in exchange for their protection. According to a Somerset County historian, "Losses ... included every description of property that an evilly-disposed enemy in war could destroy or steal—houses, crops, fences, household utensils, furniture, horses and cattle, men and women's clothing." Appraisers were later appointed to gather detailed claims, taken under oath, about the depredation. Hendrick Cortelyou reported a loss valued at 27 pounds, 7 shillings, 6 pence.

Hendrick and Johanna's oldest child, also named Hendrick, enlisted in 1777 at age 16. Young Hendrick served nine distinct terms in the Somerset County militia over five years of the war.

Lieutenant Josiah Gale A043251
(1742-1798)
Judith Marie Laney Taves and Jennifer Melissa Taves

Josiah Gale was born on June 5, 1742, in Stamford, Fairfield County, Connecticut, to Joseph and Rebecca Gale. He married Rachael Mead and the couple lived in New York.

As a young man, Josiah had served in the British Army during the French and Indian War. Despite being a veteran of the British Army, Josiah joined the side of independence early in the Revolutionary War. In 1775 he served as a first lieutenant in Captain Roger Sutherland's Company, Colonel David Southerland's 6th Regiment, Charlotte Precinct militia of New York. It is likely that he served standing ready to defend his community from Tory attacks along the Hudson River.

After the war, Josiah and Rachel lived in Stanford, New York. They had a son in 1789 and named him George Washington Gale in honor of Josiah's commander in chief during the Revolutionary War. According to family lore, George described his father as a man of remarkable strength. Josiah died at the age of 56 in 1798, in Stanford, New York, and is buried with his wife in Amenia, Dutchess County, New York. George Washington Gale went on to attend Princeton Theological Seminary and became an ordained Presbyterian minister. He founded Knox College in New York where he was an ardent abolitionist leader.

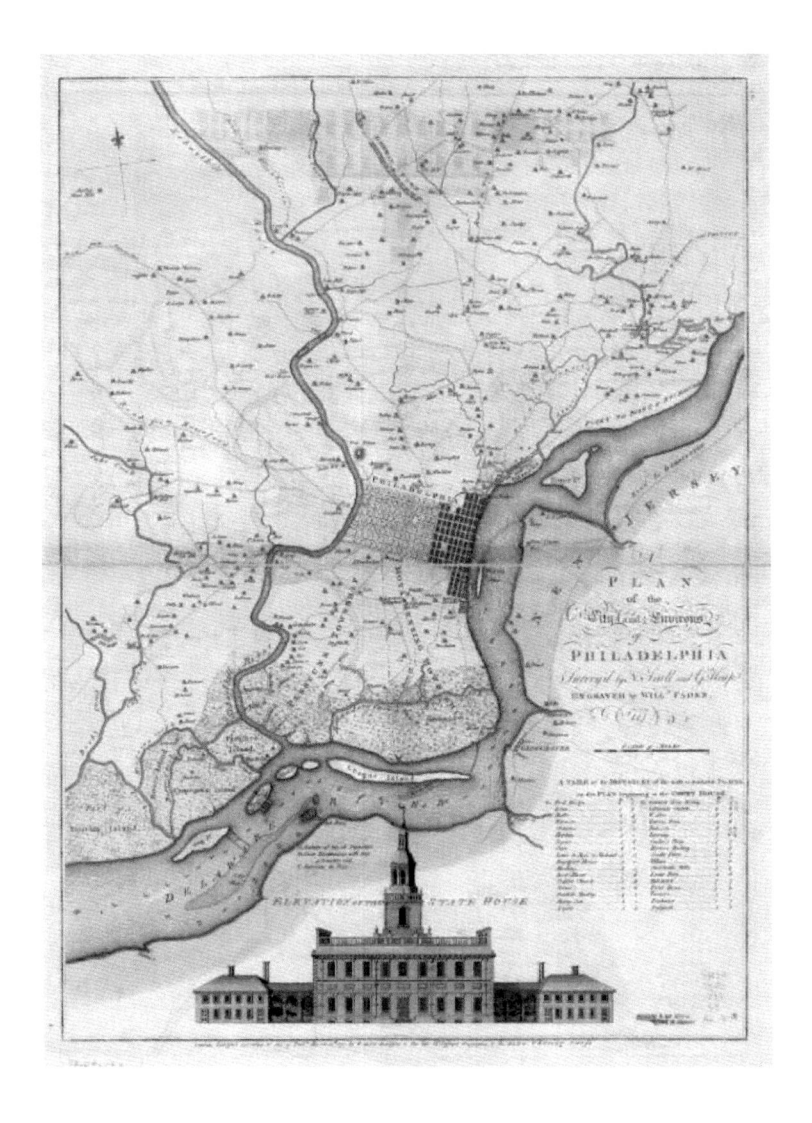

American Capital of Philadelphia in 1777[1]
Source: Library of Congress

Chapter 3:
HOPE

★

As the early military victories in Boston gave way to the devastating defeats in New York, Americans began to understand the depth of sacrifice that would be required to earn the independence they had just declared. "Summer soldiers" and "sunshine patriots" would not be sufficient. Nor would the traditional military tactics of the day. Conventional rules of engagement favored the impeccably trained and experienced British military. However, the Continental Army's gutsy strikes at British weak points in Trenton and Princeton had given the Patriots a glimpse of the kind of resourceful and audacious approaches that could succeed.

Sacrifice of a different kind was required of the soldiers' families as well. Some women remained home to manage farms and businesses on their own. Others essentially joined the army as camp followers. The resourcefulness and courage of such women was no less impressive than that of their soldier husbands and sons.

Though 1777 witnessed the devastating loss of the American capital of Philadelphia, the year also marked a stunning Continental Army victory that roused powerful support internationally and invaluable hope domestically in the battle for independence.

Divide and Conquer

When intimidation with an overwhelming show of force in New York City failed to suppress the insubordinate colonists, General John Burgoyne, commander of British forces in Canada, proposed a new approach. Burgoyne's goal was to cut off New England from the rest of the colonies by taking control of the Hudson River. In preventing the movement of troops, supplies, and information, he believed he could crush the rebellion by isolating the seditious New England colonies from the other presumably more loyal colonies.[2]

Burgoyne set out to build an alliance with the Six Nations Confederacy in upstate New York to help him. The Six Nations Confederacy had decided on a position of neutrality at the outset of the Revolution.[3] However, when Burgoyne invited them to join his side, the vote resulted in a split decision. Influenced by Mohawk leader Joseph Brant's arguments that it was necessary to support King George III to halt American encroachments on their land, the Mohawk, Onondaga, Seneca, and Cayuga Nations chose to join the British.[4] The Oneida and Tuscarora Nations chose to side with the Americans.[5]

With this First Nation alliance built, Burgoyne laid out a sweeping, three-pronged plan to accomplish his goal of dividing the American colonies. First, Burgoyne would lead a large force comprised of British regulars, German mercenaries, First Nation allies, French-Canadians, and colonial Loyalists south from Canada along Lake Champlain and the Hudson River Valley to Albany, New York. Second, British Lieutenant Colonel Barry St. Leger would march east along the Mohawk River Valley, recruiting Loyalists and capturing Fort Stanwix along the way, to join Burgoyne in Albany. Third, if necessary, British General William Howe, Commander in Chief of all British Forces in America, would reinforce Burgoyne in Albany from New York City.

Burgoyne's formidable force of 7,000 troops began its march from Canada to Lake Champlain in spring 1777.[6] On June 20, Burgoyne issued a chilling proclamation for the people living in the territory along his intended path. Unlike Howe's more conciliatory proclamation in New York offering pardons to Patriots, Burgoyne's message made clear that he would show no such mercies. His proclamation warned Patriots that his forces would "await them in the [f]ield, and devastation, famine, and every concomitant horror that a reluctant b[ut] indispensible [sic] prosecution of Military duty must occasion, will bar the way to their return."[7] To underscore that no one was beyond his reach, he warned Patriots against "disregard[ing the proclamation] by considering their distance from the immediate situation of my Camp," because, he threatened, "I have but to give stretch to the Indian Forces under my direction, and they amount to Thousands, to overtake the harden'd Enemies of Great Britain and America, (I consider them the same) wherever they may lurk."[8]

In early July, Burgoyne reached American-held Fort Ticonderoga on the southern end of Lake Champlain. Anticipating Burgoyne's arrival, a small force of Patriots under the command of Major General Arthur St. Clair was instructed to hold Fort Ticonderoga as long as possible and then retreat to Fort Independence. From Fort Independence, they were to harass and impede Burgoyne's progress south. However, the British set up heavy artillery on the high ground at Mount Defiance near Fort Ticonderoga, forcing the outnumbered and outgunned Patriots to withdraw, returning the prized fort to the British. The small number of American forces stationed along the upper Hudson River Valley were unable to slow Burgoyne's progress. He proceeded to capture the American forts in upstate New York at Crown Point, Anne, and Independence on his route south.

As Burgoyne's forces continued to march toward Albany, the Northern Department of the Continental Army planned its defense. Expeditions were sent north to stall Burgoyne's progress. Patriot forces successfully destroyed bridges and blockaded roads with trees and rocks. Behind schedule and now desperate for supplies, Burgoyne sent a detachment to Bennington, Vermont, in search of horses and food. Local militia discovered the plan and sent out alerts to respond. A New Hampshire and Massachusetts militia force led by General John Stark and reinforced by Colonel Seth Warner launched an offensive attack on August 16, 1777.[9] After a day of fierce fighting, American forces surrounded and defeated the British detachment.

New Hampshire militiaman, Thomas Mellon, participated in the Battle of Bennington and described the retreat of Burgoyne's forces stating, "We chased them till dark. We might have mastered them all, but Stark, saying he would run no risk of spoiling a good day's work, ordered a halt and return to quarters."[10] Mellon recalled that the Americans spent the night of their victory unceremoniously encamped near the battlefield, writing, "My company lay down and slept in a corn field, near where we had fought – each man having a hill of corn for a pillow."[11]

This unexpected defeat at Bennington cost Burgoyne more than the loss of supplies. His First Nation allies, who had served as valuable scouts, lost confidence in the mission and abandoned the British Army in the wilderness.[12] Further complications arose when St. Leger's march east was halted. The attempted siege of Fort Stanwix in August ended in a failure and St. Leger returned with his forces to Canada.[13] But perhaps most crippling, General Howe made the crucial decision to sail from New York City to capture Philadelphia rather than reinforce Burgoyne in Albany. Burgoyne's depleted forces were left to march to Albany on their own.

Defeat in Philadelphia

General Howe arrived in Maryland in late August to begin his strategic Philadelphia campaign. In addition to capturing the American capital, Howe intended to enlist the support of the city's considerable Loyalist community as well as take over a critical Continental Army supply site in southeastern Pennsylvania.

After wintering in Morristown, New Jersey, General Washington led the Main Continental Army to Philadelphia and prepared to defend the capital. By September the Continental Army had grown to over 10,000 strong with several capable officers including Pennsylvania politician, Anthony Wayne, and Rhode Island politician, Nathanael Greene.[14] The Americans were also joined by the newly arrived 19-year-old French nobleman, the Marquis de Lafayette, who had decided to support the American Revolution after witnessing King

George III's brother disparage the American colonists' desire for self-government.[15]

The Continental Army flew a new flag during the Philadelphia campaign. On June 14, 1777, the Continental Congress had approved a flag to symbolize the union of the 13 colonies into a new nation. The resolution instructed "that the flag of the United States be made of 13 stripes, alternate red and white; that the union be 13 stars, white in a blue field, representing a new Constellation."[16] This flag was first flown by Delaware General William Maxwell in a skirmish on September 3, 1777, near Philadelphia.[17]

By early September, the Continental Army was situated in defensive positions along the bank of Brandywine Creek near Philadelphia.[18] Washington mistakenly believed he had fortified all crossing points over the river. On September 11, the British divided their forces and attacked the entrenched Continental Army first at Chadd's Ford. Hidden by thick fog, the second British force crossed the Brandywine Creek at the undefended position and attacked the Continental flank. After a valiant resistance, the American line collapsed. Greene's forces counterattacked, allowing the rest of the Continental Army to withdraw. Though Brandywine was his first battle, the wounded Lafayette calmly led an orderly retreat of the American troops.

General Wayne's American forces stationed at Paoli, Pennsylvania, outside of Philadelphia encountered a particularly brutal attack one week after the Battle of Brandywine. After nightfall on September 20, British Major General Charles Grey ordered a surprise attack on the American garrison. In what would later be called the "Massacre at Paoli," the British soldiers destroyed the camp and routed the Americans with a brutal bayonet charge.[19]

General Howe's Philadelphia campaign successfully captured the American capital. On September 26, 1777, the British were in control of Philadelphia and the Continental Congress was once again forced to flee, this time to Lancaster and York in southeastern

Pennsylvania.[20] Howe positioned two brigades at Germantown, Pennsylvania, to defend the city. On October 4, Washington attempted a surprise attack on the British forces at Germantown but was repelled.[21]

However, the loss at Germantown did not crush the resolve of the Continental Army. Washington's account of the battle was reported in newspapers like the *Boston Gazette* where Patriot readers were assured, "[O]ur troops who are not the least dispirited by [the loss] have gained what all troops gain by being in action."[22] Washington proudly added, "I have the pleasure to inform you, that both officers and men behaved with a degree of gallantry that did them the highest honor."[23]

Although the Main Continental Army was forced to retreat to Valley Forge, Pennsylvania, their determined and disciplined engagements at Brandywine and Germantown showed a steady improvement from the chaos in New York the previous year. Potential European allies watched the Americans' progress with interest and were impressed.

Women Supporting the Cause

As Patriot men from across the states continued to join the Continental Army and local militias to fight for American independence, the role of women in American society was transformed. Colonial women had typically not been entitled to education beyond a primary level and were not allowed to handle money or even speak in public.[24] However, many women assumed the demanding task of managing their family farms and businesses when their husbands and fathers enlisted.

By 1777 approximately 2,000 women actually marched along with the Continental Army.[25] Wives of senior officers such as Martha Washington, Lucy Knox, and Catharine Greene often joined their husbands.[26] They lived comfortably in homes near camp and their role was to help uplift the morale of the officers by organizing social events. But the majority of the women who followed the Continental

Army were wives of enlisted soldiers, widows of fallen soldiers, or those tragically driven from their homes due to enemy occupation or destruction of their property.[27]

These "camp followers" performed critical roles in supporting the army. Women and children worked hard foraging for food, cooking, washing, and mending the soldiers' uniforms. Highly contagious diseases such as smallpox and dysentery were common in military camps so women also served as nurses.[28] Although they were forbidden from fighting, on rare occasions women did take part in battle. When their husbands or fathers served as artillery gunners, some women brought water to cool and clean the cannons.

Women were sometimes compensated but rarely recognized for the tremendous support they provided in Continental Army camps. In 1777 the Continental Congress resolved to pay eight dollars a month to women brave enough to take on the task of nursing.[29] However, since enlisted soldiers rarely received their pay, women serving as nurses likely did not receive their pay either. In exchange for their domestic work, women received one-half the ration a soldier received and children were given a quarter ration.[30] While their names do not appear on muster rolls, the women who performed the grueling work of supporting the Continental Army in camp are no less Patriots than their soldier husbands.

Victory at Saratoga

In September 1777, the Northern Department of the Continental Army, under the command of French and Indian War veteran, Major General Horatio Gates, moved into position near Albany to meet Burgoyne's approaching forces. Gates positioned his forces, comprised of Continental regulars and militia from Massachusetts, New York, New Hampshire, Connecticut, Virginia, and Pennsylvania, 20 miles north of Albany on the high ground on Beemis Heights above the Hudson River.[31] Gates's forces also included Colonel Daniel Morgan's fearsome corps of Virginia sharpshooters.

This was the group, Gates wrote, "General Burgoyne was the most Afraid of."[32] The American positions and breastworks on Beemis Heights were skillfully designed by talented Polish engineer, Colonel Thaddeus Kosciuszko.[33]

General Burgoyne finally crossed to the west side of the Hudson River in pursuit of Gates's army in mid-September. On September 19, he sent three columns to attack the American positions. Burgoyne's attack on the American defenses was anticipated by American Major General Benedict Arnold who counterattacked Burgoyne's western column in heavy fighting in the wooded area near Freeman's Farm. Well-suited for this non-traditional forest fighting, Morgan's regiments engaged Burgoyne's middle column. Henry Jolly, a member of Morgan's regiments, recalled,

> Colonel Morgan and his riflemen descended like a torrent upon the right wing of the British army and though I believe I have been at least 15 times engaged with the enemy, I have never seen so great a carnage, in so short a time, by the same number of men engaged.[34]

American forces retreated to their defensive positions at nightfall when the British received reinforcements of German troops.[35] After receiving word that General Howe's second in command, General Henry Clinton, could march to reinforce him from New York, Burgoyne decided to wait on further offensive attacks.

As Burgoyne waited for Clinton, militia regiments poured in to reinforce the American line that now significantly outnumbered the British.[36] Hearing nothing from Clinton and facing nearly depleted supplies, Burgoyne sent out a large detachment on October 7 to forage for food and scout American positions. Gates ordered an attack on this detachment, driving them back to their defensive line. The Americans pressed forward and attacked two British fortifications. In the face of staggering casualties, Burgoyne ordered a retreat to the nearby village of Saratoga, New York.

Gates ordered a pursuit and caught up with the retreating British on October 10. The Americans surrounded the British army in Saratoga, forcing Burgoyne to surrender. As the victorious American troops celebrated, Burgoyne handed his sword over to Gates, marking the first American victory in which an entire army had been captured.[37] Burgoyne's attempt to divide the colonies had failed.

Articles of Confederation

While the Continental Army was engaging British forces in New York and Philadelphia during the summer of 1777, the Continental Congress was at work developing a plan to govern the new United States of America.

On November 15, 1777, just one month after the American victory at Saratoga, the Continental Congress adopted the Articles of Confederation. The document had been drafted by John Dickinson and a committee with representatives from each of the 13 colonies.

The government outlined in the Articles of Confederation resembled neither the strong central government proposed by Thomas Paine in *Common Sense,* nor the more refined vision of a government with executive, two-house legislative, and judicial branches proposed by John Adams in *Thoughts on Government*. Instead, the Articles called for a relatively weak representative central Congress that would exist primarily for the common defense of the states from foreign powers and from each other. The confederation was to be "a firm league of friendship" among the 13 states "for their common defen[s]e, the security of their Liberties, and their mutual and general welfare, binding themselves to assist each other, against all force offered to, or attacks made upon them."[38] Because future disputes between the states over contested borders were anticipated, the Congress would also serve as the final court of arbitration in such disagreements.[39]

The articles specified that this Congress would meet annually and be comprised of delegates chosen by each state's legislative assembly.[40] While states could send between two and seven delegates, decisions would be made by casting one vote per state, regardless of population.[41]

The Articles of Confederation were clearly designed to ensure that the newly formed state governments would retain most of the power. Beyond the powers of common defense and arbitration of interstate disputes conferred on Congress, the Articles specified that "[e]ach state retains its sovereignty, freedom and independence, and every Power, Jurisdiction and right, which is not by this confederation expressly delegated to the United States, in Congress assembled."[42]

Ratification by all 13 states was required to authorize the Articles. Delayed for years by debates over voting and representation, the Articles would not be enacted until March 1, 1781, with Maryland's ratification. The need for stronger central powers to regulate trade and raise revenue would become clear after the Revolution, predestining the Articles to be replaced by a new Constitution in 1787. But for the balance of the war, the Articles represented a significant step forward in establishing the United States of America, positioning the new nation to negotiate and partner with other nations on the world stage.

Alliance with France

The resounding American victory at Saratoga proved to be an international turning point in the Revolution. America's lead diplomat in Paris, Benjamin Franklin, enthusiastically shared the news of the American victory at Saratoga with King Louis XVI. The convincing victory finally persuaded the French King to recognize the United States as an independent nation and join the American Revolution to help defeat France's old European rival, Great Britain. A diplomatic team comprised of Franklin, Silas Deane, and Arthur Lee negotiated the terms of *The Treaty of Alliance with France*.[43]

According to the terms of the treaty, the stated purpose of this American-French "defensive alliance" was "to maintain effectually the liberty, Sovereignty, and independ[e]nce absolute and unlimited of the said [U]nited States, as well in Matters of Gouvernement [sic] as of commerce."[44] The French agreed "not to lay down their arms, until the Independence of the [U]nited [S]ates shall have been formally or tacitly assured."[45] In exchange, the United States agreed to support France if it engaged in war with Great Britain. The two countries arranged to negotiate peace with Great Britain only with the consent of the other.[46]

The Treaty of Alliance with France, written in both French and English, was formally signed on February 6, 1778. Later that spring, proud Patriot readers of Boston's *Continental Journal* read, "At the reception of our ministers, the King [Louis XVI], addressing himself to Mr. Franklin, said he was happy in acknowledging the Independence of America, and that the condition of the treaty on the part of France should be faithfully observed."[47] Patriot spirits were bolstered when the article went on to confirm, "The Doctor [Franklin] answered to the same effect on the part of Congress."[48]

Our Patriots

Our Patriots were active participants in defending their new nation against the powerful British offensives of 1777. Those living in New York and the New Hampshire territory that would become the state of Vermont read Burgoyne's threatening proclamation with horror. Determined to resist, our Patriots participated in the defense of Fort Ticonderoga, excursions to harass and slow Burgoyne's movement down the Hudson River, and in the Battle of Bennington. They courageously took part in the Battles of Brandywine and Germantown under the command of General Washington to defend the capital city. Several of our Patriots victoriously fought in the Battle of Saratoga and were present to witness and celebrate General Burgoyne's ignominious surrender.

Drum Major Robert Polley A090288
(1752 - 1828)
Adrienne Morrison, Adrienne "Adie" Bendickson,
and Virginia "Ginny" Morrison

Music was used to uplift the morale of Continental Army soldiers during the American Revolution. However, drum majors played an even more vital role than simply encouraging the troops. A drummer communicated orders from officers to soldiers through signals on his drums. In camp, drummers signaled when to assemble. In battle, drummers signaled where and when to maneuver. Because drummers were unarmed and critical for maintaining a company's order, they became vulnerable enemy targets.

Robert Polley was born in Medford, Massachusetts, one of Paul Revere's "Midnight Ride" stops when the Revolution first began. He served as a drum major in three companies during the war. Robert first joined Captain Stephen Dana's Company, Colonel Josiah Whitney's Regiment raised to serve in Rhode Island in 1777. He enlisted again in 1778 to serve in Captain John Devereux's Company, Colonel Jacob Gerrish's Regiment of guards at the Winter Hill Camp in Charlestown, Massachusetts. He enlisted a third time later in 1778 to serve in Captain Nathan Sergant's Company, Colonel Jacob Gerrish's Regiment of guards.

Robert stayed close to home after the Revolution, settling in Charlestown when the city was rebuilt after being burned by the British in 1775 during the Siege of Boston. Robert died in Charlestown at the age of 76.

Private Eleazer Warner, Jr. A213377
(1755 - 1835)
Linda LaBelle Kline

Eleazer Warner, Jr. joined the Continental Army in 1776 to fight for American independence alongside his father, Eleazer Warner, Sr. (A121074), in Colonel Ruggles Woodbridge's Regiment. His company marched to the Continental Army's headquarters in Morristown, New Jersey, where he served during the harsh winter of 1777. He stated in his pension record that "General George Washington was at Morristown at the same time."

Food and clothing were in short supply that winter and many soldiers marched in the snow in bare feet. As a smallpox outbreak threatened to devastate the Continental Army, soldiers at Morristown were secretly inoculated with live virus collected from the sick. Eleazer, Jr. survived these hardships and marched with his father the following August to fight in the American victory in the Battle of Bennington, Vermont.

After the Revolutionary War, Eleazer, Jr. moved to Pittsford, Vermont, where he married Hannah Cox in 1783. The couple had ten children, including my ancestor, Hannah Warner Wilder. Family lore records that Eleazer, Jr. enjoyed telling his children stories of how he and his father fought for liberty during the Revolution. Perhaps Hannah shared those stories to inspire her three sons when they fought for the Union in the Civil War to extend that liberty to all Americans.

*Rebecca Marshall Cathcart
Holding Ann H. Cathcart's father
Courtesy of Ann H. Cathcart*

Captain David Marshall A073741
(1754 - 1821)
Ann H. Cathcart

Captain David Marshall, eldest son of Irish immigrants who settled near Philadelphia, was born in Cumberland County, Pennsylvania, on February 23, 1754. His granddaughter, my twice great-grandmother, Rebecca Marshall Cathcart, became a DAR member in 1911. I joined her in honoring our brave Patriot ancestor by becoming a member 108 years later.

According to Rebecca's memoir, recorded by the Minnesota Historical Society in 1913, David Marshall served throughout the American Revolution with troops under General Anthony Wayne. In his pension application, David stated he was commissioned ensign and promoted to 1st lieutenant in the 5th Regiment of the Pennsylvania Line in 1777. He was subsequently promoted to captain of the 3rd Company, 5th Battalion in 1780. He participated in numerous military conflicts including the Battles of Brandywine, Pennsylvania, in September 1777; Germantown, Pennsylvania, in October 1777; Monmouth Court House, New Jersey, in June 1778; and Green Spring, Virginia, in July 1781.

Rebecca's memoir also indicates her grandfather visited Kentucky before the war. After peace was declared, David and his wife, Sarah Graham, journeyed on horseback from Pennsylvania to make their home in Kentucky. Captain Marshall died in Bourbon County, Kentucky, and is buried in nearby Old Millersburg Cemetery.

Private Thomas McDaniel A207740
(circa 1752 - 1834)
Louise Duncan Farkas, Laura Farkas Roth,
and Haley Michelle Roth

Thomas McDaniel was among the Continental Army soldiers transformed at Valley Forge during the winter of 1778. Born around 1752, Thomas first enlisted as a private in 1776 to represent his home state of North Carolina in Captain Emmett's Company, General Francis Nash's Brigade.

Thomas participated in the Philadelphia Campaign as part of General Washington's failed attempt to prevent the British from capturing the American capital. He fought in the defeats at Brandywine and Germantown, Pennsylvania, in the fall of 1777. Following these devastating losses, Thomas presumably marched with the Continental Army to Valley Forge to receive much-needed training under Major General von Steuben. Having survived the brutal winter conditions and intense training at Valley Forge, Thomas fought in the pivotal Battle of Monmouth, New Jersey, in June 1778. Although both sides claimed victory, the tenacious and well-disciplined Continental Army's performance won international praise. When the war shifted south and threatened Thomas's home state, he fought in the Battle of Guilford Courthouse, North Carolina, in 1781.

After the war Thomas married Celia Tuggle in Patrick County, Virginia. The couple moved to Monroe County in present day West Virginia to claim the bounty land Thomas was granted for his service during the Revolutionary War.

Private Henry Maxwell A075918
(circa 1730 - circa 1792)
Barbara Strothman Rustad

Born in Scotland around 1730, Henry Maxwell was well acquainted with the oppression of the English monarchy. He emigrated to North America and settled in Pennsylvania. When the Revolutionary War began, Henry eagerly joined the side of the Patriots.

Henry enlisted as a private in Captain Thomas Church's Company, Colonel Francis Johnston's 5th Pennsylvania Regiment of Foot and served several continuous enlistments between April 1, 1777, and October 10, 1777. During this time, Henry participated with his regiment to defend the American capital of Philadelphia. Although defeated, the regiment fought valiantly at the Battles of Brandywine Creek, Pennsylvania, on September 11, 1777, and Germantown, Pennsylvania, on October 4, 1777. The following spring, Henry was stationed at Valley Forge and served additional enlistments through 1783.

The standard weapon of Henry's 5th Regiment was the long rifle, which had greater range and accuracy than the standard muskets used by the British and Continental armies. Dr. James Thatcher had observed the Pennsylvania regiments in Boston at the beginning of the Revolution and stated, "These men are remarkable for the accuracy of their aim; striking a mark with great certainty at two hundred yards distance."

Henry died sometime after 1792 in his beloved Cumberland Township, York County, Pennsylvania

Gravestone of Georg (Henry) Lutz
Friedens Church Cemetery, Pennsylvania
Courtesy of Lois Abromitis Mackin

Private Henry Lutz A131923
(1760 - 1838)
Lois Abromitis Mackin

Georg Heinrich (Henry) Lutz was born in Berks County, Pennsylvania. He was the eldest son of linen weaver Georg Heinrich Lutz and Anna Clara Roth of Ontelaunee Township.

In 1776 the teenaged Henry enlisted as a private in the Sixth Pennsylvania Line and served for about six and a half years. He fought in the battles of White Plains, Paoli, Brandywine, and Germantown. After wintering at Valley Forge, Henry's regiment fought in the battles at Monmouth, New Jersey and Stony Point, New York. In 1780 the troops were back in New Jersey, unpaid and short of rations and clothing, with many enlistments expiring. At New Years 1781 they mutinied, but the mutineers remained orderly and loyal to the Continental Congress. After their complaints were settled, the regiment was split up and sent to South Carolina.

At war's end, Henry returned to Berks County where he married Maria Margaretha Volk in 1784. The couple had two girls and two boys. In the 1790s Henry purchased land in Brunswick Township, north of Friedens Church, where he farmed and worked as a weaver. After his sons were grown, Henry purchased new land in neighboring Schuylkill Township, including a lot in Lewistown where he lived until the 1830s. Henry died in 1838 and is buried at Friedens Church Cemetery, Schuylkill County, Pennsylvania.

Private Massey Thomas A113098
(1760 - 1818)
Joanne Voigt Hagen, Laura Hagen Rickabaugh,
and Carrie Hagen Sorenson

Massey Thomas was born in 1760 in Culpeper County, Virginia, originally surveyed by a 17-year-old George Washington. At the age of 16, Massey enlisted in the Virginia militia to serve for five years in the American Revolution.

Delegates from the American colonies had met in Philadelphia beginning in 1774 to plan and execute the Revolution. In early 1777, the British launched their Philadelphia Campaign to capture the city. On September 11, 1777, American forces clashed with the British Army at Brandywine Creek between Delaware and Pennsylvania to prevent the city's capture. In what would be one of the largest engagements of the war, Massey joined General Washington's 14,600 troops and intercepted British General William Howe's 15,500 troops in the Battle of Brandywine. After hours of intense fighting and strong resistance, American forces were overrun. On September 26, the British occupied Philadelphia.

At some point during his service, Massey contracted measles during which time he was appointed to drive a medical wagon for a member of Washington's medical staff. He recovered and returned to the militia, serving until 1781.

As the *Treaty of Paris* ending the American Revolution was awaiting formal signatures, Massey married Dicey Tobert/Talbot on June 3, 1783. The couple settled in Ohio, Kentucky, where they farmed and raised five children.

Private Benjamin Sage, Jr. A099134
(1754 - 1784)
Jane Landowski Truckenbrod, Teresa Landowski, Clare Barnes, and Grace Truckenbrod

Benjamin Sage, Jr. was the first-born son of the patriotic Sage family. His father, Benjamin Sage, Sr. (A099131), had signed the New York Articles of Association calling for independence from Great Britain at the outset of the Revolution. Benjamin, Jr. and his brothers served in the military during the war.

Historians believe Benjamin, Jr. and his brother, Daniel, served together with General Benedict Arnold on the treacherous Quebec Campaign of 1775-6. Benjamin, Jr. also served as a private in Colonel Henry Killian Van Rensselaer's 4th Regiment of militia in New York under Captain David Husted. According to Husted's pension application, their company marched to Albany and then on to Forts Miller, Edward, and Anne in 1777 in response to British General Burgoyne's destructive New York Campaign. They continued to Fort Crown Point, placing trees and boulders as obstacles to hinder the British advance. In 1778, the company was stationed at Fort Dubois in Cobleskill and Middle Fort in Schoharie to protect these communities from British and indigenous ally attacks in upstate New York.

Benjamin, Jr. and his wife, Hannah Randall, were farmers. They raised six children in Connecticut and New York. Their last known residence was Rensselaerville, New York. Benjamin is said to have died in 1784 from injuries sustained in the war.

Private Thomas Eldredge A037278
(1734 - 1812)
Therese Lebens, Elizabeth Lebens Prodahl, and Melody Huttner

Thomas Eldredge was born in 1734 in North Kingstown, Rhode Island, where he married Isabel Niles in 1754. On September 7, 1777, Thomas enlisted with the Berkshire County, Massachusetts, regiment known as the "Berkshire Boys" under Colonel Benjamin Simonds. As part of this regiment, the 43-year-old Thomas joined 2,000 troops from Massachusetts, New Hampshire, and Vermont to take part in a campaign known as the Pawlet Expedition.

The purpose of the expedition was to "divide and distract" British General Burgoyne's army stationed in forts along the Hudson River Valley by attacking their supply depots and cutting off their lines of communication. Speed was imperative so the men marched with no wagons or heavy artillery and were armed with only a musket and 24 cartridges of ammunition each. They did not even bring tents, instead sleeping in makeshift shelters or in the open. The successful two-week expedition ultimately contributed to the weakening of British forces and Burgoyne's surrender to the Americans at Saratoga, New York, one month later.

After Isabel's death, Thomas married Mary Niles. The couple lived in Berkshire County, Massachusetts, and Thomas's family grew to include five sons and four daughters. Thomas died March 7, 1812, and is buried in Hancock, Massachusetts.

Private Samuel Curtis A208263
(1758 - circa 1817)
Louise Duncan Farkas, Laura Farkas Roth, and Haley Michelle Roth

Samuel Curtis was born in 1758 in Farmington, Connecticut, to Margery Andrews and Azor Curtis, Sr. (A028810). In March 1777, Samuel's father enlisted to serve in the Revolutionary War. Six months later, 19-year-old Samuel enlisted as well. He joined Lieutenant Joseph Farnam's Company on September 5, 1777, where he participated in the Pawlet Expedition designed to harass British General Burgoyne's Army on its march down the Hudson River.

Always ready to defend what he knew was right, Samuel re-enlisted in the fall of 1779, serving at Claverack, New York, and again in the fall of 1780, serving at Totoway, New Jersey. After Burgoyne's unsuccessful attempt to divide the colonies, General Washington was determined to defend the Hudson River and the crucial Fort West Point. Samuel enlisted one final time to reinforce the Continental Army at West Point during the fall of 1781. Samuel would not learn until the end of the war that his father had survived the brutal conditions at Valley Forge in 1778 only to die a few months later.

During one of his periods home, Samuel had married Elizabeth Guarnsey. Samuel is believed to have died at the age of 59 in Stockbridge, Massachusetts.

Ensign Daniel Davidson A030059
(circa 1753 - circa 1834)
Gwen Mashek, Tara Mashek, and Janea Mitcheltree

Daniel Davidson was born in Washington County in southwestern Virginia around 1753. He married at the outbreak of the American Revolution and began to raise a family. In 1777 Daniel would leave his young family to fight for independence as part of a particularly distinguished regiment.

Between January 1777 and July 1779, Daniel served in Colonel Daniel Morgan's 11th Virginia Regiment. This specially selected group of Virginia, Pennsylvania, and Maryland frontiersmen was known as "Morgan's Riflemen" and was noted for their creative tactics and excellent marksmanship. Wearing camouflage hunting shirts, they engaged in quick strike actions throughout New Jersey and New York, striking fear in the British regulars more accustomed to traditional combat. In October 1777, their skills proved instrumental in achieving an American victory of the Battle of Saratoga. In a letter informing Continental Congress President John Hancock of the victory, American General Horatio Gates wrote, "too much praise cannot be given to the Corps commanded by Col. Morgan." In his final enlistment, Daniel participated in the resounding American victory at the Battle of Kings Mountain, South Carolina, on October 7, 1780.

After surviving four years of intense military service during the Revolution, Daniel settled in Perry County, Kentucky, where he lived to the approximate age of 80.

Corporal Bartholomew (Somers) Summers A110885
(1744 - post 1794)
Meghan Grace Flannery

In 1774 Bartholomew Somers immigrated from Scotland and settled in Ryegate, Vermont. Nicknamed "Lang Bart," Somers was a jolly man who was fond of practical jokes. Like his fellow Scotsmen, Somers defended his new home by joining Captain Frye Bayley's militia company and was elected corporal.

In October 1777, the company heeded the Continental Army's call for help and marched to Saratoga, New York. Captain Bayley heard reports of 15 British supply boats they could capture. In his memoirs, Bayley recounted a brief skirmish with the British when they found these boats coming up the Hudson River. When the boats were moored for the night on an island across the river, Corporal Somers courageously volunteered to swim across to steal the first boat. When Corporal Somers returned with the vessel, the company emptied it and used it to capture the remaining boats without resistance. This significant loss of supplies could have finally pushed the British to surrender. Throughout his patriotic adventure, Somers persevered through a dangerous campaign as he fearlessly forced the British to cease their attacks on his adopted homeland.

After finishing his service, Somers returned to Vermont, married his wife, Susanna, and had a family.

Gravestone of Nathaniel Rudd
Village Cemetery, Charlemont, Massachusetts
Courtesy of Dee Brochu

Private Nathaniel Rudd A099513
(1731 - 1819)
Kristine Swanson Sittler, Janet Swanson, and Marianne L. Loftus

Nathaniel Rudd's ancestors settled in Norwich, Connecticut, in the 1600s. Nathaniel farmed, worked as a mason, and taught school in the winter. He fought in the French and Indian War in 1758. His Revolutionary War journey began after moving to Massachusetts where he and his neighbors served in the volunteer militia. The men called him "Captain" in recognition of his natural leadership skills.

In 1777 Nathaniel joined Captain Ward's Hampshire Company in Colonel Wells's Regiment as a private. On September 22, he marched 80 miles from Charlemont, Massachusetts, to New York to take part in the Battle of Saratoga. Under the command of Generals Benedict Arnold and Horatio Gates, the Americans won a resounding victory. British General John Burgoyne surrendered on October 17 and Nathaniel was discharged the following day. This decisive win convinced the French to support the cause of American independence, becoming the turning point of the Revolution.

Perhaps inspired by his father's service, Nathaniel's son, Andrew, joined the American cause. In 1780, Andrew used his skills as a blacksmith and served as a Sergeant Artificer under Colonel Jeduthan Baldwin at Morristown, New Jersey. Artificers were skilled tradesmen responsible for maintaining military equipment.

Nathaniel retained his "Captain" title after the war and it is inscribed on his headstone.

Michelle White at gravestone of David Smith
Colrain West Branch Cemetery, Massachusetts
Courtesy of Michelle Henderson White

Private David Smith A213166
(1757 - 1816)
Michelle Henderson White

David Smith was the son of Major Hezekiah Smith (A105490) and Eunice Morris Smith, and like them, was born in Woodstock, Connecticut. In 1764, as a seven-year-old child, he moved with his family to Colrain, Massachusetts. Originally known as "Boston Township #2," the town of Colrain is named for the town in Ireland from where many of the first settlers originated. David grew up in this beautiful frontier valley in western Massachusetts, surrounded by hills, trees, rivers, and abundant wildlife. War would come to Massachusetts by the time David was a teenager, and he and his family would heed the call of service.

David served as a private in Captain Hugh McClellan's Company, David Wells's Regiment, in the Continental Army. He fought at the Battle of Saratoga in the fall of 1777, along with his brother, Nathaniel (A106528), and his father. All three were present at the surrender of British General Burgoyne.

Following active duty, David served Colrain as a selectman in 1781. Then he, along with brothers Nathaniel and Calvin, married three daughters of Jennet McClellan and Patriot Joseph Thompson (A114337) after the war. David and his wife, Martha, had ten children. The family lived in Colrain and are buried in Colrain West Branch Cemetery in the Smith family plot.

Benjamin Sage, Sr. A099131
(1725 - 1813)
Jane Landowski Truckenbrod, Teresa Landowski, Clare Barnes, and Grace Truckenbrod

When the Revolutionary War began, Benjamin Sage, Sr. and his wife Abigail Blinn, lived with their family in Dutchess County, New York. Although many New Yorkers favored reconciliation with Great Britain, the Sage family chose the side of independence.

At the age of 50 in 1775, Benjamin, Sr. signed the New York Articles of Association calling for independence from Great Britain. These articles read in part,

"We, the Freeman, Freeholders, and Inhabitants of Dutchess, being greatly alarmed at the avowed design of the Ministry to raise a revenue in America, and shocked by the bloody scene now acting in Massachusetts Bay, do in the most solemn manner resolve never to become slaves, and do ... endeavor to carry into execution whatsoever measures may be recommended by the Continental Congress."

Benjamin and Abigail's four sons served in the military. Their daughter, Elsie Sage Clark, has her own unique Revolutionary War story. Heavily pregnant, Elsie courageously traveled to the Continental Army camp at Saratoga, New York, in 1777 to nurse her dying husband. While caring for him, she went into labor and gave birth to twin boys under an apple tree. American officers kindly ensured Elsie received the care she needed and named the twins "Gates" and "Arnold" in honor of the victorious American Generals in the Battle of Saratoga.

Winter Scene at Valley Forge[1]
Wood Engraving by Julian Scott
Source: Library of Congress

Chapter 4:
PERSEVERANCE

---------- ★ ----------

With the alarming news of France's alliance with the United States, King George III and Prime Minister Frederick Lord North were ready to negotiate peace. However, the American Patriots who had envisioned a new future for themselves and their descendants would agree to nothing less than full recognition of their independence.

The perseverance of the rapidly transforming Continental Army would be severely tested through hardships at the winter encampments of Valley Forge and Morristown. The perseverance of state militias would be similarly tested as they defended their settlements on the northern frontiers and New England port towns from brutal attacks. A moral victory at the Battle of Monmouth Courthouse, New Jersey, and the return of the Continental Congress to its capital in Philadelphia gave reason to believe that perseverance itself may be the key to winning the war.

Valley Forge

After the losses in the Battles of Brandywine and Germantown, General Washington ordered the Main Continental Army to encamp for the winter at Valley Forge, Pennsylvania. His goal was to rest and restore the exhausted soldiers while still remaining within striking distance of the now British-held American capital.

The army arrived at Valley Forge on December 19, 1777, and their first priority was to build their winter camp. Upon arriving, the 12,000 men set to work building the approximately 2,000 log cabins required to house them.[2] Each cabin was 14 feet by 16 feet in size and was equipped with bunk beds, a fireplace, and an oiled parchment window.[3] The soldiers also constructed a bridge over the Schuylkill River, dug miles of trenches, and built earthen redoubts.[4]

Living conditions in the camp were difficult. Although supplies were available in the region, delivery systems were inadequate to transport them to Valley Forge.[5] Food rotted enroute and much-needed blankets and clothing failed to arrive. Officers reported the soldiers were in good spirits and were resourcefully making their own clothing and shoes.[6] However, as winter wore on, thousands died from starvation and disease.[7] A frustrated Washington wrote a letter to Continental Congress President Henry Laurens on December 22 requesting assistance. "I do not know from what cause this alarming deficiency, or rather total failure of Supplies arises, [b]ut," Washington warned, "unless more vigorous exertions and better regulations take place in that line and immediately, This Army must dissolve."[8]

When the Continental Congress failed to resolve the supply problems, Washington appealed directly to the people of the surrounding states to provide food. "After three Campaigns, during which the brave Subjects of these States have contended, not unsuccessfully, with one of the most powerful Kingdoms upon Earth," he wrote in a letter to citizens on February 18, 1778, "we now find ourselves at least upon a level with our opponents; and there is the best reason to believe, Efforts adequate to the abilities of this country would enable us speedily to conclude the War and to secure the invaluable Blessings of Peace, Liberty and Safety."[9] However, he solemnly continued, "In the Prosecution of this object, it is to be feared that so large an Army may suffer for the want of Provisions" and "unless the virtuous Yeomanry of the States of New Jersey, Pennsylvania, Delaware, Maryland and Virginia will exert themselves to prepare Cattle for the use of the Army, ... great difficulties may arise in the course of the Campaign."[10]

To ensure that the citizenry understood the dangers and consequences of failure, he reminded them, "should there be any so insensible to the common Interest, as not to exert themselves upon these generous principles" they may become "immediate subjects to the Enemy's incursions" and the Continental Army would be in no position to "save their property from plunder; their families from insult, and their own persons from abuse, hopeless confinement, or perhaps a violent death."[11]

Washington also wrote letters directly appealing to the governors of each of the 13 states for help. On February 19, 1778, Washington described the army's dire conditions to Virginia Governor Patrick Henry stating, "The situation of the Commissary's department and of the army, in consequence, is more deplorable, than you can easily imagine. We have frequently suffered temporary want and great inconveniences, and for several days past, we have experienced little less than a famine in camp."[12] Washington confessed he "had much cause to dread a general mutiny" if the army could not be supplied.[13]

Despite failing to feed, cloth, and arm the Continental Army, the Continental Congress passed a resolution in February requiring members of the army to sign Oaths of Allegiance. The Oath read:

> I [blank for name] do acknowledge the UNITED STATES of AMERICA, to be Free, Independent and Sovereign States, and declare that the people thereof owe no allegiance or obedience to George the Third, King of Great-Britain; and I renounce, refuse and abjure any allegiance or obedience to him; and I do swear that I will to the utmost of my power, support, maintain and defend the said United States, against the said King George the Third, his heirs and successors and his or their abettors, assistants and adherents, and will serve the said United States in the office of [blank for rank] which I now hold, with fidelity, according to the best of my skill and understanding.[14]

Convinced he could help them understand the gravity of his situation, Washington insisted that the Continental Congress's Board of War observe conditions at Valley Forge for themselves. The visiting board saw not only the deplorable lack of supplies firsthand, but also the perseverance of the soldiers who trained and drilled despite the harsh conditions. The board was moved to appoint the talented Rhode Island merchant and administrator, Major General Nathanael Greene, to the position of Quartermaster General. Greene promptly created an efficient system to deliver much needed food and clothing to Valley Forge.[15]

Now more adequately supplied, Washington proceeded to develop the military skills necessary to deliver on his lofty promise to "conclude the War and to secure the invaluable Blessings of Peace, Liberty and Safety." At the end of February, Prussian army veteran, Friedrich Wilhelm von Steuben, arrived at Valley Forge to train the Continental Army. Starting with a model unit, Steuben taught the soldiers how to march efficiently, enter and exit a battlefield as a unit, quickly load their muskets, and use a bayonet. He adjusted his teaching tactics to accommodate the independent-minded Americans who preferred to understand the reasons behind each tactic and approach, rather than simply obey orders.[16]

In March Washington extended an invitation to the Oneida and Tuscarora Nations to join the Continental Army at Valley Forge.[17] He hoped to leverage their skills to gather intelligence on British positions and to secure supplies from British stores. Oneida Chief Oskanondonha sent an expeditionary force of 50 people, including talented Oneida medical expert, Polly Cooper.[18] The group arrived on May 15, 1778, bringing gifts of food and supplies. Cooper brought white corn and taught the soldiers how to properly prepare it so it could be eaten.[19] She remained at Valley Forge to cook for the soldiers and nurse the sick, while other Oneida members served as scouts.

By spring, the Continental Army had been transformed from a disparate collection of inexperienced militia companies to a unified, well-trained force ready to fight for their independence. In May, Washington asked his men to sign their Oaths of Allegiance.[20]

Carlisle Peace Commission

Over 3,000 thousand miles away from Valley Forge, King George III was informed by the French minister to Great Britain that King Louis XVI had recognized the United States of America as an independent nation.[21] The news of the American Alliance with France shook the British government in London, prompting a major shift in strategy. Prime Minister Frederick Lord North dispatched a three-person commission led by the Earl of Carlisle, Frederick Howard, to America in March 1778 with instructions to negotiate peace.[22]

The Carlisle Commission was prepared to present North's decision to repeal the Tea Act of 1773, the Coercive Acts of 1774, as well as his agreement that Great Britain would not tax the colonies.[23] However, the Continental Congress rejected offers to negotiate peace without certain preconditions. On June 17, Congress firmly responded to the Commission's offer unequivocally stating, "The acts of the British parliament, the commission from your sovereign, and your letter, suppose the people of these states to be subjects of the crown of Great Britain, and are founded on the idea of dependence, which is utterly inadmissible."[24] Congress further stated it was "inclined to peace" but only with "an explicit acknowledgment of the independence of these states, or the withdrawing [the King's] fleets and armies."[25] The Carlisle Commission returned to England empty handed.

Victory at Monmouth Courthouse

In addition to prompting a change in diplomatic strategy, the imminent arrival of the French military in North America necessitated a radical change in British military strategy. Forces would need to be diverted to protect British interests in the Caribbean and other parts of the empire.[26] General Howe faced harsh criticism for failing to reinforce General Burgoyne at Saratoga and was replaced as Commander in Chief of British forces in North America by General Henry Clinton. Clinton was ordered to withdraw from Philadelphia and consolidate defenses in New York City.[27] His 12-mile-long troop and supply train came under constant harassment by New Jersey militia as he marched across the state toward New York.[28]

Emboldened by the news of the French alliance and of the British evacuation of Philadelphia, the reinvigorated Continental Army marched out of Valley Forge on June 19, 1778, to pursue the British enroute to New York.[29] As the British moved from their encampment at Monmouth Courthouse, New Jersey, a detachment of Continental forces under the Command of Major General Charles Lee attacked Clinton's rear guard.[30] After a brief and confused retreat by Lee's forces, General Washington led the Main Continental Army into the attack. Intense cannon fire was deployed by both sides during a full day of fighting in sweltering heat. Fighting stopped at nightfall when exhausted forces on both sides encamped.[31] At midnight, Clinton's forces silently withdrew and proceeded to New York.

Though both sides declared victory, the Battle of Monmouth was a clear triumph for the cause of American independence, marking the first time the Main Continental Army engaged and held its own against the Main British Army.[32] Importantly, American control of the capital had been restored. The Continental Congress returned to Philadelphia in July where it would remain for the rest of the Revolution.[33] Major General Benedict Arnold was appointed Military Governor of the city by General Washington.

Life in the Continental Army

By 1778 the Continental Army was 35,000 strong.[34] Its soldiers represented families who had lived in all 13 states for generations as well as immigrants from a variety of nations.[35] Their ranks included free white people, enslaved and free African Americans, and First Nation people.[36] Most were between the ages of 15 and 30 and had worked as farmers, merchants, or laborers.[37]

Each state also maintained its own militia. Free males between 16 and 45 were required to serve and to provide their own arms.[38] Militia served to protect their own states but were also called into conflicts to serve alongside the Continental Army.

Service in the Continental Army was physically demanding. The men were required to drill and march daily.[39] Between conflicts, the soldiers served on guard duty or were put to work clearing fields, building fortifications, and digging latrines.[40] Longer marches were especially challenging. Each soldier carried 45 pounds of gear that included his haversack, firearm, bayonet, and ammunition as well as his canteen, a tin cup, and a spoon.[41] However, this important equipment was frequently in short supply.

In addition to shortages of military materiel, the soldiers often lacked basic living provisions. Official daily food rations included one and a half pounds of meat, a pound of bread or flour, and three pints of dried vegetables along with a pint of milk or spruce beer to drink and two ounces of spirits to add to their canteens to kill the bacteria in the water.[42] These rations were often unavailable and foraging was required. Privates were promised a monthly wage of $6.23 that was frequently paid in worthless paper currency or not paid at all.[43] At the start of the war, there was no standard uniform so soldiers wore their own clothes. In 1779 General Washington determined that Continental Army soldiers had earned the right to wear official uniforms. He ordered a uniform that consisted of a blue coat with facings of different colors designating each state.[44]

The persistent lack of supplies and pay paled in comparison to the brutality of the army's harsh discipline and its primitive medical care. Soldiers could be punished by lashing or execution for violations ranging from desertion to failing to use camp latrines.[45] Anesthesia was uncommon and treatments for battlefield wounds such as limb amputations or the removal of bullets with forceps were excruciatingly painful.[46] However, soldiers were understandably more afraid of diseases than battlefield wounds. Infectious diseases like typhus, malaria, and dysentery were common in camp and treated with painful bleeding, purging, or blistering, which were thought to rid the body of infection.[47]

Diversity in the Continental Army

As the Revolution wore on, such harsh conditions made it increasingly difficult for states to fill the soldier recruitment quotas set by the Continental Congress. Local loyalties compounded the recruitment problem. Town militias and state regiments often offered better pay than the Continental Army, along with the opportunity for a soldier to protect his own community.[48]

Severe recruitment shortfalls prompted the creation of new solutions to staff the Continental Army. The first strategy was to offer more enticing incentives. The Continental Congress revised its recruitment rules in 1778, requiring soldiers to serve for a term of three years or even for the duration of the war.[49] To encourage enlistment, bounties of money, clothing, or land west of the Ohio River were often offered to those who agreed to serve these longer terms.[50]

The second strategy was to expand recruitment with diversity. General Washington had explicitly forbidden the recruitment of free and enslaved African Americans in November 1775, shortly after taking command of the Continental Army.[51] However, in reality, enslaved people had already served with distinction in the Revolution prior to 1778, including at the battles of Lexington and Concord, Bunker Hill, and Saratoga. Brigadier General James Varnum, commander of the 1st Rhode Island Infantry, recommended that Washington change his position and allow the enlistment of enslaved people willing to join the Continental Army in exchange for their freedom.[52]

Anxious to bolster his depleted army, Washington agreed and wrote a recommendation in January 1778 to Rhode Island Governor Nicholas Cooke in support of Varnum's idea.[53] On February 14, 1778, the Rhode Island Assembly approved a plan to offer enlistment to enslaved people in exchange for their freedom. The preamble of the act invoked the "[p]recedent [that] the wisest, the freest, and bravest Nations have liberated their Slaves, and enlisted them as Soldiers to fight in the Defense of their Country," resolving "that every able-bodied Negro, Mulatto, or Indian Man Slave, in this State, may enlist into either of the said two Battalions to serve during the Continuance of the present War with Great-Britain."[54] The act declared that upon successful completion of service, these soldiers would "be immediately discharged from the Service of his Master or Mistress; and be absolutely FREE, as though he had never been encumbered with any Kind of Servitude or Slavery."[55]

The act was repealed four months later under pressure from Rhode Island slave owners who feared the potential consequences of arming enslaved people.[56] However, more than 100 African Americans had already enlisted and were eventually integrated into the 1st Rhode Island Infantry, ready to participate in the next battle.[57]

Battle of Newport

In addition to the fresh recruits that enlisted after the Continental Congress and Rhode Island Assembly resolutions, the French fleet arrived in North America in 1778 to support the Continental Army. The Battle of Newport, Rhode Island, was the first engagement for the allied American and French forces as well as the integrated 1st Rhode Island Infantry.

In May 1778, New Hampshire Brigadier General John Sullivan and French Admiral the comte d'Estaing designed a plan to retake Newport, Rhode Island, from the British in a siege.[58] By July Sullivan was reinforced by troops under the command of the Marquis de Lafayette and General Nathanael Greene. Militia from across New England joined as well. On August 8, d'Estaing's fleet arrived in Newport Harbor to join the gathering American forces.

British Admiral Richard Howe's fleet was dispatched from New York to meet the French fleet. However, a storm on August 10 damaged both fleets, forcing d'Estaing to abandon the attack and retreat with the French troops to Boston for repairs. Sullivan decided to abandon the siege, but the British attacked as the Americans retreated. American forces successfully held their lines and forced the British to halt the attack. Although this first military collaboration with the French had not gone smoothly, the bravery of the 1st Rhode Island Infantry at the Battle of Newport sent its detractors a strong message in favor of welcoming African Americans into the Continental Army.

Raids on the Northern Frontier

As the Continental Army engaged the British Army, conflicts more akin to a civil war erupted on the frontiers of New York and western Pennsylvania. Farms in the river valleys of these two states were critical food suppliers for the Continental Army.[59] But they were sparsely populated and heavily wooded, making them vulnerable to surprise attacks.[60] From their frontier forts, British officers encouraged their First Nation allies and Loyalists to lead destructive raids on Patriot settlements.[61] Patriot families were killed or kidnapped in these terrifying raids and their farms were burned, crops destroyed, and livestock stolen.[62] In addition to terrifying Patriot residents, these raids deprived the Continental Army of food and diverted soldiers from fighting on other fronts.[63]

On May 30, 1778, an allied Loyalist and Iroquois Nation force under the command of Joseph Brant attacked and destroyed the Cobleskill settlement in New York's Mohawk River Valley.[64] In July a particularly brutal raid led by Loyalist Colonel John Butler with local troops and Seneca Nation allies invaded the Wyoming Valley of northeastern Pennsylvania.[65] Nearly all of the 400 American militiamen who marched out to engage them were killed.[66]

In a harsh response to these raids, General Washington sent a large contingent of the Continental Army in August 1779 to destroy First Nation villages. Over 4,000 men from New York, Pennsylvania, New Hampshire, and New Jersey, along with Oneida Nation allies under the command of General John Sullivan moved up the Susquehanna River to Seneca and Onondaga Nation settlements in New York and Pennsylvania.[67] A series of raids and counter raids ensued for the next two months. By September, Sullivan's army had destroyed over 40 First Nation villages and their farms.[68]

Frontier raids intensified and continued to rage over the next five years. One account of a raid on a Schoharie Valley settlement in the fall of 1780 records the role of women who contributed to their settlement's defense. When they received news of an imminent attack, both men and women assembled at the fort and worked together to defend themselves.[69] Schoharie Patriot, Sarah Vrooman, is said to have molded bullets from an iron spoon to replenish dwindling supplies.[70] The account also states, "[a] number of fearless women are said to have stood ready at the pickets, armed with spears, pitchforks and poles, when the enemy appeared in sight."[71]

Raids on Connecticut Ports

Loyalist and First Nation raids on the northern frontiers were matched by terrifying British raids in Connecticut. Port towns along the coast bore the brunt of these brutal raids. However, American privateers operating along Connecticut's coast successfully captured nearly 500 British ships and the valuable food, supplies, and ammunition they carried.[72]

In July 1779, General Clinton ordered a naval raid on the towns of New Haven, Fairfield, and Norwalk led by former royal New York Governor Major General William Tryon. A large force of British regulars and Loyalists attacked on July 5, overwhelming the outnumbered local militiamen who defended the towns. Tryon pillaged and burned the town's warehouses and supplies.[73] In retaliation for militiamen firing on the British from their homes, Tryon also ordered the homes in Norwalk to be burned.[74]

Instead of intimidating the Patriots as the British intended, raids like those in New York, Pennsylvania, and Connecticut sparked outrage among Americans and resulted in greater support for the Patriot cause. When the news of these raids was published, enlistments in the Continental Army and local militias rose across New England.[75]

Back to Morristown

As the Revolution stood in a stalemate at the end of 1779, the Continental Army withdrew once again to their winter encampment at Morristown, New Jersey. Unlike the army that had camped at Valley Forge, these soldiers were now seasoned veterans led by experienced officers.[76] The American force of approximately 10,000 set to work constructing log cabins.[77] This winter was among the harshest on record for the state. Extreme cold and frequent snowstorms combined with food and supply shortages made camp conditions unbearable. Funds to pay the soldiers failed to materialize.[78]

Nineteen-year-old Connecticut Private Joseph Plumb Martin described the appalling conditions in the camp recording,

> At one time it snowed the greater part of four days successively, and there fell nearly as many feet deep of snow and here was the keystone of the arch of starvation. We were absolutely, literally starved. I do solemnly declare that I did not put a single morsel of victuals into my mouth for four days and as many nights, except a little black birch bark which I gnawed off a stick of wood, if that can be called victuals. I saw several of the men roast their old shoes and eat them.[79]

Over the course of the winter, desertions and deaths cut the size of the Continental Army to 8,000 men.[80] In protest of their horrific situation, Connecticut soldiers called for mutiny.[81] The revolt was quickly quashed but made a vivid statement of the extreme suffering endured by these veterans who had already contributed so much to the Revolution.

Hopeful news accompanied the spring thaw. On May 10, 1780, the Marquis de Lafayette returned to Morristown from his yearlong mission in France to lobby King Louis XVI for supplies and troops to support the Continental Army. He proudly informed Washington that a force of 6,000 French troops under the command of the comte de Rochambeau would soon arrive in America.[82]

Our Patriots

As the initial exhilaration of independence receded and gave way to the realities of war, our Patriots persevered through these particularly challenging years of the Revolution. Several survived the grueling winter camp conditions at Valley Forge and Morristown as the Continental Army was transformed into a formidable fighting force. Our soldier Patriots signed Continental Congress's Oath of Allegiance while our civil service Patriots responded to General Washington's plea for supplies.

Many of our soldier Patriots went on from these winter encampments to fight commendably in the conflicts at Monmouth Courthouse and Rhode Island. Others served in their local militias to defend their settlements against ruthless attacks on their communities on the New York and Pennsylvania frontiers and the port towns of Connecticut. Exhausted and hungry, they must have wondered how much longer the Revolution would continue.

Drummer Moses Ramsdell A093887
(1763 - 1834)
Sharon Larson Noble

Moses Ramsdell is my sixth great-grandfather and was born April 6, 1763, in Mendon, Worcester County, Massachusetts, to Moses and Mary (Wares) Ramsdell.

Moses served as a drummer in the 6th Massachusetts Regiment during the Revolutionary War, part of a music tradition that would be passed down through generations in my family. He enlisted in 1779 at the age of 17 and served through 1781 under Colonel Thomas Nixon and Colonel Smith. Muster rolls described him as five feet, eight inches tall with light hair and blue eyes.

Moses served primarily to protect American positions along the Hudson River following British General Burgoyne's defeat at the Battle of Saratoga, New York. He was stationed in New York at West Point, Highlands, and Camp Orangetown. General George Washington was at Camp Orangetown on August 11, 1780, at the time of Moses's service there.

After the Revolution, Moses married Nancy Lapham on February 20, 1784, in Providence, Rhode Island. Their son, Knight, served as a fifer in the New York militia in the War of 1812. Moses died on May 16, 1834, in Jefferson County, New York. Following my family's long-standing tradition, I played the flute and piccolo in marching band.

Private Jacob Galusha A203033
(circa 1757 – 1836)
Kathleen Barrett Huston

Jacob Galusha was born in New Milford, Connecticut, around 1757 to a family committed to military and political service. Jacob's father served in the French and Indian War and his relative, Jonas Galusha, was elected Governor of Vermont in 1809.

Jacob served in the American Revolution for five years in the Connecticut Line. In 1777 he fought in the decisive American victory at the Battle of Saratoga resulting in British General John Burgoyne's surrender. He then enrolled in Captain Ebenezer Hill's Company, Colonel Heman Swift's Regiment on April 26, 1778, joining thousands of Continental Army soldiers wintering at Valley Forge. After transformational training under Major General Friedrich von Steuben, Hill's company fought in the sweltering heat at the Battle of Monmouth Courthouse, led by General George Washington on June 28, 1778. Though inconclusive, the battle resulted in a retreat by British General Sir Henry Clinton's forces. In July 1779 Hill's company fought to defend the Connecticut cities of Fairfield and Norwalk from a raid by British Major General William Tryon. They spent the following winter at Morristown, New Jersey. Jacob was honorably discharged in February 1781.

During his service, Jacob married Dinah Matteson on May 5, 1780, in Williamstown, Massachusetts. He died on June 16, 1836, in Almond, New York.

Private Azor Curtis A028810
(1718 - 1778)
Louise Duncan Farkas, Laura Farkas Roth,
and Haley Michelle Roth

Fifty-nine-year-old Azor Curtis joined the Continental Army from Lanesboro, Connecticut, as a private in 1777, leaving his wife to care for six of their eleven children still at home. His company was at the Battle of Saratoga before being ordered to winter at Valley Forge. Just before Christmas, Azor and his company joined the 12,000 soldiers and 400 women and children who marched into Valley Forge and began building a camp the size of the fourth largest city in the colonies.

General Washington's army left Valley Forge for the Battle of Monmouth in mid-June 1778. Although family lore assumed that Azor died at Valley Forge, he was listed as having engaged in the Battle of Monmouth in Pennsylvania on June 28 and received pay for service until his death on July 17, 1778, when his regiment was near White Plains, New York. His youngest son was just three years old.

His will was not probated until May 2, 1784, so his family likely did not receive confirmation of his death until his company returned home in late 1783. Among his Revolutionary relatives, Azor was the only member of the Continental Army on continuous duty despite his advanced age.

Private Benjamin Webster A121172
(1760 - 1840)
Terry Anderson

Benjamin Webster was born on July 6, 1760, in East Hartford, Connecticut. He was a uniquely resourceful and adventuresome Patriot during the Revolution, serving in both the army and the navy.

When Benjamin was 16 years old, he enlisted in Colonel Sherman's Connecticut Regiment in April 1777, and was charged with defending the Hudson River Valley. General George Washington had ordered the new Fort West Point to be built along a particularly strategic curve in the Hudson River and Benjamin took part in its construction.

In August 1778, while serving in Captain Pipkin's militia, Benjamin was ordered to join General Sullivan's Regiment to fight in the Battle of Rhode Island, marking the first joint engagement of the American and French allies. The allies fought bravely until, recalls Benjamin in his pension application, they were "ordered off by General Washington on account of the British blockading the island."

Benjamin went on to serve as a marine in the navy on the privateer ship *Brig Dean* in 1779 and he made two voyages. When he returned, Benjamin settled in Poultney, Vermont, where he was engaged by Ethan Allen in a final Revolutionary adventure escorting Tories to the British where he was captured and held prisoner for 20 days.

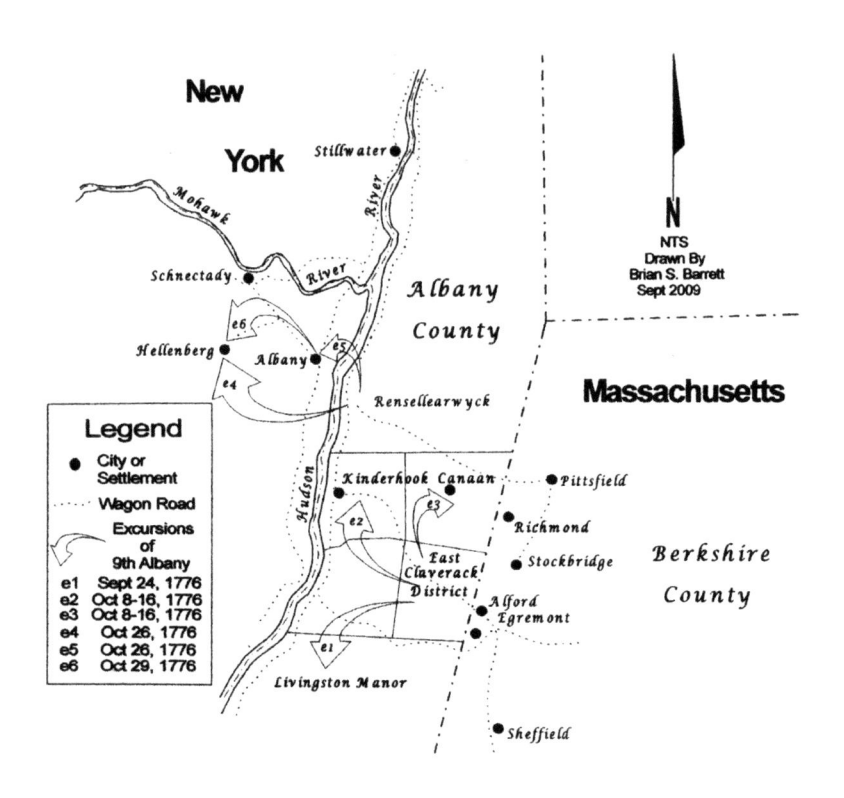

*Revolutionary Excursions
of the 9th Regiment of Hillsdale Militia
Courtesy of Brian S. Barrett*

Captain Bartholomew Barrett A208181
(1736 - circa 1788)
Kathleen Barrett Huston

Bartholomew Barrett, my fifth great-grandfather in a direct male line from my father, was born in Plainfield, Connecticut, on May 5, 1736. His ancestors immigrated from England to Braintree, Massachusetts, around 1635 and helped to settle Chelmsford, Massachusetts.

While living in Plainfield, Bartholomew's father purchased land as an original proprietor in the then wilderness of Cornwall, Connecticut. His family moved there in 1742. They continued on to Salisbury, Connecticut, where Bartholomew married Mehitable Rood in 1755.

Bartholomew fought in the French and Indian War, then relocated to the Massachusetts Berkshires. He appeared in Sheffield in 1760, and as one of the "ratable inhabitants" of Great Barrington in 1762. By 1770 he lived in Claverack, New York.

During the Revolutionary War, he helped to form the "Regiment of Hillsdale" as captain of the 4th Company, 9th Regiment Albany County militia. He also served in the Line under Colonel Philip Van Cortland and the Levies under Colonel Marinus Willett. The Albany County militia's primary duty was hunting Tories spying along the Hudson River. Part of the group also joined General Horatio Gates's army at the Battle of Saratoga.

His eloquent, pious will is recorded in Alford, Berkshire County, Massachusetts, where he died in 1788.

Private James Gaffin A042877
(circa 1746 – circa 1782)
Katherine Ann Winegar Tunheim and Kristi Jane Winegar Wieser

James Gaffin was born in 1746 in New York. In 1768 he married Catharine Van Deusen, probably in Schaghticoke, Rensselaer, New York. The couple had two sons and three daughters: Mary "Polly," Johannes "John," Abraham "Abram," Margaret, and Johanna. James belonged to the Dutch Reformed Church.

During the American Revolution, James served as a private in the Albany County militia, 16th Regiment under Colonels John Blair and Lewis Van Woert. According to family lore as recorded in an Ogle County, Illinois, biography of his great-grandson, James served as one of the Green Mountain Boys and was used as a scout to carry messages. Under the joint command of Ethan Allen and Benedict Arnold, the Green Mountain Boys captured Fort Ticonderoga from the British in May 1775. They also played central roles in the Battles of Hubbardton and Bennington in present day Vermont prior to the American defeat of General Burgoyne at Saratoga, New York, in October 1777. Scouts were not always listed on military rolls, so it is not known for certain whether James participated in these conflicts.

James died in Schaghticoke, Albany County, New York, sometime after March 1782.

Captain Edwards Bucknam A016550
(1741 - 1813)
Mary Jo Pfeifer Wulf

Edwards Bucknam was born in 1741 in Worcester County, Massachusetts. He married Susannah Page. In 1764 he was one of six men who settled Lancaster, New Hampshire. He served as the first Justice of the Peace and for many years held the offices of coroner, town clerk, and selectman.

In the fall of 1776, local residents voted to send Edwards to the General Court at Exeter, New Hampshire, to request that a company of soldiers be located at Lancaster under his command. Edwards served as captain for several years and as second major of the Twelfth (Revolutionary) Regiment of the state militia between 1782 and 1784.

Bucknam's contributions to his community are well documented. According to *History of Lancaster, New Hampshire*, "Edwards Bucknam was, in his sphere, the most universal genius of the settlement. No other man, at any time in the history of the town, has exerted so powerful an influence as he did. He kept the first stock of goods for barter among the settlers; ... surveyed their lands [...]; built the first roads that allowed the passage of loaded teams from Haverhill."

Until he died in 1813, it was recorded that "his life bore relations to about everything in the history of Lancaster."

Private Andreas (Daniel) Daniels A114883
(1757 - 1841)
Pam Daniel Petersen and Meaghan Daniel

Andreas Daniel was born in Berks County, Pennsylvania, in 1757. When the General Assembly of Pennsylvania passed the 1777 act requiring an oath of allegiance to the state during the Revolutionary War, nearly every man in Berks County complied. Signing the oath took courage. If the revolutionary cause failed, signers' properties would be confiscated and they could be imprisoned for treason. Andreas's probable brother, Henry (Daniel) Daniels (A029602), is credited with having signed this oath, making it likely that Andreas signed it as well.

After signing the oath, able-bodied Pennsylvania men aged 18-35 were required to enroll in the militia. Andreas was awarded Depreciation Pay Certificates for his service between 1777 and 1780. Andreas also served near the end of the Revolution in Lieutenant Nicholas Seybert's detachment from October 17 to December 18, 1781. Typical duties of the Berks County militia were guarding prisoners and patrolling the frontier. However, Seybert's detachment is listed as part of the Continental Army, indicating that it may have been called to reinforce American positions in the north after the Main Continental Army had marched to Virginia in September for the Battle of Yorktown.

Andreas married Susanna Hoy. They raised their family in Lykens Township, Dauphin County, Pennsylvania, where the Harrisburg Chapter DAR dedicated a plaque honoring Andreas and eight other Patriots.

Private Jeremiah Frame A041521
(1752 - 1828)
Lindal Eveland Martin, Sarah Martin Pearson, and Cheryl Lynn Stanga Despathy

Jeremiah Frame was born in Augusta County, Virginia, in 1752. He likely grew up on the Frame family-owned land in the Naked Creek area of the Shenandoah Valley. He married Elizabeth McGill in 1777.

During the Revolutionary War, Jeremiah served with the Augusta County militia under Captain Robert McCreery/McCreary. According to Peyton's *History of Augusta County, Virginia*, indigenous warriors "burning with grief and indignation at their wrongs, were easily won over by British diplomacy, and inflicted terrible sufferings on the colonists during the Revolution." To defend the settlers, Captain McCreery and his company were stationed at Fort Warwick in 1777 and at Clover Lick Fort in 1778/9.

Life in the military was difficult where even minor infractions were investigated and could incur severe penalties. In 1779 Jeremiah was acquitted of charges during an Augusta County Court Martial, presumably for failing to appear at a muster. Most soldiers listed in the minutes were either acquitted or fined for not appearing at muster.

In 1783 Jeremiah and Elizabeth relocated to Bourbon County, Kentucky. In 1815 they moved on to Preble County, Ohio, where Jeremiah achieved a level of wealth and prominence. He gave a farm to each of his nine children.

The Old Stone Fort at Schoharie, New York
Courtesy of Patricia Lynne Briley Peterson

Private Henry (Heinrich) Hitzman A211038
(circa 1741 - circa 1810)
Patricia Lynne Briley Peterson

The Schoharie Valley in northern New York was a strategically important supplier of food for the Continental Army during the American Revolution. However, the loyalties of farmers in Schoharie were deeply divided. German born Henry Hitzman chose the side of the Patriots and enlisted in Colonel Peter Vrooman's Albany militia. He experienced a particularly brutal aspect of the war.

Loyalist John Johnson joined forces with indigenous allies to conduct raids on northern Patriot farms. The Marquis de Lafayette ordered the forts in Schoharie garrisoned for their protection. In 1778 Loyalists launched a tragic raid in what would be known as the Battle of Cobleskill in Schoharie County. After engaging Patriot militia, Loyalist raiders burned all the farms in Cobleskill. According to his daughter, Christina, Henry was sent from the Lower Fort to help the victims. He discovered a massacre at the home of George Fester where several family members had been killed and viciously mangled. Henry "gathered the remains of those dead ... and buried them."

The horrific raids continued for five more years. In a November 7, 1780, letter to the Continental Congress, General Washington wrote, "The destruction of grain was so great as to threaten the most alarming consequences ... But for that event, the settlement of Schoharie, alone, would have delivered eighty thousand bushels of grain."

Letter to Enoch Eastman from Vermont Governor Thomas Chittenden
Courtesy of Manchester Historical Society, Howard Wilcox Collection

Captain Enoch Eastman A035718
(1748 - 1829)
Karen Wojahn

Enoch Eastman was one of the Green Mountain Boys during the American Revolution. He was born in Norwich, Connecticut, but settled in East Rupert, Vermont. Settlers in this area were strongly divided during the Revolution. When militia were called to defend the frontiers of Vermont from Loyalist attacks, Enoch joined the side of the Americans and served under Ethan Allen's youngest brother, Colonel Ira Allen.

Once General Burgoyne's Army evacuated the Hudson River Valley and was defeated at the Battle of Saratoga in 1777, the British strategy in the north was to raid the scattered frontier settlements of Vermont and New York. The goal of these raids was to prevent soldiers and supplies in this region from reaching the Continental Army as the war moved to the southern states. Enoch first joined the Vermont militia to defend the frontiers as a lieutenant in 1778 in Captain Noble's Company, Colonel Warren's Regiment. In the following years, he responded to raid alarms in March and October 1780. He was then promoted to captain in 1781 when he responded to alarms in October 1781 and May 1782 under Colonel Allen.

Enoch died in 1829 at the age of 81 on the Vermont land he had protected during the Revolution.

Captain Jacob Odell A204561
(circa 1737 - 1823)
Kathleen Barrett Huston

The Odells of Westerly, Rhode Island, were early settlers of the Beekman Patent in Dutchess County, New York. This part of the Hudson Valley was the site of pre-Revolutionary anti-rent rebellions between landlords and tenant farmers. These tenant uprisings were precursors to conflicts that arose when New York disputed New Hampshire's right to grant land west of the Green Mountains in present-day Vermont. The Green Mountain Boys emerged in 1770 determined to defend the property rights of residents. Drawing upon the New York rioters' resistance strategies, they perfected "a powerful form of extralegal government."

Jacob Odell had purchased land in Shaftsbury, Vermont, and his name appears on a 1765 petition to the New York Governor by Vermont settlers asking that they be allowed to keep their New Hampshire grants. He lived in Manchester, Vermont, where he was elected constable in 1768.

During the Revolutionary War, Jacob served multiple times in Colonel Ira Allen's Regiment of Vermont militia between 1780 and 1784; he was captain of one of the three companies from Manchester.

Jacob died in Manchester and is buried with first wife, Mary Millington, in Factory Point Cemetery. His name is among the Revolutionary War soldiers listed on the Soldiers' Monument in Manchester.

Asa (Cheadle) Cheedle, Sr. A021269
(1734 - circa 1792)
Cheryl Lynn Stanga Despathy and Megan Anne Stanga

Asa Cheedle was born in Connecticut in 1734. During the French and Indian War, Asa served with Connecticut soldiers, rising to the rank of sergeant. He married Martha Paddock in 1761 and their first child, Asa Jr., was born the following year.

By 1775 Asa's growing family resided in Windsor County, Vermont, where they had followed William Cheedle, one of the earliest pioneers in the town of Barnard and likely Asa's brother. In the 1779 annual town meeting, Asa was named grand jury man and one of three selectmen. Among his responsibilities, "Deacon Cheedle" was designated to plan construction of a meetinghouse, hire a minister, and be surveyor of highways.

During the American Revolution, the British Army and their indigenous allies invaded northern Vermont in 1780, burning settlements and taking prisoners. When a war party descended on Barnard in August, they carried off several citizens to Canada. The settlement's Patriot inhabitants immediately set to work building Fort Defiance in Barnard and Fort Fortitude in nearby Bethel for their protection. Asa and William were among a scouting party for Captain Benjamin Cox's Company, "pursuing after the enemy to Brookfield" in October 1780.

Fourteen-year-old Asa, Jr. (A021270) also served in the Revolution, enlisting for six tours with the militia from early 1777 to 1782.

Lieutenant Jesse Washburn, Sr. A121889
(circa 1724 - circa 1810)
Lois Abromitis Mackin

Jesse Washburn, Sr. was born about 1724 in Plymouth, Massachusetts. In Plymouth County court documents, Jesse is referred to as a yeoman or laborer. In 1748 he married Silence Washburn in Bridgewater, Massachusetts. Silence was descended from two *Mayflower* passengers, Francis Cooke and Thomas Rogers. The couple had six children. By 1759 Jesse and Silence had moved to Newtown, New Jersey, and then on to Pennsylvania, where Jesse operated a mill on McMichael's Creek.

In July 1778 Jesse was at present-day Plymouth, Pennsylvania, with his family when the Patriot militia, including Jesse's 15-year-old son Daniel, serving in place of his father, engaged British and indigenous forces at the Battle of Wyoming. Only 60 of the 400 Patriot militia members survived and the battle became known among settlers as the "Wyoming Massacre." After the massacre Jesse's family fled to the more settled parts of Northampton County.

During the Revolutionary War Jesse served as a sergeant in 1778 and lieutenant in 1780 and 1782 in the Northampton County militia. His companies were raised in Chestnut Hill Township, in the vicinity of McMichael's Creek land. In 1778 Jesse's company marched from Allentown to Feather Bed Hill, where they remained until discharged. In 1780 and 1782 the company performed guard duty on the northern frontier of Northampton County.

Ensign Leonard Stahl A206354
(ante 1755 - circa 1829)
Georgetta "Gigi" Henrichsen Hickey

Leonard Stahl was the second-born son of Henry Stahl (A095663). Leonard and two younger brothers, Henry, Jr. (A108238) and Jacob (A108244), served in the Cumberland County militia during the Revolutionary War. In 1777, 1778, and 1779, Leonard was listed as a private in Captain John Jack's Company. During at least one tour, he substituted for another frontiersman. In 1780 and 1781, Leonard served as ensign in Captain William Berryhill's Company. (Ensigns existed in the Revolutionary infantry as the lowest commissioned rank, just below lieutenants.)

Soldiers in the backcountry of western Pennsylvania were organized into geographical units. Some fought the British in the East but many protected property and families in their communities. Frontier militias guarded local farms during plowing and harvest seasons where they were less likely to encounter the British Army than attacks from local Loyalists. Consequently, the conflict on the frontier was intensely personal and violent. That Leonard Stahl volunteered for multiple military assignments showed his deep commitment to his neighbors and community.

In about 1785, Leonard married Elizabeth King, daughter of Michael King (A064689). The village of Stahlstown, Pennsylvania, was later built on land owned by Leonard Stahl, from whom the village took its name.

*Gravestone of Adam and Elizabeth Flake
Buffington Cemetery, Wilmington, Indiana
Courtesy of Justin Meyer*

Private Adam Flake A040466
(1750 - 1836)
Margie Anderson Nash

Born in Switzerland in 1750, Adam Flake arrived in Pennsylvania in 1773. He served as a private in the Cumberland County militia and was listed on four muster rolls all under the command of Captain Samuel Royer: 1779, August 1780, March 1781, and July 1781. Royer, who lived in what would later become Franklin County, led companies of soldiers living in that locale.

Detailed muster and training requirements were enacted for the Pennsylvania militias in early 1780. Exercises, marching, and inspection were to be conducted based on a rotating schedule by battalion and company. As necessary, militia units were to be called into active service to protect property, crops, and families in the community. While not commonly encountering the British Army, local militia members tried to repel attacks by Indigenous allies of the British.

In about 1782, Adam Flake married Elizabeth Stuff/Stough. Secondary sources indicate Nicholas and Michael Stuff were likely her brothers and had served multiple tours in the Cumberland County militia.

Adam and Elizabeth Flake and their growing family lived in Bedford County, Pennsylvania, until moving west to Dearborn County, Indiana, where they became the first settlers on South Hogan Creek in January 1796.

Private Jacob (Peter) Peters A205789
(1751 - 1804)
Lois Abromitis Mackin

Jacob Peter or Peters was born on March 22, 1751, in Bucks County, Pennsylvania. He was the son of Patriot Casper Peter (A089595) and Anna Elisabeth Ribsamin, immigrants from Canton Zurich, Switzerland, who were early settlers of the area that became Heidelberg Township, Northampton County, Pennsylvania.

Jacob married Susanna Rex in 1772. Jacob and Susanna had seven children born between 1773 and 1786.

During the Revolutionary War, Jacob served as a private in Captain Conrad Ritter's Company, Third Battalion (later Sixth Battalion), Northampton County militia. He is recorded on muster rolls dated 1778, 1780, and 1782.

Jacob died in April 1804 and is buried at Heidelberg Church in Lehigh County, Pennsylvania.

Gravestone of Jacob Peter
Heidelberg Church, Pennsylvania
Courtesy of Lois Abromitis Mackin

Sergeant Peter Andreas A002555
(1751 - 1834)
Lois Abromitis Mackin

Peter Andreas was a farmer from northeastern Pennsylvania. His parents came from Germany and Alsace to Pennsylvania as young children, settling on what was then the Pennsylvania frontier in Northampton County. Just before the Revolutionary War, Peter married Thankful Washburn, daughter of Patriot Jesse Washburn (A121889). The couple had ten children between 1773 and 1794.

During the war Peter served as a sergeant in the Northampton County militia and as a ranger on the frontier, likely the northern frontier of Northampton County.

Peter's war was personal but also familial. His father, Martin (A002554), served with the Pennsylvania Flying Camp at the Battle of Long Island in 1776. His brothers William (A002556), Jacob, and Martin also provided military service, as did his father-in-law Jesse Washburn (A121889) and his brothers-in-law Jesse (A121892), and Daniel Washburn. The Washburns were unfortunate enough to be close to the 1778 Wyoming Massacre. Daniel, who fought in the battle, survived, but Peter's uncle, William Wotring (A130665), was killed. William left a pregnant widow and children who fled back to Northampton County with the Washburns. Peter and his wife stood as godparents for William's posthumous infant.

After the Revolution Peter continued to serve in the militia, becoming captain of a Northampton County rifle company in 1796. He died in Luzerne County in 1834.

Private William Andreas A002556
(baptized 1757 - 1824)
Lois Abromitis Mackin

William Andreas, the second known son of DAR patriot Martin Andreas (A002554) and Anna Elisabetha Woodring, was born in Northampton County, Pennsylvania about 1757.

In 1780, William served as a private in the Fifth Company, Sixth Battalion, Northampton County militia commanded by Captain Conrad Reader. William's brothers Peter, a sergeant (A002555); Martin; and Jacob (both privates) served in the same company, which was raised in Heidelberg Township and served on the Northampton County frontier against indigenous forces.

William married Elizabeth Helfrich in 1783. The couple had ten children. Along with his brothers Peter and Martin, William farmed in Heidelberg Township on land originally warranted by their father. By 1810 William and his family had followed Peter and Jacob to East Penn Township over the Blue Mountain, where William died in 1824, leaving over 200 acres to his children.

Private Jacob Frantz A041886
(circa 1742 - circa 1827)
Lois Abromitis Mackin

Jacob Frantz was born in Bucks County, Pennsylvania. His father came to Philadelphia from Lorraine in 1738, settled on the frontier, and died about 1763, possibly in an indigenous raid. Jacob went to court two years later when his uncle petitioned for him to choose a guardian. Young Jacob chose Paul Balliet, a neighboring landowner from the same town as his father.

About 1771, Jacob married Margaretha X and had seven known children, four boys and three girls, who were born between 1772 and 1789.

During the Revolutionary War Jacob moved around within Northampton County, signing the oath of allegiance and serving in the militia companies raised in his townships. By the end of the war he was working as a blacksmith and had become a landowner. Blacksmith shops were community centers, and blacksmiths often invested in other trades. Jacob's two-story log house measured 30 by 23 feet. He also had a store, a tavern, and a distillery, in addition to his blacksmith shop. He died shortly after writing his will in April 1826.

Jacob Neifert A202310
(1735 - 1812)
Lois Abromitis Mackin

Jacob Neifert was born in Germany in 1735. He arrived in Philadelphia as a single man on the ship *Nancy* in 1752 and took the oath of allegiance. He settled between Berks and Northampton Counties about the time the French and Indian War started. In 1757 he enlisted as a private in the Pennsylvania militia for three years, serving in the company of Captain John Nicholas Weatherholt for duty east of the Susquehanna. In 1758 the company was stationed in Heidelberg Township as protection against indigenous raids.

Jacob married Elisabeth Stumpf and the couple had six children. Records show that in 1767 and 1768 Jacob was taxed only on a horse and a cow; by 1779 he had acquired land and additional livestock.

On January 4, 1778, Jacob and his father-in-law Daniel Stumpf signed the oath of allegiance to the new American government. The following year Jacob was among the Berks Countians who signed a remonstrance against calling a new Pennsylvania constitutional convention to replace the constitution adopted in 1776, described as the most democratic in America.

Jacob wrote his will in 1810, signing with a mark, and died in 1812. He left an estate of about $2,200, including a loom and weaving equipment, swarms of bees, Bibles, books, and spectacles.

Private Joseph Hunsicker A060102
(baptized 1762 - 1831)
Lois Abromitis Mackin

Joseph Hunsicker was born in 1762 and baptized in Heidelberg Township, Northampton County, Pennsylvania. He was the seventh child and fifth son of Johannes Hunsicker of Schalbach, Alsace-Lorraine, and Magdalena Pierson or Bierson. His parents emigrated to Pennsylvania on the ship *Two Brothers*, arriving in Philadelphia in 1748. They were settled in Heidelberg Township by 1750.

Joseph was a relatively young man during the Revolutionary War. He first appears on the muster roll of Captain Conrad Rader's Company, Sixth Battalion, Northampton County militia in 1782.

Joseph married Maria Barbara Ohl, daughter of another early settler, in 1783. He and Maria Barbara had four children born between 1783 and 1791 before Maria Barbara's death in 1794. The same year Joseph married Catharine Krumm; he and Catharine had six more children between 1795 and 1817.

Joseph wrote his will in May 1826 and died on December 29, 1831, leaving the widowed Catharine and ten children to inherit his land in Lehigh and Northampton Counties and other assets.

Private John George Huntzinger A060865
(1751 - 1802)
Lois Abromitis Mackin

John George Huntzinger was born on February 7, 1751, in Pennsylvania. His father, Johann George Huntzinger (1715 - 1790), had arrived in Philadelphia on the ship *Jacob* from Amsterdam in 1749, quickly moving to the Berks County frontier, settling "over the mountains" by 1754.

In 1774 John George married Anna Maria Deibert, daughter of another early settler in the area. The couple had nine children, born between 1775 and 1797.

John George, along with his father George and brother Bernard, signed the oath of allegiance to the new United States of America in 1778. During the Revolution, he served as a private in the company of Captain Jacob Whetstone, Third Battalion, Berks County militia.

John George died intestate on September 6, 1802, in Brunswick Township, Berks County, leaving the widowed Anna Maria and nine children, five still in their minority. His estate included multiple tracts of land and woodland, plus household furnishings, farm implements, livestock, and produce.

Thomas Brooks A015100
(1750 - 1790)
Miriam Erhard Kaegebein

Thomas Brooks was born in Chester County, Pennsylvania, to Quaker parents, Thomas, Sr. and Martha Brooks. As a young man in 1774, Thomas admitted to fathering an illegitimate child and was disowned from the church. He became a tailor by profession and later married Mary Richardson.

Many Quakers chose to refuse military service during the Revolutionary War because of their commitment to pacifism. Thomas did not share these views. He supported the cause of liberty by enlisting in the Cumberland County militia. He served in Captain John Orbison's Fourth Company, Fourth Battalion, commanded by Colonel Samuel Culbertson in 1780 and Captain Walter McKinnie's Eighth Company, Fourth Battalion, in 1781 and 1782. Thomas also performed patriotic service by paying supply taxes in 1780 and 1782.

Thomas died at age 40 under what appear to be difficult circumstances. His hand-written will includes a prayer, "Dearest Lord, do condescend so far to be with me in this time of tryal [sic]." He compassionately left equal shares of his estate to his children, including Lydia who is likely the child born in 1774, and thoughtfully instructed his friends to assist "my wife in settling my affairs and also finding places for my children ... as my mind is deeply exercised [sic] for my poor family."

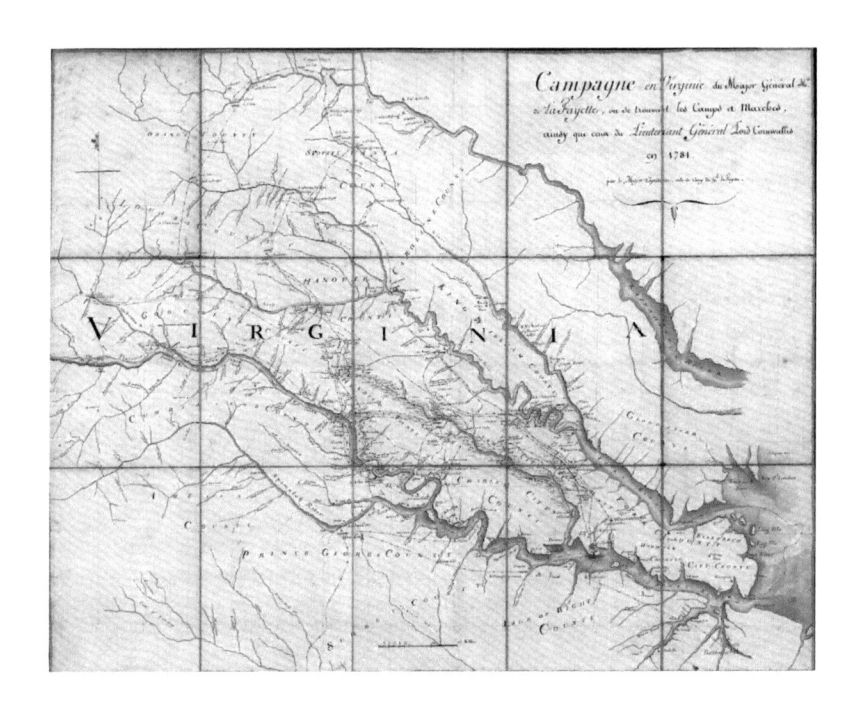

*Major General Marquis de Lafayette's Virginia Campaign Map[1]
Source: Library of Congress*

Chapter 5:
INDEPENDENCE

★

The American alliance with France changed Great Britain's perspective on the Revolutionary War. To protect its stake in its wealthiest colonies, the British redirected their military operations to the south. The southern states had faithfully sent Patriot soldiers and supplies to support the war effort but had not experienced British military attacks for the past several years while the war raged in the New England and mid-Atlantic states. Now the Carolinians and Georgians would experience bloody conflicts at home with both the British and with each other as civil war broke out between Patriots and Loyalists in the backcountry.

Early southern conflicts fought with traditional military tactics were won by the British. However, bold and inventive American military approaches led by new officers successfully deterred British efforts until the decisive American and French allied victory at Yorktown, Virginia. The surrender of the British Army at Yorktown forced King George III to conclude that the war in the American colonies was no longer worth the cost. With the *Treaty of Paris*, the Americans finally secured their long-sought independence.

The Southern Campaign

At precisely the same time Prime Minister Lord North dispatched the Carlisle Peace Commission to New York for negotiations, Colonial Secretary Lord Germain sent orders to General Henry Clinton for a dramatic change in the British military strategy in America. On March 8, 1778, Germain directed Clinton to shift the war to the southern states. Germain's directive read, "It is the King's intention that an attack should be made against the Southern Colonies with a view to the conquest and possession of Georgia and South Carolina."[2]

Germain's rationale was twofold. First, he wanted to protect the economically wealthy southern colonies and the Caribbean Islands from French capture.[3] The south's valuable rice, indigo, and tobacco cash crops were unique to the American colonies and could not be produced in Great Britain. Second, he believed reports from former royal governors informing him that the southern population was comprised predominantly of Loyalists who, along with enslaved people, could be recruited for support.[4]

Despite a delayed start, the new strategy met with initial success for the British. On November 9, 1778, General Clinton sent a sizable force under the command of Lieutenant Colonel Archibald Campbell to invade South Carolina and Georgia.[5] Campbell arrived in late December and immediately captured Georgia's capital city of Savannah, forcing the state's provincial congress to flee to Augusta. However, on January 9, 1779, the British captured the city of Augusta as well. After securing these cities, Campbell issued a proclamation repeating the terms of the Carlisle Commission offering protection "to all his Majesty's faithful subjects of the southern provinces" who "embrace the happy occasion of cementing a firm and perpetual coalition with the parent state, free from the imposition of taxes by the Parliament of Great Britain" provided "they shall immediately return to the class of peaceful citizens, acknowledge their just allegiance to the crown, and with their arms support it."[6] For those who opposed the King, Campbell threateningly declared, "We lament the necessity of exhibiting the rigours [sic] of war, and call upon God and the world to witness that they only shall be answerable for all the miseries which may ensue."[7] Thousands of southern citizens joined the side of the British.[8]

The invasion of the southern states combined with the continued hardships in the northern states to deflate energy for the revolutionary cause. Washington observed the alarming developments in the south and their impact on American morale with growing anxiety. He shared his concerns in a spring 1779 letter to New York Continental Congress delegate, Gouverneur Morris,

> The rapid decay of our currency, the extinction of public spirit, the increasing rapacity of the times, the want of harmony in our councils, the declining zeal of the people, the discontents and distresses of the officers of the army; and I may add, the prevailing security and insensibility to danger, are symptoms, in my eye of a most alarming nature.[9]

He added that in his opinion, "the relief of the S[outhern] S[tates] appears to me an object of the greatest magnitude" and accurately predicted that South Carolina's capital of Charleston, was likely "to feel the next stroke." [10]

Siege of Charleston

The following September, Washington appointed Massachusetts Patriot, Major General Benjamin Lincoln, to assume command of the Southern Department of the Continental Army and defend the southern states.[11] When Lincoln arrived in Charleston, South Carolina, he found the city's defenses in poor condition. Several fortresses were in disrepair and others remained unfinished.

On December 26, 1779, Clinton sailed from New York with a fleet of 14 warships, numerous gunner ships, and over 8,000 troops to capture Charleston.[12] British forces under the command of General Lord Earl Cornwallis set out on a difficult march over marshy terrain to Charleston, harassed on their journey by a South Carolina militia led by Brigadier General Francis Marion.[13] Despite this harassment, Cornwallis's forces arrived in Charleston to dig the first trench in a siege surrounding the city on April 1. When British warships entered Charleston Harbor, the Americans were trapped on all sides.

The following week, Lincoln and the city's leaders agreed to refuse Clinton's first demand for surrender. The British responded by bombarding the American fortifications and moving their forces closer to the city in their second parallel siege line. The outnumbered American soldiers, reinforced by 750 Virginia soldiers sent by

Washington, courageously defended the city against the oncoming British, firing broken glass and metal from their cannons when ammunition ran short.[14] Members of South Carolina's provincial government were forced to secretly flee the city. When British forces were within 25 yards of the city's defenses with every escape route cut off and the city under heavy bombardment, Clinton again demanded Lincoln's unconditional surrender. In the largest surrender of American forces during the Revolution, Lincoln was finally forced to concede on May 8.[15] On June 17, the victorious Clinton sailed back to New York City.

Clinton's threatening demand for unconditional surrender was reprinted in the *New Jersey Gazette* on June 28 where Americans read what the terrified Charleston residents faced if they had refused. Clinton's demand read, "By this last summons therefore, I throw to your charge whatever vindictive severity exasperated soldiers may inflict on the unhappy people, whom you devote by preserving your fruitless defense."[16]

Defeat at Camden

Another devastating American defeat closely followed the surrender of Charleston. Alarmed by the demoralizing losses in the southern states, the Continental Congress appointed Major General Horatio Gates to respond. Gates gathered eight Continental Army regiments along with Virginia and North Carolina militia and marched to South Carolina.[17] General Washington sent Continental soldiers from Maryland and Delaware to reinforce him.[18]

With Charleston firmly under British control, Cornwallis proceeded to secure South Carolina's backcountry by establishing a supply depot and garrison in Camden.[19] Alerted to the approaching American forces north of Camden, Cornwallis moved out to engage them. As the two armies took their positions on the field on August 16, 1780, Gates errantly set up his most inexperienced militia troops opposite Cornwallis's strongest force. The British advanced with bayonets drawn and the American militia line collapsed in retreat. Although the experienced Continental troops from Maryland and Delaware fought fiercely and held, the panicked Gates fled the field, riding all the way to Charlotte, North Carolina.[20]

In less than one hour of fighting, the Americans were routed and many were taken prisoner. Only 700 of the original American force of 4,000 escaped.[21] However, four days later, the cunning and resourceful Brigadier General Marion and his South Carolina militia launched a surprise attack on the British detachment guarding American prisoners and rescued the Maryland regiment captured at Camden.[22]

Benedict Arnold's Treason

Unfortunately, American disasters in 1780 were not limited to the battlefield. Although Major General Benedict Arnold had served with distinction in earlier battles such as the capture of Fort Ticonderoga and the Battle of Saratoga, he grew increasingly frustrated after being repeatedly passed over for promotion and accused of corruption in his position as military governor of Philadelphia.[23] Struggling with war wounds and deeply in debt, he resigned his position in Philadelphia and began to plan his defection to the British Army.

Arnold proposed to General Washington that he take command of Fort West Point on the Hudson River in New York, claiming his wounds made him unfit for a field command. Washington approved the appointment. Working through intermediaries, Arnold communicated to British General Clinton that he would be willing to turn West Point over to the British in exchange for £20,000 and an appointment in the British Army.[24] On September 21, 1780, Arnold secretly left his West Point home and met British Major John André to discuss the fort's vulnerabilities.[25]

Washington, along with General Lafayette, General Knox, and Colonel Alexander Hamilton, arrived at West Point to inspect the fort and discovered Arnold's treason. Disguised in civilian attire, André had been arrested on his attempted return to British lines by American militia who found the map of West Point in his boot. Arnold narrowly escaped capture aboard the British warship, *Vulture*. The ill-fated André was found guilty of espionage in an American military court and sentenced to be executed. When the British refused Washington's proposal to exchange André for Arnold, André was hanged as a spy. Despite his original plan's dismal failure, Arnold was appointed Brigadier General in the British Army.

The incensed General Washington informed the Continental Congress of Arnold's treason. Congress passed a resolution to expunge the traitor's name from American military records stating, "Resolved, That the Board of War be and hereby are directed to erase from the register of the names of the officers of the army of the United States, the name of Benedict Arnold."[26] Dismayed Patriot readers of the *Boston Gazette* learned of Arnold's treason. In a colorful account, the article vilified Arnold declaring, "It is not possible for human nature to receive a greater quantity of guilt than he possesses" because "in [Arnold's] most early infancy, hell mark'd him for her own, and infus'd into him a full proportion of her diabolical malice."[27]

The citizens of Richmond, Virginia, likely agreed with the *Boston Gazette's* assessment. On December 20, 1780, now-British General Arnold departed New York City for Virginia to join the British southern campaign. Within weeks, he led a Loyalist force that captured and destroyed the undefended Virginia capital of Richmond.[28]

Turning Point at Kings Mountain

By fall 1780, General Cornwallis had established British strongholds in Charlotte, North Carolina, and Camden, South Carolina. However, supply lines between the two cities suffered continual raids by Patriot militia. Hoping to move forward with his vision of capturing Virginia, Cornwallis sent Major Patrick Ferguson to the foothills between the

Carolinas to destroy the raiding militia and recruit Loyalists to join the British army.[29]

American settlers in this area, known as "Overmountain Men," lived in the territory in violation of the British Proclamation Line of 1763.[30] Ferguson issued a threatening ultimatum to the Overmountain settlers ordering them to swear allegiance to King George III or he would "hang their leaders, and lay waste to the land with fire and sword."[31] Enraged by this threat and the risk of expulsion under British rule, the Overmountain Men decided to pursue Ferguson.[32]

On October 6, 1780, Ferguson positioned his force on the high ground at Kings Mountain, South Carolina.[33] Familiar with the wooded terrain and armed with their own accurate long rifles rather than Continental Army issued short-range muskets, the skilled Overmountain marksmen launched a surprise attack and overran Ferguson's position in less than an hour.[34] This overwhelming defeat forced Cornwallis's now unprotected main army to retreat back to South Carolina.

Virginia Governor Thomas Jefferson had observed developments in the southern states with growing concern and was relieved to share news of the decisive victory at Kings Mountain with the Continental Congress. His letter to the President of the Continental Congress was reprinted in the *Pennsylvania Gazette* where he stated, "I do myself the pleasure of congratulating your Excellency on the small dawn of fortune which at length appears in the south."[35] General Clinton would later reflect that the British loss at Kings Mountain "proved [to be] the first link in a chain of evils that followed each other in regular succession until they at last ended in the total loss of America."[36]

Conflict in the Carolina Backcountry

Even with decisive early British victories, General Cornwallis's southern campaign was difficult. The southern populace was more divided than he had been advised. Before leaving Charleston for New

York, Clinton had issued a series of severe proclamations demanding that the citizens of South Carolina declare their allegiance to the British king and requiring pardoned prisoner soldiers to serve in Loyalist militias.[37] Coupled with the suffering that accompanied the southern conflicts and raids, these proclamations polarized Americans who were forced to choose sides. Other partisan differences further fueled divides. Scots-Irish immigrants who resented British treatment of their countries of origin sided with the Patriots.[38] Those who hoped the British would help defend against attacks on their settlements by First Nation forces became Loyalists.[39]

This polarization effectively incited a civil war between Loyalists and Patriots in the South Carolina, North Carolina, and Georgia backcountry.[40] The few southern Loyalists Cornwallis found were more interested in fighting their Patriot neighbors than joining British military engagements.[41] Rival Patriot and Loyalist groups developed militias and conducted brutal raids on each other's homes and farms.

In addition to difficulties recruiting Loyalists to his cause, Cornwallis had to face a formidable new American military leader. General Washington appointed the bold and tenacious General Nathanael Greene as the commander of the Southern Department of the Continental Army. Greene took command on December 2, 1780, and was joined by Brigadier General Daniel Morgan whose inventive military tactics and familiarity with the rough Carolina backcountry terrain were ideally suited to outmaneuvering the traditional British approach.[42]

Greene refused to repeat Lincoln and Gates's mistakes by fighting Cornwallis in a traditional engagement. Knowing Cornwallis's force was unfamiliar with the swampy Carolina topography and could be bogged down hauling their heavy artillery, Greene instead decided to exhaust Cornwallis in a battle of attrition by leading him deep into the backcountry and away from his supply lines.[43] To keep his forces nimble and able to launch surprise guerilla attacks, Greene divided the American forces, assigning half to Morgan.[44]

On January 17, 1781, Morgan's force of Continentals and militia engaged with a British force led by Lieutenant Colonel Banastre Tarleton at Cowpens, South Carolina. Morgan cunningly set up his forces in an unconventional three-line formation. The first line was comprised of inexperienced skirmishers who he commanded to fire two volleys focused on British officers and then to retreat.[45] Believing the Americans were fleeing, the British continued their assault and were attacked by Morgan's second and third lines of more experienced Continentals and militia. The British fled in a humiliating defeat. Wearied by long marches and guerilla attacks, Cornwallis abandoned South Carolina and pursued Greene in North Carolina.[46]

Morgan's subsequent report to Greene was reprinted in the *New Jersey Gazette* on February 14, 1781. Patriots were encouraged to read, "The troops I have the honour [sic] to command have gained a complete victory over a detachment from the British Army, commanded by Lieut. Col. Tarleton."[47] Morgan concluded, "Such was the inferiority of our numbers, that our success must be attributed, under God, to the justice of our cause, and the bravery of our troops."[48] Eager to share credit for the victory, Morgan included a list of his troops, telling Greene he did so "from a conviction that you will be pleased to introduce such characters to the world."[49]

For the next month, Greene harassed Cornwallis in a series of swift and intense raids.[50] On March 15, Greene engaged Cornwallis's exhausted and undersupplied forces at Guilford Courthouse, North Carolina.[51] Greene repeated Morgan's successful strategy at Cowpens and positioned his forces in three lines. The North Carolina militia on the first line opened fire on the advancing British and then retreated. The second and third lines of Virginians and Marylanders successfully resisted and drove the British back. When British reinforcements arrived, Greene withdrew. Although the British declared victory when the Americans retreated, they had lost a quarter of their forces in the battle and were unable to pursue Greene.[52] Unwilling to sustain more such losses, Cornwallis decided to shift his focus to Virginia.[53]

Greene's post-battle report recounting the Battle at Guilford Courthouse was printed in the Boston *Independent Chronicle* where Patriots read with interest, "The firmness of the officers and soldiers during the whole campaign has been almost unparalleled. Amidst innumerable difficulties they have discovered a degree of magnanimity and fortitude that will forever add lustre [sic] to their military reputation."[54]

As Cornwallis withdrew to Virginia in the spring, Greene's continued efforts to recapture the Carolinas proved more difficult than anticipated. After successfully capturing British-held Fort Watson and Camden, Greene began a siege of the fort and supply post at Ninety Six, South Carolina, held entirely by Loyalists from South Carolina, New York, and New Jersey.[55] Greene was reinforced by American Colonel Henry Lee who had just successfully recaptured Augusta, Georgia. After a month-long siege, Greene decided to directly attack the post's main fort on June 18, ahead of British reinforcements dispatched from Charleston. However, the Loyalists counterattacked and successfully drove back Greene's forces. After intense fighting, Greene ended the attack. The Loyalists also withdrew from Ninety Six, burning the town as they left.

Still determined to eliminate the British presence in South Carolina, Greene led his forces on a 22-day, 120-mile march to engage British Lieutenant Colonel Alexander Stewart's forces at Eutaw Springs, South Carolina.[56] Greene's Virginia and Maryland Continentals, along with North and South Carolina militia, clashed with Stewart on September 8, 1781, and fought intensely for four hours until each side was exhausted. While both sides declared victory, the Americans had successfully debilitated Loyalist forces in the Carolinas again and, most importantly, prevented them from reinforcing Cornwallis in Virginia.

Grateful Patriots read in the *Pennsylvania Packet* that the Continental Congress honored Greene with one of only six gold medals awarded during the Revolutionary War:

> Resolved, that the thanks of the [U]nited [S]tates [C]ongress assembled, he presented to major general Greene, for his wise, decisive and magnanimous conduct in the action of the 8th of September last, near the Eutaw Springs in South-Carolina; in which, with a force inferior in number to that of the enemy, he obtained a most signal victory.[57]

Economic Hardship & Resourcefulness

As welcome as news like that of Greene's success at Eutaw Springs was received, it did little to alleviate difficult living conditions experienced by many Americans across the states. Years of brutal partisan raids between Patriots and Loyalists on the northern frontiers and southern backcountry had destroyed livelihoods. Some states collected taxes and provisions from their citizens to pay and supply their soldiers. However, wherever they marched both armies were required to forage and confiscate provisions from whatever farms and towns they passed to feed their frequently starving soldiers.

General Washington was grateful to the faithful Americans who had generously provisioned his army. He expressed grave concerns about the damaging depredation that resulted from the Continental Army's foraging. In a letter to Brigadier General Anthony Wayne on November 27, 1780, Washington encouraged restraint, writing,

> I would recommend in the strongest manner the preservation of the persons and properties of the inhabitants from wanton or unnecessary violation. They have, from their situation, borne much of the bur[d]en of the War and have never failed to releive [sic] the distresses of the Army, when properly called upon.[58]

American citizens and merchants who were fortunate enough to earn income found their cash worthless. The huge quantity of paper money the Continental Congress had printed resulted in extreme inflation. By 1780, $100 dollars was equivalent to the purchasing power of 74¢ in 1775.[59] By 1781 most businesses no longer accepted Continental money as legal tender, sparking widespread protests over the worthless currency.[60] In spring 1781, the Continental Congress appointed successful Pennsylvania merchant and delegate, Robert Morris, to the newly created position of Superintendent of Finance to restore the country's financial position.[61]

The primary reason Continental currency was worthless was that Congress did not have the power to raise revenue through taxation under the Articles of Confederation and was therefore entirely reliant on the financially strained states to fund the army.[62] As General Washington made plans to march the Main Department of the Continental Army south in the spring of 1781, he again feared his unpaid soldiers may mutiny. Washington appealed to Morris for one month's pay to satisfy his soldiers.[63] The resourceful Morris swiftly responded by securing a loan in gold from France so that the soldiers could be paid in hard currency and by pledging his own personal fortune to pay Philadelphia merchants who supplied the Army for its anticipated march south.[64]

The Virginia Campaign

As General Washington's Main Continental Army remained stationed along the Hudson River to contain Clinton in the spring of 1781, he sent two of his trusted leaders, the Marquis de Lafayette and Major General von Steuben, ahead to harass the British Army and defend Virginia while Greene fought in the Carolinas.[65]

Steuben took command of the Virginia State militia in Petersburg, Virginia, where he correctly anticipated a British attack of the city on April 25.[66] Although the Virginia militia was significantly outnumbered, it successfully repulsed several British assaults before retreating. This engagement allowed Lafayette the time he needed to position his forces on the high ground at Richmond, preventing a second British assault of the city.

Lafayette and his force of New England and New Jersey Continentals were joined by Brigadier General Anthony Wayne's Pennsylvania Line. The joint forces shadowed Cornwallis as the British Army moved across Virginia in May 1781.[67] When Cornwallis decided to cross the James River, Lafayette saw an opportunity to attack. Recognizing his vulnerability during the river crossing, Cornwallis set a trap by leaking false information that led the Americans to believe only a small number of British troops remained to cross. Facing a much larger force than expected, Wayne's forces fell into the trap and engaged the British near Green Spring, Virginia. Lafayette observed Wayne's trapped troops and ordered reinforcements to join the intense battle. Severely outnumbered, the Americans were forced to withdraw.

Lafayette's report commended the performance of Wayne's troops, stating, "[I am] happy in acknowledging the spirit of the detachment commanded by General Wayne, in their engagement with the total of the British Army" and inviting "General Wayne, the officers and men under his command, to receive [my] best thanks."[68]

Victory at Yorktown

In spring 1781, General Washington met with French Lieutenant General comte de Rochambeau in Rhode Island to discuss plans for an allied engagement that could break the stalemate of the war. They considered an attack to recapture New York City, but when Rochambeau arrived in New York with news that the French fleet under the command of Admiral comte de Grasse was sailing from the West Indies to the Chesapeake Bay, they saw the opportunity for a coordinated land and sea attack on British forces in Virginia.[69] With an elaborate deception to convince Clinton that they planned to remain in New York, Washington and Rochambeau marched their combined force of 8,000 troops through New Jersey, Pennsylvania, and Delaware to join Lafayette's force in Williamsburg, Virginia.[70]

In July General Cornwallis received specific orders from General Clinton to hold a position at Yorktown on the Virginia peninsula between the York and James Rivers.[71] Upon their arrival at Yorktown, the British proceeded to construct fortifications and redoubts around the town.

At the end of August, Admiral de Grasse arrived in Chesapeake Bay and delivered another 3,000 French troops who joined the allied forces in Williamsburg.[72] On September 5, de Grasse delivered an even bigger gift when he successfully defeated the British fleet in the Battle of the Capes. While the devastated British fleet retreated back to New York for repairs, de Grasse established a blockade to cut off the British Army's escape and supply routes through the bay.

The situation developing in Yorktown was reported in newspapers across the states with keen interest. A provocative article in the September 13 issue of Boston's *Massachusetts Spy* read,

> It is not doubted but that his Excellency General Washington has marched, with 8,000 choice troops including the French, to Virginia, where the troops in that quarter will join him; lord Cornwallis is blocked up by the French fleet; by the present appearance of things we are at the eve of some important event, which God grant may be propitious to the United States.[73]

At the end of September, a massive American and French force of more than 17,000 marched to Yorktown to establish a siege around the city.[74] They set to work digging a semi-circular trench line 800 yards from the British line, followed by a constant barrage of cannon fire.[75] Two weeks later on October 11, they began to dig their second parallel trench line 400 hundred yards from British defenses.[76] However, this line could not be completed until two British fortifications, known as Redoubts 9 and 10, were neutralized. On October 14, an American force led by Lieutenant Colonel Alexander Hamilton captured Redoubt 10 after fierce hand to hand combat while a French force captured Redoubt 9. With the second parallel trench line completed, allied artillery continued its relentless pounding of the British forces trapped in Yorktown.

Although the British were outnumbered by more than two to one, Cornwallis was determined to exhaust all possibilities to prevent a loss.[77] However, after a failed counterattack on October 16 and an unsuccessful attempt to evacuate his troops across the York River, a humiliated Cornwallis requested a cease fire. Under a white flag of surrender, he sent a letter to General Washington which read, "I propose a cessation of hostilities for twenty four hours, and that two officers may be appointed by each side to meet at Mr. Moore's house, to settle terms for the surrender of the posts of York and Gloucester."[78] Washington agreed and on October 19 the British troops marched out of Yorktown between two parallel lines of American and French troops more than a mile long to surrender their arms.[79]

Three days later, General Washington sent a letter to the Continental Congress proudly announcing the victory at Yorktown and his gratitude to his allied soldiers. The letter sparked celebrations across the nation as Patriots read,

> I have the Honor to inform Congress, that a Reduction of the British Army under the Command of Lord Cornwallis, is most happily effected - The unremitting Ardor which actuated every Officer & Soldier in the combined Army on this Occasion, has principally led to this Important Event.[80]

News of the British surrender at Yorktown reached London on November 25, 1781, prompting an anguished Prime Minister Lord North to respond, "Oh God. It is all over."[81] The following March, North resigned and Parliament passed a long-awaited resolution authorizing the negotiation of peace with America.

Moore House, Yorktown, Virginia
Courtesy of Linda LaBelle Kline

Independence Won

The Continental Congress appointed seasoned diplomats Benjamin Franklin, John Adams, and John Jay to Paris to negotiate the terms of peace with Great Britain. Negotiations began on September 27, 1782, but General Washington maintained the Continental Army in case the process faltered.[82] The diplomats' primary goal was to secure recognition of an independent United States of America. They were successful in achieving that objective and a great deal more.

The *Treaty of Paris's* flowery and conciliatory introduction opened with the statement,

> It having pleased the Divine Providence to dispose the Hearts of the most Serene and most Potent Prince George the Third, by the Grace of God, King of Great Britain ... and of the United States of America, to forget all past Misunderstandings and Differences that have unhappily interrupted the good Correspondence and Friendship which they mutually wish to restore; and to establish such a beneficial and satisfactory Intercourse between the two countries upon the ground of reciprocal Advantages and mutual Convenience as may promote and secure to both perpetual Peace and Harmony.[83]

The first article of the treaty specified that the King "acknowledges the United States ... as free and sovereign independent states" and "relinquishes all claims to the Government, Propriety, and Territorial Rights of the same."[84] Subsequent articles ceded all territory east of the Mississippi River to the United States, granted the new nation fishing rights in Newfoundland, and specified the exchange of prisoners and withdrawal of British armed forces from the United States.[85] True to the terms of America's alliance with France, the *Treaty of Paris* was conditional upon the agreement of terms of peace between Great Britain and France.[86]

It is doubtful King George III felt either "serene" or "potent," let alone happy to "forget all past misunderstandings" at the signing of this treaty. It is equally doubtful his victorious American counterpart felt that way either. Judging by his simple statement to the Continental Army, Washington's prevailing emotions were likely relief and gratitude. On April 18, 1783, Washington issued general orders announcing,

> The Commander in Chief orders the Cessation of Hostilities between the United States of America and the King of Great Britain to be publickly [sic] proclaimed tomorrow at 12 o'clock at the New building, and that the Proclamation which will be communicated herewith, be read tomorrow evening at the head of every regiment and corps of the army. After which the Chaplains with the several Brigades will render thanks to almighty God for all his mercies, particularly for his over ruling [sic] the wrath of man to his own glory, and causing the rage of war to cease amongst the nations.[87]

Preliminary peace agreements were signed on November 30, 1782, and the formal *Treaty of Paris* was finally signed on September 3, 1783. In November, the last British soldiers were evacuated from New York City.[88] Almost ten years after Parliament had threatened the colonies' constitutional right to representative government in the Coercive Acts, the United States of America was a free and independent nation, doubled in size and recognized internationally by the world's most powerful nations.

Our Patriots

Our Patriots were eyewitnesses to the stunning events that brought the American Revolution to a close. They courageously fought in the pivotal battles of the southern campaign, including Kings Mountain, Eutaw Springs, Ninety Six, Guilford Courthouse, Petersburg, and Green Spring. One Patriot was even encamped outside General Benedict Arnold's headquarters at West Point when he treasonously delivered the fort's plans to the British. And one was present to witness the momentous surrender of the British Army at Yorktown.

Others suffered through the financial struggles brought on by the war. They suffered depredation, paid supply taxes, and generously contributed provisions to supply the Continental Army despite their own hardships.

When the *Treaty of Paris* was signed, our Patriots undoubtedly celebrated their nation's hard-earned independence. After enduring years of economic, political, and social upheaval, they were ready to move forward and peacefully enjoy their freedom from British rule. While many stayed in their home communities, others settled in states through which they had marched during the war. Many of their children chose to venture west to settle in the new territory ceded to the United States in the *Treaty of Paris*, including the territory that would become the state of Minnesota in 1858.

All of our Patriots have descendants who now live in Minnesota and who are privileged to honor their courage, sacrifices, and perseverance on America's 250th birthday as members of the Lake Minnetonka Chapter DAR. We hope the restoration of their stories in this book is evidence of our pride in their contribution to the formation of the United States of America and our desire to make good use of the freedom they earned for us.

"Posterity! You will never know, how much it cost the present Generation, to preserve your Freedom! I hope you will make a good Use of it." – John Adams[89]

Private William Braithwaite A013697
(circa 1751 - 1831)
Norina Dove

William Braithwaite was born in London, England, around 1751 and immigrated to the colony of Maryland. He faithfully served his new country during the American Revolution, enlisting in Captain Wright's Company, Colonel Price's Regiment in 1778.

Over the course of the next five years, William would fight in five battles across three different states. His first was the Battle of Monmouth, New Jersey, on June 28, 1778, commanded by General George Washington. His second was the Battle of Guilford Courthouse, North Carolina, on March 15, 1781. William's company then marched to South Carolina where he fought in the Siege of Ninety Six in the spring of 1781 and the Battle of Eutaw Springs on September 8, 1781. These Carolina battles successfully forced the British to shift to Virginia, setting the stage for the end of the war and American independence.

After the Revolution, William and his family settled in Virginia. At the age of 74, William stated in his pension application that although he was "very infirm with a very bad rupture," he persisted to "teach school at times." His resourceful wife, Catherine, raised chickens and saved enough money to purchase a cow and three sheep to help support their family.

Private Enos Day A030874
(1760 - 1839)
Heidi Gray Rosekrans Hust, Rosie Gray Hust,
Lori Rosekrans Klinedinst, Constance Sarah Klinedinst,
Wendy Rosekrans Marik, and Hannah Constance Marik

Enos Day was born in 1760 in Keene, New Hampshire. In 1780 he enlisted in Captain Nehemiah Houghton's company, Colonel Moses Nichols's Regiment of the New Hampshire militia. This regiment was specifically raised for the purpose of protecting Fort West Point and served there during a crucial point in the American Revolution.

West Point was a critical American stronghold, essential for controlling supply and communication lines along the Hudson River. American General Benedict Arnold was appointed commander of West Point in June 1780. Deeply disappointed when overlooked for promotion, Arnold devised a treasonous plot to help the British capture both West Point and the visiting General George Washington himself. This plot was foiled when British Major John André was captured in September carrying the plans of West Point in his boot. According to *A History of the Town of Keene*, Enos Day's regiment had encamped near Arnold's headquarters and "were there at the time of his treason."

Enos married Betsy Ann Waters at Milton, Vermont, and they had five sons. He died in New York in 1839. Enos and Ann's son, Abel, married Amanda Middlebrook. By the mid-1850s Abel and Amanda had settled in western Hennepin County, Minnesota.

In memoriam, Constance Rosekrans (1932-2022), for whom this story was written as a 90th birthday gift.

Private John Peebles A088010
(1763 - 1849)
Sandra Lamberton Sweatt Hull

John Peebles, my fifth great-grandfather, was born in the Kershaw District near Camden, South Carolina. When the Revolutionary War reached South Carolina, John eagerly volunteered to serve.

In spring 1781, John enlisted in the militia of Captain William Nettles. The following September, he fought in the Battle of Eutaw Springs, South Carolina, serving as a camp guard. He then marched to North Carolina where he was engaged in scouting parties against the Tories. John served under the renowned American Brigadier General Francis Marion. Marion was known as the "Swamp Fox" in recognition of his exceptional knowledge of the Carolina backcountry terrain and cunning military tactics against the British. John survived the fierce fighting in the Carolinas, but sadly lost an eye during one of the conflicts.

John married Wilmouth/Wilmath Owens in April 1785. After the war he settled in Hart County, Kentucky, and then removed to Chesterfield Township, Macoupin County, Illinois, around 1840 where he worked as a farmer and blacksmith. He lived to the age of 86 and is buried in the Peebles Cemetery in Chesterfield where the Ninian Edwards Chapter DAR has placed a bronze marker in honor of his patriotic service.

Colonel Thomas Wooten A130383
(circa 1740 - 1808)
Sonia Cranston Goetz

Born in North Carolina, Thomas Wooten settled in what would become Wake County where he made numerous and exceptional contributions to the revolutionary cause through civil, patriotic, and military service. He served as Justice of the Peace in 1776 and as a member of the North Carolina House of Commons in 1777. Between 1777 and 1780, Wooten occupied the office of High Sheriff of Wake, "then a station of great importance."

Serving in the Wake County militia, he achieved the rank of Lieutenant Colonel by 1779. Under Major General Nathanael Greene, Lieutenant Colonel Wooten led six Wake Regiment companies against the British at the Battle of Eutaw Springs, South Carolina, on September 8, 1781. Both sides were on short rations with little rest, and casualties were extremely high. The hard-fought and bloody Battle of Eutaw Springs proved to be the last major engagement of the war in the Carolinas. Despite winning a tactical victory, the British lost strategically and retreated to Charleston. British control of the south was broken and aid to British forces in the north was denied.

After the war, Wooten and his family moved to Georgia, where he claimed bounty land and died in 1808.

Joseph Thompson A114337
(circa 1720 - 1803)
Michelle Henderson White

Joseph Thompson was born around 1720 in Coleraine, County Londonderry, Ireland. In 1749 he married Jennet McClellan in Maghera, Ulster, Ireland. Special attention is given in several historic books to the description of his mother-in-law, Jane Henry McClellan. She is described as "a brave, resolute, red-haired woman who came from the north of Ireland" who along with husband Michael and children left for the colonies soon after daughter Jennet was married to Joseph. The extended McClellan family migrated together to western Massachusetts. In 1769 Joseph and Jennet settled on Lot #56 in Boston Township #2, also known as Colrain, Massachusetts.

Joseph served during the American Revolution as a tythingman in 1780. Tythingmen occupied a special place in 18th century New England. They were responsible for ensuring that no one worked on the Sabbath day, children paid attention in church, and parishioners did not fall asleep during sermons. They also had the unsavory task of making sure their neighbors paid their tithes to the church on time.

Joseph and Jennet had 13 children. Daughters Mary, Martha, and Ann married three sons of Hezekiah and Eunice Smith, solidifying that their family roots would be strong in the community. Joseph and Jennet Thompson are buried at the North River Cemetery in Colrain.

John Adam Roush A098982
(1711 - 1786)
Sarah Lynne Martin

Like many Europeans seeking religious freedom in the early 18th century, John Roush emigrated to the colony of Pennsylvania in America. He was born in 1711 near Darmstadt, Germany, and arrived in America on October 19, 1736, on board the brigantine *Perthamboy*, having sailed from the Dutch port of Rotterdam via Dover, England. He soon became an industrious farmer, tanner, and miller in his new country.

Three years after his arrival in Pennsylvania, John married Susannah Schlern in Philadelphia. The couple eventually settled in Shenandoah County, Virginia, and raised a large family of nine sons and three daughters.

When the American Revolution began, John and his family chose the side of independence to protect their newfound freedom. In 1780 John supported the war effort by supplying beef to the Continental Army. A record of this contribution is preserved on a payment voucher dated December 15, 1780, and signed by Captain Jacob Holeman of the Dunmore County militia. At least five of John's sons and three sons-in-law reportedly also served in the Revolution.

John died at the age of 75 just three years after the *Treaty of Paris* was ratified formally ending the war. He and his wife are buried at the Old Pine Church Cemetery in Shenandoah County, Virginia.

Portrait of George Roush
Source: History of the Roush Family in America
Lester Le Roy Roush ©1928

Private George Roush A098975
(1761 - 1845)
Sarah Lynne Martin

My third great-grandfather, George Roush, was born to John Adam Roush (A098982) and Susannah Schlern in 1761 in Shenandoah County, Virginia. George was one of nine sons, all of whom reportedly served in the American Revolution. Four of George's brothers are proven DAR Patriots: Philip (A098986), Jacob (A098978), Henry (A098977), and Jonas (A098985).

George served three enlistments as part of the war's Southern Campaign. George's Revolutionary War story is indelibly preserved in his own words; at age 71 he applied for a pension as a veteran under the 1832 Pension Act. He stated he first enlisted in fall 1779, serving as a private in his brother, Captain John Roush's, Company. In spring 1780, in Captain Joseph Pugh's Company, he "served guarding prisoners from Millerstown to Winchester." Finally, he served in summer 1780 under Captain All where "we were constantly employed watching & catching Tories."

About 1781, George married Catherine Zirkle in Shenandoah County, Virginia, where they raised twelve children. They moved to Mason County, Virginia, in 1798, and to Sutton Township, Meigs County, Ohio, in the Ohio River valley in 1807. George was by trade a mechanic – a good one – and a farmer. He died in Ohio, May 1845, and is buried in the Weldon cemetery in Meigs, Racine County, Ohio.

Nathaniel Colburn A209171
(1742 - 1788)
Tammy Wenz, Angela Coccoluto, and Amy Feldkamp

Nathaniel Colburn, a fourth-generation New Englander, was a descendant of Corporal Edward Colburn, Sr. who immigrated to the colonies during the Great Puritan Migration of the 17th century. Nathaniel was born and spent his life in the northeast corner of Connecticut where his grandfather had purchased 100 acres of land in the early 18th century.

Nicknamed "The Provision State" during the American Revolution, Connecticut's geographical location and 96 miles of coastline set it up to be a breadbasket for the colonial troops. The colony's harbors provided shelter for privateers who captured hundreds of British ships full of food, supplies, and ammunition.

Nathaniel served his country and colony during the Revolutionary War through his civic participation. He served his town as a grand juror and as a surveyor of highways. In his role of surveyor of highways, Nathaniel worked with others to see that roads were kept in good order and remained passible.

He also served his church as a tythingman. In this role, Nathaniel was responsible for enforcing the First Connecticut Code, otherwise known as Connecticut's "Blue Laws." The main purpose of the Code was to maintain religious and civil order in the community.

Collin (McKinney) McKenney A077574
(1735 - circa 1811)
Ann Wilhoite Brilley

Patriot Collin McKinney, my fourth great-grandfather, was born in Somerset County, New Jersey, in 1735. He married his wife, Rebecca (whose maiden name may have been Tuttle), in 1766. During the Revolutionary War, they lived in Washington County, Virginia.

In Spring of 1776, delegates from across Virginia met at the Virginia Conference in Williamsburg and unanimously voted to instruct their delegates attending the Second Continental Congress in Philadelphia to introduce a resolution calling for independence from Great Britain. After Virginia delegate, Richard Henry Lee, successfully proposed this resolution, another Virginian, Thomas Jefferson, was appointed to the committee to draft the formal Declaration of Independence.

Before the Declaration of Independence was even signed, delegates at the Virginia Conference also approved a new state constitution that established a representative House of Delegates and Senate, a governor, and a court system independent of royal control. Under that constitution, Thomas Jefferson was elected governor of Virginia in 1779. In this role, he appointed Justices of the Peace for the county courts. Just as British forces moved into Virginia, Collin courageously served as a juror under such justices in Washington County in 1780 and 1781.

Collin and Rebecca later moved to Pulaski County, Kentucky, where they both died in 1811.

Samuel Dyer's home, Plain Dealing
Albemarle County, Virginia
Courtesy of Mary Dyer Marszalek

Samuel Dyer A035237
(1756 - 1839)
Mary Dyer Marszalek

In 1770, at the age of 14, Samuel Dyer arrived in the Colony of Virginia with his British master, Breckinridge. Dyer was indentured for seven years. He was provided food, clothing, and shelter while he served out his contract. Breckinridge fled the colonies at the start of the Revolutionary War, leaving Dyer behind with few resources. However, under Breckinridge's tutorage, Dyer had gained an important and necessary skill: merchandising.

Dyer joined the militia formed by Patrick Henry to move against the actions of the Virginia Royal Governor Lord Dunmore. The militia forced Dunmore to pay for the colony's gunpowder he had confiscated. As Governor of Virginia, Patrick Henry granted Dyer citizenship and appointed him Assistant Commissary of the Clothing Department of the Army of Virginia in 1778. Dyer stated in his pension application that he served in New Jersey and New York as an assistant to John Moss. He declared the duties he performed "were of the most important and responsible character, and the comfort of the Troops mainly depended upon the faithful performance of the duties entrusted to him."

After the war, Dyer became a successful and respected merchant in Albemarle, Virginia, operating a store called "Plain Dealing," a name which he later also gave to his home.

Private Jeremiah Lockwood A071069
(1733 - circa 1786)
Elaine Richmond Dunn
Story prepared by her son, Kelly Dunn

Jeremiah Lockwood was born in 1733 in Greenwich, Fairfield County, Connecticut. He was the son of Hezekiah and Ruth Lockwood. His twice great-grandfather, Robert Lockwood, of Combs, Suffolk, England, came to Massachusetts as part of John Winthrop's Great Migration on the ship *Mary and John* in 1630. The family eventually settled in Greenwich as founding landowners. Jeremiah married Abigail Smith in 1758.

When the Massachusetts Provincial Congress called for assistance following the outbreak of fighting at Lexington and Concord in April 1775, Connecticut responded immediately by sending more than 3,700 men. In addition to participating in nearly every campaign from the Battle of Bunker Hill to the decisive victory at Yorktown, Connecticut Patriots provided food, cannon, and other goods to the Continental army, earning it the nickname "The Provision State" from General George Washington.

Jeremiah enlisted on September 15, 1779, at the age of 46 and served as a private in Major Benjamin Throops's Company, Colonel John Durkee's 4th Connecticut Regiment. He served until January 1, 1781. According to oral family history, Jeremiah suffered intense hunger during his service and at one time had to eat his leather shoestrings to survive. He died in November 1786, just three years after the end of the Revolutionary War.

Henry Stahl, Sr. A075663
(1707 - circa 1790)
Georgetta "Gigi" Henrichsen Hickey

Henrich Stahl, Sr. arrived in Philadelphia from Rotterdam in September 1741. The ship's list reflected the names of male Palatine passengers; other evidence indicates Henrich/Henry was accompanied by his wife and young children.

Five years later, Stahl was among 13 "German Protestants" naturalized as British citizens in Frederick County, Maryland. Between 1756 and 1785, Henry acquired property along both sides of the Maryland/Pennsylvania border and associated with the Reformed Church.

During the American Revolution, the Stahl family joined the side of independence. Three of Henry's sons – Leonard (A206354, my ancestor), Henry, Jr. (A108238), and Jacob (A213721) – served in the Cumberland County militia during the Revolutionary War. In his 70s, Henry, Sr. was too old to act in a military capacity but paid a supply tax in 1778, which was considered patriotic service.

Henry died around 1790 and his ten tracts of land, totaling over 1,000 acres, were distributed among his six sons, two daughters and a grandson. The discovery of his probate records proved both shocking and tragic. Listed in Henry's estate inventory: "1 negro woman and child." It was heartbreaking to learn this prosperous German family could deny the freedom of this woman and child after supporting the cause of American freedom.

James (Flowers) Flower A039887
(ante 1753 - 1806)
Clare Barnes and Grace Truckenbrod

James Flowers was born in Long Island and came to Bristol, Pennsylvania, in 1774. Pennsylvania was a haven for Quakers and it is likely that James was a Quaker and pacifist. He did not participate in any skirmishes during the Revolutionary War, but he was loyal and committed to the cause of independence as evidenced by the war taxes he paid during the Revolution and the years following.

James was a shoemaker. Shoemakers were well-respected during colonial times for their notable intelligence and the large number of poets and statesmen who came from the profession. In the 1770s, shoes were made entirely of leather and were straight, with neither a right nor left shoe. The leather was treated with a combination of soot, bear grease, lard, and beeswax. A tradesman often specialized in making shoes for either men or women, but boot making was considered the most prestigious.

James first married Rebecca Gosline. After her death he married Rachel Van Blunk in 1787. When James died at the age of 53, he left behind 12 children. His youngest children, George and Charles, migrated west and their children continued moving west, finally settling in Cleveland, Minnesota. Many of James's descendants are buried in Savidge Lake Cemetery in Cleveland.

Judge Samuel Chase, Sr. A021210
(1707 - 1800)
Michelle Henderson White

Samuel Chase, Sr. was born in Newbury, Essex County, Massachusetts. He married Mary Dudley in 1728 and they had ten children together. He purchased previously unsettled land in New Hampshire in 1765, directing several children to go ahead and settle the area. His daughter Anne was married to Patriot Daniel Putnam (A092404), who was among the first of those to arrive by canoe to clear the land. Two years later Samuel Chase, Sr. arrived. He subsequently became the first Justice of the Peace and called the first meeting to organize the town of Cornish, New Hampshire.

During the American Revolution, the Honorable Samuel Chase, Sr. was chosen to serve as a selectman and moderator in 1782. He represented Cornish in the struggle between towns bordering the Connecticut River. This tug of war land struggle between New York, New Hampshire, and Massachusetts would eventually abate, and the State of Vermont would be formed in 1791. The town of Cornish was integral to these discussions and Samuel Chase, Sr. was at the center of the negotiations as the representative from Cornish, attending the Provincial Convention that eventually formed the State of Vermont.

An oil on canvas portrait of Judge Chase painted by Joseph Steward in 1793 hangs in the National Portrait Gallery in Washington, D.C.

Dr. James Terman at Brewster Sisters' Memorial
Indiana University Campus
Courtesy of Ann Olson (Dr. Terman's Daughter)

Agnes Brewster A014150
(1763 - 1830)
Ann E. Terman Olson and Erin Olson

Agnes Brewster was born in 1763 and was living in Augusta County, Virginia, when the first shots of the American Revolution were fired at Lexington and Concord in 1775. When she was just 13 years old, Agnes made the courageous decision to support the cause of American independence with the skills she had learned growing up on her family's farm.

Along with her older sisters, Elenor (A034856) and Jennete (A060519), Agnes worked unceasingly to support Patriot soldiers. The sisters sheared their family's herd of sheep, spun the wool, and used their looms to weave the yarn into cloth. They cut the cloth and sewed uniforms which were sent to American soldiers. When General George Washington's men were encamped near the family farm, Agnes helped prepare food for the soldiers. According to family stories, the sisters also melted pewter household utensils to mold bullets.

After the Revolution, the Brewster family resettled to Indiana where Agnes and her sisters are buried in Dunn Cemetery on the campus of Indiana University. The Daughters of the American Revolution have honored the sisters' patriotic service with a plaque on their headstone. Hundreds of students now pass the memorial each day, many finding it a peaceful place for study and reflection.

Michael King A064689
(circa 1741 - circa 1800)
Georgetta "Gigi" Henrichsen Hickey

A first-generation American and my fifth great-grandfather, Michael King was born in Philadelphia in 1741. He married Susannah Passmore in 1762, likely in York County. In about 1782 the King family moved west to settle in Milford Township, Bedford County, near several of Michael's siblings.

Pennsylvania raised funds for the Revolutionary War effort by assessing a supply tax against the estates of property owners. In many places, however, residents suffered significant losses due to actions of Loyalists/Tories and the British Army, or ongoing conflict with indigenous people on the frontier. These losses often left residents unable to pay the taxes.

Legislation passed in 1780, titled "Relief of the Suffering Inhabitants of the Counties of Northampton, Bedford, Northumberland and Westmoreland," was in effect through the close of the war. Residents could be exonerated from paying supply tax if assessors itemized the "bona fide [losses] by the incursions of the enemy," for example, buildings or fences destroyed; livestock stolen or killed. Michael King was credited with patriotic service due to losses he sustained and the tax exoneration granted in 1783. The DAR service description is "suffered depredation" rather than "paid supply tax."

Michael's daughter, Elizabeth, married Patriot Leonard Stahl (A206354) after the war.

Ann Graves A047196
(circa 1696 - circa 1782)
Barbara Schneider

Ann Graves was 80 years old when Thomas Jefferson wrote the Declaration of Independence. Ann had deep roots in America and was born about 1696 in the Colony of Virginia. She married Thomas Graves and raised a large family.

From her home in Spotsylvania, Virginia, Ann witnessed the American Revolution shift to the southern states as the British launched their Southern Campaign. In 1780 the Virginia Assembly passed a law "for procuring a supply of provisions" to support the army. Ann made her support for the Patriot cause clear when she furnished supplies in 1781 from the farm she was granted upon her husband's death.

Ann was not the only Patriot in her family. Her son, Rice (A047369), served in Captain John Webb's Company, Colonel Alexander McChenachan's 7th Virginia Regiment of the Continental Army. Her son, David (A131996), took the Oath of Allegiance and served as Deputy Sheriff in 1778. Like their mother, sons Solomon (A047394) and Thomas (A047401) furnished supplies. Ann's daughter, Susannah, married William Pettus (A089943) who served in the Louisa County, Virginia militia.

Despite her advanced age, Ann likely survived to see the United States achieve independence. She died sometime after August 15, 1782. The preliminary articles of peace in the *Treaty of Paris* were signed on November 30, 1782.

John Grigsby A048485
(1720 - 1794)
Joanne Voigt Hagen, Laura Hagen Rickabaugh, and Carrie Hagen Sorenson

The Grigsby family immigrated to the Colony of Virginia in 1660 and became prosperous farmers. Their financial success would play an important role in helping to fund the American Revolution.

John Grigsby earned the nickname "Soldier John" from his service in the 1741 Battle of Cartagena, Columbia. John accompanied fellow Virginian, Lawrence Washington, half-brother of George Washington, on this expedition to South America. Grigsby survived the horrific 67-day battle that decimated the British Navy.

In 1779 John crossed the Blue Ridge Mountains to settle in Rockbridge County in the Valley of Virginia, joining James (A048481), the eldest of his 14 children. The history of Rockbridge County records that the Grigsbys owned several large farms and were "well-to-do, able, and influential." In 1780 the Virginia General Assembly passed an act allowing Virginia Governor Thomas Jefferson to impress its citizens for supplies needed to fund the Revolution. In 1783 John paid a supply tax and James furnished supplies. Family historians also believe John led a company of the 13th Virginia Regiment during the early years of the Revolution.

John died in 1794 and is buried in the cemetery at Falling Bridge Presbyterian Church in Rockbridge County where the family worshipped. James resettled and died in Bledsoe County, Tennessee.

Private Cottrell Lively A070741
(1763 - 1838)
Louise Duncan Farkas, Laura Farkas Roth, and Haley Michelle Roth

Cottrell Lively was born in Albemarle County, Virginia, in 1763. Like many of his peers, Cottrell enlisted to serve in the Revolutionary War when he was just 16 years old and participated in the Southern Campaign.

When Cottrell enlisted in the militia during the fall of 1780, he marched to Cabin Point, Virginia, to defend against a British attack led by the newly turned traitor, Benedict Arnold. The following spring, Cottrell served for one month defending the Virginia capital of Richmond. After the American victory at Yorktown in the fall of 1781, Cottrell enlisted in the cavalry under Colonel Charles Armand Tuffin where he served until the *Treaty of Paris* ended the Revolutionary War.

After the war Cottrell moved to Monroe County in present day West Virginia, where he married Sarah Maddy. They settled on the bounty land Cottrell received for his three continuous years of military service. Cottrell and Sarah's land was still known as "the old Lively place" over 150 years later and both are buried there. Though the land briefly passed out of the family following the death of their son at the close of the Civil War, their great-grandson later acquired the land and rebuilt the house.

Private Elijah Gray A215654
(circa 1762 - 1849)
Jane Landowski Truckenbrod, Teresa Landowski, Clare Barnes, and Grace Truckenbrod

At the age of 16, Elijah Gray tried to enlist for a three-year term to fight in the American Revolution. He was deemed unfit for service when his height of four feet ten and one-half inches fell short of the required five feet. The setback did not deter him. The tenacious Elijah enlisted in 1781 as a private in Captain William Mills's company, Lieutenant Colonel John Brook's 7th Regiment; later in Captain Reed's Company, Colonel Simond's Regiment. He served at Windsor, Massachusetts; York Hutts, New York; and West Point, New York. In December 1783, he was honorably discharged when the *Treaty of Paris* was enacted.

Troubles followed Elijah after the Revolution. In 1822 Elijah, his wife, Anna Cartwright, and their children moved to Michigan. As they crossed Lake Erie, their vessels capsized in a violent gale. One son narrowly escaped with his life, but the family's finances were lost. Elijah returned to New York where his problems persisted. The military pension he was awarded in 1818 was suspended around 1827 when a sale of land called his poverty into question. In 1829 Elijah and his son, James, were convicted of murdering a tavern owner. Elijah was imprisoned and James was hanged in what was the last public hanging in Genesee County.

Captain Edward Moseley A081969
(circa 1730 - 1808)
Barbara Schneider

Edward Moseley was a lifelong resident and influential leader of Charlotte County, Virginia. In 1765 he was a vestryman in Cornwall Parish and a Justice of the Peace. When Virginia Patriots called for independence from Great Britain in May 1776, Edward joined the cause.

Edward became captain of militia and took the oath of office in October 1778. Charlotte County's militia proved to be instrumental in slowing General Cornwallis's advance through Virginia during the British campaign to capture the southern states. While Virginia's military records are incomplete, it is likely that Edward fought in the Battle of Petersburg, just south of Virginia's capital of Richmond, in April 1781. With only 1,000 troops, the Virginia militia was badly outnumbered by the British force of 2,500. Despite this disadvantage, they put up a heroic fight and bought a full day for General Lafayette to position his army in defense of Richmond.

As the United States of America was recognized as a new nation internationally in 1783, Edward served as a member of the Virginia House of Burgesses. His daughter, Martha, married Patriot Ensign Thomas Bouldin, Jr. (A012550), who was the son of Patriot Thomas Bouldin, Sr. (A012548). Edward died in 1808 and is buried in a family cemetery near Buffalo Creek.

Thomas Paxton A211156
(circa 1719 - 1788)
Private William Paxton A209218
(1757 - 1838)
Joanne Voigt Hagen, Laura Hagen Rickabaugh, and Carrie Hagen Sorenson

The Paxton family of Virginia joined the side of independence during the American Revolution. Thomas paid a supply tax in 1783 to help fund the war. His son, William, served in the militia during the Virginia Campaign, which was part of the British campaign designed to divide the colonies.

William first volunteered to serve in 1779, patrolling the James River after a British naval raid on Norfolk, Virginia. As the Virginia Campaign intensified, General George Washington sent the Marquis de Lafayette to protect Virginia. William was drafted to serve in his uncle Captain William Paxton's Company under Lafayette's command. On June 26, 1781, William joined 300 American troops to engage 1,500 British soldiers near Williamsburg, Virginia, in the Battle of Spencer's Ordinary. William's company attacked the British rear guard, drawing cannon fire and light horse reinforcements before the outnumbered Americans received assistance. On July 6, 1781, William participated in the Battle of Green Spring, attacking the British as they attempted to cross the James River enroute to Yorktown. Though an American loss, the attack slowed the British advance.

After the Revolution, William married Jane Grigsby. The couple settled on a farm in Virginia south of the James River and raised 16 children.

Private William Gragg, Jr. A046612
(1758 - 1847)
Jessica Fritz

William Gragg, Jr. was born in Augusta County, Virginia, in 1758. He grew up just 180 miles west of Yorktown where he would witness the American victory that ended the Revolutionary War.

William recorded his Revolutionary War experience in a pension application when he was 75 years old. His first tour began in 1779 or 1780 when he guarded British prisoners captured at the Battle of Saratoga and held in Virginia. On his second tour in 1781, William's company marched to North Carolina. However, they returned when British General Lord Cornwallis moved his army to Virginia, having sustained heavy losses at the Battle of Guilford Courthouse, North Carolina. This retreat set the stage for the final battle at Yorktown.

On September 28, 1781, General Washington moved his allied American and French army from Williamsburg, Virginia, to trap the British in a siege of Yorktown. William was again drafted in September and his company "joined General Washington's army at Little York." After three weeks of conflict, the British surrendered. William recalled witnessing the momentous American victory and being there on October 19, 1781, when "Lord Cornwallis was captured by Washington."

After the Revolution, William settled in North Carolina where he had once marched, living there until he died at the age of 89.

Private Stephen Manchester A214635
(baptized 1764 - circa 1845)
Kathleen Barrett Huston

Stephen Manchester was born to Stephen and Lois Manchester in Tiverton, Rhode Island about 1762. His 1764 baptism is among the records of Tiverton's United Church of Christ. When Stephen was just 14 years old, Rhode Island became the first colony to declare independence from Great Britain on May 4, 1776.

Stephen enlisted in the Continental Army in April 1782, serving in Captain William Humphrey's Company, Colonel Jeremiah Olney's Rhode Island Battalion. Five months later, Benjamin Franklin initiated peace negotiations with Great Britain. Preliminary articles of peace were signed in Paris in November 1782, effectively ending the Revolutionary War. With American independence won, Stephen's enlistment concluded in February 1783.

Stephen married Hannah Crandall January 8, 1784. Six days later, the Continental Congress ratified the *Treaty of Paris*. Like many Rhode Islanders, the couple settled in New York's Hudson Valley before migrating to Oneida County, New York, where they died. In addition to recognizing American independence in the *Treaty of Paris*, Great Britain also ceded the Northwest Territory with land spanning from present-day Ohio to eastern Minnesota. Stephen's daughter, Betsey Manchester Galusha, was among the pioneers to capitalize on this opportunity to move west, choosing to settle in territorial Minnesota. She is buried in Houston County, Minnesota.

Portrait of Phillis Wheatley 1773[1]
Source: Library of Congress

Chapter 6:
VISION

★

The American Revolution was a struggle within a struggle for African Americans. The Patriot rhetoric of liberty compelled many free and enslaved African Americans to choose the side of independence. In exchange for the promise of personal freedom, enslaved Patriot soldiers served in nearly every conflict of the Revolution from Lexington to Yorktown. In exchange for the same promise, other enslaved African Americans escaped bondage to join the side of the British.

The Revolution successfully restored liberty to America's free, landowning men and was undeniably a monumental achievement in representative government. However, such liberty and representation were still denied to thousands of enslaved people after the war. Tragically, enslaved people who had faithfully served in the Continental Army or had escaped to British lines were often denied the personal freedom that had been promised to them. Such broken promises prompted abolitionist Frederick Douglass to ask, "What to the slave is the fourth of July?"[2]

One potential answer to that important question is *vision*. The vision of equality for all Americans written in the Declaration of Independence was certainly no consolation to those who remained enslaved at the conclusion of the war. But visions can be powerful forces for change. While the Declaration's "self-evident" arguments could not compel America's first leaders to abolish slavery, such arguments resonated with future leaders who would.

Revolutionary Petitions for Freedom

As British oppression of the colonies escalated after the French and Indian War, American Patriots devised compelling arguments to defend their rights. Widely distributed publications such as *The*

Boston Pamphlet put colonists' fears and hopes into vivid, powerful language. *The Boston Pamphlet* was distributed to every town in Massachusetts in 1772 and articulated the natural rights of the colonists including, "First, a right to Life; secondly, to Liberty; thirdly, to Property."[3] Defense of these rights was a "Law of Nature," under which all men "in Case of Intollerable [sic] Oppression, civil or religious," had the right to "leave the society they belong to and join another."[4] With the creation of Committees of Correspondence in early 1772, calls for "liberty" and "freedom" sparked by these arguments blazed across the colonies.

Revolutionary Patriots even began rhetorically equating British oppression with *slavery*. Although an enslaver himself, Thomas Jefferson argued at the Virginia Convention in 1774 that Great Britain's "oppressions … too plainly prove a deliberate and systematic plan of reducing [the colonies] to slavery."[5] That same year, Alexander Hamilton similarly wrote,

> Under the auspices of tyranny the life of the subject is often sported with, and the fruits of his daily toil are consumed in oppressive taxes, that serve to gratify the ambition, avarice, and lusts of his superiors. The page of history is replete with instances that loudly warn us to beware of slavery.[6]

Before the bloody conflicts of the American Revolution had even begun, enslaved people recognized the opportunity to leverage such arguments. In April 1773, four enslaved men from Taunton, Massachusetts, named Peter Bestes, Sambo Freeman, Felix Holbrook, and Chester Joie, petitioned the Massachusetts General Court for their manumission. "The divine spirit of freedom, seems to fire every humane [sic] breast on this continent," they wrote, adding "the efforts made by the legislat[ure] of this province in their last sessions to free themselves from slavery, gave us, who are in that deplorable state, a high degree of satisfact[i]on."[7] Echoing the rationale used in *The Boston Pamphlet*, the petitioners stated, "as the people of this province seem to be actuated by the principles of equity and justice, we cannot but expect your house will again take our deplorable case into serious consideration, and give us that ample relief which, as men, we have a natural right to."[8] This petition was ignored.

The enslaved people of Massachusetts were undeterred. Within months of British General Thomas Gage's installation as the military governor of the Massachusetts Bay Colony in 1774 to enforce the Coercive Acts, another group of enslaved people petitioned him for the freedom of those enslaved in Massachusetts. These petitioners stated, "we have in common with all other men a natur[a]l right to our freedoms without being depriv'd of them by our fellow men as we are a freeborn [People]," arguing, "we were unjustly dragged by the cruel hand of power from our dearest [friends] and others [some] of us stolen from the bosoms of our tender Parents" and as such "we [are] deprived of everything that hath a tendency to make life even tolerable."[9] With these arguments, they asked General Gage to "cause an act of the legislat[ure] to be p[a]ssed that we may obtain our Natural right our freedoms."[10] Like its predecessor, this petition was also ignored.

A Critical Choice

As the Revolution evolved from a political conflict to a military one in April 1775, enslaved people faced an important question: was freedom from slavery more achievable in an independent America or under Great Britain's continued rule? After assessing their options, enslaved people ultimately chose both sides.

In the New England colonies, many African Americans joined the side of American independence. Enslaved Patriots were among the soldiers who fought in the first conflict at Lexington, Massachusetts, on April 19, 1775.[11] Many enlisted to serve in the New England militia companies that marched to support the Siege of Boston and fight in the Battle of Bunker Hill.[12] Despite their competent contributions, newly appointed Commander in Chief George Washington forbade African Americans from serving in the Continental Army.[13] Slave owning Patriots feared that arming and training enslaved people would encourage revolts.[14]

Washington convened his generals on October 8, 1775, to revisit the question. Generals Lee, Ward, Putnam, Thomas, Spencer, Heath, Sullivan, Greene, and Gates agreed to deny enlistment to both enslaved and free African Americans.[15] However, upon hearing New England officers' complaints, Washington allowed recruitment of free African Americans in late 1775, promising to refer the issue to the Continental Congress for approval.[16] After deliberation, Congress approved only the reenlistment of free African Americans currently serving.[17]

In sharp contrast to the Continental Army, the Continental Navy recruited both free and enslaved African Americans. Many were experienced sailors and racially integrated merchant crews had been commonplace throughout the colonies.[18] The benefits were enticing. The potential financial reward was much higher for Patriot sailors than soldiers, and enslaved runaways were less likely to be recaptured while at sea.[19]

The British leaders took a decidedly stronger position on recruiting African Americans than the Patriots. After the King declared the colonies in "open and avowed rebellion" in 1775, Virginia's Royal Governor John Murray, the Earl of Dunmore, delivered a proclamation offering freedom to rebel-owned enslaved people who were willing to serve in the British Army. By December, more than 300 enslaved people joined the British Army upon hearing Dunmore's words,

> I do hereby further declare all indented servants, Negroes, or others (appertaining to rebels) free, that are able and willing to bear arms, they joining his Majesty's troops, as soon as may be, for the more speedily reducing this colony to a proper sense of their duty, to his Majesty's crown and dignity.[20]

Although the proclamation applied only to the Colony of Virginia, it was published in newspapers throughout all the colonies and inspired tens of thousands of enslaved people to escape to the protection of the British Army during the Revolution.[21]

The Continental Congress and the States

Slavery was a central topic in the early sessions of the Continental Congress. The First Continental Congress used slavery as an economic weapon. The Articles of Association included the slave trade in its wide sweeping boycott of British goods. The Articles stated,

> We will neither import nor purchase, any slave imported after the first day of December next; after which time, we will wholly discontinue the slave trade, and will neither be concerned in it ourselves, nor will we hire our vessels, nor sell our commodities or manufactures to those who are concerned in it.[22]

The Second Continental Congress contended with the moral issues of slavery. Virginian enslaver Thomas Jefferson included a strong condemnation of slavery in his original draft of the Declaration of Independence. After a clause describing slavery as a "cruel war against human nature itself, violating its most sacred rights of life and liberty," this draft criticized the King's insistence on perpetuating an "open a market where MEN should be bought & sold" and his resistance to "every legislative attempt to prohibit or restrain this execrable commerce."[23] Not surprisingly, this strong language proved divisive among the states. Rather than risk unanimity in the vote for independence, the passage was stricken from the final document.

This precedent would stand for the remainder of the war. Congress failed to address slavery when establishing the loose structure of a national government in the Articles of Confederation. In fact, the Articles made no mention of slavery whatsoever. Debates and decisions on slavery's morality and legality were left to the states.

Some states recognized slavery's obvious inconsistency with the Revolution's ideals. When the states were advised by the Continental Congress to draft constitutions following the Declaration of Independence, some began to address equality and slavery in their new laws. New Jersey's 1776 constitution granted suffrage to all residents worth a minimum of £50, regardless of race or gender, although married women were still not permitted to own the property necessary to vote.[24] Free African American property-owning male residents were granted suffrage in Maryland's 1776 constitution.[25] Vermont's 1777 constitution freed enslaved people upon their reaching the age of 21 and granted the vote to all free, adult men.[26] New York's 1777 constitution granted the vote to all property-owning men regardless of race or prior servitude.[27] After Philadelphia's Quaker community had banned its members from owning slaves in 1776,[28] the Pennsylvania General Assembly passed its own Gradual Abolition Act in 1780, freeing the state's enslaved people over time.[29]

Most states did not give their citizens the opportunity to ratify their new constitutions. However, with its deep history of participatory government and town meetings, Massachusetts did. The first Massachusetts constitution proposed in 1778 called for the legalization of slavery and was rejected in a popular vote.[30]

Many Massachusetts residents agreed with Abigail Adams who wrote to her husband, "I wish most sincerely there was not a Slave in the province. It always [sic] appear[e]d a most iniquitous [sic] Scheme to me - fight ourselfs [sic] for what we are daily robbing and plundering from those who have as good a right to freedom as we have."[31] The revised Constitution of the Commonwealth of Massachusetts authored by John Adams was approved by popular vote in 1780. This document omitted the legalization of slavery and instead included the phrase, "all men are born free and equal, and have ... the right of enjoying and defending their lives and liberties."[32]

Three years later, the Massachusetts Supreme Court applied this clause to declare slavery inconsistent with the state's constitution. At the conclusion of a series of three lawsuits known collectively as the Quoc Walker case, Supreme Judicial Court Chief Justice William Cushing declared,

> In short, without resorting to implication in constructing the constitution, slavery is in my judgment as effectively abolished as it can be by the [constitution's] granting of rights and privileges wholly incompatible and repugnant to its existence.[33]

African Americans in the Military

While state politicians grappled with the legal issue of equality, General Washington contended with the practical issue of a depleted Continental Army. Enlistments expired and states often failed to meet their recruitment quotas as the protracted war stretched into its fourth year. Some of Washington's most trusted officers recommended replenishing the army with enslaved people.

In 1778 Washington had reversed his previous position and supported Rhode Island's Brigadier General James Varnum's recommendation to offer enslaved people their freedom in exchange for military service.[34] The formerly enslaved people of the 1st Rhode Island Regiment had successfully repelled Hessian attacks at the Battle of Rhode Island and would help capture the important British fortification, Redoubt 10, in the Battle of Yorktown.[35]

When a British invasion of the south appeared imminent, South Carolina's Lieutenant Colonel John Laurens presented a plan similar to Varnum's for the southern states.[36] Though the Continental Congress initially rejected the plan, it was later revisited and approved in 1779, under the condition that it must also be approved by the Georgia and South Carolina legislatures.

Colonel Alexander Hamilton wrote a letter to the Continental Congress in support of Laurens's plan. "I foresee that this project will have to combat much opposition from prejudice and self-interest," he wrote, because "[t]he contempt we have been taught to entertain for the blacks, makes us fancy many things that are founded neither in reason nor experience."[37] He continued, "An essential part of the plan is to give them freedom with their muskets. This will secure their fidelity, animate their courage, and I believe will have a good influence upon those who remain, by opening a door to their emancipation."[38]

Georgia and South Carolina ultimately rejected Laurens's plan. Nevertheless, free African Americans joined integrated military units in the northern states and Virginia in increasing numbers.[39] Unlike their white farmer counterparts, these African American soldiers frequently reenlisted when their typical 90-day enlistments expired.[40] By the final years of the war, New York and New Hampshire both offered freedom to enslaved people willing to enlist and awarded land bounties to their owners as payment.[41] However, in other states enslaved people were forced to serve in the place of their conscripted owners.[42]

British General Henry Clinton capitalized on the Patriots' reluctance to enlist enslaved people. On June 30, 1779, he issued the Philipsburg Proclamation offering freedom and protection to enslaved people from any state who were willing to join the British side. The proclamation had the twin objectives of weakening the Patriots' supply of plantation labor as well as potential soldiers.[43] The proclamation stated,

> I do most strictly forbid any Person to sell or claim Right over any NEGROE, the property of a Rebel, who may take Refuge with any part of this Army; And I do promise to every NEGROE who shall desert the Rebel Standard full security.[44]

The proclamation also contained a threat. To deter their enlistment in the American military, Clinton warned African American Patriot soldiers that they would be sold upon capture, stating "I do hereby give notice That all NEGROES taken in arms, or upon any military Duty, shall be purchased for the public service."[45]

As a result of Clinton's proclamation, many successfully escaped slavery. Thousands of enslaved people joined the British during the capture of Charleston, South Carolina.[46] Thousands more escaped to British lines when General Cornwallis moved his army into Virginia.[47] Among those joining the British were enslaved people from George Washington and Thomas Jefferson's plantations.[48]

Freedom Gained and Freedom Denied

Both American and British promises to enslaved African Americans were put to the test when the American Revolution ended in 1783. Far too few of these promises were fulfilled.

The promise of freedom made to the enslaved soldiers who served the Patriot cause in the 1st Rhode Island Regiment was faithfully fulfilled. However, immediately following the American victory at Yorktown, Washington issued orders stating the enslaved people who had been promised freedom by the British must be returned to their former owners.[49] The terms of the *Treaty of Paris* echoed this order, requiring the British to return enslaved people to their former owners.[50]

However, Sir Guy Carleton, the newly appointed Commander of British forces, nobly refused to break the promise of the Philipsburg Proclamation. As the British evacuated the new United States of America, Carleton ensured the safe passage of thousands of African American Loyalists to Nova Scotia, Jamaica, and Great Britain.[51]

Another Generation

Although clearly contradictory to the ideals cast in the Declaration of Independence, the appalling institution of slavery persisted beyond the Revolution. But the vision of equality and liberty endured. Decades after the *Treaty of Paris* was signed, future President Abraham Lincoln delivered a speech imploring Americans to recall the vision embodied in the Declaration of Independence,

> Now, my countrymen, if you have been taught doctrines conflicting with the great landmarks of the Declaration of Independence; if you have listened to suggestions which would take away from its grandeur, and mutilate the fair symmetry of its proportions; if you have been inclined to believe that all men are not created equal in those inalienable rights enumerated by our chart of liberty, let me entreat you to come back. Return to the fountain whose waters spring close by the blood of the Revolution.[52]

Lincoln's call proved undeniable. Another war far bloodier than the Revolution transformed the Declaration's vision into personal freedom with equal protection under the law for African Americans. And courageous American women would similarly invoke the Declaration's vision of equality to win the right to vote decades later. The depth of sacrifice made in these subsequent struggles is itself proof of the enduring force of America's founding vision of equality and liberty.

Our Patriots

African American Patriots played critical roles in securing American independence. Their invaluable contributions as soldiers, orators, and writers have been too often overlooked. The National Society Daughters of the American Revolution has undertaken efforts to discover and celebrate these contributions. An extensive research effort was launched in the 1980s to document the service of African Americans with a project entitled *Forgotten Patriots*. In 2020 the DAR launched the *E Pluribus Unum Educational Initiative* to promote awareness of the diverse Patriots the *Forgotten Patriots* project had identified.

To honor their considerable contributions, we have researched and written the stories of ten remarkable African Americans proven to be Patriots in the American Revolution as part of the *Forgotten Patriots* project. Though none of the current members of the Lake Minnetonka Chapter DAR descend from these Patriots, our ancestors fought together with them in conflicts such as Bunker Hill, Long Island, Saratoga, Monmouth, Eutaw Springs, and Yorktown. We hope publication of these stories inspires their descendants to discover their lineage to these heroes and share our pride in their notable contributions to American history.

Prince Estabrook
(circa 1740 - c. 1830)

Prince Estabrook served in the American Revolution from the very first shots fired on Lexington Green until 1783 when the *Treaty of Paris* ended hostilities. Estabrook was likely born enslaved in Lexington, Massachusetts, around 1740. In 1775 he was a member of the Lexington militia commanded by Captain John Parker. Estabrook assembled with his militia on Lexington Green on April 19, 1775, when the town received warning that British troops were advancing to capture a munitions store. As the "shot heard 'round the world" was fired, Estabrook was hit in the shoulder by a British musket ball, making him among the first to be wounded in the fight for independence.

Estabrook recovered and served several more enlistments until his discharge in October 1783. He returned to Lexington and at that point was a free man. While details of Estabrook's manumission are unknown, Massachusetts had begun recognizing the incongruency between slavery and the freedoms for which the Revolution was fought. Quoting the new Massachusetts constitution, Massachusetts Chief Justice William Cushing stated in a 1783 ruling that "Our Constitution of government declares that all men are born free and equal. Slavery in my judgment is as effectively abolished as it can be."

William Lee
(circa 1750 - 1810)

Until recently, the Minnesota Marine Art Museum was home to one of three original Emanuel Leutze paintings entitled *Washington Crossing the Delaware*. In 2022 the painting was auctioned for over $45,000,000. Leutze was an ardent abolitionist and painted several diverse characters into this famous work.

While the identity of the African American man sitting in the boat with General George Washington is unknown, he is very likely William Lee. Lee was born around 1750 and was purchased by Washington in 1767 to serve as his valet. When Washington was named commander of the Continental Army, Lee accompanied him throughout the entire Revolutionary War. Lee was responsible for maintaining the General's confidential papers and delivering messages. Armed with a pistol, Lee accompanied Washington into battle, standing ready to provide Washington with his sword or field glass. Among other events, Lee survived the difficult winter at Valley Forge and witnessed the Battle of Yorktown at the end of the war.

In addition to persuasive anti-slavery arguments from Washington's military confidantes such as Alexander Hamilton and John Laurens, Lee's courageous war service likely contributed to the gradual change in Washington's perspective toward slavery. After the war, Washington made a new will in which Lee was immediately freed upon Washington's death and given an annual life-time annuity "for his faithful services during the Revolutionary War."

Salem Poor
(1747 - 1802)

Salem Poor was born into slavery in Andover, Massachusetts, in 1747. By the age of 22, Poor had saved enough money to purchase his own freedom. Six years later, Poor enlisted with Captain James Frye's regiment of Minutemen and joined the Siege of Boston in protest of the British occupation of the city.

On June 16, 1775, Poor marched with his regiment to Charleston and courageously fought in the Battle of Bunker Hill, repulsing several British attacks and covering the retreat of American soldiers. He performed so heroically that Colonel William Prescott and 13 of his fellow commanders made a petition to the General Court of Massachusetts calling for Poor to receive an award. The petition recognized him as a "brave and gallant soldier" who had "behaved like an experienced officer, as well as an excellent officer." Unfortunately, the petition was ignored. Despite this omission, Poor reenlisted in the Continental Army and continued to fight for American independence. He fought in the Battles of Saratoga and Monmouth and survived the difficult winter at Valley Forge before being discharged in 1780.

Two hundred years later, Poor's bravery was commemorated in the 1976 bicentennial celebration stamp series, *Contributors to the Cause*.

Phillis Wheatley
(circa 1753 - 1784)

Phillis Wheatley was captured as a young child in West Africa and shipped to Boston where she was sold into slavery to the Wheatley family. The Wheatley family discovered her intellectual ability and taught her to read, exposing her to the Bible and classical British, Greek, and Latin literature. She began writing powerful poetry while still in her teens. In 1773 Wheatley became the first African American woman in America to publish a book, *Poems on Various Subjects – Religious and Moral,* with a forward written by John Hancock. In that same year, Wheatley was given her freedom.

Believing that liberty for the enslaved would inevitably follow liberty for America, Wheatley used the power of her eloquent words to support simultaneously the causes of the American Revolution as well as the freedom of enslaved people. In a 1774 letter she passionately wrote, "In every human Breast, God has implanted a Principle, which we call Love of Freedom." As the first conflicts of the Revolution unfolded in 1775, Wheatley wrote a poem to encourage General George Washington as he assumed leadership of the Continental Army. After reading this poem, Washington requested to meet the "person so favored by the Muses" at his headquarters in Cambridge, Massachusetts.

Peter Salem
(1750 - 1816)

Peter Salem was born into slavery in Framingham, Massachusetts, in 1750. Enslaved people had been legally barred from joining colonial militias for more than a century prior to the Revolution. Salem's Patriot owner, Major Lawson Buckminster, freed him so he could join Buckminster's regiment. As a result, Salem fought in the first engagement of the Revolution at Lexington and Concord in April 1775. One month later, he fought in the Battle of Bunker Hill and was subsequently introduced to General George Washington as "the man who shot [British Major John] Pitcairn" in that engagement.

The newly appointed General Washington vehemently opposed enlistment of African American soldiers in the Continental Army. However, his perspective began to change when Virginia Royal Governor Lord Dunmore issued a proclamation encouraging enslaved people to join the British Army in exchange for their freedom. Washington ultimately supported the enlistment of African American soldiers.

Despite this prejudice, Salem enlisted in January 1776 and fought in the Battles of Harlem Heights and Trenton. He reenlisted in January 1777, and fought in the Battles of Saratoga, Monmouth, and Stony Point, serving until his discharge in 1780. Salem's enduring contributions impactfully challenged the prejudices of his time.

Lemuel Haynes
(1753 - 1833)

Lemuel Haynes was a gifted orator and minister who wrote a poignant poem describing the value of freedom at the Battle of Lexington and Concord. Haynes was born in West Hartford, Connecticut, in 1753. When his mother, an indentured servant from Scotland, and his father, an enslaved African American, abandoned Haynes as an infant, he entered indentured servitude in Granville, Massachusetts. Despite receiving limited formal education, Haynes avidly read the Bible and theology books.

Once freed at age 21, he enlisted in his local militia of Minutemen. He was assigned to Captain Lebbeus Ball's unit just one day after the Battle of Lexington and Concord and marched to participate in the Siege of Boston in 1775. He went on to participate in the capture of Fort Ticonderoga.

Haynes likely wrote his ballad, *"The Battle of Lexington,"* while stationed at Cambridge during the siege. He eloquently captured the spirit of the revolutionary cause writing, "For Liberty, each Freeman Strives/As it's a Gift of God/And for it willing yield their Lives/And Seal it with their Blood. Thrice happy they who thus resign/Into the peacefull [sic] Grave/Much better there, in Death Confin'd/Than a Surviving Slave."

James Forten
(1766 - 1842)

James Forten dedicated his life to the cause of liberty, first for America and then for the disenfranchised. The grandson of enslaved people, Forten was born free in 1766 in Philadelphia, Pennsylvania. When Forten was nine years old, he heard the Declaration of Independence read for the first time outside Independence Hall. Two years later, he witnessed the British Army invade his city.

Having worked as a sailmaker since the age of eight, Forten volunteered to serve in the defacto American Navy aboard the privateer ship, *Royal Louis*, carrying gun powder to the ship's cannons. When his ship was captured, he became a prisoner of war aboard the *HMS Jersey* for several months. Conditions were wretched, earning the notorious *Jersey* the nickname, "Hell." Forten survived and was released in 1782 in a prisoner exchange.

After the Revolution, Forten returned to Philadelphia where he became a successful businessman. His sail innovations achieved financial success and he used his wealth to advance the rights of those left out of the new American constitution. With his wife and daughters, Forten spent the remainder of his life leading political campaigns calling for the abolition of slavery, African American civil rights, and women's suffrage.

Agrippa Hull
(1759 - 1848)

Agrippa Hull's distinguished six-year service in the Continental Army uniquely spanned both the northern and southern campaigns. Hull was born free to formerly enslaved parents in 1759 in Northampton, Massachusetts. In 1777 he joined the cause of American liberty and served as an orderly to General John Paterson in the Massachusetts Line. With this unit, Hull served at the Battle of Saratoga, Valley Forge, and the Battle of Monmouth Courthouse.

In 1779, Hull was reassigned to serve as the personal aide to Polish military engineer, Tadeuz Kosciuszko, in the southern campaign. The two developed an enduring friendship, participating together in the battles of Cowpens, Eutaw Springs, Ninety Six, Guilford Courthouse, and the Siege of Charleston. At each engagement, they witnessed examples of what would ultimately become an estimated 20,000 people fleeing enslavement to join the British Army in response to Virginia Royal Governor Lord Dunmore's promise of freedom. At the conclusion of the war, Hull was discharged from service with the signature of General George Washington.

After the war, Hull returned to Stockbridge, Massachusetts, where he bought a farm and worked with abolitionist lawyer, Theodore Sedgwick. Sedgwick successfully worked to free Jane Darby, whom Hull married in 1785.

James Armistead Lafayette
(circa 1760 - 1832)

James Armistead's powers of observation and his knowledge of the Virginia terrain were ideally suited to his role as a spy for the Americans during the Revolution. Armistead was born into slavery and lived in New Kent, Virginia. In 1781 he received permission from his owner to join the Marquis de Lafayette's unit. Posing as a runaway slave, Armistead infiltrated British General Benedict Arnold's camp and reported back intelligence.

He so convincingly played this role that the British subsequently recruited him to spy on the Americans. Double Agent Armistead informed Lafayette of the British Army's planned move to Yorktown with expected reinforcements. In response, the Americans and French set up a successful siege of Yorktown, resulting in the British surrender and American independence.

Tragically, Armistead was forced back into slavery after the war. Virginia's Act of 1783 stated that enslaved Patriots who had contributed to American independence "should enjoy the blessings of freedom as a reward." Armistead's spy work was not deemed an acceptable contribution. His several petitions were ignored. Lafayette attested to Armistead's "essential services" in a letter stating his "intelligence from the ennemy's [sic] camp were [sic] industriously collected and most faithfully delivered." Armistead's petition for freedom was finally granted and he adopted the surname Lafayette in gratitude. During Lafayette's 1824 tour of the United States, the commander and his spy were reunited in Richmond, Virginia.

Prince Hall
(circa 1735 - 1807)

Prince Hall was among Massachusetts's earliest and most fervent promoters of African American liberty during the American Revolution. He was most likely born in 1735 in either Boston, Massachusetts, or Barbados, and enslaved by Boston resident, William Hall. William freed Prince in 1770. After obtaining his freedom, Prince owned a leather workshop, paid taxes, and voted in Boston.

Hall is likely one of six men named "Prince Hall" listed in the Massachusetts Revolutionary War military records and possibly fought at the Battle of Bunker Hill. His leather shop crafted five drumheads for the Boston Regiment of Artillery in April 1777.

On January 13, 1777, Hall became the first recorded person to apply the *"all men are created equal"* argument written in the Declaration of Independence to the abolition of slavery. Hall authored a petition to the Massachusetts General Court, calling for the emancipation of slaves by age 21, arguing that "Blackes [sic] detained in a State of slavery … have in Common with all other men a Natural and Unali[en]able Right to that freedom which the Gr[e]at Parent of the Universe that Bestowed equalley [sic] on all m[a]nkind."

Hall remained an advocate of African American rights for the remainder of his life.

Appendix

★

Chapter Endnotes	233
Patriot Stories Works Cited	257
List of Additional Chapter Patriots	299
Index of Images	303
Index of Featured Chapter Patriots	305

Endnotes
Introduction: PATRIOTS

[1] Desjardins, Jeff. "Mapped: The world's oldest democracies." *World Economic Forum*. Aug. 8, 2019. https://www.weforum.org/agenda/2019/08/countries-are-the-worlds-oldest-democracies/.

[2] Ibid.

[3] Letter from John Adams to Abigail Adams, 26 April 1777 [electronic edition]. Adams Family Papers. *Massachusetts Historical Society*. http://www.masshist.org/digitaladams/.

[4] Paine, Thomas. *The American Crisis* (1776-1783). Bill of Rights Institute. https://billofrightsinstitute.org/primary-sources/the-american-crisis.

[5] Zagarri, Rosemary, PhD. "Slavery in British North America." teachinghistory.org. 2018. https://teachinghistory.org/history-content/ask-a-historian/25577.

[6] Grant, George. *The American Patriot's Handbook*. Naperville, IL: Cumberland House Publishing, 2009. Pg. 125.

Endnotes
Chapter 1: RESOLVE

[1] The massacre perpetrated in King Street Boston on March 5th. United States Boston Massachusetts, 1770. [Photograph] Retrieved from the Library of Congress. Free to use and reuse collection. https://www.loc.gov/item/2004670035/. Free to use and reuse collection.

[2] "The First Charter of Virginia; April 10, 1606." Avalon Project. Lillian Goldman Law Library. *Yale Law School*. Original source: The Federal and State Constitutions Colonial Charters, and Other Organic Laws of the States, Territories, and Colonies Now or Heretofore Forming the United States of America Compiled and Edited Under the Act of Congress of June 30, 1906, by Francis Newton Thorpe Washington, DC: Government Printing Office, 1909. https://avalon.law.yale.edu/17th_century/va01.asp.

[3] "Magna Carta." National Archives Foundation. 2023. www.archivesfoundation.org/documents/magna-carta/; also, English Translation of Magna Carta. *The British Library*. G.R.C. Davis, Magna Carta. (London: British Museum, 1963). Pgs. 23–33. https://www.bl.uk/magna-carta/articles/magna-carta-english-translation.

[4] "The First Legislative Assembly." Historic Jamestown. *National Park Service*. United States Department of the Interior. Last Updated Sept. 4, 2022. https://historicjamestowne.org/history/the-first-general-assembly/.

[5] Ibid.

[6] Ibid.

[7] "Mayflower Compact: 1620." Avalon Project. Lillian Goldman Law Library. *Yale Law School*. The Federal and State Constitutions Colonial Charters, and Other Organic Laws of the States, Territories, and Colonies Now or Heretofore Forming the United States of America Compiled and Edited Under the Act of

Congress of June 30, 1906, by Francis Newton Thorpe Washington, DC: Government Printing Office, 1909.
https://avalon.law.yale.edu/17th_century/mayflower.asp.
[8] "The Charter of Massachusetts Bay: 1629." Avalon Project. Lillian Goldman Law Library. *Yale Law School*. The Federal and State Constitutions Colonial Charters, and Other Organic Laws of the States, Territories, and Colonies Now or Heretofore Forming the United States of America Compiled and Edited Under the Act of Congress of June 30, 1906, by Francis Newton Thorpe. Washington, DC: Government Printing Office, 1909.
https://avalon.law.yale.edu/17th_century/mass03.asp.
[9] "Colony." National Geographic. 2003.
https://education.nationalgeographic.org/resource/colony/; also, Brooks, Rebecca Beatrice. "The 13 Colonies in the Revolutionary War." History of Massachusetts Blog. Dec. 12, 2017.
https://www.digitalhistory.uh.edu/teachers/lesson_plans/pdfs/unit1_3.pdf.
[10] Ibid.
[11] Ibid.
[12] "The Reign of James II." *UK Parliament*. 2023.
www.parliament.uk/about/living-heritage/evolutionofparliament/parliamentaryauthority/revolution/overview/reignofjames/.
[13] "English Bill of Rights 1689." The Avalon Project. Lillian Goldman Law Library. *Yale Law School*. https://avalon.law.yale.edu/17th_century/england.asp.
[14] Ibid.
[15] "The speech of Edmund Burke, Esq; on moving his resolutions for conciliation with the colonies, March 22, 1775:
Burke, Edmund, 1729-1797." London: printed for J. Dodsley, 1775. Eighteenth Century Collections Online. *University of Michigan Library*.
https://quod.lib.umich.edu/e/ecco/004895777.0001.000.
[16] History.com Editors. "The 13 Colonies." HISTORY. *A&E Television Networks*. Original: June 17, 2010; Updated: Aug. 22, 2022.
https://www.history.com/topics/colonial-america/thirteen-colonies.
[17] "The Six Nations Confederacy during the American Revolution." *National Park Service*. United States Department of the Interior. Last updated: Feb. 23, 2023.
https://www.nps.gov/articles/000/the-six-nations-confederacy-during-the-american-revolution.htm.
[18] "Benjamin Franklin." A film by Ken Burns. *Public Broadcasting Service (PBS)*. First aired April 2022.
[19] "Motivations for Colonization." *National Geographic Society*. 2003.
https://education.nationalgeographic.org/resource/motivations-colonization/.
[20] Ibid.
[21] "French and Indian War/Seven Years' War, 1754-63." Office of the Historian, Foreign Service Institute. *United States Department of State*.
https://history.state.gov/milestones/1750-1775/french-indian-war.
[22] Smith, Laverne Y. "Seven Years' War." *George Washington's Mount Vernon*. 2023. https://www.mountvernon.org/library/digitalhistory/digital-encyclopedia/article/seven-years-war.

[23] "French and Indian War/Seven Years' War, 1754-63."
[24] "Confronting the National Debt: The Aftermath of the French and Indian War." *OpenStaxCollege*. May 7, 2014. https://pressbooks-dev.oer.hawaii.edu/ushistory/chapter/confronting-the-national-debt-the-aftermath-of-the-french-and-indian-war.
[25] Ibid.
[26] Ibid.
[27] Triber, Jayne E. "Britain Begins Taxing the Colonies: The Sugar and Stamp Acts." *National Park Service*. United States Department of the Interior. Last updated: Jan. 13, 2023. www.nps.gov/articles/000/sugar-and-stamp-acts.
[28] Ibid.
[29] "Great Britain: Parliament - The Sugar Act: 1764." Preamble. Avalon Project. Lillian Goldman Law Library. *Yale Law School*. Original source: Great Britain; The statutes at large ... [from 1225 to 1867] by Danby Pickering Cambridge: Printed by Benthem, for C. Bathhurst; London, 1762-1869. https://avalon.law.yale.edu/18th_century/sugar_act_1764.asp.
[30] "The Sugar Act." *Massachusetts Historical Society*. 2023. https://www.masshist.org/revolution/sugar.php.
[30] Shumate, Ken. "The Sugar Act: A Brief History." *Journal of the American Revolution*. Sept. 17, 2018. https://allthingsliberty.com/2018/09/the-sugar-act-a-brief-history/.
[31] "Great Britain: Parliament - The Sugar Act: 1764." Article XLI.
[32] Shumate, Ken. "The Sugar Act: A Brief History."
[33] "Petition from the Massachusetts House of Representatives to the House of Commons; November 3, 1764." Avalon Project. Lillian Goldman Law Library. *Yale Law School*. Original source: Bradford, Alden; Speeches of the Governors of Massachusetts from 1765 to 1775: and the answers of the House of Representatives to the same; with their resolutions and addresses for that period and other public papers relating to the dispute between this country and Great Britain which led to the independence of the United States. Boston: Printed by Russell and Gardner, proprietors of the work, 1818.https://avalon.law.yale.edu/18th_century/petition_mass_1764.asp.
[34] Qtd. Shumate, Ken. "The Sugar Act: A Brief History."
[35] Qtd. Ibid.
[36] "The Currency Act." US History.org. *Independence Hall Association*. 2023. https://www.ushistory.org/declaration/related/currencyact.html.
[37] "The Sugar Act." *Massachusetts Historical Society*.
[38] "Great Britain: Parliament - The Stamp Act, March 22, 1765." Preamble. Avalon Project. Lillian Goldman Law Library. *Yale Law School*. Original source: Great Britain; The statutes at large ... [from 1225 to 1867] by Danby Pickering; Cambridge: Printed by Benthem, for C. Bathhurst; London, 1762-1869. https://avalon.law.yale.edu/18th_century/stamp_act_1765.asp.
[39] "Patrick Henry's Resolutions Against the Stamp Act." *Red Hill Patrick Henry National Memorial*. 2023. https://www.redhill.org/primary-sources/patrick-henrys-resolutions-against-the-stamp-act/.
[40] "Braintree Instructions." *Braintree Historical Society*. https://www.braintree-historical.org/event-3031909.

[41] Adams, John. "Instructions to the Representative of Braintree against the Stamp Act 1765," Adams' Original Draft, 24 Sept. 1765." *National Archives*. Founders Online. https://founders.archives.gov/documents/Adams.
[42] Ibid.
[43] Zeilinski, Adam E. "What Was the Stamp Act Congress and Why Did It Matter." *American Battlefield Trust*. Original: Nov. 17, 2020; Updated: June 15, 2021. https://www.battlefields.org/learn/articles/what-was-stamp-act-congress.
[44] Nesnay, Mary. "The Stamp Act – A Brief History." *Journal of the American Revolution*. July 29, 2014. https://allthingsliberty.com/2014/07/the-stamp-act-a-brief-history/.
[45] Zeilinski, Adam. E. "What Was the Stamp Act Congress and Why Did It Matter."
[46] Ibid. Virginia did not attend after the Lieutenant Governor disbanded its assembly. New Hampshire, Georgia, and North Carolina also did not attend.
[47] "The Declaration Of Rights Of The Stamp Act Congress, 19 October 1765." *University of Wisconsin Madison*. https://archive.csac.history.wisc.edu/8_THE_DECLARATION_OF_RIGHTS_OF_THE_STAMP_ACT_CONGRESS.pdf.
[48] "The Quartering Act." *The Boston Tea Party Ships & Museum*. 2023. https://www.bostonteapartyship.com/the-quartering-act.
[49] Ibid.
[50] "The Declaratory Act." The Colonial Williamsburg Foundation. 2023. https://www.ouramericanrevolution.org/index.cfm/page/view/p0062.
[51] "Great Britain: Parliament - The Townshend Act, November 20, 1767." Article X. Avalon Project. Lillian Goldman Law Library. *Yale Law School*. Original source: Great Britain; The statutes at large ... [from 1225 to 1867] by Danby Pickering; Cambridge: Printed by Benthem, for C. Bathhurst; London, 1762-1869. https://avalon.law.yale.edu/18th_century/townsend_act_1767.asp.
[52] History.com Editors. "Townshend Acts." HISTORY. *A&E Television Networks*. Original: Nov. 9, 2009; Updated: Jan. 15, 2020. https://www.history.com/topics/american-revolution/townshend-acts.
[53] Andrlik, Todd. *Reporting the Revolutionary War*. Pg. 33. Naperville, IL: Source Books Inc., 2012.
[54] "John Dickinson, Letters from a Farmer in Pennsylvania, 1767–1768." *Bill of Rights Institute*. 2023. https://billofrightsinstitute.org/activities/john-dickinson-letters-from-a-farmer-in-pennsylvania-1767-1768.
[55] "Massachusetts Circular Letter (1768). Samuel Adams and James Otis." *National Constitution Center*. 2023. https://constitutioncenter.org/the-constitution/historic-document-library/detail/samuel-adams-and-james-otis-massachusetts-circular-letter-february-11-1768.
[56] Ibid.
[57] Qtd. Cecere, Michael. "Take Them at their Word: Virginia's Opposition to the Townshend Duties." *Journal of the American Revolution*. 2018. https://allthingsliberty.com/2018/03/take-them-at-their-word-virginias-opposition-to-the-townshend-duties/.
[58] Ibid.
[59] Ibid.

[60] History.com Editors. "Townshend Acts."
[61] Brooks, Rebecca Beatrice. "The Daughters of Liberty: Who Were They and What Did They Do?" *History of Massachusetts Blog*. Dec. 9, 2015.
[62] History.com Editors. "Townshend Acts."
[63] Ibid.
[64] Ibid.
[65] "The Formation of Committees of Correspondence." *Massachusetts Historical Society*. 2023. https://www.masshist.org/revolution/committees.php.
[66] Treesh, Catherine. "Committees of Correspondence." *George Washington's Mount Vernon*. 2023. https://www.mountvernon.org/library/digitalhistory/digital-encyclopedia/article/committees-of-correspondence.
[67] Andrlik, Todd. Pg. 70.
[68] History.com Editors. "Committees of Correspondence." HISTORY. *A&E Television Networks*. Original Oct. 27, 2009; Updated Oct. 26, 2021. https://www.history.com/topics/american-revolution/committees-of-correspondence.
[69] *Boston and the American Revolution*. Boston National Historic Park. *National Park Service*. United States Department of the Interior. Division of Publications, 1998. Pg. 44.
[70] Ibid.
[71] "The Boston Tea Party." *Massachusetts Historical Society*. 2023. www.masshist.org/revolution/teaparty.php.
[72] History.com Editors. "British Parliament passes unpopular Tea Act." HISTORY. *A&E Television Networks*. Original: Oct. 27, 2009; Updated: Sept. 20, 2022. https://www.history.com/this-day-in-history/parliament-passes-the-tea-act.
[73] "The Boston Tea Party." Extract of a Letter from Philadelphia, Dec. 4, 1773. *Massachusetts Historical Society*. 2023. www.masshist.org/revolution/teaparty.php.
[74] Ibid.
[75] "The Tea Act." *Boston Tea Party Ships & Museum*. 2023. https://www.bostonteapartyship.com/the-tea-act.
[76] "The Body of the People." *Boston Tea Party Ships & Museum*. 2023. https://www.bostonteapartyship.com/the-body-of-the-people.
[77] Ibid.
[78] "The Secret Meeting." *Boston Tea Party Ships & Museum*. 2003. https://www.bostonteapartyship.com/the-secret-plan.
[79] Ibid.
[80] "The Destruction of the Tea." *Boston Tea Party Ships & Museum*. 2003. https://www.bostonteapartyship.com/the-destruction-of-the-tea.
[81] Ibid.
[82] "The Boston Tea Party." *Massachusetts Historical Society*.
[83] History.com Editors. "Boston Tea Party." HISTORY. *A&E Television Networks*. Original: Oct. 27, 2009; Updated: Sept. 20, 2022. https://www.history.com/topics/american-revolution/boston-tea-party.
[84] Franklin, Benjamin. Letter on February 2, 1774, to Thomas Cushing, Sam'l Adams, John Hancock, William Phillips, Esquires. *Boston Tea Party Ships &*

Museum. 2003. www.bostonteapartyship.com/tea-blog/benjamin-franklins-views-on-the-*boston*-tea-party.

[85] Qtd. Brooks, Rebecca Beatrice. "The Boston Tea Party." History of Massachusetts Blog. Sept. 27, 2011. https://historyofmassachusetts.org/the-boston-tea-party/.

[86] Adams, John. "[December 1773]," Founders Online. *National Archives.* https://founders.archives.gov/documents/Adams/01-02-02-0003-0008. [Original source: The Adams Papers, Diary and Autobiography of John Adams, vol. 2, 1771–1781, ed. L. H. Butterfield. Cambridge, MA: Harvard University Press, 1961, pp. 85–87.] https://founders.archives.gov/documents/Adams.

[87] Ibid.

[88] "Great Britain: Parliament - The Boston Port Act: March 31, 1774." Avalon Project. Lillian Goldman Law Library. *Yale Law School.* Original source: Great Britain; The statutes at large ... [from 1225 to 1867] by Danby Pickering; Cambridge: Printed by Benthem, for C. Bathhurst; London, 1762-1869. https://avalon.law.yale.edu/18th_century/boston_port_act.asp.

[89] "Great Britain: Parliament - The Massachusetts Government Act; May 20, 1774." Article 1. Avalon Project. Lillian Goldman Law Library. *Yale Law School.* Original source: Great Britain; The statutes at large ... [from 1225 to 1867] by Danby Pickering; Cambridge: Printed by Benthem, for C. Bathhurst; London, 1762-1869. https://avalon.law.yale.edu/18th_century/mass_gov_act.asp.

[90] "Great Britain: Parliament - The Administration of Justice Act; May 20, 1774." Avalon Project. Lillian Goldman Law Library. *Yale Law School.* Original source: Great Britain; The statutes at large ... [from 1225 to 1867] by Danby Pickering; Cambridge: Printed by Benthem, for C. Bathhurst; London, 1762-1869. https://avalon.law.yale.edu/18th_century/admin_of_justice_act.asp.

[91] *Boston and the American Revolution.* National Park Service. Pg. 53.

[92] "Great Britain: Parliament - The Quartering Act; June 2, 1774." Avalon Project. Lillian Goldman Law Library. *Yale Law School.* Original source: Great Britain; The statutes at large ... [from 1225 to 1867] by Danby Pickering; Cambridge: Printed by Benthem, for C. Bathhurst; London, 1762-1869. https://avalon.law.yale.edu/18th_century/quartering_act_1774.asp.

[93] Andrlik, Todd. Reporting the Revolutionary War. Pg. 88. Source Books Inc.: Naperville, IL. 1012.

[94] Ibid. Pg. 88.

[95] "Virginia's House of Burgesses, British America's First Elected Legislature." Americana Corner. 2022. https://www.americanacorner.com/blog/house-burgesses.

[96] Letter from George Washington to George William Fairfax; Friday, June 10, 1774. *George Washingtons' Mount Vernon.* 2023. https://www.mountvernon.org/library/digitalhistory/past-projects/quotes/article.

[97] "The Intolerable Acts." *American Battlefield Trust.* 2023. www.battlefields.org/learn/articles/intolerable-acts.

[98] Ibid. See also: Resolution of the House of Burgesses Designating a Day of Fasting and Prayer, 24 May 1774. Founders Online. National Archives. 2023. https://founders.archives.gov/documents/Jefferson/01-01-02-0082.

[99] *Boston and the American Revolution*. National Park Service. United States Department of the Interior. Pg. 53-4. 1998.
[100] Andrlik. Pg. 101.
[101] Ibid. Pg. 86.
[102] Ibid. Pg. 106.
[103] "Provincial Congress." Repository of the Massachusetts Archives. Record Group Number: PC1. https://www.sec.state.ma.us/arc/arcpdf/collection-guides/FA_PC.pdf.
[104] Qtd. "The Militia and Minute Men of 1775." *National Park Service*. United States Department of the Interior. www.nps.gov/mima/learn/historyculture/the-militia-and-minute-men-of-1775.
[105] *Boston and the American Revolution*. National Park Service. Pg. 55.

Endnotes
Chapter 2: DECLARATION

[1] *Thomas Jefferson, Rough Draft of the Declaration of Independence*. June 1776. [Manuscript/Mixed Material] Retrieved from the Library of Congress. Free to use and reuse collection. https://www.loc.gov/item/mtjbib000156/.
[2] "Declaration and Resolves of the First Continental Congress." Avalon Project. Lillian Goldman Law Library. *Yale Law School*. 2008. Original source: Documents Illustrative of the Formation of the Union of the American States. Government Printing Office, 1927. House Document No. 398. Selected, Arranged and Indexed by Charles C. Tansill. https://avalon.law.yale.edu/18th_century/resolves.asp.
[3] Ibid.
[4] Ibid.
[5] Cecere, Michael. "The First Continental Congress Responds to the Intolerable Acts." *Journal of the American Revolution*. 2018. https://allthingsliberty.com/2014/09/the-first-continental-congress-responds-to-the-intolerable-acts/.
[6] Horan, Karen. "First Continental Congress." *George Washington's Mount Vernon*. 2023. https://www.mountvernon.org/library/digitalhistory/digital-encyclopedia/article/first-continental-congress/.; Georgia did not send delegates to the First Continental Congress.
[7] Cecere, Michael. "The First Continental Congress Responds to the Intolerable Acts."
[8] "Continental Association, 20 October 1774." Founders Online. *National Archives and Records Administration*. Jefferson Papers. https://founders.archives.gov/documents/Jefferson/01-01-02-0094.
[9] Ibid.
[10] Adams, John. "John Adams diary 22A, includes notes on Continental Congress, September - October 1774." Adams Family Papers. Massachusetts Historical Society. https://www.masshist.org/digitaladams/archive/doc?id=D22A.
[11] *Boston and the American Revolution*. Pg. 58.
[12] Ibid. Pgs. 56 & 58.

[13] Ibid. Pg. 58.
[14] Palmer, Joseph, Originator; Tyler, Daniel, Jr. Originator of copy. "Lexington Alarm Letter, 1775 April 19." *Digital Commonwealth*. Massachusetts Collections Online. Original Tyler copy at Scottish Rite Masonic Museum and Library. www.digitalcommonwealth.org/search/commonwealth-oai:8p58ps57m.
[15] Berthelson, Robert L. "An Alarm from Lexington." Nov. 16, 2021. *The Massachusetts Society Sons of the American Revolution*. https://www.massar.org/2012/11/16/alarm-from-lexington/.
[16] *Boston and the American Revolution*. Pg. 57.
[17] Qtd. Ibid. Pg. 58.
[18] Andrlik. Pg. 120.
[19] Ibid. Pg. 122.
[20] Ibid.
[21] "Lexington and Concord." *American Battlefield Trust*. 2023. www.battlefields.org/learn/revolutionary-war/battles/lexington-and-concord.
[22] "Fort Ticonderoga (1775)." *American Battlefield Trust*. 2023. https://www.battlefields.org/learn/revolutionary-war/battles/fort-ticonderoga-1775.
[23] *Boston and the American Revolution*. Pg. 61.; the militia accidentally built the redoubt on nearby Breeds Hill.
[24] Ibid. Pg. 62.
[25] Brown, Peter. "Letter from Peter Brown to Sarah Brown, 25 June 1775." *Massachusetts Historical Society*. https://www.masshist.org/database/viewer.
[26] Ibid.
[27] Andrlik. Pgs. 132.
[28] Ney, Diane. *Sites of the American Revolution*. Barnes and Noble. Berenson Design & Books Ltd.: New York. Pg. 149.
[29] "American Revolutionary War Continental Regiments." Revolutionary War.us. 2017. https://revolutionarywar.us/continental-army/.
[30] Frayler, John. "Privateers in the American Revolution." *National Park Service*. United States Department of the Interior. Last updated: March 23, 2023. https://www.nps.gov/articles/privateers-in-the-american-revolution.htm.
[31] Ibid.
[32] "Journals of the Continental Congress - Petition to the King; July 8, 1775." Avalon Project. Lillian Goldman Law Library. *Yale Law School*. Original source: Journals of the Continental Congress 1774-1779; Vol. II Pages 158-172. Edited from the original records in the Library of Congress by Worthington Chauncey Ford; Chief, Division of Manuscripts. Washington, DC: Government Printing Office, 1905. https://avalon.law.yale.edu/18th_century/contcong_07-08-75.asp.
[33] Ibid.
[34] "By the KING, A PROCLAMATION, For suppressing Rebellion and Sedition." *Massachusetts Historical Society*. https://www.masshist.org/database/viewer.
[35] Ibid.
[36] Ibid.
[37] "In Congress March 23, 1776. Whereas the Petitions of these United Colonies to the King, for the Redress of great and manifest Grievances ..." *Massachusetts Historical Society*. https://www.masshist.org/database/viewer.
[38] Andrlik. Pg. 187.

[39] Ibid.
[40] Page, T. H. & Faden, W. (1777) A plan of the town of Boston, with the intrenchments &c. of His Majestys forces in: From the observations of Lieut. Page of His Majesty's Corps of Engineers; and from the plans of other gentlemen. [London; Engraved & printed for Wm. Faden] [Map] Retrieved from the Library of Congress. Free to use and reuse collection. https://www.loc.gov/item/gm71000620/.
[41] "Quebec." *American Battlefield Trust*. 2023. https://www.battlefields.org/learn/revolutionary-war/battles/quebec.
[42] Andrlik. Pg. 170.
[43] Paine, Thomas. *Common Sense*. Edited by Edward Larkin. Broadview Editions. Pg. 50. www.sjsu.edu/people/ruma.chopra/courses/H174_MW_F12/s1/Wk7_A.pdf.
[44] Ibid.
[45] Ibid. Pg. 56.
[46] Ibid. Pg. 64.
[47] Ibid. Pgs. 65 & 66.
[48] Ibid. Pgs. 74 & 75.
[49] Ibid. 77.
[50] Adams, John. *Thoughts on Government, April 1776*. Adams Papers. Founders Online. *National Archives and Records Administration*. https://founders.archives.gov/documents/Adams/06-04-02-0026-0004.
[51] Ibid.
[52] Ibid.
[53] Ibid.
[54] Ibid.
[55] Ibid.
[56] Ibid.
[57] Adams, Abigail. "Letter from Abigail Adams to John Adams, 31 March - 5 April 1776." Adams Family Papers. *Massachusetts Historical Society*. https://www.masshist.org/digitaladams/archive/doc?id=L17760331aa.
[58] Ibid.
[59] Andrlik. Pg. 186. Also, "Fort Ticonderoga (1775)." *American Battlefield Trust*. 2023. https://www.battlefields.org/learn/revolutionary-war/battles/fort-ticonderoga-1775.
[60] "Siege of Boston." *American Battlefield Trust*. 2023. https://www.battlefields.org/learn/revolutionary-war/battles/boston. General Gage had been recalled to London and replaced by Howe as Commander in Chief of British Armed Forces in North America.
[61] "The Second Continental Congress." *Massachusetts Historical Society*. https://www.masshist.org/revolution/congress2.php.; See also, Andrlik. Pg. 135.
[62] Andrlik. Pg. 194.
[63] "The Declaration of Independence." *U.S. National Archives and Records Administration*. 2023. www.archives.gov/founding-docs/declaration-history.
[64] "Documents from the Continental Congress and the Constitutional Convention, 1774 to 1789." *Library of Congress*. https://www.loc.gov/collections/continental-

congress-and-constitutional-convention-from-1774-to-1789/articles-and-essays/timeline/1776/.
[65] "Lee Resolution (1776)." Founders Online. *National Archives and Records Administration*. 2023. https://www.archives.gov/milestone-documents/lee-resolution.
[66] "The Declaration of Independence." *U.S. National Archives and Records Administration*.
[67] Declaration of Independence: A Transcription. *U.S. National Archives and Records Administration*. https://www.archives.gov/founding-docs/declaration-transcript.
[68] Ibid.
[69] Ibid.
[70] Ibid.
[71] Ibid.
[72] "First Public Reading of the Declaration of Independence." *National Park Service*. U.S. Department of the Interior. Updated: Feb. 26, 2015. https://www.nps.gov/inde/learn/news/first-public-reading-of-the-declaration-of-independence.
[73] Adams, Abigail. "Letter from Abigail Adams to John Adams, 21 - 22 July 1776." Adams Family Papers. *Massachusetts Historical Society*. https://www.masshist.org/digitaladams/archive.
[74] Trickey, Erick. "Mary Katharine Goddard, the Woman who Signed the Declaration of Independence." *Smithsonian Magazine*. Nov. 14, 2018. https://www.smithsonianmag.com/history/mary-katharine-goddard-woman-who-signed-declaration-independence-180970816/.
[75] Ibid.
[76] NCC Staff. "On this day, the name 'United States of America' becomes official." *National Constitution Center*. Sept. 9, 2023. https://constitutioncenter.org/blog/today-the-name-united-states-of-america-becomes-offici#:
[77] "Documents from the Continental Congress and the Constitutional Convention, 1774 to 1789." *Library of Congress*. https://www.loc.gov/collections/continental-congress-and-constitutional-convention-from-1774-to-1789/articles-and-essays/timeline/1776/.
[78] Stockwell, Mary Ph.D. "Declaration of Independence." *George Washington's Mount Vernon*. 2023. https://www.mountvernon.org/library/digitalhistory/digital-encyclopedia/article/declaration-of-independence/.
[79] Stockwell, Mary Ph.D. "Battle of Long Island." *George Washington's Mount Vernon*. 2023. https://www.mountvernon.org/library/digitalhistory/digital-encyclopedia/article/battle-of-long-island/. See also Andrlik. Pg. 202 and "Brooklyn Long Island." American Battlefield Trust American Battlefield Trust. 2023. https://www.battlefields.org/learn/revolutionary-war/battles/brooklyn. Troop estimates vary across sources.
[80] Andrlik. Pg. 202.
[81] Ibid.
[82] Ibid.

[83] "Lord Howe's Conference with the Committee of Congress, 11 September 1776." Founders Online. *National Archives and Records Administration.* https://founders.archives.gov/documents/Franklin/01-22-02-0358.
[84] Howe, William. "A Proclamation. By His Excellency the Honorable William Howe." New York Historical Society. https://digitalcollections.nyhistory.org/islandora/object/islandora.
[85] Ibid.
[86] "Documents from the Continental Congress and the Constitutional Convention, 1774 to 1789." *Library of Congress.* https://www.loc.gov/collections/continental-congress-and-constitutional-convention-from-1774-to-1789/articles-and-essays/timeline/1776/.
[87] Paine, Thomas. *The American Crisis* (1776-1783). Bill of Rights Institute. https://billofrightsinstitute.org/primary-sources/the-american-crisis.
[88] Ibid.
[89] "Trenton." *American Battlefield Trust.* 2023. https://www.battlefields.org/learn/revolutionary-war/battles/trenton.
[90] Qtd. Andrlik. Pg. 212.
[91] Washington, George. "Proclamation concerning Persons Swearing British Allegiance, 25 January 1777." Founders Online. *National Archives and Records Administration.* https://founders.archives.gov/documents/Washington/03-08-02-0160.
[92] Ibid.

Endnotes
Chapter 3: HOPE

[1] Scull, N., Heap, G. & Faden, W. A plan of the city and environs of Philadelphia. London, W. Faden. 1777. [Map] Retrieved from the Library of Congress, https://www.loc.gov/item/74692193/. Free to use and reuse collection.
[2] "Burgoyne's Campaign: June-October 1777." *National Park Service.* U.S. Department of the Interior. www.nps.gov/articles/burgoyne-s-campaign-june-october-1777.htm.
[3] "The Six Nations Confederacy During the American Revolution." *National Park Service.* U.S. Department of the Interior. Updated Feb. 3, 2023. https://www.nps.gov/articles/000/the-six-nations-confederacy-during-the-american-revolution.htm.
[4] McCutchen, Shannon C. "Breaking the Great League of Peace and Power: The Six Iroquois Nations During and After the American Revolution." Pg. 4. www2.umbc.edu/che/tahlessons/pdf/The_League_of_Peace_and_Power_PF.pdf.
[5] Ibid.
[6] Ney, Diane. Pg. 134.
[7] Burgoyne, John. "By John Burgoyne Esq'r; Lieut Gen'l of His Majesties Armies in America, Col. of the Queens Reg't of Lt. Dragoons, Governor of Fort William in North Britain, one of the Representatives of the Commons of Great Britain in Parliament, and Commanding an Army and Fleet employed on an expedition from Canada." Camp at Bouquet Ferry June 20th, 1777. *Teaching American History.*

2023. https://teachingamericanhistory.org/document/general-burgoynes-proclamation/.
[8] Ibid.
[9] "Bennington." *American Battlefield Trust*. 2023. https://www.battlefields.org/learn/revolutionary-war/battles/bennington.
[10] Mellon, Thomas. "Primary Sources for The Battle of Bennington: Excerpts from Thomas Mellon." *Bennington Museum*. https://benningtonmuseum.org/wp-content/uploads/2018/09/primary-source-booklet-for-teachers.pdf.
[11] Ibid.
[12] "Bennington." *American Battlefield Trust*.
[13] "Burgoyne's Campaign: June-October 1777." *National Park Service*. U.S. Department of the Interior. Updated: Aug. 8, 2022. https://www.nps.gov/articles/burgoyne-s-campaign-june-october-1777.htm.
[14] Ney, Diane. Pgs. 178-9.
[15] Stockwell, Mary Ph.D. "Marquis de Lafayette." *George Washington's Mount Vernon*. 2023. https://www.mountvernon.org/library/digitalhistory/digital-encyclopedia/article/marquis-de-lafayette/.
[16] Qtd. "Facts About the United States Flag." *Smithsonian Institution*. Last revised: Sept. 2001. https://www.si.edu/spotlight/flag-day/flag-facts.
[17] History.com Editors. "The Stars and Stripes flies in battle for the first time." HISTORY. *A&E Television Networks*. Original date: Feb. 9, 2010; Last updated: Aug. 30, 2021. www.history.com/this-day-in-history/the-stars-and-stripes-flies."
[18] "Brandywine." *American Battlefield Trust*. 2023. https://www.battlefields.org/learn/revolutionary-war/battles/brandywine.
[19] "Paoli." *American Battlefield Trust*. 2023. https://www.battlefields.org/learn/revolutionary-war/battles/paoli.
[20] Andrlik. Pg. 223. And "Meeting Places for the Continental Congresses and the Confederation Congresses, 1774-1789." History, Art & Archives. *United States House of Representatives*. https://history.house.gov/People/Continental-Congress/Meeting-Places.
[21] "Germantown." *American Battlefield Trust*. 2023. https://www.battlefields.org/learn/revolutionary-war/battles/germantown.
[22] Qtd. Andrlik. Pg. 228.
[23] Ibid.
[24] Ney, Diane. Pg. 230.
[25] Mellaci, Taylor. "Camp Followers." *George Washington's Mount Vernon*. 2023. https://www.mountvernon.org/library/digitalhistory/digital-encyclopedia/article/camp-followers/.
[26] "Women with the Continental Army." *The American Revolution Institute*. 2023. https://www.americanrevolutioninstitute.org/women-with-the-continental-army/.
[27] Mellaci, Taylor. "Camp Followers."
[28] "Women of the Continental Army." *National Park Service*. U.S. Department of the Interior. https://www.nps.gov/articles/000/women-of-the-army.htm.
[29] Mellaci, Taylor. "Camp Followers."
[30] "The Fighting Man of the Continental Army." *American Battlefield Trust*. https://www.battlefields.org/learn/articles/fighting-man-continental-army.
[31] Ibid.

[32] Gates, Horatio. "To George Washington from Major General Horatio Gates, 5 October 1777." Founders Online. *National Archives and Records Administration.* https://www.founders.archives.gov/documents/Washington/03-11-02-0418.
[33] Ney, Diane. Pg. 150.
[34] Jolly, Henry. "The Battle of Saratoga - A First-Hand Account." Varsity Tutors. 2023. https://www.varsitytutors.com/earlyamerica/early-america-review/volume-8/the-battle-of-saratoga.
[35] "The Northern Campaign of 1777." *National Park Service.* U.S. Department of the Interior. Aug. 4, 2021. https://www.nps.gov/fost/blogs/the-northern-campaign-of-1777.htm.
[36] "Saratoga." *American Battlefield Trust.* https://www.battlefields.org/learn/revolutionary-war/battles/saratoga.
[37] Andrlik, Pg. 230.
[38] "Articles of Confederation (1777)." *National Archives and Records Administration.* Jan. 3, 2023. Art. III. https://www.archives.gov/milestone-documents/articles-of-confederation.
[39] Ibid. And Simner, Marvin L. "A Further Evaluation of the Carlisle Peace Commission's Initiative." *Journal of the American Revolution.* https://allthingsliberty.com/2021/09/a-further-evaluation-of-the-carlisle-peace-commissions-initiative/.
[40] Ibid. Art. V.
[41] Ibid.
[42] Ibid. Art. II.
[43] "Treaty of Alliance with France (1778)." *National Archives and Records Administration.* https://www.archives.gov/milestone-documents/treaty-of-alliance-with-france.
[44] Ibid. Art. 1.
[45] Ibid. Art. 8.
[46] Ibid. Art. 8.
[47] Qtd. Andrlik. Pg. 247.
[48] Ibid.

Endnotes
Chapter 4: PERSEVERANCE

[1] *Valley Forge.* 1877. [Photograph] Retrieved from the Library of Congress, https://www.loc.gov/item/2004676940/. No known restrictions.
[2] "What Happened at Valley Forge." *National Park Service.* United States Department of the Interior. https://www.nps.gov/vafo/learn/historyculture/valley-forge-history-and-significance.htm.
[3] Ney, Diane. Pg. 194.
[4] "What Happened at Valley Forge." *National Park Service.*
[5] Ibid.
[6] Ibid.
[7] Ney, Diane. Pg. 194.

[8] Washington, George. "From George Washington to Henry Laurens, 22 December 1777." Founders Online. *National Archives and Records Administration.* https://founders.archives.gov/documents/Washington/03-12-02-0611.

[9] Washington, George. "George Washington to New Jersey, Pennsylvania, Maryland, and Virginia Citizens, February 18, 1778." Valley Forge Headquarters. George Washington Papers. *Library of Congress.* https://www.loc.gov/resource/mgw3c.002/?sp=247&st=text.

[10] Ibid.

[11] Ibid.

[12] Washington, George. "George Washington to Patrick Henry, February 19, 1778." Valley Forge Headquarters. George Washington Papers. *Library of Congress.* https://www.loc.gov/resource/mgw3c.002/?sp=249&st=text.

[13] Ibid.

[14] Kratz, Jessie. "My Name is Alex Hamilton." *National Archives and Records Administration.* July 1, 2020. https://prologue.blogs.archives.gov/2020/07/01/my-name-is-alex-hamilton/.

[15] Ney, Diane. Pg. 195.

[16] Trickey, Erick. "The Prussian Nobleman Who Helped Save the American Revolution." *Smithsonian Magazine.* April 27, 2017. https://www.smithsonianmag.com/history/baron-von-steuben-180963048/https://www.smithsonianmag.com/history/baron-von-steuben-180963048/.

[17] Greenwalt, Phillip S. "George Washington's Integrated Army." *American Battlefield Trust.* 2023. https://www.battlefields.org/learn/articles/george-washingtons-integrated-army.

[18] "Polly Cooper." *American Battlefield Trust.* 2023. https://www.battlefields.org/learn/biographies/polly-cooper.

[19] Ibid.

[20] "Broadsides." *The American Revolution Institute of the Society of the Cincinnati.* 2023. https://www.americanrevolutioninstitute.org/discover-the-collections/broadsides/.

[21] "The American Revolution." George Washington Papers. *Library of Congress.* https://www.loc.gov/collections/george-washington-papers/articles-and-essays/timeline/the-american-revolution.

[22] "Documents from the Continental Congress and the Constitutional Convention, 1774 to 1789." *Library of Congress.* https://www.loc.gov/collections/continental-congress-and-constitutional-convention-from-1774-to-1789/articles-and-essays/timeline/1777-to-1778/.

[23] Ibid.

[24] "Journals of the Continental Congress, 1774-1789." Wednesday, June 17, 1778. Edited from the original records in the Library of Congress by Worthington Chauncey Ford, Chief, Division of Manuscripts. Vol. XI. May 2-Sept. 1. Washington: Government Printing Office. 1908. https://memory.loc.gov/cgi-bin/query/r?ammem/hlaw:@field(DOCID+@lit(jc01141)).

[25] Ibid.

[26] Andrlik. Pg. 249.

[27] "Henry Clinton." *National Park Service*. United States Department of the Interior. 2023. htttps://www.nps.gov/people/henry-clinton.
[28] Ney, Diane. Pg. 87.
[29] "What Happened at Valley Forge." *National Park Service*.
[30] Ney, Diane. Pg. 88.
[31] Ibid.
[32] Andrlik. Pg. 249.
[33] "Meeting Places for the Continental Congresses and the Confederation Congress, 1774–1789." History, Art & Archives. *United States House of Representatives*. https://history.house.gov/People/Continental-Congress/Meeting-Places.
[34] "American Revolutionary War Continental Regiments." *Revolutionary War*. 2017. https://revolutionarywar.us/continental-army.
[35] "Continental Army Historical Facts." *Boston Tea Party Ships and Museum*. 2023. https://www.bostonteapartyship.com/facts-continental-army.
[36] Ibid.
[37] "The Fighting Man of the Continental Army." *American Battlefield Trust*. 2023. https://www.battlefields.org/learn/articles/fighting-man-continental-army.
[38] Ibid.
[39] Ibid.
[40] Ibid.
[41] Ibid.
[42] "The Fighting Man of the Continental Army." *American Battlefield Trust*. And "Continental Army Historical Facts." *Boston Tea Party Ships and Museum*.
[43] Ibid.
[44] Washington, George. "General Orders, 2 October 1779." Founders Online. *National Archives and Records Administration*. https://founders.archives.gov/documents/Washington/03-22-02-0489.
[45] "The Fighting Man of the Continental Army." *American Battlefield Trust*.
[46] Ney, Diane. Pg.107.
[47] Ibid.
[48] Matheny, Mike. "The Predicament we are in: How Paperwork Saved the Continental Army." *American Journal of the Revolution*. May 3, 2021. https://allthingsliberty.com/2021/05/the-predicament-we-are-in-how-paperwork-saved-the-continental-army/.
[49] "The Fighting Man of the Continental Army." *American Battlefield Trust*.
[50] Ibid.
[51] Greenwalt, Phillip S. "George Washington's Integrated Army."
[52] Partin, Elliot. "1st Rhode Island Regiment." *Black Past*. Nov. 17, 2010. https://www.blackpast.org/african-american-history/first-rhode-island-regimenthttps://www.blackpast.org/african-american-history/first-rhode-island-regiment.
[53] Ibid.
[54] "Act creating the 1st Rhode Island Regiment, also known as the 'Black Regiment', 1778." Rhode Island State Archives, C#0210 – Acts & Resolves of the General Assembly, Vol. 17 #14.

https://docs.sos.ri.gov/documents/civicsandeducation/teacherresources/Black-Regiment.pdf.
[55] Ibid.
[56] Ibid.
[57] Ibid.
[58] "Rhode Island." *American Battlefield Trust*. 2023. https://www.battlefields.org/learn/revolutionary-war/battles/rhode-island.
[59] Aikey, Michael. "Ballston Raid of 1780." *Journal of the American Revolution*. Dec. 6, 2017. https://allthingsliberty.com/2017/12/ballston-raid-1780-military-operation-time-settle-old-scores.
[60] Ibid.
[61] Makos, Isaac. "Roles of Native Americans during the Revolution." *American Battlefield Trust*. Original: Jan. 21, 2021; Updated: April 13, 2021. https://www.battlefields.org/learn/articles/roles-native-americans-during-revolution.
[62] Aikey, Michael. "Ballston Raid of 1780."
[63] Ibid.
[64] "Battle of Cobleskill." *Mohawk Valley Region Path Through History*. https://www.mohawkvalleyhistory.com/destinations/listing/Battle-of-Cobleskill.
[65] Schenawolf, Harry. "Battle of Wyoming – American Defeat or Massacre?" July 12, 2021. *Revolutionary War Journal*. https://www.revolutionarywarjournal.com/battle-of-wyoming-american-defeat-or-massacre/.
[66] Ibid.
[67] "The Clinton-Sullivan Campaign of 1779." *National Park Service*. Last updated: April 17, 2022. United States Department of the Interior. www.nps.gov/articles/000/the-clinton-sullivan-campaign-of-1779.htm.
[68] "The Clinton-Sullivan Campaign of 1779." *National Park Service*.
[69] Greene, Nelson, Ed. "History of the Mohawk Valley: Gateway to the West 1614-1925." Chapter 69: Johnson's Great Raid. S.J. Clarke Publishing Co.: New York. 1925.
[70] Ibid.
[71] Ibid.
[72] Fernandez, Juan Miguel. "Connecticut Raids." *George Washington's Mount Vernon*. 2023. https://www.mountvernon.org/library/digitalhistory/digital-encyclopedia/article/connecticut-raids/.
[73] Ibid.
[74] "The American Revolution." George Washington Papers. *Library of Congress*. https://www.loc.gov/collections/george-washington-papers/articles-and-essays/timeline/the-american-revolution/.
[75] Fernandez, Juan Miguel. "Connecticut Raids."
[76] "Washington's Encampment at Morristown, New Jersey and the 'Hard Winter' of 1779-1780." *American Battlefield Trust*. 2023. https://www.battlefields.org/learn/articles/washingtons-encampment-morristown-new-jersey-and-hard-winter-1779-1780.
[77] Ibid.
[78] Ibid.

[79] Qtd. "The Encampment at Morristown: Summary and Quotes." *National Park Service*. United States Department of the Interior. Last updated: Sept. 24, 2022. https://www.nps.gov/morr/learn/historyculture/encampment-summary.htm.
[80] "Washington's Encampment at Morristown, New Jersey and the 'Hard Winter' of 1779-1780." *American Battlefield Trust*.
[81] "Morristown." *National Park Service*. United States Department of the Interior. Last updated: Nov. 23, 2022. http://npshistory.com/publications/morr/index.htm.
[82] Seidel, Maria. "Morristown, NJ." *George Washington's Mount Vernon*. 2023. https://www.mountvernon.org/library/digitalhistory/digital-encyclopedia/article/morristown-nj/.

Endnotes
Chapter 5: INDEPENDENCE

[1] Capitaine Du Chesnoy, M. & Lafayette, M. J. P. Y. R. G. D. M. (1781) Campagne en Virginie du Major Général M'is de LaFayette: ou se trouvent les camps et marches, ainsy que ceux du Lieutenant Général Lord Cornwallis en. [Map] Retrieved from the Library of Congress. Free to use and reuse collection. https://www.loc.gov/item/00558784/.
[2] Qtd. "Siege of Charleston 1780." *National Park Service*. United States Department of the Interior. Last updated: March 30, 2021. https://www.nps.gov/articles/siege-of-charleston-1780.htm.
[3] Ibid. And "Cowpens." *American Battlefield Trust*. 2023. https://www.battlefields.org/learn/articles/cowpens.
[4] "Revolutionary War: Southern Phase, 1778-1781." *Library of Congress*. www.loc.gov/classroom-materials/united-states-history-primary-source-timeline/american-revolution-1763-1783/revolutionary-war-southern-phase-1778-1781/.
[5] "The American Revolution." George Washington Papers. *Library of Congress*. And "Siege of Charleston 1780." *Library of Congress*.
[6] Andrlik. Pg. 275.
[7] Ibid.
[8] McBrayer, Rachel. "Southern Strategy." *George Washington's Mount Vernon*. 2023. https://www.mountvernon.org/library/digitalhistory/digital-encyclopedia/article/southern-strategy/.
[9] Washington, George. "George Washington to Gouverneur Morris, May 8, 1779." *Library of Congress*. https://www.loc.gov/resource/mgw3h.001/?sp=281&st=text.
[10] Ibid.
[11] Scott, Joseph C. "Siege of Charleston - 1780." *George Washington's Mount Vernon*. 2023. www.mountvernon.org/library/digitalhistory/digital-encyclopedia/article/siege-of-charleston--1780/.
[12] "Siege of Charleston 1780." *National Park Service*.
[13] Scott, Joseph C. "Siege of Charleston - 1780."
[14] Ibid. And "Siege of Charleston 1780." *National Park Service*.
[15] Andrlik. Pg. 278.
[16] Andrlik. Pg. 278.

[17] Andrlik. Pg. 286.
[18] "The American Revolution." George Washington Papers. *Library of Congress.*
[19] "Camden." *American Battlefield Trust.* 2023. https://www.battlefields.org/learn/articles/camden.
[20] Ibid.
[21] "The American Revolution." George Washington Papers. *Library of Congress.*
[22] Ibid.
[23] Uva, Katie. "Benedict Arnold." *George Washington's Mount Vernon.* 2023. https://www.mountvernon.org/library/digitalhistory/digital-encyclopedia/article/benedict-arnold/.
[24] "Major John André and Brigadier General Benedict Arnold." *Library of Congress.* Today In History – October 2. https://www.loc.gov/item/today-in-history/october-02.
[25] "Spy Letters of the American Revolution – Timeline." *William M. Clements Library.* University of Michigan. 2023. https://clements.umich.edu/exhibit/spy-letters-of-the-american-revolution/timeline/#1780.
[26] Qtd. "Major John André and Brigadier General Benedict Arnold." *Library of Congress.* Today In History – October 2. https://www.loc.gov/item/today-in-history/october-02.
[27] Andrlik. Pg. 296.
[28] History.com Editors. "Benedict Arnold captures and destroys Richmond." HISTORY. *A&E Television Networks.* Original: Nov. 13, 2009; Updated: Jan. 4, 2021. https://www.history.com/this-day-in-history/benedict-arnold-captures-and-destroys-richmond.
[29] Ney. Pg. 213.
[30] Andrlik. Pg. 290.
[31] Qtd. "Over Mountain Victory." *National Park Service.* United States Department of the Interior. Last updated: Sept. 16, 2021. https://www.nps.gov/blri/learn/historyculture/overmountain-men.htm.
[32] Andrlik. Pg. 290.
[33] Ney. Pg. 213.
[34] Ibid.
[35] Qtd. Andrlik. Pg. 292.
[36] Qtd. Ney. Pg. 212. And "The Battle of Kings Mountain: A Story of Memories". *American Battlefield Trust.* Original: Oct. 6, 2020; Updated Feb. 14, 2023. https://www.battlefields.org/learn/articles/battle-kings-mountain-story-memories.
[37] "Siege of Charleston 1780." *National Park Service.*
[38] Ney. Pg. 215.
[39] Ibid.
[40] Andrlik. Pg. 282.
[41] "Cowpens." *American Battlefield Trust.*
[42] "The American Revolution." George Washington Papers. *Library of Congress.*
[43] Ibid.
[44] "Cowpens." *American Battlefield Trust.*
[45] Ibid.
[46] Ibid.
[47] Qtd. Andrlik. Pg. 306.

[48] Ibid.
[49] Ibid.
[50] Ney. Pg. 168.
[51] "Guilford Courthouse." *American Battlefield Trust*. 2003. www.battlefields.org/learn/revolutionary-war/battles/guilford-court-house.
[52] Ibid.
[53] Ibid.
[54] Andrlik. Pg. 314.
[55] Ney. Pg. 216. And "Ninety Six." *American Battlefield Trust*. 2023. https://www.battlefields.org/learn/articles/ninety-six.
[56] Andrlik. Pg. 328-9.
[57] Qtd. Andrlik. Pg. 329.
[58] Washington, George. "George Washington to Anthony Wayne, November 27, 1780." *Library of Congress*. https://www.loc.gov/resource/mgw3b.012/?sp=377&st=text.
[59] Matheny, Mike. "'The Predicament We Are In': How Paperwork Saved the Continental Army." *Journal of the American Revolution*. May 3, 2021. https://allthingsliberty.com/2021/05/the-predicament-we-are-in-how-paperwork-saved-the-continental-army/.
[60] Ibid. And "History of the Treasury." *United States Department of the Treasury*. https://home.treasury.gov/about/history/history-overview/history-of-the-treasury.
[61] Ibid.
[62] Adams, Jonathan. "Department of the Treasury." *George Washington's Mount Vernon*. 2023. https://www.mountvernon.org/library/digitalhistory/digital-encyclopedia/article/department-of-the-treasury/.
[63] Matheny, Mike. "'The Predicament We Are In': How Paperwork Saved the Continental Army."
[64] Ibid. And Ney. Pg. 257.
[65] Leepson, Marc. "George Washington and the Marquis de Lafayette." *George Washington's Mount Vernon*. 2023. https://www.mountvernon.org/library/digitalhistory/digital-encyclopedia/article/george-washington-and-the-marquis-de-lafayette/. And Stockwell, Mary PhD. "Baron von Steuben." *George Washington's Mount Vernon*. 2023. https://www.mountvernon.org/library/digitalhistory/digital-encyclopedia/article/baron-von-steuben/.
[66] "The Battle of Petersburg." *Revolutionary War.us*. 2017. https://revolutionarywar.us/year-1781/battle-of-petersburg/.
[67] "Lafayette and the Virginia Campaign 1781." *National Park Service*. Unites States Department of the Interior. Last updated: Feb. 26, 2015. https://www.nps.gov/york/learn/historyculture/lafayette-and-the-virginia-campaign-1781.
[68] Qtd. Ibid.
[69] Andrlik. Pg. 332.
[70] "Yorktown National Battlefield." Park Net. *National Park Service*. United States Department of the Interior. Last Modified: Dec. 2, 2002. https://www.nps.gov/parkhistory/online_books/hh/14/hh14f.htm.

[71] "Yorktown National Battlefield." Park Net. *National Park Service.*
[72] "History of the Siege." Yorktown Battlefield. *National Park Service.* United States Department of the Interior. Last updated: Feb. 26, 2015. https://www.nps.gov/york/learn/historyculture/history-of-the-siege.htm.
[73] Andrlik. Pg. 334.
[74] "History of the Siege." Yorktown Battlefield. *National Park Service.*
[75] Ibid.
[76] Ibid.
[77] Ibid.
[78] Qtd. "Yorktown National Battlefield." Park Net. *National Park Service.* And Ney. Pg. 258.
[79] Ibid.
[80] Washington, George. "From George Washington to Thomas McKean, 19 October 1781." Founders Online. *National Archives and Records Administration.* https://founders.archives.gov/documents/Washington/99-01-02-07206.
[81] "Yorktown." *American Battlefield Trust.* 2023. https://www.battlefields.org/learn/revolutionary-war/battles/yorktown.
[82] "Treaty of Paris, 1783." *United States Department of State.* Office of the Historian. https://history.state.gov/milestones/1776-1783/treaty.
[83] "The Definitive Treaty of Peace 1783." *National Archives and Records Administration.* https://www.archives.gov/milestone-documents/treaty-of-paris.
[84] Ibid.
[85] Ibid.
[86] Ibid.
[87] Washington, George. "George Washington Papers, Series 3, Varick Transcripts, 1775 to 1785, Subseries 3G, General Orders, 1775 to 1783, Letterbook 7: Jan. 1, 1783." Manuscript/Mixed Material. *Library of Congress.* https://www.loc.gov/item/mgw3g.007/.
[88] History.com Editors. "Last British Soldiers Leave New York." HISTORY. *A&E Television Networks.* Original: Nov. 13, 2009; Updated: Nov. 23, 2020. www.history.com/this-day-in-history/last-british-soldiers-leave-new-york-2.
[89] Adams, John. Letter from John Adams to Abigail Adams, 26 April 1777. Adams Family Papers: An Electronic Archive. *Massachusetts Historical Society.* https://www.masshist.org/digitaladams/archive/doc?id=L17770426ja.

Endnotes
Chapter 6: VISION

[1] Wheatley, Phillis, et al. Poems on Various Subjects, Religious and Moral. [London: Printed for A. Bell, bookseller, Aldgate and sold by Messrs. Cox and Berry ... Boston, MDCCLXXIII, 1773] Image. Retrieved from the Library of Congress. Free to use and reuse collection. www.loc.gov/item/30020911/.
[2] Douglass, Frederick. "July 5, 1852, address to the Rochester Ladies' Anti-Slavery Society in Rochester, New York." *National Endowment for the Humanities.* https://edsitement.neh.gov/student-activities/frederick-douglasss-what-slave-fourth-july#:~:text.

[3] *The Votes and Proceedings of the Freeholders and Other Inhabitants of the Town of Boston*. Boston, MA: Printed by Edes and Gill, in Queen Street, and T. and J. Fleet, in Cornhill, 1772. Pg. 2. *Historical Society of Massachusetts*. https://www.masshist.org/database/viewer.
[4] Ibid.
[5] Jefferson, Thomas. *A Summary View of the Rights of British America*. Thomas Jefferson Library Collection. *Library of Congress*. Williamsburg, VA: Clementina Rind, 1774. Pg. 11. https://tile.loc.gov/storage-services/service/rbc/rbc0001/2003/2003jeff16823/2003jeff16823.pdf.
[6] "The Revolutionary Writings of Alexander Hamilton." Qtd. From "A Full Vindication of the Measures of Congress (1774)" by Alexander Hamilton. *Online Library of Liberty*. 2023. https://oll.libertyfund.org/title/appleby-the-revolutionary-writings-of-alexander-hamilton.
[7] "Boston, April 20th, 1773. Sir, The efforts made by the legislative [sic] of this province..." Circular letter signed 'In behalf of our fellow slaves in this province, and by order of their committee ...' *Historical Society of Massachusetts*. https://www.masshist.org/database/viewer.php?item_id=443&mode=large&img_step=1&&pid=2&br=1.
[8] Ibid.
[9] "Petition for freedom to Massachusetts Governor Thomas Gage, His Majesty's Council, and the House of Representatives, 25 May 1774." From the Jeremy Belknap papers. *Historical Society of Massachusetts*. https://www.masshist.org/database/viewer.php?item_id=549&mode=large&img_step=1&&pid=4&br=1.
[10] Ibid.
[11] Zielinski, Adam E. "Fighting For Freedom: African Americans Choose Sides During the American Revolution." Original: Nov. 30, 2020; Updated: Aug. 24, 2021. *American Battlefield Trust*. www.battlefields.org/learn/articles/fighting-freedom-african-americans-during-american-revolution.
[12] Ibid.
[13] "Give Me Liberty: African Americans in the Revolutionary War." Adapted from *Give Me Liberty: African Americans in the Revolutionary War*, a temporary exhibition in 2020. *George Washington's Mount Vernon*. 2023. https://www.mountvernon.org/george-washington/the-revolutionary-war/african-americans-in-the-revolutionary-war/.
[14] Collins, Elizabeth M. "Black Soldiers in the Revolutionary War." March 4, 2013. *U.S. Army*. www.army.mil/article/97705/black_soldiers_in_the_revolutionary_war.
[15] Schenawolf, Henry. "African Americans in the American Revolution: Black Soldiers' Did Not Quit Whose Percentage was Much Higher than Previously Reported." *Revolutionary War Journal*. Oct. 14, 2018. https://revolutionarywarjournal.com/arm-negroes-to-the-principles-of-liberty-never-to-be-lost-in-a-contest-for-liberty-the-black-presence-in-the-american-revolutionary-army-was-much-larger-than-what-weve-tho/.
[16] Ibid.
[17] Ibid.

[18] "Black Revolutionary Seamen." Africans in America. *PBS Online.* https://www.pbs.org/wgbh/aia/part2/2p51.html.
[19] Ibid.
[20] "Lord Dunmore's Proclamation, 1775." *The Gilder Lehrman Institute of American History.* https://www.gilderlehrman.org/history-resources/spotlight-primary-source/lord-dunmores-proclamation-1775.
[21] Ibid.
[22] "Journals of the Continental Congress - The Articles of Association; October 20, 1774." Article 2. Edited from the original records in the Library of Congress by Worthington Chauncey Ford; Chief, Division of Manuscripts, Washington, DC: Government Printing Office, 1905. Avalon Project. Lilian Goldman Law Library. *Yale Law School.* https://avalon.law.yale.edu/18th_century/contcong_10-20-74.asp.
[23] Boyd, Julian P. Boyd, Ed. *The Papers of Thomas Jefferson.* Vol. 1, 1760-1776. Princeton: Princeton University Press, 1950, pp 243-247. Library of Congress. https://www.loc.gov/exhibits/declara/ruffdrft.html.
[24] "Did You Know: Women and African Americans Could Vote in NJ before the 15th and 19th Amendments?" *National Park Service.* United States Department of the Interior. Updated: July 3, 2018. https://www.nps.gov/articles/voting-rights-in-nj-before-the-15th-and-19th.htm.
[25] Constitution of Maryland - November 11, 1776. Article II. Avalon Project. Lilian Goldman Law Library. *Yale Law School.* Original source: The Federal and State Constitutions Colonial Charters, and Other Organic Laws of the States, Territories, and Colonies Now or Heretofore Forming the United States of America Compiled and Edited Under the Act of Congress of June 30, 1906, by Francis Newton Thorpe Washington, DC: Government Printing Office, 1909. https://avalon.law.yale.edu/17th_century/ma02.asp.
[26] Vermont Constitution – 1777. Chapter 1, Articles II and VIII. *Vermont Secretary of State.* https://sos.vermont.gov/vsara/learn/constitution/1777-constitution/#:~:text.
[27] The Constitution of New York: April 20, 1777. Article VII. Avalon Project. Lilian Goldman Law Library. *Yale Law School.* Original source: The Federal and State Constitutions Colonial Charters, and Other Organic Laws of the States, Territories, and Colonies Now or Heretofore Forming the United States of America Compiled and Edited Under the Act of Congress of June 30, 1906, by Francis Newton Thorpe Washington, DC: Government Printing Office, 1909. https://avalon.law.yale.edu/18th_century/ny01.asp.
[28] "Quaker Activism." History Detectives. *Oregon Public Broadcasting System.* 2003-2014. https://www.pbs.org/opb/historydetectives/feature/quaker-activism/#:~:text=.
[29] Cannon, Alexandria. "Gradual Abolition Act of 1780." *George Washington's Mount Vernon.* 2023. www.mountvernon.org/library/digitalhistory/digital-encyclopedia/article/gradual-abolition-act-of-1780.
[30] "Massachusetts Constitution and the Abolition of Slavery." *Commonwealth of Massachusetts.* 2023. https://www.mass.gov/guides/massachusetts-constitution-and-the-abolition-of-slavery#:~:text.

[31] Letter from Abigail Adams to John Adams, 22 September 1774. Adams Family Papers. *Massachusetts Historical Society*. https://www.masshist.org/digitaladams/archive/.
[32] "Massachusetts Constitution and the Abolition of Slavery." *Commonwealth of Massachusetts*. 2023. https://www.mass.gov/guides/massachusetts-constitution-and-the-abolition-of-slavery#:~:text.
[33] Ibid.
[34] Partin, Elliot. "1st Rhode Island Regiment." *Black Past*. Nov. 17, 2010. https://www.blackpast.org/african-american-history/first-rhode-island-regimenhttps://www.blackpast.org/african-american-history/first-rhode-island-regiment.
[35] Collins, Elizabeth M.
[36] Fitzpatrick, Siobhan. "John Laurens." *George Washington's Mount Vernon*. 2023. www.mountvernon.org/library/digitalhistory/digital-encyclopedia/article/john-laurens/.
[37] Hamilton, Alexander. "Alexander Hamilton to John Jay, March 14, 1779." The Papers of Alexander Hamilton, ed. Harold C. Syrett. New York, NY: Columbia University Press, 1961. Vol. 2. Pgs. 17-19. Accessed at https://shec.ashp.cuny.edu/items/show/674.
[38] Ibid.
[39] Schenawolf, Henry.
[40] Ibid.
[41] Ibid.
[42] "African American Service during the Revolution." *American Battlefield Trust*. 2023. https://www.battlefields.org/learn/articles/african-american-service-during-revolutionhttps://www.battlefields.org/learn/articles/african-american-service-during-revolution. See also Collins, Elizabeth M. and Schenawolf, Henry.
[43] "The Philipsburg Proclamation (June 30, 1779)." The American Revolution. *Colonial Williamsburg*. 2023. https://www.ouramericanrevolution.org/index.cfm/page/view/p0422.
[44] "The Phillipsburg Proclamation, 1779." *The Bill of Rights Institute*. 2023. https://billofrightsinstitute.org/activities/the-phillipsburg-proclamation-1779.
[45] Ibid.
[46] "The Philipsburg Proclamation (June 30, 1779)."
[47] Ibid.
[48] Ibid.
[49] "George Washington, October 25, 1781, General Orders." George Washington Papers. *Library of Congress*. https://www.loc.gov/resource/mgw3g.006/?sp=67.
[50] "The Definitive Treaty of Peace 1783." Article 7th. *National Archives and Records Administration*. https://www.archives.gov/milestone-documents/treaty-of-paris.
[51] "The Revolutionary War." Africans in America. *PBS Online*. https://www.pbs.org/wgbh/aia/part2/2narr4.html#:~:text.
[52] Lincoln, Abraham. "Speech on the Declaration of Independence at Lewiston, Illinois on August 17, 1858." *National Park Service*. United States Department of the Interior. https://www.nps.gov/liho/learn/historyculture/declaration.htm.

Patriot Stories Works Cited

All Patriot Stories include information from: National Society Daughters of the American Revolution. "Ancestor Database." Genealogical Research System. Accessed 2023. https://services.dar.org/public/dar_research/.

Patriot Stories Works Cited
Chapter 1: RESOLVE

Eliakim Weller A214108
- "Weller Family." *The American Genealogist*. New England Historic Genealogical Society. Pgs. 145-6. Accessed at AmericanAncestors.org.
- Vail, William Penn M.D. *Moses Vail of Huntington, L.I.; Showing his Descent from Joseph Vail, son of Thomas Vail at Salem Massachusetts 1640*. Blairstown, NJ: 1947. Pg. 241. Accessed at Ancestry.com
- Deed: Manchester, VT, 1769. Accessed at FamilySearch.org.
- Aldrich, Lewis Cass. *History of Bennington Co, VT*. Syracuse, NY: D. Mason & Co., 1889. Pgs. 55, 346-9, 355-358. Accessed at Google Books.
- Smith, Richard B. *Ethan Allen & the Capture of Fort Ticonderoga*. Arcadia Publishing, 2010. Pgs. 65-66, 79-80.
- Plaque from Weller Tavern. www.josiahallen.com/listing/4650923/3116-route-7a-manchester-vt-05254/.
- National Register of Historic Places Inventory. *National Park Service*. United States Department of the Interior. 1983. https://npgallery.nps.gov/GetAsset/066492f8-3ce8-4bf1-9b96-1f98ac3f2911.
- Probate Manchester, Bennington Co, VT. Oct. 10, 1780, Eliakim Weller. Accessed at FamilySearch.org.
- Photo courtesy of Manchester Historical Society.

Captain Edward Converse A025168
- Converse, Charles Allen, Comp. and Ed. *Some of the Ancestors and Descendants of Samuel Converse*. Vol. 1. Pgs. 53-54. Boston, MA: Eben Putnam Publisher. And Salem, MA: Salem Press, Co., 1905. Accessed at Google Books.
- Lockwood, Rev. John H. et. al., Ed. *Western Massachusetts A History 1636-1925*. Vol. II. Boston, MA and Chicago, IL: Lewis Historical Publishing Company Inc., 1926. Pgs. 555-556. Accessed at Google Books.

Richard Langhorn (Clarke) Clark A134150
- Beitzell, Ewin Warfield. "St. Mary's County, Maryland in the American Revolution: calendar of events." Leonardtown, MD: St. Mary's County, Maryland Bicentennial Commission, 1975. Pgs. 44, 79, 125, 126.
- Flaherty, Carol Gibson. *Following a Kentucky Trace*. 2nd Ed. Author Published, 1999. Pgs. 92, 94.

- O'Rourke, Timothy J. *Catholic Families of Southern Maryland: Records of Catholic Residents of St. Mary's County in the Eighteenth Century*. Baltimore, MD: Genealogical Publishing Company, 1985. Pg. 78.
- Editors, History.com. "The Settlement of Maryland." HISTORY. *A&E Television Networks*. www.history.com/this-day-in-history/the-settlement-of-maryland.
- Papenfuse, Edward C., et. al. "A Biographical Dictionary of the Maryland Legislature 1635 – 1789 John Allen Thomas." *Maryland State Archives*. www.msa.maryland.gov/megafile/msa/speccol/sc3500/.
- "Committees of Correspondence." *Boston Tea Party, Ships & Museum*. www.bostonteapartyship.com/committees-of-correspondence.
- "Declaration and Resolves of the First Continental Congress." First Continental Congress. Oct. 14, 1774. Government Printing Office, 1927. House Document No. 398. Selected, Arranged and Indexed by Charles C. Tansill. www.avalon.law.yale.edu/18th_century/resolves.asp.
- Treesh, Catherine. "Committees of Correspondence." *George Washington's Mount Vernon*. 2023. https://www.mountvernon.org/library/digitalhistory/digital-encyclopedia/article/committees-of-correspondence/.
- Editors, History.com. "Committees of Correspondence." HISTORY. *A&E Television Networks*. www.history.com/topics/american-revolution/committees-of-correspondence.

Major Hezekiah Smith A105490
- *Massachusetts Soldiers and Sailors of the Revolutionary War*. Vol. 14. Prepared by the Secretary of the Commonwealth. Boston, MA: Wright 7 Potter Printing Co., 1908. Pg. 412. Accessed at Ancestry.com.
- Patrie, Lois McClennan. *A History of Colrain Massachusetts, with Genealogies of Early Families*. Higgonson Book Co., 1974. Pg. 75.
- McClellan, Charles H. *The Early Settlers of Colrain Massachusetts*. Speech. 1885. Reprinted by Heritage Books, 2011. Pgs. 82, 84.

Thomas Johnson A063768
- *William & Mary Quarterly*. Series 1. Vol. 5. Richmond, VA: Whittet & Shepperson, General Printers, 1897. Pg. 106. Accessed at Google Books.
- Harris, Malcom H. *A History of Louisa County, Virginia*. Genealogical Press, 1963. Pgs. 116 – 116D.
- Cooke, Patty. *Louisa County Virginia, A Brief History*. History Press, 2008. Pgs. 17-21.
- "Delegate Patrick Henry of Virginia." History, Art & Archives. *United States House of Representatives*. June 6, 1799. https://history.house.gov/Historical-Highlights/1700s/Delegate-Patrick-Henry-of-Virginia.

- "Give Me Liberty or Give Me Death!" *Colonial Williamsburg*. March 3, 2020. https://www.colonialwilliamsburg.org/learn/deep-dives/give-me-liberty-or-give-me-death/.

Captain John Fox A215188
- McAllister, J. T. *Virginia Militia in the Revolutionary War*. Hot Springs, VA: McAllister Publishing, Co., 1913. Pgs. 213-4. Library of Congress. https://www.loc.gov/item/13023910.
- Abercrombie, Janice L. and Richard Slatten, Comp. & Tr. *Virginia Revolutionary Publick [sic] Claims*. Vol II. Athens, GA: Iberian Publishing House, 1992. Pg. 625. Accessed at Library of Virginia online.
- "Virginia Legislative Papers (Continued)." *The Virginia Magazine of History and Biography*. Vol. 13, No. 1. July 1905. Pgs. 36-50. https://www.jstor.org/stable/4242723.
- Bentley, Elizabeth Petty. "Virginia Military Records." From the *Virginia Magazine of History and Biography, The William and Mary College Quarterly* and *Tyler's Quarterly*. Baltimore, MD: Genealogical Publishing Company, 1983. Pg. 467.
- "The Second Virginia Convention." Historic St. John's Church, 1741. https://saffron-fennel-ern6.squarespace.com/2nd-virginia-convention.
- "Virginia, Historical Society Papers, 1607-2007." *Virginia Historical Society*. Accessed at FamilySearch.org.
- Fox, James Wallace. "Fox Family." *The William and Mary Quarterly*. Vol. 26, No. 2. Oct. 1917. Published by Omohundro Institute of Early American History and Culture. Pgs. 129-138.
- "Fox Family of King William County, Va." *The William and Mary Quarterly*. Vol. 20, No. 4. April 1912. Published by Omohundro Institute of Early American History and Culture. Pgs. 262-266.

John Ragland A132445
- Abercrombie, Janice L. and Richard Slatten, Comp. & Tr. *Virginia Revolutionary Publick [sic] Claims*. Vol II. Athens, GA: Iberian Publishing House, 1992. Pg. 627. Accessed at Library of Virginia online.
- "Getting Food in the Continental Army." *American Battlefield Trust*. 2023. https://www.battlefields.org/learn/articles/getting-food-continental-army.
- "Virginia Legislative Papers (Continued)." *The Virginia Magazine of History and Biography*. Vol. 13, No. 1. July 1905. Pgs. 36-50. https://www.jstor.org/stable/4242723.
- "The Second Virginia Convention." Historic St. John's Church, 1741. https://saffron-fennel-ern6.squarespace.com/2nd-virginia-convention.
- "Historical and Genealogical: Ragland-Hopson or Hobson." *The Constitution" Atlanta, GA*. Oct. 13, 1901. Pg. 32.

- "General Orders, 8 August 1775." Founders Online. *National Archives and Records Administration.* https://founders.archives.gov/documents/Washington/03-01-02-0173.

Patriot Stories Works Cited
Chapter 2: DECLARATION

Captain Abraham Winsor A128863
- Smith, Joseph Jencks, Comp. *Civil & Militia Lists of Rhode Island, 1647-1800.* Vol. 1. Providence, RI: Preston & Rounds Co., 1900. Pgs. 367, 377. Accessed at Ancestry.com.
- Robertson, John K. "The Organization of the Rhode Island Militia 1774–1783." *Journal of the American Revolution.* Jan. 13, 2016. www.allthingsliberty.com/2016/01/the-organization-of-the-rhode-island-militia-1774-1783/.
- *Yearbook of the Sons of the Revolution in the State of New York.* Sons of the Revolution in New York, 1899. Pg. 263. Accessed at Google Books.
- Perry, Elizabeth A. *A Brief History of the Town of Glocester, Rhode Island.* Providence, RI: Providence Press Company, 1886. Pgs. 18-9, 22. Accessed at Google Books.
- Photo courtesy of Nate Bramlett.

Private Burkhardt Musser A083545
- Linn, John B. and Egle, Dr. William Henry, Eds. *Pennsylvania Archives.* Second Series, Vol. 14. Pgs. 594, 625–627. Issued 1874-1890. Accessed at Ancestry.com.
- Montgomery, Dr. Thomas Lynch, Ed. *Pennsylvania Archives.* Fifth Series, Vol. 8. Pgs. 228, 504. Issued in 1906. Accessed at Ancestry.com.
- "Northampton County Revolutionary War Militia." *Pennsylvania Historical & Museum Commission.* https://www.phmc.pa.gov/Archives/Research-Online/Pages/Revolutionary-War-Militia-Northampton.aspx.
- Mott, Anita L. *Mosser/Musser Family.* Westminster, MD: Heritage Books, 2008.
- Mattfeld, Walter R. "Some Descendants of Johann Christian Moser of Berks County, Pennsylvania." *The American Genealogist.* Pgs. 62, 82–88.
- Weiser, Frederick S., Tr. *The Record Book of Daniel Schumacher.* Camden, ME: Picton Press, 1993.
- Oswald, Rev. Charles E. C. *The Descendants of Henry Oswald.* New York, 1907. Accessed at Ancestry.com.
- Fox, Francis S. *Sweet Land of Liberty: The Ordeal of The American Revolution in Northampton County, Pennsylvania.* University Park, PA: Pennsylvania State University Press, 2000.

Private David Haskell A052362
- U.S., Revolutionary War Pension and Bounty Land Warrant Application Files, 1800-1900. Haskell, David. S*W7650. Accessed at Fold3.com.
- Child, William. *History of the town of Cornish, New Hampshire with Genealogical Record*. Concord, NH: Rumford Press, 1911. Pg. 72. Accessed at Google Books.
- Kidder, Frederic. *History of the 1st New Hampshire Regiment in the War of the Revolution*. Albany, NY: Joel Munsell, 1808. Pg. 164. Accessed at Google Books.
- Hammond, Isaac Weare, Ed. *Town Papers. Documents Relating to Towns in New Hampshire*. Vol. 11. Pgs. 438-439, 445-446. New Hampshire State Papers. https://scholars.unh.edu/propapers/.
- All Massachusetts, U.S., Compiled Birth, Marriage, and Death Records, 1700-1850. Online Database. Pg. 179. Accessed at Ancestry.com.
- The New England Historical and Genealogical Register. Online Database. Pg. 284. Accessed at Ancestry.com.

Corporal Jacob Barber A005849
- Johnston, Henry P., Ed. *The Record of Connecticut Men in the Military and Naval Service During the War of the Revolution 1775-1783*. Vol. I-III. Hartford, CT.: 1889. Pgs. 3,4, 21, 473. Accessed at Google Books.
- Barber, Donald S. M.D. *The Connecticut Barbers: a genealogy of the descendants of Thomas Barber of Windsor, Conn*. Middlefield, CT: Donald S. Barber, c1992. Pgs. 19-20.

Captain Eleazer Warner, Sr. A121074
- *Massachusetts Soldiers and Sailors of the Revolutionary War*. Vol. 16. Prepared by the Secretary of the Commonwealth. Boston, MA: Wright 7 Potter Printing Co., 1908. Pgs. 582-3. Accessed at Ancestry.com.
- Massachusetts Town and Vital Records, 1620-1988; Granby 1710-1900. Town Records. Pgs. 5, 7, 19, 29, 31, 36-38, 44-45, 59. Accessed at Ancestry.com.
- Massachusetts, U.S., Town and Vital Records, 1620-1988. Granby, Massachusetts. Town Records, with Births, Marriages, and Deaths. Pg. 866. Accessed at Ancestry.com.
- "Sword of a Massachusetts Minute Man." The American Revolution Institute. *The Society of the Cincinnati*. 2023. https://www.americanrevolutioninstitute.org/recent-acquisitions/minute-man-sword/. And "Benjamin Ruggles Woodbridge - Revolutionary War - Battle of Bunker Hill." *Liquisearch*. 2020. http://www.liquisearch.com/benjamin_ruggles_woodbridge/revolutionary_war/battle_of_bunker_hill. [Eleazer Warner, Sr. served in Colonel Benjamin Ruggles Woodbridge's Regiment in 1775.]

- "The Battle of Bunker Hill." The Coming of the American Revolution. *Massachusetts Historical Society*. 2020. www.masshist.org/revolution/bunkerhill.php.
- Goodway, Frank. "American Participants in the Battle of Saratoga." Original: Aug. 1997; Updated: Nov. 2012. http://saratoganygenweb.com/batlda.htm.
- Wilder, Justin E. *The Descendants of Harvey Wilder*. Goshen, IN: Justin E. Wilder, 1974. Printed by Light and Life Press, Winona Lake, IN. Pgs. 157-9.

Private David Glazier A045383
- Massachusetts Town Records, Hardwick, MA. Births. Pgs. 49 and 89; Marriage. Pg. 180. Accessed at Ancestry.com.
- Paige, Lucius. *History of Hardwick, Massachusetts*. Boston, MA: Houghton Mifflin Co., 1883. Pgs. 263-7, 383-4. Accessed at archive.org.
- Hibbard, George Sayre. *Rupert, Vermont: A History, Historical and Descriptive 1761-1898*. Rupert, VT: Tuttle Co., 1889. Pg. 12. Accessed at Archive.org.
- Hammond, Isaac Weare, Ed. *Rolls of the Soldiers in the Revolutionary War*. New Hampshire State Papers. *University of New Hampshire Scholars Repository*. Vol. 14. Pgs. 84-5. Vol. 15. Pgs. 223-5. https://scholars.unh.edu/propapers/14/.
- Vermont Vital Records, Death Certificates. David Glazier, Nov. 17, 1824. Sarah Glazier April 7, 1821. Manchester, Bennington, VT. Accessed at Ancestry.com.
- Fay, Orlin P. *Fay Genealogy: John Fay of Marlborough and His Descendants*. Cleveland, OH: J.B. Savage, 1898. Pgs. 21-22. Accessed at Ancestry.com.
- Levine, Rachel Scharf. *Captain Jacob Odell and Mary Millington of Manchester, VT*. 2003. Fairbanks, AK: Self-published, 2003. Pg. 33. Rachel Levine, PO Box 72349, Fairbanks, AK 99707. Also available at DAR Library.
- Batchellor, Albert Stillman. *Miscellaneous Revolutionary Documents of New Hampshire*. Manchester, NH: John B. Clarke Co., 1910. Pgs. 156-157. Accessed at Archive.org.

Private Ard Godfrey A045896
- *Massachusetts Soldiers and Sailors of the Revolutionary War*. Vol. 6. Prepared by the Secretary of the Commonwealth. Boston, MA: Wright 7 Potter Printing Co., 1908. Pg. 525. Accessed at Ancestry.com.
- U.S., Revolutionary War Pension and Bounty-Land Warrant Application Files, 1800-1900. Godfrey, Ard. *W14798. Accessed at Ancestry.com.
- "Pioneers of St. Anthony: Men Who Helped Build a City." *Minneapolis Daily Times*. May 20, 1899. Pg. 14. Accessed at Newspapers.com.

Commodore Thomas Truxtun A116510
- Clark, William Bell. *Naval Documents of the American Revolution*. Vol. 8. Washington, DC: Naval History Division, Dept. of the Navy, 1964-2005. Pg. 1024.

- Ferguson, Eugene S. "TRUXTUN of the CONSTELLATION." Baltimore, MD: The John Hopkins Press, 1956. Pgs. 52-59. www.penelope.uchicago.edu/Thayer/E/Gazetteer/People/Thomas_Truxtun/.
- Chisholm, Hugh, ed. "Truxtun, Thomas." *Encyclopædia Britannica*. Vol. 27, 11th ed. New York, NY: Cambridge University Press, 1911. Pg. 339.
- "Commodore Thomas Truxtun, USN. 1755-1822." www.navysite.de/people/ttruxtun.htm.
- "The Militia of the Sea Privateering in the American Revolution and the War of 1812." *American Battlefield Trust*. 2022. www.battlefields.org/learn/articles/militia-sea.
- Fryler, John. "Privateers in the American Revolution." *National Park Service*. United States Department of the Interior. Dec. 15, 2016. www.nps.gov/articles/privateers-in-the-american-revolution.htm.
- Editors, History.com. "Congress Authorizes Privateers to Attack British Vessels." HISTORY. *A&E Television Networks.* Original: Nov. 13, 2009; Updated: Apr. 1, 2021. www.history.com/this-day-in-history/congress-authorizes-privateers-to-attack-british-vessels.
- Klein, Christopher. "How a Rogue Navy of Private Ships Helped Win the American Revolution." HISTORY. *A&E Television Networks*. Sept. 10, 2020. www.history.com/news/american-privateers-revolutionary-war-private-navy.
- NCC Staff. "On this day, the name 'United States of America' becomes official." *National Constitution Center*. Sept. 9, 2021. www.constitutioncenter.org/interactive-constitution/blog/today-the-name-united-states-of-america-becomes-official.
- Truxtun, Thomas. "To Thomas Jefferson from Thomas Truxtun, 18, May 1801." *The Papers of Thomas Jefferson.* Vol. 34, *1* May–31 July 1801. ed. Barbara B. Oberg. Princeton University Press, 2007. Pgs. 138–140. www.founders.archives.gov/documents/Jefferson/01-34-02-0108.
- "Mount Vernon Truxtun Defender Bowl." *George Washington's Mount Vernon.* 2023. www.shops.mountvernon.org/products/mount-vernon-truxtun-defender-bowl.
- "1785: Observations on the Gulf Stream by Benjamin Franklin." *National Oceanic and Atmospheric Administration*. U.S. Department of Commerce https://oceanexplorer.noaa.gov/history/docs/gulf.htmlhttps://oceanexplorer.noaa.gov/history/docs/gulf.html.
- Portrait: Saint-Mémin, C. B. J. F. D. (1799) *Thomas Truxtun, head-and-shoulders portrait, right profile*. 1799. [Philadelphia:] [Photograph] Retrieved from the Library of Congress, https://www.loc.gov/item/2007676943/. No known restrictions.

Private Jonathan Hall A049847
- U.S., Revolutionary War Pension and Bounty-Land Warrant Application Files, 1800-1900. Hall, Jonathan. S*W23230. Accessed at Ancestry.com.

- "Revolutionary Cannons." AmRevNC, LLC., 2021-2023. https://amrevnc.com/revolutionary-cannons/.
- "Artillery." *American Revolution.org*. The JDN Group, LLC., 2014 – 2020. https://www.americanrevolution.org/artillery.php
- Find A Grave. Hall, Jonathan. Memorial 32567767. Includes transcription of "Revolutionary War Veteran," *Palladium Times*, June 3, 1941. Accessed at findagrave.com.

Private Charles Hilton A056408
- Hammond, Isaac Weare, Ed. *Rolls of the Soldiers in the Revolutionary War*. New Hampshire State Papers. *University of New Hampshire Scholars Repository*. Vol. 15, Pgs. 283, 285, 290-1. https://scholars.unh.edu/propapers/14/.
- "Quebec." *American Battlefields Trust*. 2023. www.battlefields.org/learn/revolutionary-war/battles/quebec.
- Desjardin, Thomas A. *Through a Howling Wilderness: Benedict Arnold's March to Quebec, 1775*. New York, NY: St. Martin's Press, 2006. Pg. 99.
- Kiger, Patrick J. "Battle of Quebec: When Benedict Arnold Tried to Invade Canada." HISTORY. *A&E Television Networks*. Original: Nov. 26, 2018; Updated: Sept. 29, 2021. www.history.com/news/benedict-arnold-canada-invasion-revolutionary-war.

Private Daniel Putnam A092404
- Child, William. *History of the town of Cornish, New Hampshire with Genealogical Record*. Concord, NH: Rumford Press, 1911. Pgs. 13, 18, 19, 61, 72, 77.
- Kidder, Frederic. *History of the First New Hampshire Regiment in the War of the Revolution*. Albany, NY: Joel Munsell, 1808. Pg. 164. Accessed at Google Books.
- Hammond, Isaac Weare, Ed. *Rolls of the Soldiers in the Revolutionary War*. Vol. 14. Pgs. 264, 265, 607, 608. Vol. 16. Pgs. 223, 267, 269. New Hampshire State Papers. https://scholars.unh.edu/propapers/.

Private Nathaniel Webster A121332
- U.S., Compiled Revolutionary War Military Service Records, 1775-1783. Webster, Nathaniel. Pgs. 2224-7. Accessed at Ancestry.com.
- New Hampshire, U.S., Revolutionary War Records, 1675-1835. List of Captain Everit's [sic] Company in Colonel Bedel's Regiment. Pg. 590. Accessed at Ancestry.com.
- New Hampshire, U.S., Marriage Records, 1700-1971. Pg. 3233. Accessed at Ancestry.com.

- Hammond, Isaac Weare, Ed. Part I. Rolls and documents relating to soldiers in the revolutionary war. Part II. Miscellaneous provincial papers from 1629 to 1725. Volume IV of the war rolls. Volume XVII of the series. Provincial and State Papers. List of Captain Tolton's [sic] Company in Colonel Bedel's Regiment. Pg. 251. Manchester, NH: John B. Clarke, Public Printer, 1889. https://scholars.unh.edu/propapers/17.
- Wheeler, Sandra L., Form. "Guide to the Timothy Bedel Papers, 1763-1787." Collection Number 1880.001. *New Hampshire Historical Society*. https://www.nhhistory.org/finding_aids/finding_aids/Bedel_Timothy_Papers_1880.001.pdf.
- Scott, Joseph C. "Battle of White Plains." *George Washington's Mount Vernon*. 2022. www.mountvernon.org/library/digitalhistory/digital-encyclopedia/article/battle-of-white-plains/.
- Goodway, Frank. "American Participants in the Battle of Saratoga." Original: Aug. 1997; Updated Nov. 2012. http://saratoganygenweb.com/batlwe.htm.
- U.S. Revolutionary War Rolls, 1775-1783. Webster, Abell. Pg. 109. Labeled Valley Forge. Accessed at Ancestry.com.

Captain Thomas Alexander A001253
- Mackenzie, George Norbury. *Colonial Families of the United States of America, Volume VI.* Originally seven volumes, 1912. Reprinted Baltimore, MD: Genealogical Publishing Co. Inc., 1995. Pgs. 19-20. Accessed at Ancestry.com.
- Temple, J. H. and Sheldon, George. *A History of the Town of Northfield, Massachusetts*. Albany, NY: Joel Munsell, 1875. Pgs. 303, 388. Accessed at Google Books.
- *Massachusetts Soldiers and Sailors of the Revolutionary War*. Vol. 10. Prepared by the Secretary of the Commonwealth. Boston, MA: Wright 7 Potter Printing Co., 1908. Pg. 77. Accessed at FamilySearch.org.
- *North America, Family Histories, 1500-2000*. DAR Lineage Book. National Society Daughter of the American Revolution. 1917-1918. Vol. 137. Pg. 268. Lineage papers for Miss Florence Margaret Alexander. Accessed at Ancestry.com.
- Find A Grave. Alexander, Mary Lyman. Memorial 33556039. Accessed at Findagrave.com.
- *Journals of the House of Representatives of Massachusetts 1779*. Vol. 55. Original from University of Michigan. Digitized by Google. Pgs. 35, 221. https://www.sec.state.ma.us/arc/arcdigitalrecords/housejournals.htm.
- New Hampshire, U.S. Birth Records, 1631-1920. Azubah Alexander born 1778. Accessed at Ancestry.com.
- Passenger and Immigration Index, 1500s-1900. Alexander, George/John. Accessed at Ancestry.com.
- Photo courtesy of Mary Helen Ellison Peterson.

Private Hugh (Osborne) Osborn A084449
- *Massachusetts Soldiers and Sailors of the Revolutionary War*. Vol. 11. Osborn, Osborne; Osburn; Osburne, George. Osborne; Osbourne; Osbun, Hugh. Prepared by the Secretary of the Commonwealth. Boston, MA: Wright 7 Potter Printing Co., 1908. Pgs. 686, 687, 690, 692, 693, 696. Accessed at Ancestry.com.
- U.S., Revolutionary War Pension and Bounty-Land Warrant Application Files, 1800-1900. Osbourne, Hugh. S*W6889. Accessed at Ancestry.com.
- Bolander, Louis H. *The Frigate Alliance: The Favorite Ship of the American Revolution*. Vol. 63/9/415. Sept. 1937. *U.S. Naval Institute*. www.usni.org/magazines/proceedings/1937/september/frigate-alliance-favorite-ship-american-revolution https:.
- Kellogg, Lucy Mary. *Mayflower Families Through Five Generations: Descendants of the Pilgrims who landed at Plymouth, Mass., December 1620*. Plymouth, MA: General Society of *Mayflower* Descendants, 1975-2015. Vol. 15. Chilton, James. Pg.1; Furner, Susanna. Pg. 2; Chilton, Mary. Pg. 3.

Captain John Willoughby A127077
- New England Families, Genealogical and Memorial. Pg. 1256. Accessed at Ancestry.com.
- Gazetteer of Grafton County, N.H., 1709-1886. Town of Plymouth. Pg. 581. Accessed at Ancestry.com.
- Historical discourse commemorative of the centennial anniversary of the Congregational Church, Plymouth, N.H. Pg. 7. Accessed at Ancestry.com.
- Stearns, Ezra Scollay. *History of Plymouth, New Hampshire*. Cambridge, MA: Cambridge University Press, 1906. Vol. 1. Pgs. 110, 119, 121, 124, 177-8, 250, 426. Accessed at Ancestry.com.
- Jaquith, George Oakes and Walker, Georgetta Jaquith. *The Jaquith Family in America*. Boston, MA: New England Historical Genealogical Society, 1982.
- New Hampshire, U.S., Revolutionary War Records, 1675-1835. Accessed at Ancestry.com.
- Hammond, Isaac Weare, Ed. *Rolls of the Soldiers in the Revolutionary War*. Concord, NH: Parsons B. Cogwell, State Printer. 1885-1889. Pgs. 124, 381, 385, 586. Accessed at Google Books.

Private Zebulon Sutton A111425
- *U.S., Revolutionary War Pension and Bounty Land Warrant Application Files, 1800-1900*. Sutton, Zebulon. *S16265. Ohio, Knox Co. 19.790. Book E, Vol. 8. June 7, 1832. Pg. 25.
- Phillips, Joseph. "Letter to George Washington from Colonel Joseph Phillips, 12 October 1776." Founders Online. *National Archives and Records Administration*. https://founders.archives.gov/documents/Washington/.

- Scott, Joseph C. "Battle of White Plains." *George Washington's Mount Vernon.* 2022. www.mountvernon.org/library/digitalhistory/digital-encyclopedia/article/battle-of-white-plains/.
- Stockwell, Mary, Ph.D. "Battle of Long Island." *George Washington's Mount Vernon.* 2022. www.mountvernon.org/library/digitalhistory/digital-encyclopedia/article/battle-of-long-island/.
- History.com Editors. "British Capture Fort Washington." HISTORY. *A&E Television Networks.* Original: Nov. 13, 2009; Updated: Nov. 16, 2020. www.history.com/this-day-in-history/fort-washington-is-captured.
- Photo courtesy of Terry Anderson.

Private Levi Hayden A052558
- Hayden, Jabez H. *Records of the Connecticut Line of the Hayden Family.* The Case, Lockwood & Brainard Company, 1888. Pgs. 132-3.
- Johnston, Henry P., Ed. *Connecticut Men in the Revolutionary War.* Hartford, CT: 1889. Pgs. 480, 482. Accessed at Ancestry.com.
- *Roll of State Officers and Members of the General Assembly of Connecticut from 1776 to 1881.* Hartford, CT: Published by order of the General Assembly, 1881. Pg. 204. www.cga.ct.gov/hco/books/Sylvanus_Backus_Roll_Call_1811-1814_1881.pdf.

Private Jabez Tuttle A131803
- Connecticut Men in the Revolutionary War. Tenth Regiment of Militia. Pg. 460. Accessed at Ancestry.com.
- *North America, Family Histories, 1500-2000.* Lineage Book, NSDAR, Vol. 151. Jabez Tuttle. 1919. #150001. Accessed at Ancestry.com.
- "The descendants of William and Elizabeth Tuttle, who came from old to New England in 1635, and settled in New Haven in 1639." Image 339. Accessed at Ancestry.com.
- Stockwell, Mary Ph.D. "Battle of Long Island." *George Washington's Mount Vernon.* 2023. https://www.mountvernon.org/library/digitalhistory/digital-encyclopedia/article/battle-of-long-island/.
- "Brooklyn Long Island." *American Battlefield Trust.* 2022. https://www.battlefields.org/learn/revolutionary-war/battles/brooklyn.

Corporal Elisha Clark A022276
- U.S., Revolutionary War Pension and Bounty-Land Warrant Application Files, 1800-1900. Clark, Elisha. S*W17630. Accessed at Ancestry.com.
- Bryant, George Clarke. *Deacon George Clark(e) of Milford, Connecticut, and Some of His Descendants.* Prepared for publication by Donald Lines Jacobus. Portland, ME: Anthoensen Press, 1949. Pg. 88.
- United States Rosters of Soldiers and Sailors, 1775-1783. Connecticut. Fifth Battalion, Wadsworth's Brigade. Accessed at FamilySearch.org.
- U.S., The Pension Roll of 1835. Vol 1. Connecticut. Accessed at Ancestry.com.

Private Michael Zirkle A131099
- Abercrombie, Janice Luck & Slatten, Richard. *Virginia Revolutionary Publick [sic] Claims.* Vol III. Athens, GA: Iberian Publishing House, 1992. Pg. 840. (DAR Library Photocopy.)
- Find A Grave. Zirkle, Michael. Memorial 36755623. Accessed at Findagrave.com.
- Brumbaugh, Gaius Marcus. *Revolutionary War Records Virginia.* Lancaster, PA: Lancaster Press, 1936. Pg. 607. Accessed at Archive.org.
- Wayland, John Walter. *A History of Shenandoah County, Virginia.* Strasburg, VA: Shenandoah Publishing House, 1927. Pgs. 168, 223, 437, 732. Accessed at Ancestry.com.
- Harpine, J. William, Comp. *Zirkle Family History.* Madison, WI: University of Wisconsin, 1963. Pgs. 9,12. Accessed at FamilySearch.org.
- Wust, Klaus. *Old Pine Church Baptisms, 1783-1828, Mill Creek, Virginia.* Edinburg, VA: Shenandoah History, 1987. Pg. 7. Accessed at FamilySearch.org.
- Note: In 1885, Dunmore County was renamed Shenandoah County. Dunmore was named for a British Earl.

Hendrick Cortelyou A026240
- Cortelyou, John Van Zandt. *The Cortelyou Genealogy: A Record of Jaques Corteljou and of many of his Descendants.* Lincoln, NE: Brown Printing Service, 1942. Pg. 106.
- "Millstone History." Millstone Borough, Somerset County, New Jersey. https://millstoneboro.org/about/millstone-history/2/.
- Messler, Abraham. *Centennial History of Somerset County.* Somerville, NJ: C.M. Jameson Publisher, 1878. Pg. 75. Accessed at Google Books.
- "The Ten Mile Run Cemetery Is Both Very Old and Very Quaint." *The Sunday Times*, New Brunswick, New Jersey. May 18, 1930.
- Honeyman, A. Van Doren, Ed. *Somerset County Historical Quarterly.* Vol 1. Somerset County Historical Society. 1912. Pgs. 280-282, 232, 62. Accessed at Google Books.
- Photo courtesy of Lindal Martin.

Lieutenant Josiah Gale A043251
- White, Lorraine Cook, Ed. *Connecticut, U.S., Town Birth Records, pre-1870 (Barbour Collection).* Vol. 42. Baltimore, MD: Genealogical Publishing Co., 1994-2002. Pg. 80. Accessed at Ancestry.com.
- Fernow, Berthold, Ed. *Documents Relating to the Colonial History of New York.* Vol. 15. Albany, NY: Weed, Parsons and Company, Printers, 1887. Pg. 282. Accessed at Archive.org.
- Calendar of Historical Manuscripts Relating to War of the Revolution. Vol. 1. Albany, NY: Weed Parsons and Company, Printers, 1868. Pg. 136.
- Find A Grave. Gale, George Washington. Memorial 5578846. Accessed at Findagrave.com.

- Connecticut Soldiers, French and Indian War, 1755-62. Accessed at Ancestry.com.
- Mead, Spencer P. *History and Genealogy of the Mead Family of Fairfield County, Connecticut, Eastern New York, Western Vermont, and Western Pennsylvania, from A.D. 1180 to 1900.* New York: Knickerbocker Press. 1901. Pg. 332. Accessed at Google Books.
- "The Origins of Knox College." *Knox College.* https://www.knox.edu/about-knox/our-history/perspectives-on-knox-history/origins-of-knox-college.

Patriot Stories Works Cited
Chapter 3: HOPE

Drum Major Robert Polley A090288

- *Massachusetts Soldiers and Sailors of the Revolutionary War.* Vol. 12. Prepared by the Secretary of the Commonwealth. Boston, MA: Wright 7 Potter Printing Co., 1908. Pgs. 508-9. Accessed at Ancestry.com.
- "Music in the Revolutionary War." *George Washington's Mount Vernon.* 2022. www.mountvernon.org/george-washington/the-revolutionary-war/music/.

Private Eleazer Warner, Jr. A213377

- Massachusetts, U.S. Town and Vital Records, 1620-1988; Granby. Town Records with Births, Marriages and Deaths. Pg. 866. Accessed at Ancestry.com.
- U.S., Revolutionary War Pension and Bounty-Land Warrant Application Files, 1800-1900. Warner, Eleazer. S22571. Accessed at Ancestry.com.
- *Massachusetts Soldiers and Sailors of the Revolutionary War.* Vol. 16. Prepared by the Secretary of the Commonwealth. Boston, MA: Wright 7 Potter Printing Co., 1908. Pg. 583. Accessed at Ancestry.com.
- "The First Winter Encampment in Morris County." *Morristown National Historic Park.* U.S. Department of the Interior. Dec. 2002. www.nps.gov/parkhistory/online_books.
- Brown, Leonard E. "Morristown Winter Encampment 1777." *National Park Service.* U.S. Department of the Interior. June 1967. http://npshistory.com/publications/morr/winter-encampment.pdf.
- Roos, Dave. "How Crude Smallpox Inoculations Helped George Washington Win the War." Original: May 13, 2020; Updated: May 18, 2020. HISTORY. *A&E Television Networks.* www.history.com/news/smallpox-george-washington-revolutionary-war.
- Wilder, Justin E. *The Descendants of Harvey Wilder.* Goshen, IN: Justin E. Wilder, 1974. Printed by Light and Life Press, Winona Lake, IN. Pgs. 49, 81, 85, 159, 161, 166.
- McNitt, William. "The Warner Family of Pittsford, Vermont" and "Family Members who Served in the Civil War." www.wmcnitt.net/wilder/cw.htm.

Captain David Marshall A073741
- National Society Daughters of the American Revolution. *Daughters of the American Revolution Lineage Books*. Provo, UT. Accessed at Ancestry.com.
- "Memoir of Rebecca Marshall Cathcart." 1913. *Minnesota Historical Society*.
- Linn, John B. and Egle, Dr. William Henry, Eds. *Pennsylvania Archives*. Second Series, Vol. 14. Pg. 421. Issued 1874-1890. Accessed at Ancestry.com.
- Egle, Dr. William Henry and Reed, Dr. George Edward, Eds. *Pennsylvania Archives*. Third Series, Vol. 23. Pg. 714. Issued 1894-1899. Accessed at Ancestry.com.
- Montgomery, Dr. Thomas Lynch, Ed. *Pennsylvania Archives*. Fifth Series, Vol. 6. Pg. 339. Issued in 1906. Accessed at Ancestry.com.
- Scott, Joseph C. "Anthony Wayne." *George Washington's Mount Vernon*. 2023. www.mountvernon.org/library/digitalhistory/digital-encyclopedia/article/anthony-wayne/.
- Harris, C. Leon, Tr. Eastern District of Pennsylvania Pension Applications. Marshall, David. W3571. Jan. 15, 1819. www.revwarapps.org/w3571.pdf.
- Photo: Harris, C. Leon, Tr. Eastern District of Pennsylvania Pension Applications. Marshall, David.
- Photo courtesy of Ann H. Cathcart

Private Thomas McDaniel A207740
- U.S., Revolutionary War Pension and Bounty-Land Warrant Application Files, 1800-1900. McDaniel, Thomas. *S38192. Accessed at Ancestry.com.
- Tuggle, Vivian S. *Tuggle Family of Virginia*. Baltimore, MD: Gateway Press, Inc., 1970. Pg. 46.

Private Henry Maxwell A075918
- Thatcher, James M.D. *A Military Journal during the American Revolutionary War from 1775 to 1783*. Boston, MA: Cotton & Barnard Printer, 1827. Pg. 33. Accessed at Google Books.
- U.S., Compiled Revolutionary War Military Service Records, 1775-1783. Maxwell, Henry; Maxfield, Henry. *National Archives and Records Administration*. Online Database. Accessed at Ancestry.com. [NOTE: The file for Henry Maxwell contains records for "Henry Maxwell" and "Henry Maxfield" who are presumed to be one and the same person.]

Private Henry Lutz A131923
- U.S., Compiled Revolutionary War Military Service Records, 1775–1783. Pennsylvania 6th Regiment. Images 138-141. Accessed at Ancestry.com.
- Revolutionary War Pensions. Lutz, Henry (Pvt., Capt. Bowyer's Company, Sixth Pennsylvania Reg.). S4537. Record Group 15: Records of the Department of Veterans Affairs. *National Archives and Records Administration*. Accessed at Fold3.com.

- U.S., Revolutionary War Pension and Bounty-Land Warrant Application Files, 1800-1900. Moyer, Leonard (Pvt., Capt. Bankoen's Company, Col. Stewart's Reg.). S41898. Record Group 15: Records of the Department of Veterans Affairs. *National Archives and Records Administration.* Accessed at Fold3.com.
- Revolutionary War Pensions. Bower, Jacob (Capt., Sixth Pennsylvania Reg.). W3212. Record Group 15: Records of the Department of Veterans Affairs. *National Archives and Records Administration.* Accessed at Fold3.com.
- U.S., Revolutionary War Pension and Bounty-Land Warrant Application Files, 1800-1900. Harmar, Josiah (Col., Sixth Pennsylvania Reg.). W3246. Record Group 15: Records of the Department of Veterans Affairs. *National Archives and Records Administration.* Accessed at Fold3.com.
- Trussell, John B., Jr. *The Pennsylvania Line: Regimental Organization and Operations, 1776–1783.* Harrisburg, PA: Commonwealth of Pennsylvania, 1977.
- Yordy, Charles S. "The Pennsylvania Line Mutiny, Its Origins and Patriotism." *Unearthing the Past: Student Research on Pennsylvania History.* https://libraries.psu.edu/about/collections/unearthing-past-student-research-pennsylvania-history/pennsylvania-line-mutiny-0.
- History.com Editors. "Mutiny of the Pennsylvania Line." HISTORY. *A&E Television Networks.* Original: Nov. 13, 2009; Updated: Dec. 22, 2020. https://www.history.com/this-day-in-history/mutiny-of-the-pennsylvania-line.
- "Itinerary of the Pennsylvania Line from Pennsylvania to South Carolina, 1781-1782." *Pennsylvania Magazine of History and Biography*, 36. 1912. Pgs. 273-292. https://www.jstor.org/stable/20085599.
- Boatner, Mark M. *Encyclopedia of the American Revolution.* Mechanicsburg, PA: Stackpole Books, 1994.
- Berks County, Pennsylvania, Deeds. https://www.countyofberks.com/departments/recorder-of-deeds.
- Schuylkill County, Pennsylvania, Deeds. Accessed at FamilySearch.org.
- Van Doren, Carl. *Mutiny in January.* New York, NY: Viking Press, 1943.
- Photo courtesy of Lois Abromitis Mackin.

Private Massey Thomas A209218
- U.S., Pension and Bounty-Land Warrant Application Records, 1800-1900. Thomas, Massey. W.8785. *National Archives and Records Administration.* Accessed at Ancestry.com.
- "Brandywine." *American Battlefield Trust.* 2023. www.battlefields.org/learn/revolutionary-war/battles/brandywine.
- "George Washington and the History of Culpeper. *Culpeper VA Economic Development.* Last updated: Oct. 16, 2018. www.culpeperva.org/news/george-washington-and-the-history-of-culpeper/.
- Find A Grave. Thomas, Massey. Memorial 69155048. Accessed at Findagrave.com.
- North America, Family Histories, 1500-2000. James Thomas born 1786. Accessed at Ancestry.com.

Private Benjamin Sage, Jr. A099134
- Fernow, Berthold, Ed. *Documents Relating to the Colonial History of New York*. Vol. 15. Albany, NY: Weed, Parsons and Company, Printers, 1887. Pg. 461. Accessed at Google Books.
- U.S., Revolutionary War Pension and Bounty-Land Warrant Application Files, 1800-1900. Husted, David. S.29248. Accessed at Ancestry.com.
- Frazee, Frederick L., Ed. "Albert C. Mayham Series Blenheim Hill." Published in *The Jefferson Courier* and *Schoharie County Chronicle* in Jefferson, NY, between 1905 and 1907. Pg. 35. Photocopies of originals are available at the "Old Stone Fort Museum", Schoharie County Historical Society Library, Schoharie, Schoharie County, NY.
- Sage, Elisha L. and Charles Sage, Comp. & Ed. *Genealogical Record of the Descendants of David Sage*. Batavia, NY: Charles H. Sage, 1919. Pg. 109.

Private Thomas Eldredge A037278
- *Massachusetts Soldiers and Sailors of the Revolutionary War*. Vol. 5. Prepared by the Secretary of the Commonwealth. Boston, MA: Wright 7 Potter Printing Co., 1908. Pg. 267. Accessed at Ancestry.com.
- Hoyt, Edward A. "The Pawlet Expedition, September 1777." *Vermont History*. Vol. 75, No. 2 (Summer/Fall 2007). Pgs. 69-100. www.vermonthistory.org/journal/75/10_Hoyt.pdf.
- Smith, Joseph and Thomas Cushing, ed. *History of Berkshire County, Massachusetts, with Biographical Sketches of its Prominent Men*. Vol. II. New York: J.B. Beers & Co. 1885. Pg. 70. Accessed at Google Books.
- Find A Grave. Eldredge, Thomas. Memorial 94022945. Accessed at Findagrave.com.

Private Samuel Curtis A208263
- Curtiss, Frederic Haines. *A Genealogy of the Curtiss Family; Being a Record of the Descendants of Widow Elizabeth Curtiss, Who Settled in Stratford, Conn., 1639-1640*. Boston: Rockwell and Churchill Press, 1903. Pg. 34.
- *Massachusetts Soldiers and Sailors of the Revolutionary War*. Vol. 4. Prepared by the Secretary of the Commonwealth. Boston, MA: Wright 7 Potter Printing Co., 1908. Pg. 250. Accessed on Ancestry.com.
- Auburn, Emma. "West Point." George Washington's Mount Vernon. 2023. https://www.mountvernon.org/library/digitalhistory/digital-encyclopedia/article/west-point/.
- New York, Wills and Probate Records, 1659-1999 for Solomon Guarnsey, Saratoga, County, New York. Wills. Vol. 0001-0002, 1799-1815. Image 92. Accessed at Ancestry.com.

Ensign Daniel Davidson A030059
- Summers, Lewis Preston. *Annals of Southwest Virginia, 1769-1800*. Baltimore, MD: Genealogical Publishing Co., 1996. Pgs. 1053-4, 1387. Accessed at Ancestry.com.
- National Archives Military Service Records, Company Payroll Papers. Disk No. D8. Payroll vouchers June-July 1777; Aug.-Oct. 1777; Nov.-Dec. 1777; Jan.-March 1778; Nov.-Dec. 1778; April 1778. *National Archives and Records Administration*. Accessed in person, 2022.
- Gwathmey, John Hastings. *Historical Register of Virginians in the Revolution*. Richmond, VA: Dietz Press, 1938. Pg. 209.
- Wilkes, Ariel. "Daniel Morgan." *George Washington's Mount Vernon*. 2022. https://www.mountvernon.org/library/digitalhistory/digital-encyclopedia/article/daniel-morgan/.
- "Daniel Morgan." *American Battlefield Trust*. 2022. https://www.battlefields.org/learn/biographies/daniel-morgan.
- Letter to John Hancock from Horatio Gates. American Revolutionary War Manuscripts Collection. *Boston Public Library*. https://archive.org/details/lettertojohnhanc00gate/page/n1/mode/2up.
- Find A Grave. Davidson, Daniel Sr. Memorial 34969255. Accessed at Ancestry.com.
- "Brigadier General Daniel Morgan." The American Revolution in North Carolina. www.carolana.com/NC/Revolution/continental_army_daniel_morgan.html.
- Goodway, Frank. "American Participants in the Battle of Saratoga." Original: Aug. 1997; Updated: Nov. 2012. http://saratoganygenweb.com/batlda.htm.

Corporal Bartholomew (Somers) Summers A110885
- Goodrich, John E. *Rolls of the Soldiers in the Revolutionary War, 1775-1783*. Rutland, VT: The Tuttle Company, 1904. Pg. 53. Accessed at Archive.org.
- Miller, Edward and Wells, Frederic P. *History of Ryegate, Vermont: From its Settlement by the Scotch-American Company of Farmers to the Present Time with Genealogical Records of Many Families*. St. Johnsbury, VT: The Caledonian Company, 1913. Pgs. 85-87, and 528-529.
- Bailey, Frye. "Reminiscences of Frye Bayley." In Proceedings of the Vermont Historical Society for the Years 1923, 1924, and 1925, 22-86. Bellows Falls, VT: The P.H. Gobie Press, Inc., 1926. Pgs. 22, 23, 46, 49, 52-53, and 54-55. Accessed from the Vermont Historical Society at VermontHistory.org.
- Vermont Vital Records, 1760-1954. Database with images. Bartholomew Sommers and Susanna Harvey, 1777. Accessed at FamilySearch.org.

Private Nathaniel Rudd A099513
- Brown, Coralynn, Tr. "Vital Records of Norwich 1659-1848" and "Society of Colonial Wars in the State of Connecticut 1913." Second Book of Records – Norwich.

- *Massachusetts Soldiers and Sailors of the Revolutionary War*. Vol. 13. Prepared by the Secretary of the Commonwealth. Boston, MA: Wright 7 Potter Printing Co., 1908. Pg. 643. Accessed at Ancestry.com.
- Rudd, Horace. *A Genealogical Sketch of the Rudd Family*. 1858. Additions by Jabez Rudd, 1888. Submitted by Janet (Barns) Rudd.
- Massachusetts, Revolutionary War, Index Cards to Muster Rolls, 1775-1783. *Massachusetts State Archives*. Accessed at FamilySearch.org.
- "Saratoga." *American Battlefield Trust*. 2022. www.battlefields.org/learn/revolutionary-war/battles/saratoga.
- Connecticut Archives Revolutionary War Accounts. Ser. 2, 1763-1789. Also, Connecticut State Library, Connecticut Archives, Record Group 1: Connecticut Archives Revolutionary War Ser. 2; Connecticut Revolutionary War Papers and Private Collections. Accessed at FamilySearch.org.
- Photo courtesy of Dee Brochu.

Private David Smith A213166

- *Massachusetts Soldiers and Sailors of the Revolutionary War*. Vol. 14. Prepared by the Secretary of the Commonwealth. Boston, MA: Wright 7 Potter Printing Co., 1908. Pg. 372. Accessed at Ancestry.com.
- Patrie, Lois McClennan. *A History of Colrain Massachusetts, with Genealogies of Early Families.* No Publisher, 1974. Pg. 75. Accessed at Google Books.
- McClellan, Charles H. *The Early Settlers of Colrain Massachusetts.* Speech. 1885. Reprinted by Heritage Books, 2011. Pgs. 82, 84. Accessed at Google Books.
- Photo courtesy of Michelle Henderson White.

Benjamin Sage, Sr. A099131

- Hasbrouck, Frank Ed. *The History of Dutchess County, New York.* Poughkeepsie, NY: S.A. Matthieu, 1909. Pgs. 95, 98. Accessed at Archive.org.
- Find A Grave. Sage, Benjamin. Memorial 36608194. Accessed at Findagrave.com.
- Records of Births, Marriages and Deaths, Middletown Land Records, Connecticut, 1640-1775. Vol.1. Pgs. 11, 24. Accessed at Ancestry.com.
- Cutter, William. *Families of Western New York, "Peaslee."* Pg. 265. Accessed at Ancestry.com.
- Sage, Elisha L. and Charles Sage, Comp. & Ed. *Genealogical Record of the Descendants of David Sage*. Batavia, NY: Charles H. Sage, 1919. Pgs. 109-110.

Patriot Stories Works Cited
Chapter 4: PERSEVERANCE

Drummer Moses Ramsdell A093887
- U.S., Revolutionary War Pension and Bounty-Land Warrant Application Files, 1800-1900. Ramsdell, Moses. S*W26945. Accessed at Ancestry.com.
- *Massachusetts Soldiers and Sailors of the Revolutionary War.* Vol. 12. Prepared by the Secretary of the Commonwealth. Boston, MA: Wright 7 Potter Printing Co., 1908. Pg. 921. Accessed at Ancestry.com.
- Case Files of Pension and Bounty-Land Warrant Applications Based on Revolutionary War Service, compiled ca. 1800 - ca. 1912, documenting the period ca. 1775 - ca. 1900. Ramsdell, Moses. W. 26,945. Record Group 15 Roll 1995. Image Pg. 98. Accessed at Fold3.com.
- Compiled Service Records of Soldiers Who Served in the American Army During the Revolutionary War, 1775 – 1783. M881. Record group 93. National Archives and Records Administration. Accessed at Fold3.com.
- Baldwin, Thomas W., Comp. "Vital Records of Mendon, Massachusetts, to the Year 1850." Boston, MA: New England Historic Genealogical Society, 1920. Pg. 143. Accessed at FamilySearch.org.
- Massachusetts, Town Clerk, Vital and Town Records, 1626-2001. Accessed at FamilySearch.org.
- United States War of 1812 Index to Service Records, 1812-1815. Ramsdale, Knight. March 8, 2021. National Archives and Records Administration. M602. Roll 170. FHL Microfilm 882,688. Accessed at FamilySearch.org.
- "George Washington to Major Henry Lee, Jr., 20 August 1780." Founders Online. *National Archives and Records Administration.* https://founders.archives.gov/documents/Washington/03-27-02-0523. [Original source: The Papers of George Washington, Revolutionary War Series, vol. 27, 5 July–27 August 1780, ed. Benjamin L. Huggins. Charlottesville, VA: University of Virginia Press, 2019. Pgs. 571–574.]

Private Jacob Galusha A203033
- Still, Mark Sumner. *The Genealogy of the Gould Family containing a record of one line of descendants of Francis Goole of Braintree and Chelmsford, Mass.* 1971. Pg. 4. Accessed at Ancestry.com.
- Bates, Edward C., Ed. *Rolls of Connecticut Men in the French and Indian War, 1755-1762.* Vol. 1. Hartford, CT: Connecticut Historical Society, 1903. Pgs. 57-58. Accessed at Archive.org.
- Hudson-Mohawk Genealogical and Family Memoirs: Galusha. *Schenectady County Public Library Digital History Library.* www.schenectadyhistory.org/families/hmgfm/galusha.html.

- "What Happened at Valley Forge." *National Park Service.* U.S. Department of the Interior. Last updated: Nov. 7, 2022. www.nps.gov/vafo/learn/historyculture/valley-forge-history-and-significance.htm.
- "The Valley Forge Muster Roll." *Valley Forge Muster Roll Legacy Project.* 2021. https://valleyforgemusterroll.org/search-the-muster-roll/.
- "Captain Ebenezer Hill/Hills." *The Society of the Cincinnati in the State of Connecticut.* 2022. http://theconnecticutsociety.org/hillhills-ebenezer/.
- "Monmouth." *American Battlefield Trust.* 2023. www.battlefields.org/learn/revolutionary-war/battles/monmouth.
- U.S., Pension and Bounty-Land Warrant Application Records, 1800-1900. Galusha, Jacob. S*W24270. *National Archives and Records Administration.* Accessed at Ancestry.com.

Private Azor Curtis A028810
- Curtiss, Frederic Haines. *A Genealogy of the Curtiss Family; Being a Record of the Descendants of Widow Elizabeth Curtiss, Who Settled in Stratford, Conn., 1639-1640.* 1903. Pg. 34.
- *Massachusetts Soldiers and Sailors of the Revolutionary War.* Vol. 4. Prepared by the Secretary of the Commonwealth. Boston, MA: Wright 7 Potter Printing Co., 1908. Pg. 252. Accessed at Ancestry.com.
- U.S., Revolutionary War Rolls, 1775-1783. Microfilm Series M246, Massachusetts, 2nd Reg., 1777-81, Folder 3. Pg. 251. *National Archives and Records Administration.* Accessed at Ancestry.com.
- Will of Azor Curtis, Apr. 29, 1777. www.wikitree.com/wiki/Curtis-2251#_note-FCCrtiss.

Private Benjamin Webster A121172
- Revolutionary War Pension & Bounty-Land Warrant Application Files. Webster, Benjamin. W.22562. Pgs. 356-405. Accessed at Fold3.
- "West Point: The Gibraltar of the Hudson." *American Battlefield Trust.* 2023. www.battlefields.org/learn/articles/west-point.
- "Rhode Island: Siege of Newport/Battle of Quaker Hill." *American Battlefield Trust.* 2023. www.revolutionarywar.us/year-1778/battle-rhode-island/.

Captain Bartholomew Barrett A208181
- Barbour Collection. Connecticut, U.S., Town Birth Records, pre-1870. Vol. 1. Pg. 65. Accessed at Ancestry.com.
- Barbour Collection. U.S., Town Marriage Records, pre-1870. Marriage March 6, 1755; Barret, Bartholomew and Mahittable Rood; by J. Lee. Pg. 30. Accessed at AmericanAncestors.com.
- Barrett, Joseph Hartwell. "Thomas Barrett of Braintree, William Barrett of Cambridge, and Their Early Descendants." *The New England Historical and Genealogical Register.* Vol. 42. Boston, MA: David Clapp & Son, 1888. Pgs. 257-259.

- Barrett, Brian S. Barrett. *The Eleazer Barrett Identity Puzzle: An Historical Account of Five Men Named Eleazer Barrett.* 2006. Pg. 4-7. Accessed at BSB Technical Services, 805 Minaka Dr., Waukesha, WI 53188.
- *Rolls of Connecticut Men in the French and Indian War.* Vol. 1. 1755-1762. Campaign of 1756. Hartford, CT: Connecticut Historical Society, 1903. Pgs. 140, 243. Accessed at Archive.org.
- Clifford, John Henry, Ed.; et al. *The Acts and Resolves, Public and Private, of the Province of the Massachusetts Bay.* Vol. XVI. Boston, MA: Wright & Potter, 1909. Pg. 450.
- 1779 Supply Tax List Albany Co., NY. www.learnwebskills.com/lineage/albany1779taxag.htm.
- Smith, H. P. *Columbia County at the End of the Century.* Hudson, NY: The Record Printing & Publishing Co., 1900. Pg. 32.
- Roberts, James Arthur, *New York in the Revolution as Colony and State.* Comptroller's Office. Albany, NY: Weed-Parsons Printing Co., 1897. Pgs. 30, 88, 116.
- U.S., Compiled Revolutionary War Military Service Records, 1775-1783. M881. Roll #761. *National Archives and Records Administration.* Accessed at Ancestry.com.
- Berkshire County, Massachusetts Will Testators: Barrett, Bartholomew, Alford, MA-3-6-210. Will written June 2, 1788. Probated Oct. 7, 1888. Alford MA Probate Records. Pg. 1403. Accessed at Familysearch.org.
- Image courtesy of Brian S. Barrett.

Private James Gaffin A042877
- Roberts, James A. *New York in the Revolution as Colony and State.* Albany, NY: Weed-Parsons Printing Company, Printers, 1897. Pgs. 123-4. Accessed at Google Books.
- VanDeusen, Capt. Albert H. *Van Deursen Family.* Vol. 1. New York, NY: 1912. Pg. 122. Accessed at My Heritage.com.
- *Portrait and Biographical Album of Ogle County, Illinois.* Chicago, IL: Chapman Brothers, 1886. Pg. 299. Accessed at Google Books.
- "Hubbardton." *American Battlefield Trust.* 2023. https://www.battlefields.org/learn/revolutionary-war/battles/hubbardton.
- "Bennington." *American Battlefield Trust.* 2023. https://www.battlefields.org/learn/revolutionary-war/battles/bennington.
- U.S., Dutch Reformed Church Records in Selected States, 1639-1989. James Gaffin. Accessed at Ancestry.com.

Captain Edwards Bucknam A016550
- Compilation of Military Service Records. Roll #564. M881. *National Archives and Records Administration.* Accessed at Ancestry.com.

- Somers, Rev. Amos Newton. *History of Lancaster, New Hampshire*. Concord, NH: Rumford Press, 1899. Qtd. pgs. 20-21. Accessed at Archive.org.
- Massachusetts Society Sons of the American Revolution, *Historical Memoranda*. Cambridge, MA: The University Press, 1899. Pg. 139. Accessed at Google Books.
- Jackson, James R. *History of Littleton, New Hampshire*. Vol. II. Cambridge, MA: The University Press, 1905. Pgs. 544, 548, 633. Accessed at Google Books.
- New Hampshire State Papers Index. *New Hampshire Secretary of State Archives*. Accessed at https://sos.nh.gov/archives-vital-records-records-management/archives/publications-collections/new-hampshire-state-papers/.

Private Andreas (Daniel) Daniels A114883
- Montgomery, Dr. Thomas Lynch, Ed. *Pennsylvania Archives*. Fifth Series, Vol. 4. Pgs. 254, 257. Fifth Series, Vol. 5. Pgs. 284. Issued in 1906. Accessed at Ancestry.com.
- Elliott, Ella Zerbey. "Schuylkill County War of the Revolution." *Blue Book of Schuylkill*. Pottsville, PA: Republican, 1916. Chapter transcribed by Debbie Ovechka. http://genealogytrails.com/penn/schuylkill/military/revwar.html
- Fox, Francis S. "Pennsylvania's Revolutionary Militia law: the statute that transformed the state." *Pennsylvania History*. Vol. 80, Issue 2. Spring 2013. Pgs. 204-214. https://scholarlypublishingcollective.org/psup/pa-history/issue/80/2.
- Montgomery, Morton, L. *History of Berks County, Pennsylvania, in the Revolution, from 1774 to 1783*. Berks Co., PA: C.F. Haage Printer, 1894. Pgs. 135-142. https://archive.org/details/cu31924028852220/mode/2up.
- "Depreciation Pay." *Pennsylvania Historical and Museum Collection*. 2023. https://www.phmc.pa.gov/Archives/Research-Online/Pages/Revolutionary-War.aspx.
- Lykens Township – Revolutionary War Monument. Photo available at: https://www.lykensvalley.org/lykens-township-revolutionary-war-monument/.

Private Jeremiah Frame A041521
- Chalkley, Lyman. *Chronicles of the Scotch-Irish Settlement of Virginia*. Published by Mary S. Lockwood, NSDAR. Vol. I, Pg. 337; Vol. II, Pg. 424; Vol. III. Pg. 395. Accessed at Google Books.
- Peyton, John Lewis. *History of Augusta County, Virginia*. Staunton, VA: Samuel M. Yost & Son, 1882. Pg. 180. Accessed at Google Books.
- Green, Henry S. *Biennial Report of the Department of Archives and History of the State of West Virginia*. Appendix: Proceedings of the Eighth Annual Meeting, Vol. 1911-1914. Charleston, WV: Department of Archives and History, 1915. Pgs. 17, 19. Accessed at Archive.org.
- Creel, Bevin J. *Selected Virginia Revolutionary War Records, Vol. 2, Augusta County Court Martial Minutes*. Self-published, 2008. Pg. 36. Copy in DAR Library.

- Lowry, Robert Eaton. *History of Preble County, Ohio*. Indianapolis, IN: B. F. Bowen & Co. Inc., 1915. Pg. 874. Accessed at Google Books.

Private Henry (Heinrich) Hitzman A211038
- U.S., Compiled Revolutionary War Military Service Records, 1775-1783. Roll #769. M881. *National Archives and Records Administration*. Accessed at ancestry.com.
- Greene, Nelson, Ed. *History of the Mohawk Valley: Gateway to the West 1614-195*. Chapter 65: 1778 - Mohawk Valley Raids. Vol. I. Pgs. 885-901. Chapter 69: Johnson's Great Raid. Vol. II. Pgs. 1009-1048. S.J. Clarke Publishing Company, 1925.
www.schenectadyhistory.org/resources/mvgw/history/069.html.
- Pension Application for Jacob Foster. R3.520. Schoharie County, State of New York. Testimony of Christina Norman, daughter of Henry Hitzman. Accessed in person.
- Photo courtesy of Patricia Lynne Briley Peterson.

Captain Enoch Eastman A035718
- Goodrich, John E., Ed. *Rolls of the Soldiers in the Revolutionary War, 1775-1783*. Rutland, VT: The Tuttle Company, 1904. Pgs. 100, 170, 225, 452, 597, 787. Accessed at Ancestry.com.
- Bushnell, Mark. "Then Again: In a raid on Royalton in 1780, Native Americans allied with the British." *VTdigger*. Oct. 13, 2019. https://vtdigger.org/2019/10/13/then-again-in-a-raid-on-royalton-in-1780-native-americans-allied-with-the-british/.
- "Freedom & Unity." Vermont History. *Vermont Historical Society*. 2006. https://vermonthistory.org/freedom-unity-revolutionary-war.
- Image courtesy Manchester Historical Society, Howard Wilcox Collection.

Captain Jacob Odell A204561
- Doherty, Frank J. *Settlers of the Beekman Patent, Dutchess County, New York*. Vol. IX. Pleasant Valley, NY: Self-published, 1990. Pgs. 609-10; 620-22. Accessed at AmericanAncestors.org.
- Smith, Donald A. *Proceedings of the Vermont Historical Society*. "Green Mountain Insurgency: Transformation of New York's Forty-Year Land War." Vol. 64, No. 4. Fall 1996. Pgs. 197-231.
https://vermonthistory.org/journal/misc/GreenMountainInsurgency1.pdf.
- Levine, Rachel Scharf. *Captain Jacob Odell and Mary Millington of Manchester, VT*. Fairbanks, AK: Self-published, 2003. Pgs. 11-31. Rachel Levine, PO Box 72349, Fairbanks, AK 99707. Also available at DAR Library.
- Hemenway, Abby Maria. *The Vermont Historical Gazetteer*. Vol. 1. "Manchester" by Henry E. Miner, Esq. Burlington, VT: Self-published, 1867. Pgs. 199-202. Accessed at Archive.org.

- Goodrich, John E., Ed. *Rolls of the Soldiers in the Revolutionary War, 1775-1783*. Rutland, VT: The Tuttle Company, 1904. Pgs. 230, 459, 631. Accessed at Ancestry.com.
- Editors of Encyclopedia Britannica. "Green Mountain Boys." www.britannica.com/topic/Green-Mountain-Boys.
- Find A Grave. Odell, Jacob. Memorial 32537053. Accessed at Findagrave.com.

Asa (Cheadle) Cheedle, Sr. A021269
- Connecticut Soldiers, French and Indian War, 1755-1762. Muster rolls under Colonel Lyman (1757) and Colonel Fitch (1758). Accessed at Ancestry.com.
- Aldrich, Lewis Cass and Frank R. Holmes, Ed. *History of Windsor County, Vermont*. Syracuse, NY: D. Mason and Co., 1891. Pgs. 577-578. Accessed at Google Books.
- Newton, William Monroe. *History of Barnard, Vermont, Volume 1-Historical*. Burlington, VT: Vermont Historical Society, 1928. Pgs. 313-314. Accessed at FamilySearch.org.
- Child, Hamilton. *Gazetteer and Business Directory of Windsor County, VT for 1883-1884*. Syracuse, NY: The Journal, 1884. Pg. 84. Accessed at Google Books.
- Goodwin, Neil. "The Narrative of the Captive, George Avery, 1780–1782." *Vermont Historical Society*. https://search.yahoo.com/search?fr=mcafee&type=E211US105G0&p=fort+fortitude+vermnot.
- U.S., Revolutionary War Pension and Bounty-Land Warrant Application Files, 1800-1900. Cheedle, Asa. S*W14464. Accessed at Ancestry.com.
- Goodrich, John E., Ed. *Rolls of the Soldiers in the Revolutionary War, 1775-1783*. Rutland, VT: The Tuttle Company, 1904. Pg. 293. Accessed at Ancestry.com.

Lieutenant Jesse Washburn, Sr. A121889
- Olney, Elaine Washburn. *Our Washburn Heritage*. Manhattan, KS: 1986. Accessed at Archive.org
- Maltby, John. "Families of the Children of John Washburn (Jr.) and Sarah Cornell." *Maltby Family Genealogy*. www.maltbyfamily.net/genealogies/washburn/washburn_hempstead_3.html#Jesse858.
- Cooke, Francis. *Mayflower Families Through Five Generations*. Vol. 12. Plymouth, MA: General Society of *Mayflower* Families, 1996. Pgs. 268–269. And Rogers, Thomas. Vol. 19. Pgs. 431-433.
- *Vital Records of Bridgewater, Massachusetts To the Year 1850*. New England Historic Genealogical Society. 1916. Vol. 2. Pg. 387. Also, *Vital Records of East Bridgewater, Massachusetts To the year 1850*. New England Historic Genealogical Society. 1917. Vol. 1. Pgs. 314-315.

- Merrick, Barbara Lambert. "Which Josiah Washburn Married Sarah Richmond?" *Mayflower Quarterly*, 48:1. February 1982. Pgs. 12–17.
- Montgomery, Dr. Thomas Lynch, Ed. *Pennsylvania Archives*. Fifth Series, Vol. 8. Pgs. 281, 305, 561, 565. Issued in 1906. Accessed at Ancestry.com.
- "Daniel Washburn's Account of the Wyoming Massacre, 1846." *Luzerne County [Pennsylvania] GenWeb*. http://www.pagenweb.org/~luzerne/towns/wyoming.htm.
- Plymouth Court Records, 1686-1859. *AmericanAncestors.org*. http://www.americanancestors.org.
- "Northampton County Revolutionary War Militia." *Pennsylvania Historical & Museum Commission*. https://www.phmc.pa.gov/Archives/Research-Online/Pages/Revolutionary-War-Militia-Northampton.aspx.
- U.S., Revolutionary War Pension and Bounty-Land Warrant Application Files, 1800-1900. Gregory, John (Capt., Third and Fourth Battalions, Northampton, Pennsylvania, militia, Revolutionary War). S.23671. *National Archives and Records Administration*. Microfilm Publication M804. Accessed at Ancestry.com.
- Hollenbach, Raymond E. *Heidelberg Church, Heidelberg Township, Lehigh County, PA: A History and the Church Records, 1740-1978*. 1977.
- Hinke, William, Copier. "Records of Schlosser's or Union Reformed Church, Unionville North Whitehall Township, Lehigh County, Pennsylvania, 1765-1846." *Lehigh County GenWeb*. Accessed at Ancestry.com.
- Schenawolf, Harry. "Battle of Wyoming – Battle or Massacre?" *Revolutionary War Journal*. July 21, 2021. https://www.revolutionarywarjournal.com/battle-of-wyoming-american-defeat-or-massacre/.

Ensign Leonard Stahl A206354
- Bedford County (PA) Orphan's Court Records, Nov. 1791. Transcribed at www.frankstahlbio.net/Bedford%20Co%20LOA%201792%20typewritten.pdf.
- Montgomery, Dr. Thomas Lynch, Ed. *Pennsylvania Archives*. Fifth Series, Vol. 6. Pgs. 69, 79, 100, 169, 517, 519, 536, 586, 599, 600. Issued in 1906. Accessed at Ancestry.com.
- "Ensign." *ENCYCLOpedia.com*. May 29, 2018. www.encyclopedia.com/social-sciences-and-law/political-science-and-government/military-affairs-nonnaval/ensign.
- "Revolutionary War Overview." *Pennsylvania Historical and Museum Commission*. www.phmc.pa.gov/Archives/Research-Online/Pages/Revolutionary-War.aspx.
- Knouff, Gregory T. *An Arduous Service: The Pennsylvania Backcountry Soldiers' Revolution, Pennsylvania History*. Vol. 61. No. 1. January 1994. www.journals.psu.edu/phj/article/view/25116.
- Pennsylvania, U.S., Wills and Probate Records, 1683-1993. Franklin County. Henry Stahl. Accessed at Ancestry.com.

- Pennsylvania, U.S., Wills and Probate Records, 1683-1993. Westmoreland County. Leonard Stahl. Accessed at Ancestry.com.
- Albert, George Dallas, Ed. *History of the County of Westmoreland, Pennsylvania, with biographical sketches of many of its prominent men.* Philadelphia: L. H. Everts & Co. 1884. Pg. 717.

Private Adam Flake A040466
- Immigration list transcribed at the Germantown Historical Society and abstracted from five principal German newspapers published in Germantown and Philadelphia. Accessed at Ancestry.com.
- Montgomery, Dr. Thomas Lynch, Ed. *Pennsylvania Archives*. Fifth Series, Vol. 6. Pgs. 90, 98, 113, 543 (Flake); Pgs. 73, 80-81, 101-102, 540 (Stuff). Issued in 1906. Accessed at Ancestry.com.
- Pennsylvania U.S. Tax and Exoneration, 1768-1801. Accessed at Ancestry.com.
- Clarke, William P. *Official History of the Militia and National Guard of the State of Pennsylvania.* Captain Charles J. Hendler, Third Infantry, N.G.P., 1909. Pg. 23. https://www.loc.gov/item/09029138/.
- Fendrick, Virginia Shannon and Daughters of the American Revolution, Franklin County Chapter. *American Revolutionary Soldiers of Franklin County, Pennsylvania.* Historical Works Committee of the Franklin County Chapter, 1944. Pg. 208. https://www.loc.gov/item/57051550/.
- Shaw, Archibald. *History of Dearborn County, Indiana.* Indianapolis, IN: B.F. Bowen & Company, Inc., 1915. Pg. 173. Accessed at Google Books.
- Photo courtesy of Justin Meyer.

Private Jacob (Peter) Peters A205789
- Montgomery, Dr. Thomas Lynch, Ed. *Pennsylvania Archives*. Fifth Series, Vol. 8. Issued in 1906. Pgs. 233, 234, 236, 442, 448, 450, 502, 509, 510. Accessed at Ancestry.com.
- Roberts, Charles Rhoads; John Baer Stoudt; Thomas H. Krick; William J. Dietrich. *History of Lehigh County, Pennsylvania.* Allentown, PA: Lehigh Valley Publishing Co., 1914. Vol. 1. Pgs. 721–723.
- Hollenbach, Raymond E. *Heidelberg Church, Heidelberg Township, Lehigh County, PA: A History and the Church Records, 1740–1978.* 1977. Pg. 5.
- Hinke, William J. Records of Schlosser's or Union Reformed Church, Unionville, Lehigh County, Pennsylvania. DGS 7596969, Item 2. Accessed at FamilySearch.org.
- Photo courtesy of Lois Abromitis Mackin

Sergeant Peter Andreas A002555
- Montgomery, Dr. Thomas Lynch, Ed. *Pennsylvania Archives*. Fifth Series, Vol. 8. Pgs. 233, 449, 465. Issued in 1906. Accessed at Ancestry.com.

- Stauffer, William Tilden. "Sergeant Peter Andreas." *Annals of the Sugarloaf Historical Association II*. 1935. Pgs. 24-25.
- Wentink, Anna Andreas. "Descendants of Martin Andreas and Anna Elizabeth Vautrin, Part 2." *The Detroit Society for Genealogical Research Magazine*. VI. 1942. Pgs. 3-6.

Private William Andreas A002556
- Montgomery, Dr. Thomas Lynch, Ed. *Pennsylvania Archives*. Fifth Series, Vol. 8. Pgs. 442, 448, 450, 459. Issued in 1906. Accessed at Ancestry.com.
- "Northampton County Revolutionary War Militia." *Pennsylvania Historical & Museum Commission* https://www.phmc.pa.gov/Archives/Research-Online/Pages/Revolutionary-War-Militia-Northampton.aspx.
- Hollenbach, Raymond E. *Heidelberg Church, Heidelberg Township, Lehigh County, PA: A History and the Church Records, 1740–1978*. 1979.
- Hinke, William, Copier. "Records of Schlosser's or Union Reformed Church, Unionville North Whitehall Township, Lehigh County, Pennsylvania, 1765–1846." *Lehigh County GenWeb*. www.rootsweb.ancestry.com/~palehigh/Schlosserschurch.html.
- Roberts, Charles R. *Records of Egypt Reformed Church, Lehigh County, Pennsylvania, 1734–1834*. Westminster, MD: Heritage Books, 2010.
- Hendricks, Nancy. *The Frantz Family of Alsace, Lorraine*. 2nd Ed. Vero Beach, FL: 2007.
- Rice, Phillip A. and Dellock, Jean A. *Circuit and Circuit Riders*. Apollo, PA: Closson Press, 1996.
- Northampton County, Pennsylvania, Orphans Court Dockets. Accessed at FamilySearch.org.
- Bell, Raymond M. and Granquist, Mabel G. *The Vautrin--Wotring--Woodring family: Lorraine--Alsace--Pennsylvania, 1640-1790*. Washington, PA: Bell, 1953. Pg. 11.

Private Jacob Frantz A041886
- Montgomery, Dr. Thomas Lynch, Ed. *Pennsylvania Archives*. Fifth Series, Vol. 8. Pgs. 54, 116. Issued in 1906. Accessed at Ancestry.com.
- "Northampton County Revolutionary War Militia." *Pennsylvania Historical & Museum Commission*. https://www.phmc.pa.gov/Archives/Research-Online/Pages/Revolutionary-War-Militia-Northampton.aspx.
- Hendricks, Nancy Joy. *The Frantz Family of Alsace, Lorraine*. 2nd Ed. Vero Beach, FL: 2007.

Jacob Neifert A202310
- Marx, Henry F., Ed. *Oaths of Allegiance, Northampton County, Pennsylvania, 1777-1784*. Easton Public Library, 1932. Pg. 43.
- Linn, John B. and Dr. William Henry Egle, Ed. *Pennsylvania Archives*. Second Series, Vol. 3. Pg. 327. Issued 1874-1890. Accessed at Ancestry.com.

- Montgomery, Dr. Thomas Lynch, Ed. *Pennsylvania Archives*. Fifth Series, Vol. 1. Pgs. 118-119. Issued in 1906. Accessed at Ancestry.com.
- Pennsylvania, U.S., Tax and Exoneration, 1768–1801. Berks County, Pennsylvania. Accessed at Ancestry.com.
- Pennsylvania, Wills and Probate Records, 1683–1993. Berks County, Pennsylvania. Daniel Stump, Albany Township and Jacob Neifert, Albany Township. Accessed at Ancestry.com.
- Neifert, William Washington. "The Neiferts of Rush Township, Schuylkill County, Pennsylvania, 1906." *USGenWeb Archives*. http://usgwarchives.net/pa/schuylkill/famhist.htm.
- Kistler, John Levan. "The History of Jerusalem 'Allemaengel' Church." Albany Township, Berks Co., PA. Two Hundredth Anniversary, 1747-1947. Accessed at FamilySearch.org.
- Waddell, Louis M. and Bruce D. Bomberger. *The French and Indian War in Pennsylvania, 1753–1763*. Harrisburg, Pennsylvania Historical and Museum Commission. 1996.

Private Joseph Hunsicker A060102
- Montgomery, Dr. Thomas Lynch, Ed. *Pennsylvania Archives*. Fifth Series, Vol. 8. Pgs. 502, 510. Issued in 1906. Accessed at Ancestry.com.
- Hollenbach, Raymond E. *Heidelberg Church, Heidelberg Township, Lehigh County, PA: A History and the Church Records, 1740–1978*. 1977. Pg. 5.
- Roberts, Charles Rhoads; John Baer Stoudt; Thomas H. Krick; William J. Dietrich. *History of Lehigh County, Pennsylvania*. Allentown, PA: Lehigh Valley Publishing Co., 1914. Vol. 1. Pgs. 721-723. Vol. 2. Pgs. 593-594.
- Burgert, Annette Kunselman. *Eighteenth Century Emigrants from the Northern Alsace to America*. Camden, ME: Picton Press, 1992. Pgs. 272–273.

Private John George Huntzinger A060865
- Nolan, James Bennett. *Southeastern Pennsylvania: A History of the Counties of Berks, Bucks, Chester, Delaware, Montgomery, Philadelphia, and Schuylkill*. Lewis Historical Publishing Co., 1923. Vol. 2. Pgs. 1064 - 1065.
- Turnbach, Richard. "Family History: George Huntzinger Descendants: Berks/Schuylkill Co., PA." *Berks County GenWeb Archives*. http://files.usgwarchives.net/pa/schuylkill/othcourt/oath0001.txt.
- Turnbach, Richard. "Military: Rev War: Company Rosters/Pay Records 1778–1780: Berks/Schuylkill Co., PA." *Berks County GenWeb Archives*. http://files.usgwarchives.net/pa/berks/military/revwar/rev0001.txt.
- Turnbach, Richard. "Miscellaneous: Oath of Allegiance, 'Northeastern Berks,' 1778: Berks/Schuylkill Co., PA." *Berks County GenWeb Archives*. http://files.usgwarchives.net/pa/schuylkill/othcourt/oath0001.txt.
- Pennsylvania, U.S. Wills and Probate Records, 1683–1993. Berks County, Probate Estate File for George Huntzinger, 1802. Accessed at Ancestry.com.

Thomas Brooks A015100
- U.S., Quaker Meeting Records, 1681-1994. (parents' 1748 marriage; father's 1767 death; illegitimate child in 1774; disowned 1775; burial 1790; widow & children 1791). Accessed at Ancestry.com.
- Egle, Dr. William Henry and Reed, Dr. George Edward, Eds. *Pennsylvania Archives.* Third Series, Vol. 20. Pgs. 347, 632. And, Third Series, Vol. 23. Pg. 768. Issued 1894-1899. Accessed at FamilySearch.
- Montgomery, Dr. Thomas Lynch, Ed. *Pennsylvania Archives.* Fifth Series, Vol. 6. Pgs. 304-305. Issued in 1906. Accessed at FamilySearch.
- North America, Family Histories, 1500-1900. #54568. Accessed at Ancestry.com.
- Estate Papers, 1713-1810; Author: Chester County (Pennsylvania). Accessed at Ancestry.com.

Patriot Stories Works Cited
Chapter 5: INDEPENDENCE

Private William Braithwaite A013697
- U.S., Pension and Bounty-Land Warrant Application Records, 1800-1900. Braithwaite, William. S*W5934. *National Archives and Records Administration.* Accessed at Ancestry.com.
- Find A Grave. Braithwaite, William Sr. Memorial 15867569. Accessed at Ancestry.com.
- "Battle of Eutaw Springs." *American Battlefield Trust.* 2022. www.battlefields.org/learn/revolutionary-war/battles/eutaw-springs.
- "Ninety Six." *American Battlefield Trust.* 2022. www.battlefields.org/learn/revolutionary-war/battles/ninety-six.
- "Guilford Courthouse." *American Battlefield Trust.* 2022. www.battlefields.org/learn/revolutionary-war/battles/guilford-court-house.
- "Camden." *American Battlefield Trust.* 2022. www.battlefields.org/learn/articles/camden.
- "Monmouth." *American Battlefield Trust.* 2022. www.battlefields.org/learn/revolutionary-war/battles/monmouth.

Private Enos Day A030874
- U.S., Compiled Revolutionary War Military Service Records, 1775-1783. Daye, Eneas. M881. Roll #548. *National Archives and Records Administration.* Accessed at Ancestry.com.
- *A History of the Town of Keene [New Hampshire].* Chapter IX: Revolutionary War – Concluded 1778-1783. Keene, NH: Sentinel Print. Co., 1904. Pgs. 11, 244. www.keenenh.gov/sites/default/files/chapter9.pdf.
- Auburn, Emma. "West Point." *George Washington's Mount Vernon.* 2023. www.mountvernon.org/library/digitalhistory/digital-encyclopedia/article/west-point/.

- Vermont, Vital Records, 1720-1908. Lewis Day born 1799. Accessed at Ancestry.com.
- 1810 United States Federal Census. Household of Enos Day. Accessed at Ancestry.com.
- 1860 United States Federal Census. Household of A.W. Day. Accessed at Ancestry.com.

Private John Peebles A088010
- Southern Campaigns Revolutionary War Pension Statements & Rosters. Peebles, John. R8074. https://revwarapps.org/r8074.pdf.
- "The Southern Theater of the American Revolution." American Battlefields Trust. 2023. https://www.battlefields.org/learn/articles/southern-theater-american-revolution.
- Find A Grave. Peebles, John. Memorial 38615008. Accessed at findagrave.com.
- Illinois, U.S., Revolutionary War Veteran Burials Index, 1775-1850. Peebles, John. Online Database. Accessed at Ancestry.com. See also https://github.com/kwhershey/rev_soldiers/blob/master/spouse/bookv3.txt.
- U.S. and International Marriage Records, 1560-1900. Owens, Wilmouth. Online Database. Accessed at Ancestry.com.
- Walker, Hon. Charles A., Ed. *History of Macoupin County, Illinois*. Vol. II. Chicago, IL: S.J. Clarke Publishing Company, 1911. Pg. 166-9. http://livinghistoryofillinois.com/pdf_files/.

Colonel Thomas Wooten A130383
- Clark, Walter. *State Records of North Carolina*. Goldsboro, NC: Nash Brothers Book and Job Printers, 1904. Vol. 23. Pg. 992, 995; Vol. 12. Pg. 265, 337; Vol. 17. Pgs. 849, 944-5. Accessed at Google Books.
- Haywood, Marshall DeLancey. *Joel Lane, Pioneer and Patriot, Including Notes about the Colonial and Revolutionary History of Wake County North Carolina*. Creative Media Partners, LLC, 2015. Pg. 15.
- Lewis, J.D. *NC Patriots: Their Own Words, 1775-1783*. Published by Author, 2012. Vol. 2. Part 1, Pgs. 188-9. Part 2, Pgs. 20, 34, 77, 201, 397,408,462, 473, 503, 573, 555, 567, 792, 800, 849, 1004 and 1020. Accessed at Google Books.
- "The Battle of Eutaw Springs." 2017. www.revolutionarywar.us/year-1781/battle-eutaw-springs/.
- "Eutaw Springs." *American Battlefield Trust*. 2022. www.battlefields.org/learn/revolutionary-war/battles/eutaw-springs.
- Editors, History.com. "Bloody Battle Begins at Eutaw Springs, South Carolina." HISTORY. *A&E Television Networks*. Original: Nov. 13, 2009; Updated: Sept. 29, 2021. www.history.com/this-day-in-history/bloody-battle-begins-at-eutaw-springs-south-carolina.

Joseph Thompson A114337
- Patrie, Lois McClennan. *A History of Colrain Massachusetts, with Genealogies of Early Families.* Higgonson Book Co., 1974. Pg. 75.
- McClellan, Charles H. *The Early Settlers of Colrain Massachusetts.* Speech. 1885. Reprinted by Heritage Books: 2011. Pgs. 40, 83, 84.
- Eldridge, William Henry. *Henry Genealogy.* T. Marvin and Son, 1915. Pgs. 105-106.
- Holbrook, Massachusetts. Vital Records (Births and Deaths). https://www.holbrookma.gov/town-clerk/pages/vital-records-births-and-deaths.
- "The Puritan Tithingman – The Most Powerful Man in New England." *New England Historical Society.* 2022. https://newenglandhistoricalsociety.com/puritan-tithingman-powerful-men-new-england/.

John Adam Roush A098982
- Roush, Lester Le Roy. *History of the Roush Family in America, from Its Founding by John Adam Rausch in 1736 to the Present Time.* Strasburg, VA: Shenandoah Publishing House Inc., 1928. Pgs. 2, 16.
- Abercrombie, Janice L. and Slatten, Richard, Comp & Tr. *Virginia Revolutionary Publick [sic] Claims.* Vol III. Athens, GA: Iberian Publishing House, 1992. Pg. 115. Accessed at Library of Virginia online.
- Brumbaugh, Gaius Marcus. *Revolutionary War Records Virginia.* Lancaster, PA: Lancaster Press, 1936. Pg. 607. Accessed at Archive.org.
- "Virginia Public Services Claims." Family History Library #8574721. Image 554. (DAR Library photocopy)
- Abstract of Graves of Revolutionary Patriots. Accessed at Ancestry.com.
- "A collection of upwards of thirty thousand names of German, Swiss, Dutch, French and other immigrants in Pennsylvania from 1727." Pg. 104. Accessed at FamilySearch.org.
- Find A Grave. Roush, John. Memorial 14655408. Accessed at Findagrave.com.
- Pennsylvania, Land Warrants, 1733-1987. Accessed at Ancestry.com.
- U.S. and International Marriage Records, 1560-1900. Accessed at Ancestry.com.

Private George Roush A098975
- U.S., Revolutionary War Pension and Bounty-Land Warrant Application Files, 1800-1900. Roush, George. *S18579. Accessed on Ancestry.com.
- Roush, Lester Le Roy. *History of the Roush Family in America, From Its Founding by John Adam Rausch in 1736 to the Present Time.* Strasburg, VA: Printed by Shenandoah Publishing House Inc., 1928. Pgs. 61, 412, 413, 415, 417, 418.
- Ohio, County Marriage Records, 1774-1993. Accessed at Ancestry.com.
- Abstracts of Graves of Revolutionary Patriots. Accessed at Ancestry.com.

- Portrait: Roush, Lester Le Roy. *History of the Roush Family in America, From Its Founding by John Adam Rausch in 1736 to the Present Time*. Pg. 418. Copyright 1928 by Lester LeRoy Roush.

Nathaniel Colburn A209171
- Mullen, Jolene Roberts. *Connecticut Town Meeting Records during the American Revolution*. Vol. II. Westminster, MD: Heritage Books, 2011. Pgs. 577, 580-584.
- Lederer, Richard M. *Colonial American English: A Glossary*. Verbatim Book, 1985.
- Clark, Emily. "The Storied History behind Connecticut's Nicknames." *Connecticuthistory.org*. Oct. 14, 2021. https://connecticuthistory.org/the-storied-history-behind-connecticuts-nicknames.
- Fernandez, Juan Miguel. "Connecticut Raids." *George Washington's Mount Vernon*. 2023. www.mountvernon.org/library/digitalhistory/digital-encyclopedia/article/connecticut-raids.
- Brooks, Rebecca Beatrice. "The Great Puritan Migration." *Historyofmassachusetts.org*. May 24, 2017. https://historyofmassachusetts.org/the-great-puritan-migration/.
- Coburn, Silas Roger; Gordon, George Augustus. *Genealogy of the descendants of Edward Colburn/Coburn*. Lowell, MA: W. Coburn, 1913. Accessed at Archive.org.

Collin (McKinney) McKenney A077574
- "Governor of Virginia." *Thomas Jefferson Monticello*. www.monticello.org/research-education/thomas-jefferson-encyclopedia/governor-virginia/.
- "Virginia Constitutions: Constitution 1776." *Library of Virginia*. 2019. www.lva.virginia.gov/constitutions/discover/#constitution-1776.
- Summers, Lewis Preston. *Annals of Southwest Virginia, 1769-1800*. Part 2. Pgs. 1060-1, 1073, 1083. Baltimore, MD: Genealogical Publishing Co., 1996. Accessed at Ancestry.com.

Samuel Dyer A035237
- Obituary of Samuel Dyer, Southhall of Staunton, Virginia. Transcribed copy in the possession of Mary Marszalek's family.
- Harris, C. Leon, Tr. Southern Campaign American Revolution Pension Statements & Rosters. Dyer, Samuel Dyer. *S8378. www.revwarapps.org/s8378.pdf.
- Johnson, Maxwell. "Plain Dealing, Keene." *Scottsville Museum*. Scottsville, Virginia. 2018. www.scottsvillemuseum.com/esmont/esmonthomes/plaindealinghome.html.

- Kukla, Jon. "Patrick Henry (1736-1799)." *Encyclopedia Virginia*. Virginia Humanities. www.encyclopediavirginia.org/entries/henry-patrick-1736-1799/.
- Wolfe, Brendan. "Indentured Servants in Colonial Virginia." *Encyclopedia Virginia*. Virginia Humanities. www.encyclopediavirginia.org/entries/indentured-servants-in-colonial-virginia/.
- Photo courtesy of Mary Dyer Marszalek.

Private Jeremiah Lockwood A071069
- Mullen, Jolene Roberts. *Connecticut Town Meeting Records During the American Revolution*. Vol. 2. Westminster, MD: Heritage Books Inc., 2011. Pg. 365.
- U.S., Revolutionary War Rolls 1775-1783. M246. Roll #12. *National Archives and Records Administration*. Accessed at Ancestry.com.
- *North American Family Histories, 1500-2000*. Jeremiah Lockwood. Accessed at Ancestry.com.
- Clark, Ellen McCallister Powers, Sandra L. "Connecticut in the American Revolution." An Exhibition from the Library and Museum Collections of The Society of the Cincinnati. 2001. www.americanrevolutioninstitute.org/wp-content/uploads/2018/09/Connecticut-in-the-American-Revolution-2001.pdf.
- Lockwood, James. *Descendants of Robert Lockwood: Colonial and Revolutionary History of the Lockwood Family in America, from A.D. 1630*. Self-published. 1889. Pgs. 1, 143. Accessed at Google Books.
- Banks, Charles Edward. *The Winthrop Fleet of 1630: an Account of the Vessels, the Voyage, the Passengers and Their English Homes, from Original Authorities*. Boston: Houghton Mifflin, 1930. Accessed index on Ancestry.com.

Henry Stahl, Sr. A075663
- Strassburger, Ralph Beaver. *Pennsylvania German Pioneers*. Vol. 1 (1727-1775). Second Printing. Baltimore, MD: Genealogical Publishing Company, 1980. Pgs. 299-300. Accessed at Ancestry.com.
- Shinn, Benjamin, Ed. *Biographical Memoirs of Blackford County*. Chicago, IL: The Bowen Publishing Company, 1900. Pgs. 294-296. Accessed at Google Books.
- Maryland colonial naturalization records, liber DD-6. Pgs. 285-286. Accessed at www.frankstahlbio.net/.
- Meredith, John D. *Summary of land transactions in Frederick County, MD, and Cumberland & Bedford Counties, PA*. Accessed at www.frankstahlbio.net/.
- Egle, Dr. William Henry and Reed, Dr. George Edward, Eds. *Pennsylvania Archives*. Third Series, Vol. 20. Pgs. 3, 9. Issued 1894-1899. Accessed at Ancestry.com.
- Church records (1772-1774) of the Salem Reformed Church, Hagerstown, MD, researched by John D. Meredith. Accessed at https://frankstahlbio.net/.
- Orphan Court Records, Bedford County, PA. 1791. Accessed at www.frankstahlbio.net/.

- Probate records, Estate of Henry Stahl, Franklin County, PA, 1790. Accessed at www.frankstahlbio.net/.

James (Flowers) Flower A039887
- Egle, Dr. William Henry and Reed, Dr. George Edward, Eds. *Pennsylvania Archives*. Third Series, Vol. 13. Pgs. 123-124, 315-316. Issued 1894-1899. Accessed at Ancestry.com.
- Davis, William Watts Hart; Warren Smedley Ely, Ed.; John Woolf Jordan, Ed. *History of Bucks County, Pennsylvania*. Vol. 3. Chicago, IL and New York, NY: Lewis Publishing Company, 1905. Flowers, Thomas Kitching Pg. 554-5. Accessed at Google Books. http://pagenweb.org/~bucks/BIOS_DAVIS/flowers_thomasK.htm.
- Tax Records of Bucks County, Pennsylvania. 1776, 1781, 1783, 1785, 1786. Accessed at Ancestry.com.
- Pennsylvania, Revolutionary War Battalions and Militia Index, 1775-1783. Accessed at Ancestry.com.
- Pennsylvania, U.S., Tax and Exoneration, 1768-1801. Accessed at Ancestry.com.
- Pennsylvania, U.S., Direct Tax Lists, 1798. Accessed at Ancestry.com.
- Pennsylvania, Wills and Probate Records, 1683-1993. Accessed at Ancestry.com.
- Find A Grave. Flowers, George. Memorial 107996647. Accessed at Findagrave.com.
- Schenawolf, Harry. "Cordwainers & Cobblers, Shoemakers in Colonial America." *Revolutionary War Journal*. March 8, 2016. www.revolutionarywarjournal.com/cordwainers/.

Judge Samuel Chase, Sr. A021210
- Child, William. *History of the town of Cornish, New Hampshire with Genealogical Record*. Concord, NH: Rumford Press, 1911. Pgs. 13, 18,19, 49, 53, 60, 61. Accessed at Google Books.
- Hammond, Isaac Weare, Ed. *Town Papers. Documents Relating to Towns in New Hampshire*. Vol. 11. Pg. 438-9, 445-6. Accessed at Ancestry.com.
- Peck, Thomas Bellows. *The Bellows genealogy, or, John Bellows the boy emigrant of 1635 and his descendants*. Keene, NH: Sentinel Printing Co., 1898. Pgs. 43-46. Accessed at Ancestry.com.
- Judge Samuel Chase. National Portrait Gallery. *Smithsonian Institute*. https://npg.si.edu/object/npg_NH900001?destination=edan-search/catalog_of_america.

Agnes Brewster A014150
- Affidavit of Grandchildren Brewster Sister Describing Revolutionary Service. April 1913. In documentation with DAR #884403.

- Ley, Janet. "Brave Sisters Helped Militia Men." *Bloomington Herald Times*. Bloomington, IN. July 17, 2000. www.cwcfamily.org/sisters.htm.
- Schwierhttps, Carrie. "A Spot Called 'God's Acre' and the Remains of Three Revolutionary War Heroines." Blogging Hoosier History. *Indiana University Libraries*. Oct. 30, 2012. www.blogs.libraries.indiana.edu/iubarchives/2012/10/30/gods-acre/.
- Photo: Courtesy of Ann Olson.

Michael King A064689
- Perrin, William Henry, Ed. *History of Stark County Ohio*. Chicago, IL: Baskin & Battey, 1881. Pg. 960. Accessed at Google Books.
- Flaningam, Ora L. et al. *A Cramer-King History: Some Descendants of Philip King, Sr and Catherine ? of Somerset County, Pennsylvania*. Self-published. 2001. Pgs. 6-7. Copy provided by author.
- Pennsylvania, U.S., Tax and Exoneration, 1768-1801. Bedford County. King surnames. Accessed at Ancestry.com.
- Egle, Dr. William Henry and Reed, Dr. George Edward, Eds. *Pennsylvania Archives*. Third Series, Vol. 22. Issued 1894-1899. Pg. 238. Accessed at Ancestry.com.
- Pennsylvania Probate Records, 1683-1994. Somerset County, Estate file and Orphan's Court record for Michael King, 1801. Accessed at FamilySearch.org.
- Pennsylvania, U.S. Land Warrants and Applications, 1733-1952. Bedford County, Michael King, 1785. Accessed at Ancestry.com.
- 1790 U.S. Census, Milford Township, Bedford County, Pennsylvania, Pg. 259. Accessed at Ancestry.com
- Burns, Brendon S. "Suffering What?" The Ancestral Clark. April 24, 2019. www.vtcrewcat.wordpress.com/2019/04/24/suffering-what/.
- Revolutionary War Damage Claims, 1776-1783. State of New Jersey Department of State. https://wwwnet-dos.state.nj.us/DOS_ArchivesDBPortal/RevWarDamages.aspx.
- "Chester County Register of Revolutionary War Damages (British Depredations)." 1782. www.chesco.org/DocumentCenter/View/9395/Chester-County-British-Depredations?bidId=.

Ann Graves A047196
- Revolutionary War Public Service Claims Index. *Library of Virginia Online*. Revised 2021. https://lva-virginia.libguides.com/public-service.
- Abercrombie, Janice L. and Slatten, Richard, Comp. & Tr. *Virginia Revolution Public Service Claims*. Impressed Property. Vol. 3. Athens, GA: Iberian Publishing Co., 1992. Pg. 855. Accessed at Library of Virginia online.
- Drexler, Ken. "*Treaty of Paris*: Primary Documents in American History." *Library of Congress*. Original: Feb. 11, 2021; Updated: March 9, 2021. https://guides.loc.gov/treaty-of-paris.

- U.S., Wills and Probate Records, 1652-1900. Will Book, Vol D, 1761-1772. Graves, Thomas. Probate date Oct. 7, 1767. Accessed at Ancestry.com.

John Grigsby A048485
- Personal Property Tax 1782-1783. Reel #299. Vol. II. Pgs. 112-119. *Library of Rockbridge*.
- Abercrombie, Janice L. and Richard Slatten, Comp. & Tr. *Virginia Revolution Public Service Claims. Impressed Property*. Vol. 3. Athens, GA: Iberian Publishing Co., 1992. Pgs. 821, 825. Accessed at Library of Virginia online.
- Morton, Oren F. *A History of Rockbridge County, Virginia*. Staunton, VA: The McClure Company Inc., 1920. Pgs. 256, 286. Accessed at Google Books.
- National Register of Historic Places. "Hickory Hill, Rockbridge County, Virginia." *National Park Service*. United States Department of the Interior. www.dhr.virginia.gov/wp-content/uploads/2018/04/081-0022_HickoryHill_2006_NRfinal.pdf.
- Martin, Juan; Hanselmann, Frederick H; Horrell, Christopher and Espinosa, Jose. "Investigation of Shipwrecks from the Battle of Cartagena de Indias in 1741." *The Digital Archaeological Record*. 2020. https://core.tdar.org/document/457336/investigation-of-shipwrecks-from-the-battle-of-cartagena-de-indias-in-1741.
- "Record of the Grigsby Family of Rockbridge County, Virginia." Hand-written document written by Mary Davidson from transcribed Paxton/Grigsby family Bibles. Part of Rockbridge Historical Society's genealogy collection; copy secured from Washington and Lee University, Lexington, Virginia.

Private Cottrell Lively A070741
- U.S., Revolutionary War Pension and Bounty-Land Warrant Application Files, 1800-1900. Lively, Godrell [Cottrell]. *SR6389. Accessed at Ancestry.com.
- "Grave Markers to be Unveiled." *The Monroe Watchman Newspaper*. Aug. 27, 1929. Pg. 5.
- Bockstruck, Lloyd DeWitt. *Revolutionary War Bounty Land Grants*. Baltimore, MD: Genealogical Publishing Co., 1998. Pg. 318. Accessed at Ancestry.com.
- Morton, Oren F. *A History of Monroe County, West Virginia*. Dayton, VA: Ruebush-Elkins Co., 1916. Pg. 59. Accessed at Google Books.

Private Elijah Gray A215654
- U.S., Revolutionary War Pension and Bounty-Land Warrant Application Files, 1800-1900. Gray, Elijah. S*W1854. (92-page application is also numbered BLWT 19605-160-55.) Accessed at Ancestry.com.
- *Massachusetts Soldiers and Sailors of the Revolutionary War*. Vol. 6. Prepared by the Secretary of the Commonwealth. Boston, MA: Wright 7 Potter Printing Co., 1908. Pg. 768. Accessed at Ancestry.com.
- *Huron Reflector* Newspaper. Norwalk, Ohio. Nov. 2, 1830, Image 3. Accessed at Ancestry.com.

- *LeRoy Gazette* Newspaper. LeRoy, New York. Feb. 6, 1955, Pg. 2; Aug. 21, 1986, Image 7. Accessed at Ancestry.com.
- *Republican Compiler* Newspaper. Gettysburg, Pennsylvania. Feb. 16, 1830, Image 3. Accessed at Ancestry.com.
- New York, U.S., Wills and Probate Records. 1659-1999. Elijah Gray. Accessed at Ancestry.com.
- North, Stafford E. *Our County and Its People: A Descriptive and Biographical Record of Genesee County, New York*. Batavia, NY: Batavia History Co., 1899. Pg. 95. Accessed at Archive.org.

Captain Edward Moseley A081969
- Abercrombie, Janice L. and Slatten, Richard, Comp. & Tr. *Virginia Revolutionary Publick [sic] Claims*. Vol. II. Athens, GA: Iberian Publishing Co., 1992. Pg. 235. Accessed at Google Books.
- "Battle of Petersburg." Revolutionary War.com. 2017. https://revolutionarywar.us/year-1781/battle-of-petersburg/.
- "History." *County of Charlotte, Virginia*. 2023. https://www.charlottecountyva.gov/visitors/history.php.
- McAllister, J. T. *Virginia Militia in the Revolutionary War*. Hot Springs, VA: McAllister Publishing, Co., 1913. Pgs. 173. Library of Congress. https://www.loc.gov/item/13023910.
- Abstract of Graves of Revolutionary Patriots. Accessed at Ancestry.com.

Thomas Paxton A211156 & Private William Paxton A209218
- U.S., Pension and Bounty-Land Warrant Application Records, 1800-1900. Paxton, William. *S5873. *National Archives and Records Administration*. Accessed at Ancestry.com.
- *Personal Property Tax Records for Rockbridge County, 1782-1786*. Henings Statutes, Vol. XI. Pgs. 112-129. Accessed at Library of Virginia online.
- "NPS Historical Handbook: Yorktown." Yorktown National Battlefield. *National Park Service*. Last modified Dec. 2, 2002. www.nps.gov/parkhistory/online_books/hh/14/hh14b.htm.
- Grubner, Kate Egner. "The History of Williamsburg." *American Battlefield Trust*. 2023. www.battlefields.org/learn/articles/history-williamsburg.
- "Record of the Grigsby Family of Rockbridge County, Virginia." Hand-written document written by Mary Davidson from transcribed Paxton/Grigsby family Bibles. Part of Rockbridge Historical Society's genealogy collection; copy secured from Washington and Lee University, Lexington, Virginia.

Private William Gragg, Jr. A046612
- U.S., Pension and Bounty-Land Warrant Application Records, 1800-1900. Gragg, William. *S5873. *National Archives and Records Administration*. Accessed at Ancestry.com.

- "NPS Historical Handbook: Yorktown." Yorktown National Battlefield. *National Park Service*. Last modified Dec. 2, 2002. www.nps.gov/parkhistory/online_books/hh/14/hh14b.htm.

Private Stephen Manchester A214635
- U.S., Revolutionary War Pension and Bounty-Land Warrant Application Files, 1800-1900. Manchester, Stephen. *S42908. Accessed at Ancestry.com.
- Tiverton, RI Vital Records: Baptism and marriage record, Stephen Manchester. Accessed at Ancestry.com.
- "*Treaty of Paris*, 1783." *U.S. Office of the Historian*. https://history.state.gov/milestones/1776-1783/treaty.
- "*Treaty of Paris*: Primary Documents in American History." *Library of Congress*. https://guides.loc.gov/treaty-of-paris.
- History.com Editors. "Rhode Island." HISTORY. *A&E Television Networks*. Original: Nov. 9, 2009; Updated: April 17, 2020. www.history.com/topics/us-states/rhode-island.
- Deed Stephen and Hannah Manchester, Washington Co., NY. Vol. B. Pgs. 335-337. Accessed at FamilySearch.org.
- 1800 U.S. Census Rensselaerville, Albany, NY. Pg. 168. Accessed at Ancestry.com.
- 1830 U.S. Census Rensselaerville, Albany, NY. Pg. 428. Accessed at Ancestry.com.
- 1840 U.S. Census Remsen, Oneida, NY. Pg. 243-244. Accessed at Ancestry.com.
- New York 1840 Pensioners List. Stephen Manchester, Oneida Co., NY, Age 78, Remsen. New York, U.S., Compiled Census and Census Substitutes Index, 1790-1890. Accessed at Ancestry.com.
- Houston, Houston Co., MN Death Records. Vol. A. Pg. 18. Line 3, Betsey Galusha, 17 May 1870; Also, Johnston Cemetery Burial Records, "Betsy Galutia" died 7 May 1870, unmarked. Accessed at Houston County Historical Society.

Patriot Stories Works Cited
Chapter 6: VISION

Prince Estabrook
- Fikes, Robert. "Prince Estabrook." *Black Past*. Oct. 11, 2020. www.blackpast.org/african-american-history/prince-estabrook-1740-1830/.
- Poole, Bill and Charles Price. "Prince Estabrook." The Lexington Minute Men. 2018. www.lexingtonminutemen.com/prince-estabrook.html.
- "Prince Estabrook of Lexington." *National Park Service*. United States Department of the Interior. www.nps.gov/people/prince-estabrook-of-lexington.htm.

- "The Revolutionary War." Africans in America. *PBS Online*. www.pbs.org/wgbh/aia/part2/2narr4.html.
- "The Revolution and the End of Slavery in Massachusetts." *Royall House and Slave Quarters*. https://royallhouse.org/the-revolution-and-the-end-of-slavery-in-massachusetts/.

William Lee
- Fikes, Robert. "William Lee." *Black Past*. September 6, 2021. www.blackpast.org/african-american-history/people-african-american-history/william-lee-aka-billy-lee-will-lee-1752-1810/.
- MacCleod, Jessica. "William 'Billy' Lee." African Americans in the Revolutionary War. *George Washington's Mount Vernon*. www.mountvernon.org/george-washington/the-revolutionary-war/african-americans-in-the-revolutionary-war/.
- "William 'Billy' Lee." *American Battlefield Trust*. https://www.battlefields.org/learn/biographies/william-billy-lee.
- "William Lee." *Valley Forge National Historic Park*. December 22, 2020. www.nps.gov/vafo/learn/historyculture/william-lee.htm.

Salem Poor
- Coleman, Collette. "7 Black Heroes of the American Revolution." History.com. *A&E Television Networks*. February 11, 2020. www.history.com/news/black-heroes-american-revolution.
- Nielsen, Euell A. "Salem Poor." *Black Past*. Jan. 21, 2007. www.blackpast.org/african-american-history/poor-salem-1747-1780/.
- "Salem Poor." *Valley Forge National Historic Park*. Dec. 30, 2020. www.nps.gov/vafo/learn/historyculture/salem-poor.htm.
- "Salem Poor." *American Battlefield Trust*. www.battlefields.org/learn/biographies/salem-poor.
- "Salem Poor War Hero." *Smithsonian National Postal Museum*. https://postalmuseum.si.edu/exhibition/the-black-experience-early-pioneers/salem-poor.

Phillis Wheatley
- Coleman, Collette. "7 Black Heroes of the American Revolution." HISTORY. *A&E Television Networks*. Feb. 11, 2020. www.history.com/news/black-heroes-american-revolution.
- "Phillis Wheatley." *Poetry Foundation*. 2022. www.poetryfoundation.org/poets/phillis-wheatley.
- Michaels, Debra Ph.D. "Phillis Wheatley." 2015. www.womenshistory.org/education-resources/biographies/phillis-wheatley.
- "African Americans and the End of Slavery in Massachusetts." *Massachusetts Historical Society*. www.masshist.org/features/endofslavery/wheatley.

- Wheatley, Phillis. "His Excellency General Washington." 1776. https://poets.org/poem/his-excellency-general-washington.
- Winkler, Elizabeth. "How Phillis Wheatley Was Recovered Through History." July 30, 2020. www.newyorker.com/books/under-review/how-phillis-wheatley-was-recovered-through-history.
- "Portraits of American Women Writers." *The Library Company of Philadelphia.* 2005. https://librarycompany.org/women/portraits/wheatley.htm.

NOTE: The date of Wheatley's release from slavery is disputed. According to one source she states in a 1773 letter that she had been freed. According to other sources, she was freed in John Wheatley's will in 1778 or upon Susannah Wheatley's death in 1774.

Peter Salem
- Coleman, Collette. "7 Black Heroes of the American Revolution." HISTORY. *A&E Television Networks.* Feb. 11, 2020. www.history.com/news/black-heroes-american-revolution.
- Nielsen, Euell A. "Peter Salem." *Black Past.* Jan. 19, 2007. www.blackpast.org/african-american-history/salem-peter-ca-1750-1816/.
- "Peter Salem." *American Battlefield Trust.* www.battlefields.org/learn/biographies/peter-salem.
- "Peter Salem and the Battle of Bunker Hill." *National Museum of African American History and Culture.* Smithsonian. June 17, 2016. https://nmaahc.si.edu/explore/stories/peter-salem-and-battle-bunker-hill.
- "Peter Salem." *National Park Service.* www.nps.gov/people/peter-salem.htm.
- Schenwolf, Harry. "Peter Salem – African American Patriot During the American Revolutionary War." *Revolutionary War Journal.* July 10, 2016. www.revolutionarywarjournal.com/peter-salem/.

Lemuel Haynes
- "The Revolutionary War." Africans in America. *PBS Online.* www.pbs.org/wgbh/aia/part2/2p29.html.
- Ney, Diane. *Barnes & Noble Illustrated Guide to Sites of the American Revolution.* New York, NY: Berenson Design & Books, Ltd., 2004, Pg. 219.
- Nielsen, Euella A. "Lemuel Haynes." *Black Past.* Jan. 18, 2007. www.blackpast.org/african-american-history/haynes-lemuel-1753-1833/.
- "Lemuel Haynes's Patriotic Poem." *For the Church.* June 26, 2017. https://ftc.co/resource-library/blog-entries/lemuel-hayness-patriotic-poem/.

James Forten
- "The HMS Jersey." Staff editors. HISTORY. *A&E Television Networks.* Updated Aug. 21, 2018; Original March 19, 2010. www.history.com/topics/american-revolution/the-hms-jersey.

- "James Forten – One of America's Founding Fathers." The Constitutional Walking Tour. June 30, 2020. www.theconstitutional.com/blog/2020/06/30/james-forten-one-americas-founding-fathers.
- "James Forten Discovery Cart." *Museum of the American Revolution*. www.amrevmuseum.org/james-forten-discovery-cart.
- "The Revolutionary War." Africans in America. *PBS Online*. www.pbs.org/wgbh/aia/part2/2p29.html.
- Watson, Elwood. "James Forten." *Black Past*. Jan. 17, 2007. www.blackpast.org/african-american-history/forten-james-1766-1842/.

Agrippa Hull
- "Agrippa Hull." *Valley Forge National Historic Park*. Feb. 4, 2021. www.nps.gov/vafo/learn/historyculture/agrippa-hull.htm.
- Knisley, Kendra. "Agrippa Hull: Lover of Liberty." *Berkshire Museum*. https://explore.berkshiremuseum.org/digital-archive/agrippa-hull-lover-of-liberty.
- Nash, Gary. "Agrippa Hull: Revolutionary Patriot." *Black Past*. July 2, 2008. www.blackpast.org/african-american-history/agrippa-hull-revolutionary-patriot/.
- "The Revolutionary War." Africans in America. *PBS Online*. www.pbs.org/wgbh/aia/part2/2p13.html.

James Armistead Lafayette
- Coleman, Collette. "7 Black Heroes of the American Revolution." HISTORY. *A&E Television Networks*. February 11, 2020. www.history.com/news/black-heroes-american-revolution.
- "James Armistead Lafayette." *American Battlefield Trust*. www.battlefields.org/learn/biographies/james-armistead-lafayette.
- Morgan, Thad. "How an Enslaved Man-Turned-Spy Helped Secure Victory at the Battle of Yorktown." History.com. *A&E Television Networks*. Original Feb. 4, 2010; Updated July 9, 2020. www.history.com/news/battle-of-yorktown-slave-spy-james-armistead.
- Salo, Jessica. "James Armistead Lafayette." *Black Past*. www.blackpast.org/african-american-history/lafayette-james-armistead-1760-1832/.
- "Lafayette's Testimonial to James Armistead Lafayette." *George Washington's Mount Vernon*. www.mountvernon.org/george-washington/the-revolutionary-war/spying-and-espionage/american-spies-of-the-revolution/lafayettes-testimonial-to-james-armistead-lafayette/.
- "Spies of the American Revolution." *George Washington's Mount Vernon*. www.mountvernon.org/george-washington/the-revolutionary-war/spying-and-espionage/american-spies-of-the-revolution/.

Prince Hall
- Allen, Danielle. "A Forgotten Black Founding Father." *The Atlantic*. Feb. 10, 2021. www.theatlantic.com/magazine/archive/2021/03/prince-hall-forgotten-founder/617791/.
- "Petition for freedom (manuscript copy) to the Massachusetts Council and the House of Representatives, [13] January 1777." *Massachusetts Historical Society*. https://www.masshist.org/database/557.
- "Petition 1/13/1777." Africans in America. *PBS Online*. Courtesy of Massachusetts Archives. www.pbs.org/wgbh/aia/part2/2h32t.html.
- "Prince Hall – Bound for Greatness." *Medford Historical Society & Museum*. www.medfordhistorical.org/medford-history/africa-to-medford/prince-hall/.
- Swanson, Abigail. "Prince Hall." *Black Past*. Jan. 18, 2007. www.blackpast.org/african-american-history/hall-prince-c-1735-1807/.

List of Additional Lake Minnetonka DAR Chapter Patriots

Patriot and Ancestor Number	Member Descendant
Adams, Robert A000555	Sharon Rice
	Donni Torres
Annis, Daniel A002843	Dolores Scanlon
Anson, Silas* A128654	Julie Schaefer
Atwood, Jesse A003702	Nancy Steege
Austin, Joab* A003813	Julie Schaefer
Austin, Nathaniel* A003837	Julie Schaefer
Avery, Gardiner A003956	Rebecca Wilkens
	Susan Wilkens
Babcock, Oliver A004275	Elizabeth Isaacson
Baker, John A004967	Katherine Bell
Ballard, Josiah A005539	Nancy Azzam
Baltzly, Christian A005616	Sally Jacquemin
Bell, Thomas A008802	Elizabeth Murphy
Bisbee, Hopestill A010409	Shirleen Hoffman
Bouldin, Thomas, Jr. A012550	Barbara Schneider
Bouldin, Thomas, Sr. A012548	Barbara Schneider
Brower, Nicholas A015214	Janet DeJonge
Burden, Nathan A212505	Barbara Rustad
Capen, Ephraim A018979	Samantha Muldoon
Carnine, Andrew A019339	Ann Olson
	Erin Olson
Cheedle, Asa, Jr.* A021270	Cheryl Despathy
	Megan Stanga
Churchill, Nathaniel, Sr. A021950	Shirleen Hoffman
Claiborne, Jonas A022038	Manuela Witczek
Claiborne, Leonard A022039	Manuela Witczek
Connor, Richard A025095	Kelly Saporito
	Jill Weber
	JoAnn Zaspel
Corey, Hezekiah* A026020	Barbara Rustad
Cutler, Joseph A029170	Helen VonGrossman

List of Additional Lake Minnetonka DAR Chapter Patriots

Patriot and Ancestor Number	Member Descendant
Dreisbach, Jacob A033632	Libby Brahmbhatt
Dupree, William A035156	Ann Olson
	Erin Olson
Everett, Andrew A037811	Christina McGuire
Farnsworth, Henry* A038735	Sarah Martin
Faust, Baltzer A039369	Sandra Johnson
Felt, Samuel A038906	Erin Nardo
Fisk, John A039796	Sandra Duerre
Flower, Ithuriel A039886	Sandra Eldred
	Mary Nelson
	Nikki Nelson
Folsom, Daniel* A040248	Julie Schaefer
Force, Thomas Palmer* A040711	Lindal Martin
George, John A044219	Barbara Rustad
George, Yost* A044271	Sarah Martin
Giltner, John George* A048286	Lois Mackin
Gortner, David* A046294	Sarah Martin
Gortner, Michael* A046297	Sarah Martin
Grigsby, James* A048481	Joanne Hagen
Hale, Amos A049203	Barbara Schneider
Hale, Barnard A049207	Barbara Schneider
Hanson, John A051290	Krysina Grussing
Hathaway, Silas A053067	Christine Stephansen
Heady, James A053731	Ann Olson
	Erin Olson
Herring, Ludwig, Jr. A054411	Natalie Lembeck
	Terra Lembeck
Hills, Elisha A056324	Teresa Anderson
Holben, Jacob* A201606	Sarah Martin
Holman, Jonathan A056954	Phyllis Cox
Hurlburt, Adam A060970	Penney Birdsong
	Jessica Powell

List of Additional Lake Minnetonka DAR Chapter Patriots

Patriot and Ancestor Number	Member Descendant
Jewell, Benjamin A062641	Diana Bauerly
Johnson, Archibald A062974	Harriet Teiken
Kinney, Reuben A065333	Mary Ellis Peterson
Knowles, Willard A066762	Kristin Chalberg
Leedy, Abraham A068862	Cathryn Nelson
Lemley, George A069519	Kari Winning
Livezey, George A070780	Madalene McMahon
Lyman, Seth A072622	Mary Ellis Peterson
Mason, Philip A074977	Heather Pfeiffer
McLarty, Alexander A077840	Barbara Michael Baker
	Melissa Gregerson
	Sara Michael
Mears, Meshack A209537	Dee Eva
Miller, William A079655	Kathryn Fischer
Montgomery, Thomas A079094	Blair Brown
	Colleen Brown
Morrison, John III A081114	Alyse Cullen
Newell, Simeon A082820	Thomasin Rouner
Nickerson, Issacher A083733	Arlene Johnson
Ohl, Michael, Sr.* A085938	Lois Mackin
Palmer, Ephraim* A086525	Lindal Martin
Pennock, Overton A032516	Jill Albrecht
Plumb, Adam A216816	Marilyn Hein
Rothermel, Jacob A098779	Madeline Mithun
	Mary Mithun
Selby, Mordecai A101655	Elizabeth Stearns
Sheple, Joseph A207798	Amy Norheim
	Elizabeth Norheim
	Jill Trites
Sherburne, Job A103194	Alexandra Houck
Sherman, James A103261	Judith Taves
Slaght, Mathias A104982	Judy Whitlock

List of Additional Lake Minnetonka Chapter Patriots

Patriot and Ancestor Number	Member Descendant
Smith, Stephen A105943	Kimberlee Murphy Olson
Southworth, Constant A107398	Peggy Watson
Spalding, Jesse A107621	Theresa Stadheim
Stevenson, Abiathar A109210	Nancy Azzam
Tyler, William A117724	Kelly Schnell
Tyler, Major A117683	Cheryl Tibesar
Veeder, Cornelius A118445	Darienne McNamara
Viets, John A118759	Mary Theresa Kiihn
	Kathleen Melnychuk
Webster, Abel* A121122	Julie Schaefer
Webster, Stephen, Sr. A121365	Mary Ellis Peterson
Weed, John A205067	Lisa Woodard
Weeks, Matthias, Jr.* A121565	Julie Schaefer
Weeks, Matthias, Sr.* A121564	Julie Schaefer
Wentz, John* A123036	Lindal Martin
West, Alva A123083	Carol Ebbecke
Wiggins, Thomas A126002	Victoria Ahlquist
Wiley, John A201653	Shelby Banken
Williams, William* A215148	Barbara Rustad

Member's lineage to this Patriot is pending as of August 2023

Index of Images

Description of Photograph/Image	Page
DAR Memorial Continental Hall, Washington, D.C.	2
Paul Revere's Engraving of the Boston Massacre	12
Weller Tavern in Manchester, Vermont	32
Original Draft of the Declaration of Independence	40
Map of Seige of Boston, 1775	48
Gravestone of Abraham Winsor	58
Portrait of Thomas Truxtun	66
Gravestone of Real Daughter Mary Lyman Alexander	72
Gravestone of Zebulon Sutton's wife, Sarah	76
Gravestone of Hendrick Cortelyou	82
American Capital of Philadelphia in 1777	86
Rebecca Marshall Cathcart and her great-grandchildren	100
Gravestone of Georg (Henry) Lutz	104
Gravestone of Nathaniel Rudd	112
Gravestone of David Smith	114
Valley Forge	118
9th Regiment of Hillsdale Militia Excursions	136
The Old Stone Fort at Schoharie, New York	142
Letter to Enoch Eastman from Governor Chittenden	144
Gravestone of Adam and Elizabeth Flake	150
Gravestone of Jacob Peter	152
Lafayette's Virginia Campaign Map	160
Moore House, Yorktown, Virginia	176
Portrait of George Roush	186
Samuel Dyer's home, Plain Dealing	190
Brewster Sisters' Memorial	196
Portrait of Phillis Wheatley & Title Page of Poems, 1773	208

Index of Featured Lake Minnetonka Chapter DAR Patriots

Patriot and Ancestor Number	Pages	Member Descendant
Alexander, Thomas A001253	72, 265	Mary Ellis Peterson
Andreas, Peter A002555	153, 282	Lois Mackin
Andreas, William A002556	154, 283	Lois Mackin
Barber, Jacob A005849	62, 261	Michelle White
Barrett, Bartholomew A208181	136, 276	Kathleen Huston
Braithwaite, William A013697	180, 285	Norina Dove
Brewster, Agnes A014150	196, 290	Ann Olson
		Erin Olson
Brooks, Thomas A015100	159, 285	Miriam Kaegebein
Bucknam, Edwards A016550	139, 277	Mary Jo Wulf
Chase, Samuel, Sr. A021210	195, 290	Michelle White
Cheedle, Asa, Sr. A021269	147, 280	Cheryl Despathy
		Megan Stanga
Clark, Elisha A022276	80, 267	Jacqueline Anderson
Clark, Richard Langhorn A134150	35, 257	Charlotte Jenkins
Colburn, Nathaniel A209171	188, 288	Angela Coccolutto
		Amy Feldkamp
		Tammy Wenz
Converse, Edward A025168	34, 257	Nina Bentley
Cortelyou, Hendrick A026240	82, 268	Cheryl Despathy
		Sarah Pearson
Curtis, Azor A028810	134, 276	Haley Roth
		Laura Roth
		Louise Farkas
Curtis, Samuel A208263	109, 272	Haley Roth
		Laura Roth
		Louise Farkas
Daniels, Andreas A114883	140, 278	Pam Petersen
		Meaghan Daniel
Davidson, Daniel A030059	110, 273	Gwen Mashek
		Tara Mashek
		Janea Mitcheltree

Index of Featured Lake Minnetonka Chapter DAR Patriots

Patriot and Ancestor Number	Pages	Member Descendant
Day, Enos A030874	181, 285	Heidi Hust
		Rosie Hust
		Lori Klinedinst
		Constance Klinedinst
		Wendy Marik
		Hannah Marik
Dyer, Samuel A035237	190, 288	Mary Marszalek
Eastman, Enoch A035718	144, 279	Karen Wojahn
Eldredge, Thomas A037278	108, 272	Melody Huttner
		Therese Lebens
		Elizabeth Prodahl
Estabrook, Prince	219, 294	*DAR Forgotten Patriot*
Flake, Adam A040466	150, 282	Marjorie Nash
Flower, James A039887	194, 290	Clare Barnes
		Grace Truckenbrod
Forten, James	225, 296	*DAR Forgotten Patriot*
Fox, John A215188	38, 259	Michelle White
Frame, Jeremiah A041521	141, 278	Cheryl Despathy
		Lindal Martin
		Sarah Pearson
Frantz, Jacob A041886	155, 283	Lois Mackin
Gaffin, James A042877	138, 277	Katherine Tunheim
		Kristi Wieser
Gale, Josiah A043251	84, 268	Jennifer Taves
		Judith Taves
Galusha, Jacob A203033	133, 275	Kathleen Huston
Glazier, David A045383	64, 262	Kathleen Huston
Godfrey, Ard A045896	65, 262	Barbara Burwell
Gragg, William, Jr. A046612	205, 293	Jessica Fritz
Graves, Ann A047196	199, 291	Barbara Schneider

Index of Featured Lake Minnetonka Chapter DAR Patriots

Patriot and Ancestor Number	Pages	Member Descendant
Gray, Elijah A215654	202, 292	Clare Barnes
		Teresa Landowski
		Grace Truckenbrod
		Jane Truckenbrod
Grigsby, John A048485	200, 292	Joanne Hagen
		Laura Rickabaugh
		Carrie Sorenson
Hall, Jonathan A049847	68, 263	Shirleen Hoffman
		Vicki Musech
Hall, Prince	228, 298	*DAR Forgotten Patriot*
Haskell, David A052362	61, 261	Michelle White
Hayden, Levi A052558	78, 267	Marjorie Brinkley
		Leilani Peck
Haynes, Lemuel	224, 296	*DAR Forgotten Patriot*
Hilton, Charles A056408	69, 264	Deborah Blum
Hitzman, Henry A211038	142, 279	Patricia Peterson
Hull, Agrippa	226, 297	*DAR Forgotten Patriot*
Hunsicker, Joseph A060102	157, 284	Lois Mackin
Huntzinger, John George A060865	158, 284	Lois Mackin
Johnson, Thomas A063768	37, 258	Michelle White
King, Michael A064689	198, 291	Georgetta Hickey
Lafayette, James Armistead	227, 297	*DAR Forgotten Patriot*
Lee, William	220, 295	*DAR Forgotten Patriot*
Lively, Cottrell A070741	201, 292	Haley Roth
		Laura Roth
		Louise Farkas
Lockwood, Jeremiah A071069	192, 289	Elaine Dunn
Lutz, Henry A131923	104, 270	Lois Mackin
Manchester, Stephen A214635	206, 294	Kathleen Huston
Marshall, David A073741	100, 270	Ann Cathcart
Maxwell, Henry A075918	103, 270	Barbara Rustad

Index of Featured Lake Minnetonka Chapter DAR Patriots

Patriot and Ancestor Number	Pages	Member Descendant
McDaniel, Thomas A207740	102, 270	Haley Roth
		Laura Roth
		Louise Farkas
McKenney, Collin A077574	189, 288	Ann Brilley
Moseley, Edward A081969	203, 293	Barbara Schneider
Musser, Burkhardt A083545	60, 260	Lois Mackin
Neifert, Jacob A202310	156, 283	Lois Mackin
Odell, Jacob A204561	146, 279	Kathleen Huston
Osborn, Hugh A084449	74, 266	Martha Mason
Paxton, Thomas A211156	204, 293	Joanne Hagen
		Laura Rickabaugh
		Carrie Sorenson
Paxton, William A209218	204, 293	Joanne Hagen
		Laura Rickabaugh
		Carrie Sorenson
Peebles, John A088010	182, 286	Sandra Hull
Peters, Jacob A205789	152, 282	Lois Mackin
Polley, Robert A090288	98, 269	Adrienne Bendickson
		Adrienne Morrison
		Virginia Morrison
Poor, Salem	221, 295	*DAR Forgotten Patriot*
Putnam, Daniel A092404	70, 264	Michelle White
Ragland, John A132445	39, 259	Michelle White
Ramsdell, Moses A093887	132, 275	Sharon Noble
Roush, George A098975	186, 287	Sarah Martin
Roush, John Adam A098982	185, 287	Sarah Martin
Rudd, Nathaniel A099513	112, 273	Marianne Loftus
		Kristine Sittler
		Janet Swanson

Index of Featured Lake Minnetonka Chapter DAR Patriots

Patriot and Ancestor Number	Pages	Member Descendant
Sage, Benjamin, Jr. A099134	107, 272	Clare Barnes
		Teresa Landowski
		Grace Truckenbrod
		Jane Truckenbrod
Sage, Benjamin, Sr. A099131	116, 274	Clare Barnes
		Teresa Landowski
		Grace Truckenbrod
		Jane Truckenbrod
Salem, Peter	223, 296	*DAR Forgotten Patriot*
Smith, David A213166	114, 274	Michelle White
Smith, Hezekiah A105490	36, 258	Michelle White
Stahl, Henry, Sr. A075663	193, 289	Georgetta Hickey
Stahl, Leonard A206354	149, 281	Georgetta Hickey
Summers, Bartholomew A110885	111, 273	Meghan Flannery
Sutton, Zebulon A111425	76, 266	Teresa Anderson
Thomas, Massey A113098	106, 271	Joanne Hagen
		Laura Rickabaugh
		Carrie Sorenson
Thompson, Joseph A114337	184, 287	Michelle White
Truxtun, Thomas A116510	66, 262	Adrienne Bendickson
		Virginia Morrison
Tuttle, Jabez A131803	79, 267	Pamela Greinke
Warner, Eleazer, Jr. A213377	99, 269	Linda Kline
Warner, Eleazer, Sr. A121074	63, 261	Linda Kline
Washburn, Jesse, Sr. A121889	148, 280	Lois Mackin
Webster, Benjamin A121172	135, 276	Teresa Anderson
Webster, Nathaniel A121332	71, 264	Julie Schaefer
Weller, Eliakim A214108	32, 257	Kathleen Huston
Wheatley, Phillis	222, 295	*DAR Forgotten Patriot*
Willoughby, John A127077	75, 266	Ann Winegar
		Katherine Tunheim
		Kristi Wieser

Index of Featured Lake Minnetonka Chapter DAR Patriots

Patriot and Ancestor Number	Pages	Member Descendant
Winsor, Abraham A128863	58, 260	Kathleen Petit
Wooten, Thomas A130383	183, 286	Sonia Goetz
Zirkle, Michael A131099	81, 268	Sarah Martin